THE
OUTLANDER

GIL ADAMSON

LARGE PRINT

Oxford

Copyright © Gil Adamson, 2007

First published in Great Britain 2008
by
Bloomsbury Publishing Plc

Published in Large Print 2009 by ISIS Publishing Ltd.,
7 Centremead, Osney Mead, Oxford OX2 0ES
by arrangement with
Bloomsbury Publishing Plc

British Library Cataloguing in Publication Data
Adamson, Gil, 1961–
   The outlander
   1. Women murderers - - Fiction.
   2. Widows - - Fiction.
   3. Frontier and pioneer life - - Canada - - Fiction.
   4. Canada - - History - - 1867–1914 - - Fiction.
   5. Adventure stories.
   6. Large type books.
   I. Title
   813.6–dc22

ISBN 978-0-7531-8408-0 (hb)
ISBN 978-0-7531-8409-7 (pb)

Printed and bound in Great Britain by
T. J. International Ltd., Padstow, Cornwall

For Adrian, the good father

Now goes the sun under the wood,
I pity, Mary, thy fair face.
Now goes the sun under the tree,
I pity, Mary, thy son and thee.
— ANON, THIRTEENTH CENTURY

We could be meeting Jacob and the angel
We could be meeting our sleeplessness
— CHARLES SIMIC

ACKNOWLEDGEMENTS

Love and gratitude to Kevin Connolly, for pretty much everything. Thanks to Lynn Henry, Sarah McLaughlin, Ken Babstock, Laura Repas, Matt Williams and the folks at Anansi for their warmth and incredible energy. To Elyse Friedman for being honest and kind — a rare combo. To the amazing Alexandra Pringle and everyone at Bloomsbury — I am so very proud to be with you. To David Mann for his gorgeous cover design. To Del Shinkopf and Simo Von Wolff for German translations, and to Alix Bortolotti and Carmine Starnino for Italian translations. And to Jack Brink, Curator of Archaeology at the Royal Alberta Museum, for information on Aboriginal names in 1903. Any inaccuracies regarding historical Aboriginal life and customs are mine. To Rauleigh Webb and Sam Webb for their information on carbide mining lamps. William Moreland's collection of newspaper clippings have been taken from Wisconsin Death Trip, though their texts have been altered.

The author acknowledges the following books: J. Frank Dobie, *Cow People*, University of Texas Press, 1964; Michael Lesy, *Wisconsin Death Trip*, University of New Mexico Press, 1973; Eliot Wigginton, The Foxfire series, Anchor Books, various dates; Cort Conley, *Idaho Loners*, Backeddy Books, 1994; *The Book of Common Prayer*, 1662.

This is a work of the imagination. Although I refer to actual events and people, I have endeavoured to make this my own creation.

PART ONE

NOW GOES THE SUN

CHAPTER
ONE

It was night, and dogs came through the trees, unleashed and howling. They burst from the cover of the woods and their shadows swam across a moonlit field. For a moment, it was as if her scent had torn like a cobweb and blown on the wind, shreds of it here and there, useless. The dogs faltered and broke apart, yearning. Walking now, stiff-legged, they ploughed the grass with their heavy snouts.

Finally, the men appeared. They were wordless, exhausted from running with the dogs, huffing in the dark. First came the boy who owned the dogs, and then two men, side by side, massive redheads so close in appearance they might be twins. Dabs of firefly light drifted everywhere; the night was heavy with the smell of manure and flowering apple and pear. At last, the westernmost hound discovered a new direction, and dogs and men lurched on.

The girl scrambled through ditchwater and bulrushes, desperate to erase her scent. For a perilous moment she dared to stop running, to stand motionless, listening, holding her dark skirts out of the water. In the moonlight, her beautiful face was hollow as a mask, eyes like holes above the smooth cheeks. The booming in her ears faded slowly, and she listened to the night air. No wind through the trees. The frogs had stopped shrilling. No sound except the dripping of her skirts and, far away, the dogs.

Nineteen years old and already a widow. Mary Boulton. Widowed by her own hand.

The girl stood in her ditch under a hard, small moon. Pale foam rose from where her shoes sank into mud. No more voices inside her head, no noise but these dogs. She saw her own course along the ground as a trail of bright light, now doused in the ditchwater. She clambered up the bank and onto a road, her stiff funeral skirt made of bedspread and curtain, her hair wild and falling in dark ropes about her face. The widow gathered up her shawl and fled witchlike down the empty road.

At daybreak she was waiting for a ferry, hooded and shivering in her sodden black clothes. She did not know where she was but had simply run till the road came to an end, and there was the landing. A grand, warning sunrise lay overhead, lighting the tips of the trees, while the ground was in shadow and cold. The hem of her skirt was weighed down by mud. She whispered in camaraderie with herself, the shawl about her ears, while another woman stood uneasy by the empty ticket booth and held her children silent. They all watched her with large eyes. Even the smallest seemed to know not to wake the sleepwalker. Out above the river's surface, fat swallows stabbed at unseen bugs and peeped to one another in emotionless repetition. The ferry sat unmoving on the other side, a great flat skiff with a pilot's cabin in the rear.

The widow considered the ticket booth, realizing suddenly that she had no money. Behind her was the long, vacant road she had come down. It was stick-straight and lined with trees, and at the limit of sight it bent to the left where no movement, no human shape was yet visible. Her mind had cleared a little because she felt less afraid, and she now saw the world around her in a sharper, simpler way. Even the wind, rising and subsiding and fluttering her collar, followed a less ornamented rhythm than before. She could see it blowing, an infinite number of slack lines waving before her.

A boy on the other side of the river came to the edge of the bank and waved. One of the children waved back. He put his hands to his mouth and hollered. A man's voice hollered back. The widow turned to see a tall figure in coveralls coming down the road, his hand aloft. He must have emerged from an unseen path through the trees. He unlocked the door to the booth, stepped inside, slid back a tiny window, and leaned on his elbows. The woman and her children crowded in at the window and together they debated in hushed voices. A child's hand reached up to finger the dull coins and was slapped away. Once they had paid, the woman moved her children away to the dock. The river swept by in lavish, syrupy whorls, over which the ferry now laboured. The sky was withering with morning, whiter by the second, and over the shallows and the

5

slim line of sand, insects could be seen gliding, carried giddy on the wind.

The widow roused herself, tucked a strand of hair under her shawl, and went up to the tiny booth with its window. Inside, the ticketman's racoon face floated in the dim, close air.

"I haven't . . ." she began.

He said nothing, simply waited. His hand lay on the counter before him, knuckles heavy and cracked.

The widow gazed in disgust at his fingernails, pale and sunk into the flesh, with a rim of dirt about each one. A cluster of slumbering things, and above them, darkness and the man's watching eyes.

"I haven't any money," she managed.

"Can't get over if ye can't pay."

Her mouth fell open. Part desperation, part surprise at hearing an actual human voice. "Please, I need to get to the other side. I'm . . . late getting home."

"Out late, eh?"

The feral face came a little farther out of the gloom, fixing her with eyes that were clouded and small. He seemed to be considering an alternative meaning to her statement. She held her collar tight and waited as he gathered the unknown thoughts together.

"Been visiting?" His face took on the shadow of a smile. It was not an unkind face, exactly. The widow nodded, her heart beating hugely.

"Your mother will miss ye, won't she, if ye don't get home?"

The widow had never known a mother, and yet she nodded vigorously.

The ticketman's smile became a leer. "Can't have that."

He rose and stepped from the wooden booth, taking the widow's elbow in his massive hand. They walked together down to the river. The ferry, now docked, churned and roared and dug up the river mud. A scarf of cloudy water made its way downriver, where the current stirred the clear and the murky together. Black smoke issued from the ferry's funnel and was snatched away by wind. The man helped her to the railing, then went back to the shore.

The widow looked down into the boil of water, wood, and parts of fish churning in the soup, the ferry rocking deeply as if trying to tip her in. Her stomach lurched and she moved over by the engine-room door. Inside, the ferryman, who couldn't have been more than sixteen, struggled with various levers. She closed her eyes and clutched her hands together as the boat backed away from the shore, leaving solid ground, and swung slowly out into the current. The horn bawled suddenly, then again, acknowledging the ticketman left on the shore, and he raised his hand, standing among the flowering trees.

An hour later, two men stood waiting at the river's edge — red-headed brothers with rifles across their backs. Large men, identical in every way, standing close by each other, not speaking. Each with huge chest and arms, sleeves rolled up, like two lumberjacks in a rustic play. But these were not lumberjacks. The pallor of their faces, the close trim of their beards, belied any suggestion of work. And they wore fine black boots.

The ticketman, like most superstitious country people, mistrusted twins, disliked the puzzle of them, the potential for trickery, the sheer unnaturalness. He'd been to sideshows to see the horrors in which twins figured as highlights: bottled "punks" and rubber replicas, conjoined monsters melted together by the breath of hell. He'd stood with his neighbours, scandalized, all of them sharing the barker's opinion that human birth is a treacherous thing, and woman is its greatest dupe. Now, studying the brothers from the gloom of his little booth, he tsk-ed in sour disapproval. Twins or not, he overcharged them anyway.

CHAPTER
TWO

The widow headed down an empty cart track with the river to her right. She was two hours from the ferry and already the day promised to be scorching. So keen was the sun's heat that she was forced to pause in the shadows of trees to cool herself. Once, she sat on a fallen trunk and cracked the mud from her hems and shook them hard, sitting back to watch the dust eddy about her like fairies. Even in shade the ground griddled back the day's heat; it came through the soles of her shoes. She brushed dust from her bodice, smoothed the dark fabric over her hollow stomach. She tried not to look at her hands. Who knew what was painted there?

Roosters crowed in the distance. She regarded the river passing by in its curious patterns and tried to deduce the shape of the riverbed by its gurgling signs. Her eye naturally followed any floating thing, then the next, moving as if reading line by line, watching a leaf or any small body scrolling along the surface.

They would come after her, follow her, even across the river. Of course they would. She stood up and hurried on. Past massive oaks, and in the ditches and hollows, sumac tufts with their blood-red cobs, the morning grand and white and arid over the scrawny maples. At a wide bend in the river she passed a stone house where a caramel-coloured dog exploded against the rickety slats of a fence. The widow stood in a comic posture, hand at her breast, while the animal abused her in its own tongue, spittle flying. Finally a human voice shouted from inside the echoing house. "Shut up, you bastard. I said shut up!"

The widow staggered into the hot morning, invective fading in her ears. There had always been something about her that disturbed animals. She knew how to ride well enough, but the horses always reared and shied at first, jerked their heads and did not want her to mount. Domestic animals merely tolerated her. Cats watched anything in a room but her. Birds seemed not to know she existed. Bread tossed from her hand was invisible to them. She remembered a girl from her youth standing on the sidewalk with cubes of bread on her hat while sparrows alighted and squabbled, jostling with their papery bodies. The smile on the girl's face had made her seem like an expensive doll, dreamy and staring, her hair in doll's ringlets.

Now the widow was passing bigger houses and more garbage strewn about the riverbank. The cart track broke in two and one branch forded a shallow swill that flowed across the imaginary lines of property. The other track climbed a whitish and crumbling hill above the river that meandered through scraggy trees. The widow chose the second way, and she clambered between rutted cart tracks holding her skirts up in front. The heat was leaden now, and she felt the blackness of the

10

fabric draping her shoulders. In the shallows fish ran in idle patterns, churning up little blooms of reddish clay, and turtles lay dripping on the warm rocks, unseen in their camouflage.

She heard the voices of men and, later, children from below her, but she could not bring herself to look over the bank to see whether anyone was really there. There or not, they called to her as she passed, and their words were not words but accusations and longing. The river opened into wide pools where one massive catfish strafed in wearied bursts against the current and drifted in the shadows. She found a backless chair set out upon the grassy edge, dragged to this spot perhaps by someone who wished to fish or be thoughtful or watch a sunset. The widow sat herself within her damp clothes and felt an ants-crawl of sweat down her belly. Her mouth open, panting. She removed the shawl and shook it out and bent to pick at dollops of mud and crusted vegetation that clung to it.

She looked closely at the bits of flora hiding in the shawl's nap. The world is full of stowaways. Frowsy little flowered weeds that dry out and crumble and float on the air to reproduce. Burrs carried on an animal's body until chewed or scratched away; any dog trotting through underbrush wears clusters that cling to clusters, and carries them far from home. She found each hooked fibre and picked it free and dropped it to the grass. There at her feet were the knockings of a man's pipe tobacco.

Her father had smoked a pipe. How many times had she divined her own father's nocturnal wanderings by

11

the signs he left behind. The quiet, melancholy man drifting away to be by himself in the dark, leaving a scattering of spent matches, a splatch of tobacco ash. Not so secretive, not so private. The nests of dried filaments seemed to the widow to be left deliberately by men to mark their presence. Here the grass was trampled down and the chair legs sunk immovable into the soil. She shifted from side to side and the chair legs did not loose themselves from their sockets. A heavy man, she thought, who sits and smokes. She smiled and spread her legs and fanned her skirts to cool herself.

Raspberries, strawberries. These were easy, but if eaten too often would cause cramping. She hoped soon to see an orchard, wondered about this part of the world and whether people grew fruit. Behind some of the houses she had seen leggy chickens. She knew how to deal with poultry; but where to find a knife and something to cook them in? She had noted the chicks hovering about the scaly knee bones of their mothers, ignoring the widow's warning shadow, running after their dams as if tugged by little threads.

There was renewed booming in her ears. Her pulse huge and painful, racketing in her head. She must not think of babies. Must not think at all.

The widow gripped her knees in apprehension, stared down at the dreaming surface of the river, and held her breath. Would she see figures there? She hummed a short hymn to stave them off. Rocked back and forth. A small breeze rose. The booming subsided slowly. In the end, the river did nothing.

It was with grinding certainty that her mental lapses came, sometimes accompanied by noises — a booming in her ears, yes, but also voices, strange and distorted. Terrible things were imparted to her in non-words, in senseless howling. Or the sound of a cricket chirruping. Or a clatter, like a spoon thrust into a fan. She would press her hands over her ears — pointlessly, because the noise came from within — press her palms there as if to keep the horrors from leaking out of her into the room. First the sounds, then the visions. And every time, she suffered a sense of fatedness, of punishment. She was like a woman forever woken from a nightmare, afraid to go back to sleep lest it pick up where it left off. *The world has gone black before, and surely will again — because you make it so.* What spooks will come? What hand come to startle the sleepwalker? She knew there was a truth or near-truth in those terrifying moments, a lesson she must undergo. She suffered the stuffing in of it all, while her body remained in the world, exposed, her flesh in its clothes and shoes, going about its business, an empty, drifting engine.

So now she hummed her little hymn, her incantation to stave off the rolling darkness. Sometimes it worked.

The rest of the day the widow hurried along through the heat, clutching her shawl. There were no houses now, only fields with roads crossing them. Slowly her eyes fell till she was simply watching her boots swing forward and then back, crescent puffs of dust in each footfall. Unslept for several days, she simply walked, the regular pulse of her breath in her ears all that hollow afternoon, her life reduced to rhythm. When the light faded entirely, she became part of the night. The dark was heaven, and heaven was the night. She mouthed incantations to it: *As it was in the beginning, is now, and ever shall be . . . world without end.* Walking slowly now, she still followed the river. Trees stood in grand postures over the bank, bushes in pools of their own shadow.

Finally, she found herself standing still. How long had she been here? Swaying slightly, her mind vacant. After a moment, she crawled under a cascading bush to sleep. But she could only lie awake, her eyes closed while ants explored her face. Eventually she scrambled out again. The moon lay small and not quite full over the river, a pale lamp. Crickets thrilling in the grass. She skidded down the riverbank to the sandy beach and stood there by the nearly silent flow, then squatted and drank palmfuls of cold water.

Behind her there came a light exhalation of breath.

She whirled around to see two small figures sitting together under the earthen overhang of the riverbank: two little girls holding hands, their eyes huge.

"Hello," one said, her voice strangely deep. The child brought something to her lips. A red spot glowed by her knuckles.

The widow sighed with relief and put a hand to her breast to calm her leaping heart. "Goodness, girls! What are you two doing out of bed?" she said.

The children looked at each other in obvious mirth and exchanged the cigarette.

"What time is it? Do your parents know you're here?"

"Yes," they said together. "Everyone knows."

"I can't say I believe that," the widow said, noticing the fine little nightdresses, the delicate slippers in the sand. Beloved and privileged children, alone in the dark.

"We always come here," said the other girl, squinting one eye against the ascending smoke. "This is our place." Plump cheeks and pursed lips, a wintery look of assessment in her eyes, a ridiculous mime of adulthood.

"You should be at home, in bed," said the widow.

"So should you!" laughed the first girl.

"And you oughtn't to smoke. It's unattractive, and you might form the habit."

"Or we'll end up like you, I suppose."

"I don't smoke."

"Sure you do!" one said, and they both shrieked with laughter. This impudence caught the widow off guard. She felt like a child trying to best another child and failing. The widow did indeed smoke, when she was alone and no one was likely to see.

"We lie on the beach sometimes, if it's not raining," said the first child. "Feel the sand. It's still warm from the sun."

All three now put their palms to the soft white sand, which radiated a gorgeous heat. The widow stood again and looked down at the girls' little heads, the small bare arms coming out of their nightdresses, hands passing the cigarette between them.

"We lie, but we don't sleep." The deep voice was almost like a man's now.

"And what does that makes us?" the other girl sang out, as if in a familiar chant.

"Tired, tired, always tired," they said together.

"You girls wouldn't happen to have anything . . . any food?" the widow faltered. "I only ask because —"

"No food."

"Oh. I see."

"Are you terribly hungry?" one asked, her smile distinctly not innocent.

A question began to form in the widow's mind, a muted warning, like a drone from another room, getting louder. As if in answer, one of the children said, "We came up just to see you."

There was a long silence, the only sound the river's sluicing beyond and the hiss of wind through dry bushes. When the widow spoke again, her voice was a dilute and timorous whisper. "Up from where?"

They pointed together at the dark river. Their eyes like coals.

The widow's heart leaped and pounded painfully in her throat. "Oh no," she said.

She forced her eyes down, away from the vision, and as she did, tears surged up. Defeated again by an imagined thing. And yet, she could not quite believe this solid thing had come from within.

Nothing mattered but the fact of them, two children in white, their huge eyes watching her. One moved a foot, and she could hear it on the sand. How alive the illusions always were — there is art in madness, in its

16

disastrous immediacy. Four little slippers resting in the sand, one of the toes cocked slightly inward, the way any child's foot might.

She turned sharply and made her way back up the embankment, grasping roots and tufts of grass with trembling hands as she went, her eyes wide and terrified. For a moment, the white nightdresses of the girls were there in the corner of her eye. And then, just as surely, they were gone.

The widow remembered how, as a child, she had snuck out one night with a young Scottish maid, carrying a pair of her late mother's shoes. The girl had whispered, "You do it. It has to be you." In the soft, wet summer earth, they had dug a hole with their hands and the widow had dropped the shoes into the hole.

"May her spirit never walk," whispered the maid, and spat on them. It never had. Of all the apparitions the widow had seen in her nineteen years, her mother had never been among them.

Over the next many hours she trudged sadly along, following the moon that rose and withered, finally melting into nothing among the blown pink clouds of morning. She did not have the slightest idea where she was. She was hungry. Dogs barked in the distance. She heard the rapid chittering of swifts far above in the damp air. Then a church carillon began to peal nearby.

The widow paused. So it was Sunday. She hadn't known the day of the week for some time.

The widow sat in the third row along the wide aisle of the church, crammed in among other women and their volumes of skirts. To her left, a tiny bird lady held a gloved hand before her nose because the widow smelled of ditches. The occasional curious face turned to look at her. She was sweating and vaporous but deeply content, shifting eagerly in her seat. She was the child of a former minister, and so was comfortable in church, an admirer of trappings, but, to her grandmother's annoyance, she'd been immune to the divine and had a child's disinterest in any father but her own. She never prayed unless compelled to, and when she did, she sensed no listening ear, no wise counsel whispering back. She hadn't been in a church since she'd been married in one, because where she and her husband had lived there hadn't been a church close by, nor a town, nor even neighbours. But now, what surging happiness! She was well used to life in this house, the privacy of it, the promise of remedy.

To her right, the serene Christ was revealed in murals along the wall. In one, his Book was held up over the heads of many children and deer and their fauns, the tiny pages marked with painted dots and squiggles not meant to be read. Behind this group, the purple swell of impending storm clouds. *Suffer the children.* In another, women knelt at Christ's feet while monstrously hunched humans staggered before the doors of the temple, where their wares lay broken about the square. *The moneylenders.* Then there was Lazarus — luckless and desolate, called to rise by a booming voice. The stone, like a conjuror's hand, moved aside to reveal the horror: Life . . . again. Mary in blue, always in blue, inclined for mourning. Peter, confronted, denies his Christ, a rooster beside him in pedigreed plumage. Peter is always pictured with a rooster, but the widow had forgotten why. Finally, the martyred Christ in agony on a grey day with high wind. *Redemption*. Light suffuses the sky.

The widow sighed, enraptured. The little church was a cool, dim museum infused with the comfort of stale incense. She sat back and ceased her ogling and elbowing, and the bird lady beside her huffed with relief. The organ drew a breath and barked once, and the faithful women jerked to attention. A fluttering of fans. A murmur came from somewhere up front . . . no, not a murmur but a man's voice. An old minister droning. How long had he been talking? The widow strained to hear.

". . . And the first of these is charity." The minister's voice was barely audible from the pulpit, he himself so small as to be almost invisible. The widow eventually spied the man, shrouded in his fine little wooden tower. A lectern carved from the same dark wood that raised before him. A cloth canopy stretched over his head — *In case it rains*, her father would joke. Even before his withdrawal from the church, her father called himself Jack in the Pulpit, a black-clad pistil hiding in God's green underbrush.

". . . Second is faith. Last is charity." This was greeted with a peeved sigh or two from the assembly.

"He's forgotten hope," chuckled a female voice to her left.

"It's the same sermon as *last week*," hissed another in disbelief.

19

"Shh!"

"He's getting old, is all. Who isn't?"

"Ladies, *shh!*"

The service meandered along, eddying occasionally in a hymn, pausing for the united shifting of the congregation to kneel and pray. The widow was happy to be among these women, everyone wilting in their rarely washed Sunday clothes, seated among the murals and statuettes and stone flourishes. Though she was filthy and unslept, she had the compensating poise of youth. Her skin was clear, her cheeks rosy. The dark shadows under her eyes only made them seem deeper, clearer. She stood up with the rest of the women to sing, holding her hymnal before her and gazing at the minister as he waited impatiently for them to finish.

"Christ in you, the hope of glory. This is the gospel we proclaim."

Every word was like a comforting dream to the widow, and she sang her lungs out. She didn't look at her page, she didn't need to; she knew this and most of the hymns and psalms and lessons and prayers by heart. Nevertheless, a hand reached up and flipped pages for her.

"You're on the wrong one." A raspy whisper from the old lady. When the widow turned to thank her, there was a keen intelligence peering back, a question lingering there.

At the end of the service, the organ remained silent until the minister had fled behind his barricades. Then a lengthy bawl of mismatched chords that resolved slowly, mingled, and formed a sluggish processional.

20

The more sciatic participants struggled to their feet. The racket sufficient to drive guests from the house.

People stood outside, chatting in loose federation on the church steps. The widow moved among them like a spectre at the feast, and tongues fell silent. Even the tiny, hump-backed minister gaped rudely and adjusted his pince-nez. Pigeons clapped overhead like angels gleeful at such a sight: a pretty girl done up in rags, a ridiculous creature in her black curtain-cloth and haggy hair, a child's dress-up of a witch, hurrying down the stairs and out across the yard toward the dry dirt street. Though she understood the effect she had produced, the widow stepped lightly, leavened and rested. *Sins endure, yet we see the place of their atonement.*

It was a windless, humid day, the sun rising as the widow walked. As carts and carriages passed, she was obliged to leave the road and step over to where earth had been scraped and piled to grade the thoroughfare. Grasses grew on the heaped soil like hair on a bee-stung dog, and the widow struggled along from clot to tuft. She saw houses far away by the river and shining between them the sparkle of the water. She saw hen houses, wooden seats of swings roped to high tree limbs and hanging motionless, flat stones laid out to form paths and walkways, rail fences, wells and pumps set in stone rings upon uneven, sprouted lawns.

Presently, she came upon a clutch of little stores. Dry goods, apothecary, photographer. Each establishment was closed and dark, its front stoop recently swept. The widow stepped beneath an awning and puffed in the heat. Above her, bats clung like seed pods to folds in the awning. And then, in near silence, a tiny, opulent carriage glided slowly past, its occupant hidden. The widow lingered in the shade a while, her eyes closed, a smile on her lips.

When she started on again, she soon found the tiny carriage stopped at the side of the road with two admirable horses waiting and the door swung open. The carriage presented a bizarre, relic air — it was a filigreed old thing with brass handles and cracking paint. And within this sarcophagus sat the bird lady from church, now wearing a veil.

"Will you come with me," the raspy voice said. It was not a question. The old lady extended her gloved hand into the sunlight and gestured for the widow to get in.

The widow stayed where she was.

"Jeffrey," the voice said. "Compel her to come here."

Weight shifted above the carriage and a large man stepped down beside the horses. He was screwing his cap into his back pocket. The widow stepped away from him, which caused him to stop and raise his hands in acquiescence.

"Madam," he said, pointing at the open door, "will you come?"

"Why?"

"Oh, why not," the voice came from within. "What else have you got planned?"

The widow held her shawl out in front of her like a decoy, but finally she let her arms drop to her sides and licked her dry lips.

"Get in," came the voice.

"I have to be home soon."

"Lie to me in here where it's cool, can't you?"

She could run, but where would she go? And what was the point? She stood uncertainly, until she saw Jeffrey's eyes take on a different expression, one she recognized. *Compel her to come here.* The widow hurried forward and got in. The door slammed behind her.

And there was the bird lady again, even smaller than she had looked in church. The little eminence sat on its hard bench and regarded the widow as Jeffrey's bulk clambered aboard. Slowly, without a sound, the lacquered box swung on its oiled springs and jollied out into the road again. The two women sat in silence. A gentle breeze played about them.

"You do know," said the old lady, "that you appeared to those pious people back there to be mad?"

The widow looked at the woman's wasted cheeks and quilted lip. She nodded her head. Indeed, she knew.

"What do you think? Are you mad?"

"No."

"Glad to hear it. I can't help a lunatic. I am Mrs. Cawthra-Elliot."

"How do you do."

The gnome chuckled at this preposterous attempt at civility. "Better than you, apparently. You must know that you are in a fetid condition. You are very much in need of a bath. All right, I have a bath. I also have food and any number of beds for you to sleep in. You can pick and choose. I have two women who are just dying to change sheets, and I never give them enough to do."

"Thank you, that's very kind, but . . . you see, I . . ." A likely excuse did not arrive.

"But what? Go on. What is it? You'd rather run about like an animal? You're wallowing in grief?"

"I'm sorry. It's just that I have to be home soon."

"Absurd. You have no home, no husband. Anyone can see that. You're foolish even to pretend."

The widow forced a miserable, polite smile and wished herself back in church. Today hope had been with her for a brief time, but this woman snuffed it out with a knobby thumb.

"If you think I don't know what you feel like, you're wrong. I know exactly the state you're in. It feels like the end, no matter what kind of marriage you had. I loved my husband well enough. Widowhood is not a choice; life forces it upon you. It is a burden to be alone, and a worse burden to be old and alone."

"Please let me out."

This seemed to dumbfound the old woman. She sat in her dim corner, scowling, and then leaned back against the unyielding upholstery and cast her eyes about as if scouring the air for a way to deal with this rare, wild girl. "I've been rough with you. I can see that. But I really would like to help you. It is my Christian duty, I believe, to help you." She was suddenly looking tired and elderly.

The widow watched as fatigue and uncertainty took over. This is what awaits everyone, the widow thought: the body like a caved-in greenhouse, this struggle to do anything simple, to talk or plan or worry, the shallow, panting breath of anxiety and a worn heart.

24

"What I would offer you is this: a place to sleep, some meals and exercise, a chance to get well. I believe that you are mistrustful, so I won't frighten you by telling anyone that you are living with me. You can do whatever you like to occupy yourself. Feed the chickens. Polish windows. There's not much to do around the place. It's falling apart, and I don't care. Do whatever you like. Don't agree to anything; I'll let you see the place first. Who knows, you may bolt the second that door opens. I can't stop you." With this, the gnome looked down sadly for a time. She sighed weakly, the scrawny chest rising and falling. She said nothing more, and the carriage rolled on in the hot day. Soon, the papery eyelids closed and the hands composed themselves. The widow watched the frail old woman grow slack and unguarded with real sleep. It was a wonder how fast nature induced the thin lips to part and the hands to fall wide in a kind of supplication.

Outside, the day began to bake. The widow gazed upon the slow scrolling of lawns, parched trees, and the bluish heap of foothills that came nearer with each mile. She gazed at those foothills and imagined the mountains beyond as a kind of heaven, devoid of people, silent, a place to stop and think.

The widow put her face in her hands. Was it goodness the old lady shrouded with such bitter words? A fond person afraid to appear so? Christian charity ladled out upon the ground? The widow did not know where she was being taken. Perhaps to be kept as a kind of pet. Perhaps something worse. But she wasn't afraid for her own safety. Far from it. In this equation, she was the unexpected, the sudden dark. This Samaritan had no idea what kind of criminal sat across from her as she slept, but slept on.

The grocer emerged from his unlighted store with sleeves rolled up and began cranking the bent metal pole that unfurled his awning. As usual, with the first few cranks, several bats dropped from it and swooped away across the scorched street to a nearby stand of trees.

"Goddamn little bastards," he said. And then he noticed the two men standing to his left. They stood together with rifles across their backs, looking down at a small girl. The grocer couldn't see the men's faces exactly, but the little slow girl stood there with her silly smile, fascinated by the men's red hair. Her tongue stuck out.

"Help you, gentlemen?" The grocer adopted his usual business tone.

First one man turned, then the other.

Unlike the idiot child, the grocer could not muster a smile. In fact, he took a stagger-step back, for these men had the keen, predatory look of hyenas, and they were enormous.

"We're looking for a woman," said one.

"Our sister-in-law," said the other in exactly the same voice.

CHAPTER
THREE

Jeffrey held the door open. The old lady and the widow stepped from the rocking coach and climbed some wide stone steps into a darkened hall where two maids stood by with sour faces and hands crossed apron-wise. Full of "Madam" and "Right away," they hurried about, collecting the old woman's shawl and bringing her house shoes. One maid was small and mousy and never met anyone's eye. This was Emily. The other was tall and wide-shouldered and had the bearing of a man. She was Zenta. Emily went off down the hall, shuffling her feet. The hall windows had been darkened by heavy curtains. The widow stood in the cool gloom and they listened to Mrs. Cawthra-Elliot discuss her case while the widow's eyes adjusted and objects rose up out of nothingness. A ticking clock upon the hall table. A chair with petit point backing that featured a unicorn kneeling in a garden. A Persian runner carpet at her feet. A convex mirror above the hall table in which the old lady and her maids appeared in remote tableau, small and hunched together as if conspiring.

"What's her name?" Zenta was saying.

"Goodness, I don't know," said the old woman. She turned to the widow. "What is your name?"

The widow was about to say "Mary Boulton" but realized in time that she must not use her real name. "Mrs. Tower," she said.

The old lady's intelligent eyes scoured her again, just as in church, and again wintry suspicion crept into them. "Are you lying to us?"

"No."

"She's lying," announced Zenta.

"What is your first name, then?"

The widow's head was pounding. There was no answer; nothing came to her.

"I told you!" said Zenta, triumphant.

The widow went to the chair by the stairs and sat on its edge. She put her head down. "I'm sorry," she said. "I'm hungry, and I feel a bit faint." This statement caused a great excitement in the women. Together they hurried down the hall crying, "Emily!"

The widow could hear the old woman's peeved voice from the kitchen, then Zenta's rough reply. A small pot bonged. A cupboard door slammed shut. The widow saw the front door, still open, where the day burned upon the stone landing. On the stoop was a rough grass mat crusted with dried mud. She sat upright again and her eyes darted toward the sounds coming from the kitchen. She did not know where she was, or how far from the road she might be. She stood up, light-headed, swaying beside the hall table. On its surface lay a pair of gloves, a shoehorn, some envelopes. An enamelled Chinese bowl held keys and coins. On her way to the door the widow clawed up a handful of coins. She pulled out a little velvet pouch she kept hung about her neck on a black sash under her clothes, and into this she dropped the coins, adding theft to her list of crimes.

She rushed to the threshold but stopped and went no further, for there on the gravel drive was the coach, and next to the horses was Jeffrey. Crows high up in the trees made craggy calls. If not for this man standing in the way of her flight, those crows would have seen another black thing moving into the trees.

Jeffrey stood with his back to her, idly polishing some brass harness ornament, and he spoke to the mare, a poor-looking blue roan, as gently and reasonably as if it were a woman he loved. His hand swept in pacifying strokes over the mare's shoulder, and traces lay loose upon its speckled grey hide. The widow's heart pounded. She felt a braid of intention unravelling within her. Ghostly plans of flight, so recently formed, unformed themselves. A wandering puff of cooking smells came to her, and her stomach answered with a terrible pang. She could hear women's voices somewhere in the unknown house. Were they coming back to get her? Surely they would not leave her alone for long. Someone heavy-footed was coming down the hall.

Still, the widow was unable to take her eyes from the brightness of the day, from freedom. Someone called out, "Mrs. Tower!" At that sound, both horse and man looked around to where she stood in half darkness, their eyes moving like twin shotgun barrels. The widow let her knees go out from under her and fell unresisting to the floor.

★ ★ ★

She had been carried up the stairs by Jeffrey, the women behind him shouting orders as he went. She had not fainted, nor was she unconscious: twice he knocked her ankles on door frames and twice she tucked her feet in. The women sat her on the bed and shooed the man out before setting about a feminine reclamation of this wreck. They stripped the outlandish funeral costume from her body. Among its folds they discovered a pocket containing the widow's small Bible, very expensive and of fine paper, which Zenta thumped onto the bedside table without comment. The old woman flipped a few translucent pages and stopped. She stared at the minute marginalia therein — inscrutable symbols and signs drawn by an inexpert hand.

"How queer," she murmured and put it aside.

The widow sipped some clear broth from a double-handled soup bowl, and then they made her eat a little buttered toast off a napkin. As soon as the widow lifted the slice of toast, Zenta retrieved the napkin, inspected it for butter stains, then popped it in the pocket of her apron. The widow recognized the motive. Linen napkins might go a month without washing if you were careful. They were laid across your lap only to catch disastrous spills on skirts and pants, which were far worse trouble to clean. Seeing Zenta's hard hands, the widow had a sudden vision of yellowed squares of cloth laid out upon the grass to bleach in the sun.

Finally, she was taken to a bath and washed by Zenta, who scrubbed her as if she were a child, lifting limbs and pulling hair and swivelling her about for a better grip as the widow's buttocks squalled against the glazed metal tub. Water sloshed and a wooden brush bobbed upon the waves. She could not remember the last time someone had washed her. And Zenta was strong. It caused in the widow a fleeting sense of the physical submissions of her own childhood, the helplessness of it. Then later, the sudden onslaught of her husband's hands and face and body. The way he might seize her in the midst of his urgency and roll her over to get at her from behind, like she were a doll or some other invulnerable thing.

"That weren't a real spell you had. I know that much." Zenta scrubbed at her shoulder blades, the back of her neck. "And you're not the first one she's brought home."

"The first what?" the widow asked but was yanked by the upper arm to twist and face her keeper.

"Don't be smart. I despise a smartarse. You remember where you are, missy."

"Yes, ma'am."

"Hand me that brush."

The widow handed the wooden brush over her shoulder and submitted to a brutal currying of her hair, her scalp pulled taut and her eyebrows raised. She was obliged to hold on to the edge of the tub with both hands.

"She takes it too far, I say. Bringing home all manner of rubbish so Emily and I have to deal with them. Charity is one thing. Letting 'em steal the silverware's another. Pissing in the coal room. Making off with my

Sunday roast in their jackets. And guess who doesn't like it when there in't any dinner?" Zenta's hands were like hooves pounding a flinty road, her breath stormy on the widow's cheek. "And now it's you, little miss sly-boots. I'll tell you one thing: if you hurt that old woman's feelings or abuse her kindness, it'll be a damnation on you. I'm not like her, you know. I don't believe you're mad. I don't think there's anything wrong with you a'tall."

"I'm not mad," the widow said.

"I don't wonder you're weak, though," the woman said. "You've had a baby. I can tell by the look of you." She gestured at the widow's sore and laden breasts. They had been used, then abruptly unused, and the widow had had no clue how to remedy the disaster.

Zenta's eyes shone unkindly, she was pleased with her cleverness. "How long ago? I'd guess two months. Where is he now?"

There was no answer, which indeed was the answer. No lie could touch the question. The widow's mind shut off the image that had grown up before her, ghastly and sudden. She met Zenta's eye, a ragged, hot attention forming where before there had been nothing. Zenta saw it and her face fell.

"Oh no. You didn't . . ." Her voice became soft and peculiar. "Did you lose it?"

The widow's long hair dripped, strewn in weedy patterns across her back. "Yes."

"Did it live long?" Zenta asked with a strange eagerness. How precious news of suffering is, how collectible.

The widow looked down to where her toes were splayed out against the tub and saw for the first time that several nails were dark with blood. One middle toe was badly cut. She did not know what had caused this. She felt no pain there, nor anywhere else in her body. Did he live long? How far away from here? How long ago?

She brought the heel of her hand to her mouth and bit down hard, waiting to feel the yank of pain. The hand was not numb, in fact she knew she had broken the skin, but the throb that came afterward was distant, a fretful voice floating on the air. Both women gazed at the ring of marks left there on her palm, a pink stain forming slowly.

Zenta's scrub cloth hung frozen in the air. "You can get up now," she said, wholly unnerved. "Get up."

Before supper, a storm gathered to the east. Clouds dimmed the air and smears of rain angled near the horizon. A blue haze of humidity hung everywhere. Inside the house it was cool, the hallways shadowy. Evening seemed to fall, then fall again. They had taken supper early, the old lady alone in the dining room, mirthless, as if eating were a chore. The widow ate in the kitchen, sitting on a high stool, holding her plate on her lap. Food! She was so grateful for it.

When the dinner platters came back, Zenta and Emily quickly devoured what was left. Without seeming to do so, the widow watched them carefully. She remembered from her father's house that maids did this. Ordering a little too much at the meat counter, cooking a few too many potatoes, then scavenging afterward. She remembered one thin girl who had been caught pocketing boiled eggs wailing, "But how else am I to *eat*?" And it was a good question, considering the pay. Her father had counselled tolerance; her grandmother had fired the girl. Secretly she watched Emily scoop up broken potatoes with a serving spoon and shovel them into her mouth. It must have been hard to manage when the old woman ate so little. But, as a guest of sorts, the widow was given her own heaping plate, then begged a glass of wine, and to her surprise was given one. Despite her bluster, Zenta believed everyone deserved a good meal.

The widow lay that night in the wide, cool bed. It was so much like her old bed, in father's house, so familiar. The room around her was silent, dull as an unrung bell. No wind outside, no rain yet. Just a heaviness in the air that yearned to break. Was she safe here? Could she stay? Would the old lady keep her word? The widow shivered in the heat. Silence invites the mind to murmur; a dark wall waits like a canvas for imagined shapes. As a little girl, she had lain awake at night, staring hard into her lightless bedroom, imagining that the darkness congealed and shifted — a shadow play, black on black — and she had waited for what chimera might show itself. A strange child, she had been unafraid of these things, monstrous figures reaching for one another, sickly shapes boiling up like dumplings in dark broth. Her only fear was that they pantomimed her flaws and sins. Some nights she said her own name over and over again, as protection, as explanation.

She had often been an insomniac, alone in a house of sleepers. Her father could sleep anywhere, even sitting up at the table if he wanted; her grandmother, with her creams and hairnets and blindfolds, snored raucously. Even the dogs lay like corpses by the door, not a tremor betraying them. But she would be awake, wandering the house or leaning on her windowsill to watch the moon rise and wither, to follow the predations of foxes and cats. And then later, when she was married, sleeping in tents with her husband and all the men, she would sit at the tent flap hugging her knees, following with her eyes the wide paths of wolves round the camp. Praying that they would not yip, that the men would not wake, that there would be no rifles.

In the cabin, with her husband asleep and late-spring snow blown under the door and across the floor in sugary whorls, she had lain awake, standing over the baby as he tried to breathe.

The widow shot up, nearly weeping, and staggered from the bed, hands out in front of her. She hurried into the hall and felt her way downstairs to the drawing room, finally opening the French doors. She rushed outside, panicked and stunned. Lightning burst behind the hills, silvering them. She closed her eyes and saw an image burned there, a hole-punch moon above. *In your underclothes, where will you run, barefoot and half-dreaming?*

35

Finally, distant thunder came riding down the atmosphere, booming, and the widow stepped back indoors.

During the next two afternoons the widow would peep into rooms to see if anyone was there and, if not, tiptoe in and look around. In this way, she familiarized herself with the house and the private habits and details of the women who lived there. She scrutinized the blotter in the old woman's library and saw incredible sums mirrored and crawling its lower border. The old lady's bedroom was as simple as a nun's cell — two single beds separated by a bedside table and nothing else. All her feminine clutter, what little there was, was packed into the large closet, her late husband's clothes stuffed to the back. Of the two beds, only one seemed to have borne any weight, and this was the husband's bed — now dusty and yellowed.

Emily, it seemed, was an amateur artist. Among fallen cardigans and tumbled blankets, the floor was littered with pencil drawings of children: girls in bonnets, boys at the seaside poking sticks into the waves.

Zenta's room had a strange, unpleasant smell to it, the odour of perfume gone bad with age. An inept alphabet sampler hung over her bed — the widow looked up close with an expert's eye and saw a thousand minor struggles there. *Bless This House Lord*. Her father had often rolled his eyes at women and their petitions to God for blessings. "Shout down a well, and tell the frogs what you want," he'd say, and her grandmother would huff and scold. He had teased her once that he would do his own sampler: *Blast This House.* "And not one of your tea cronies will notice, because none of them can read."

He had been completely unaware that his own daughter did not, strictly speaking, read. She read the way others might make their way through a mathematical equation, each part decoded in turn, held in the memory while the next was decoded, the whole revealing itself over a long time. As a child, she was never expected to write anything. Her small hands got better at needlepoint, forming rows of letters; she listened as a young maid sang the alphabet song in the kitchen; she watched as her father set up block letters on the church sign. L-U-K-E. She suspected that for other people words might come fully formed and recognizable, not a jumble of parts, but as familiar as faces. For her, there were only letters, dull and flat as cars in a train. Words sounded out letter by letter, the sound often defying meaning. *Friend. Enough.* Go back and try again.

All she was ever asked to read from was the Bible, and that rarely, so she had relied on her memory, and had devised a way to mark the pages so that she could remember. And in this way she managed to hide her weakness. Asked to read from her own Bible, sing a hymn, or chirp along with other parishioners at the minister's call and reply, she could give a good recitation. If her father had known, what would he have said?

The widow looked now at the woollen letters of Zenta's sampler. She tried to tamp down a bloated B, plucking at a frowsy thread, but it was hopeless. She listened for the sound of footsteps and, hearing nothing, proceeded to dig through the maid's closet. She discovered that Zenta's bedslippers, faded and ugly, fit her very well. The skirts were all short, above the ankle, but this was true of all maids. A servant could not carry a tray upstairs if her skirts were too long.

She went through the little boxes and cloth bags and wrapped packages in Zenta's cupboard, and she could guess what item of feminine arcana lay in each. She herself had had masses of them. When she had found herself finally in the cabin with her new husband and she had unpacked her trousseau, the dresses with silk-covered buttons had lain in her hands like artifacts from another world. She had stood in the damp bedroom and gazed upon these clothes as if her body still stood in them. She could see herself posing at parties, sitting by a lamp and listening to her father, or huddling under a blanket in a sleigh at night as a lantern swung back and forth behind her. It had been obvious what she must do. She had packed away her former self and begun sewing clothes, rough simple things to fit her new life.

And now here she was, peering into a maid's cupboards and trying on a maid's slippers. How shocked her father would be to see his daughter now. She could almost conjure up his uncomprehending, questioning face. And yet he had believed so firmly in the alchemical nature of existence — that the path of a person's life could be predicted down to the last breath, if only one could see human interaction for what it was: a collusion of physics and chemistry.

What, then, would be his explanation for this? What billiard ball had come along to knock her into this decaying house? Could he have foreseen his daughter running through fields, dogs in pursuit? Or his son-in-law struggling on the cabin floor in his own blood while she stood watching? Could he have even imagined the small grave? The child dying, his breath fading? Surely that crisis should have wrung some forewarning from the very air, from the clouds. It should have come to her in dreams, raging. And yet there had been no warning, and no remedy. From that small devastation, all this had followed. Alchemy, physics, prophecy. Darkness erased them all.

They would come soon, her husband's brothers. She could almost feel it in the air. There would be gossip among the church people, news travelling like a smouldering fire, driven by vindictive tongues. They could not fail to find her. And yet, she could not run away in the night as she had before, without thinking. She must have a plan, give no warning, take useful things. She picked up Zenta's boots and slipped one on.

That evening, she met Mrs. Cawthra-Elliot in the gloomy hallway, the bird lady stepping like a feeble djinn out of the murk. The widow was again in her black clothes, which were now clean.

"Go and get your Bible. Come and see me in the drawing room," came the order. "You can read to me."

A few minutes later, the widow came through the drawing-room door. The fire was blazing against a perfectly mild August night, and the old woman sat near it, dandling a glass of amber liquor.

"Sit," she said. "I'll get you a drink."

The old woman went to a table and unstoppered a crystal bottle. Beside it was a bowl filled with huge shards of ice hacked by Emily from the icebox. Each piece was perfectly clear and too big to float. It was not lost on the widow that she was being served by the old woman, as if she were an equal. So, with tinkling glasses, they sat together by the fire. The widow smoothed the fabric of her dress over her knee and sniffed the scotch in her glass. "I don't drink usually," she said.

"You will. You'll find it helps. The way some people talk, you'd think the stuff was rat poison. For women, at least."

The old woman became thoughtful, patted the overstuffed arm of the chesterfield. "You know, I don't hold with the view that women can't live like men. We're not all that unalike, the two sexes. Drinking injures us no more than it does men. Neither does a year or two at university, as I had. Of course, my husband used to say that men are stronger and so must do the heavy work. I say fiddlesticks. Look at Zenta. That woman could throw a horse over a fence."

The widow snorted and covered her mouth in glee.

"Well," the old lady laughed, "it's true, isn't it?"

"It is. Zenta frightens me a little."

"If I were you, I'd be afraid too." The old woman gazed into the fire. "She's a spiteful woman. And clever. For some reason, she dislikes you more than any other person I've brought to the house."

The fire wheezed in the grate and settled, gushing a renewed brightness into the room. A door to the forecourt stood open and moths floated in, seeking the brighter indoors. It was unearthly quiet.

"Where are you from, my dear?"

The question was unexpected, and it startled the widow. She had not yet constructed a plausible deception, and so she froze, the question unanswered. A lie might have ended things, shrouded her in a dull, forgettable fog. But now, inescapably, she had been silent long enough to call suspicion on herself. There was nothing for it. She simply clammed up. For a few moments, the women sat awkwardly side by side on the massive chesterfield.

"Can you at least tell me where you were born?" The old woman's voice was unexpectedly gentle.

Still, no lie rose to the widow's mind.

The old woman simply carried on. "I was born in Dauphin. Do you know Dauphin? No? I'm not surprised. It used to take us a week by ox cart to visit Winnipeg. I thought Winnipeg very grand. Can you believe it? We had a hundred acres, a team of oxen, a large house — well, large for those days — and a barn. My father was a doctor, and my uncle farmed. We were all in the same house. I slept in a bed with my sister until the age of fifteen, at which point I feigned a sleepwalking habit and was given my own bed. That was wicked, I know, but it was the only way. We had no toilet, no plumbing at all. They melted snow in winter for water."

The widow, too, had melted snow in the cabin. She remembered the taste of it, shovelfuls melting away to mere cups in the pan. She saw the metal pot on the stove, a lavish mist rising into the frigid air, bricks of snow skating the rounded edges as they hissed and melted. A basket of her husband's long johns waiting to be washed. The baby nearly silent now, needing nothing, wanting nothing, his crying done, his life winding down. And her husband sitting, eating a bowl of soup. Humming. The widow brought the glass to her lips, her hand hovering, then drifting back down to her lap.

"I remember," the old lady continued, "that all eight of us slept for a while on a large pallet, supported by beams. And we were separated by blankets, for privacy. Since I was at the end, the hired man slept next to me. I could hear him breathing. He had a little dog that snapped at me through the blanket every time I rolled over. It was a wretched dog, named Grenadier. As I recall, it was a hideous colour, like tobacco."

The widow realized she had been only half listening. She glanced at her benefactor, expecting to see her lost in her own thoughts too. But there was the feral face, watching intently, the eyes moving back and forth as if reading a book. The old woman only talked so that she could observe.

42

"It was dark much of the winter, and cold. We women spent time in our beds after the chores, just to keep warm. We sat together with the sheets pulled up to our chins, and the dogs lay at our feet and the cats crawled in under the blankets. We all had fleas. You simply lived with that fact.

"One spring, we went off to Winnipeg to buy a new stove. We had a cart and two massive oxen that together could pull almost a ton. They had the ridiculous names of Maxwell and Minnie. I was terrified one of them might step on me and kill me. As they walked past you, the ground shook. My father had purchased this pair of monsters from a man outside Russell. They were tremendously stupid, gentle animals with huge woolly heads. They looked prehistoric. Well, we lumbered along all day and through the dusk into night. There was no moon overhead, nothing to show us our way, but we all trusted in my father. I remember we were lying under many blankets, and the moon was completely blurred by mist, and beautiful, you know? So I went to sleep. Now, when I awoke, it was to the most terrific uproar, my parents shouting, the other girls screaming, and the cart leaping as if the ground itself had begun to tear apart. I realized that we were charging through the trees at top speed, the oxen apparently gone mad. It was all I could do to seize my younger sister and hold us both to the floor of the cart."

"What was it?" the widow said.

The bird lady smiled to see how well her tale had taken hold. "Well, I peeped my head over the railing and realized the oxen were charging toward a small light, a house perhaps, I couldn't tell at first. And then I could see it was a barn. Alone on a frozen field, surrounded by trackless forest, was a farm, and the oxen had found it. In fact, it was their home. This was the very same farmer who had sold them to my father. Without the moon to guide him, my father had drifted too close to Russell, and the oxen had smelled home and made for it, with a vengeance. A pair of oxen can move pretty quickly when they see oats in their future. It makes sense now, doesn't it?

"The farmer and his wife were nice people, but perhaps a little childish. They put us up for the night and fed our oxen. The wife gave us biscuits and told my sister ghost stories that failed to frighten her but kept her up all night pondering the mysteries of death. She wouldn't let me sleep, and I was at my wits' end to shut her up. I remember sitting up and hissing, 'Why don't you just go ahead and die then, and let me sleep!' Finally, in the morning, my mother's beloved cat could not be found. We all went searching without success for almost an hour, until finally a plaintive mewing was heard, and we found him pressed between our hosts' mattresses. The wife had hoped to keep him. I still remember her tears as my mother carried the miserable, limp animal to the cart in the frigid morning and placed him in his cage."

"Your mother kept the cat in a cage?"

"That strikes you as odd? I suppose it was odd. But we'd be here all night if I tried to explain my mother's mind. I'm not even sure I could."

The bird lady sat stiffly on the soft couch by the roaring fire, her drink almost finished. The thought of her own mother seemed to wither her, to redirect her mind along a sadder path.

"I remember only cold," she said, "snow against the doors. My father on the roof shovelling it off. Even in spring it was unbearable. My sister was put outside to play one day, missing one mitten. My mother ignored her cries to be let in. You see, in those days children were supposed to get fresh air whether they wanted it or not. By the time she got back in her hand was frostbitten. Almost frozen through. Her fingers never grew properly after that." The old lady drew a line across the pads of her fingertips. "Never grew past here."

"Did it hurt?"

"Oh yes. Frostbite hurts a great deal, especially once the flesh begins to thaw."

"No. I mean, the rest of your body growing and your fingers not growing."

"No. Well . . . I don't know." The old woman smiled. "What a queer question."

The widow took a little sip of her Scotch, and it burned slowly all the way down.

"You might read to me now." The old woman's voice was fading. She seemed to have shrunk even farther somehow, as if she were a miniature version of her already small self, sitting lightly on the soft cushions.

Obediently, the widow put down her drink and took up her Bible. She opened it to a page — it seemed like any page but was, in fact, a deliberate choice — and she began to read in a plain, loud voice. "The Lord roars from Zion and thunders from Jerusalem; the shepherd's pastures are scorched and the top of Carmel is dried up." The recitation went on from there.

The bird lady tried to conceal her fascination, but it proved impossible. Finally, she leaned closer to peek over the widow's arm at the book. The page was covered in marks and illuminations, strange symbols and pictures. The widow read in halting rushes. She only looked at the book once in a while, as a navigator does to check a map. The rest, clearly, was recited from memory. Well rehearsed and dreamy, it went on and on, rote memory never failing, a formidable performance. Like watching a sparrow dip and surge in the air, resting as it flies, tireless, without thought. Slowly, there came into the old woman's eyes the pall of doubt. This pet was not turning out as expected, but was following perverse lines, unknown and covert routes. The old lady looked away, and let the widow babble as she wished. "Enter the narrow gate. The gate that leads to perdition is wide, and many go that way; but the gate that leads to life is small and the road narrow, and those who find it are few."

When sometime later Emily arrived with a tray of hot chocolate, the old lady bolted from her seat and scolded, "Not now, Emily, not now!" So, the recitation went on unhindered, until the weird symbols petered out, and memory failed, finally, and the lesson died away senselessly, and the book was closed.

★   ★   ★

In the morning, they came up the drive under a canopy of tall oak, walking in the wheel ruts with their rifles across their backs. August dandelion seeds floated across their path, as if nature itself hoped to bewitch them from their purpose and dream them into the trees. But still they came on, over the tufts in their path, through floated cobwebs, their identical faces vigilant and sober. The first building to rise into view was the barn, a wide, unpainted structure with two massive doors standing open, a tin roof, and wooden filigree along its eaves. A little cupola on top watched them come. They could see the house now too but made for the barn, because it was closer.

Jeffrey was in the stalls sorting through old bridles when the door went dim, as if a cloud had passed over. He looked up to see the silhouettes of two large men standing side by side. They had guns. Jeffrey slowly removed his cap and held it uncertainly, his eyes assessing them; then, making a decision, he screwed the cap into his back pocket. He didn't speak, he didn't move. He waited. He was a man accustomed to waiting. And slowly, the men, who had been stiff and unmoving as statues, began to shift and shuffle as doubt overtook and annoyed them, impelled them forward on their fine black boots into the gloom of the barn. Two horses watched them come, the animals' long faces hanging over the stall doors with the guileless, expectant gaze common to all horses, even the hellraisers.

What Jeffrey saw were two men as similar as twins. And yet, after a moment, he could tell they were not the same at all. To his eye one was a follower, a second, identical perhaps in size and shape, and certainly colouring, standing abreast of his brother as if he were his equal, but he was not. He was somehow subordinate, in shadow, a copy not entirely faithful to the original. As if to illustrate, the other spoke first.

"We're after a girl. People say she came through here. Your missus maybe picked her up."

"I don't have a missus," said Jeffrey. The two redheads moved closer — and he was right, one moved first and the other followed.

Their eyes were the problem, he could see that now — never mind the dour and brutal cast of their faces, the sheer size of their bodies — but in their eyes, a profound cunning. Of course people would talk, yammer helplessly looking into those eyes. The people in this town, normally clannish and suspicious of strangers, would find themselves suddenly blithering. Usually, when you saw that glint in a man's eye he was a small man, mean, and resentful of being small. How calamitous, then, to see it in a big man, and doubled.

"Who is she then?"

"Who?"

"The woman of the house."

"My employer. What do you want with her?"

"We told you. We're after this girl."

"And people told you what? That we had her?"

"That you might. That your missus picks up lame ducks sometimes." Jeffrey knew he'd said *missus* deliberately. "If she's got our girl, we want to know it."

"You don't look like policemen," Jeffrey said, taking in the cut of their fine clothes, their freshly barbered beards.

"We've been deputized, if that's what you mean. Now, have you seen her?"

One of the horses began to stamp in its dry stall. It jerked its head. Jeffrey's face registered the movement, as if saying, *I agree. Let's get rid of them.*

"She hasn't taken in anybody for weeks," Jeffrey said. "Yes, she sometimes picks up the poor, or as you say, lame ducks, people needing help. But we haven't any girl. Now, if you don't mind . . ."

The two men shifted a little in the doorway, almost spreading out, enormous impediments. Strong as he was, if Jeffrey had tried to get past them he couldn't have done it.

"I'm asking you to leave the property," he said firmly.

A long, tense moment followed, but finally they did turn to go, stepping out onto the grass, where the distaff twin, the copy, turned and said, "She's our sister-in-law. Does that make any difference to you?"

"None."

"Nor that she killed our brother?" This from the first twin.

Jeffrey held his hands out in an appeasing gesture and said, "I'm sorry" in exactly the same way he'd said it to butchers and wheelwrights and vagrants looking for a handout, the same way he told the old woman she couldn't have things before they were fixed, the way he'd said it a hundred times to a hundred other people. He said it the way one jerks the reins on a defiant horse, one hard yank that means *no*. But in that moment, all was lost, because it *did* make a difference to him. The girl he'd had in the carriage, the girl who the last two nights had slept under the benevolent old woman's roof, the dark, furtive girl he'd held in his arms and carried upstairs was a murderess. It made a difference all right. And they saw it in his eyes as clearly as if he'd spoken. Like everyone else, Jeffrey had given them what they wanted.

CHAPTER
FOUR

That same morning, standing at the library window, the widow dandled a blue glass paperweight in her palm and listened. She heard a strange scuffling sound from the forecourt below. Then it came again. She leaned out the window and looked down. Emily's head appeared, just visible beyond the confusion of ivy. She turned, turned again, disappeared. Then her head swung out again. Emily was dancing by herself on the forecourt, her arms held stiffly before her, as if around a companion's neck. The widow regarded the bobbing head — would the imagined companion be a gentleman or another girl?

"*Here* you are!" a voice barked behind her. The widow jumped. Zenta was bearing down on her with a look of satisfied determination. The widow had the distinct impression she was about to be spanked, but instead she was seized by the upper arm and dragged downstairs.

"Time to make yourself useful, missy. No more creeping around like a cat. I told Madam you'd been going through people's rooms, through their private things. Yes I did! 'Thinks she can get away with anything,' I says. 'Put her to work,' she says. And that's what I'm about to do."

They entered the basement, a damp, sweet-smelling room with other rooms coming off it. A massive antique stove slumbered against one wall. In another room was an empty pantry with slate-lined shelves and counters that were surmounted by glass-fronted cupboards, within which sat stacked dishes of various ornate designs. A set of gaudy gold and peach, another one greenish, yet another set in a deep navy blue. A tureen capable of feeding a platoon occupied its own cupboard, a visible beard of greasy dust round its edges like feathered coral. Zenta impelled the widow into a mudroom and made her stand still while she scrounged for a particular broom among many brooms and mops and dusters. She fetched up a miscreant and scraggy loser, with straw fibres sticking out sideways and patches missing, like a madman's hair.

Zenta leaned close, her milky breath on the widow's cheeks. "Little miss sly-boots," she whispered, grinning widely with malice. "You'll have a job, you will."

The widow was assigned a thorough sweeping of the forecourt: the fool sweeps the beach. Formerly a grand and imperious platform above manicured garden depths, the forecourt, like the house itself, was now swooning into a gorgeous, natural chaos. Rain-sluiced mud and blown debris lay in deep drifts and runnels along the borders. Between the heaved-up flagstones that formed the floor, seedlings and woody tufts pushed up and knotted together, the growth following a vaguely geometric pattern of broken green lines, like a mouse's maze. On every flat surface lay the gluey fossil impressions of maple keys. Expired beetles hid in the loam. Spiders slung their nets among the blown roses.

With her decayed broom the widow laboured gamely. After suffering the chores her husband had taught her to do, and her grandmother's marmish tutoring, she could be obedient as a dog. The skin of her hands tellingly rough and her back strong, the widow wore the ratted broom down to a nub, contented in her work.

At dinner, she sat again in the kitchen, sipping leftover soup and picking at a sliver in her palm. The murmur of the old woman's voice could be heard through the thick doors, then a grunt from Zenta, who was waiting at table. Emily bent over the washbasin and tested the water with her thumb, casting a wary glance from time to time in the widow's direction. A kettle of water was heating on the stove, a merry bong issuing as the old bowed metal expanded.

"Did . . . did you . . . ?" Emily's voice was timid and ghostly, a fretful whisper.

The widow might have thought she hadn't spoken, except the girl's pale eyes were staring.

"Hmm?"

"I meant to say . . . did you ever go to school?"

"No," the widow said firmly, "no school."

"But, miss, you can read!"

"My grandmother taught me," she said, digging again at the splinter. "She taught me everything."

"Oh, I see," came the sad reply. "Just a grandmother. Well, I always wisht I could go to school. I prayed I could. I don't care what they say about it being bad for you."

The widow's own grandmother had believed that education was damaging — too much blood to a woman's brain would cause reproductive malfunction. To prove her point, she had invoked the spectre of university women who were childless. "Why don't they have children?" she'd said. "Because they *can't*." And since no one in the family, including her grandmother, had ever met a woman with a degree, the lesson went unchallenged, filed along with other dubious claims: ghosts cause spontaneous combustion in people (the spirit world giving wrongdoers their just desserts); spilled salt is thrown over the left shoulder directly into the devil's eye; a phrenologist can identify a criminal in childhood, before he causes any damage, so he can be sent immediately to reform school; the monkfish is so named because it looks just like a little monk, complete with cowl. Thinking about it now, the widow couldn't see how a girl like Emily would be harmed by reading. In fact, for her, the agony lay in half-measures, in knowing how little she herself knew.

"If I could only go to school and be with other girls my age. Sometimes I even dream I am at school, and everyone knows me. There's the reading, of course. You could read all the books in Madam's library, if you wanted to. But it's the friendship, the society of it. I think it's just grand, and, and important, and . . ." The girl sputtered to a stop, frozen in embarrassment at having spoken so much. She turned quickly back to work, as if she hadn't spoken at all, then slipped a roasting pan into the water and began a vigorous scraping. Hollow grinding issued from under the water's surface as the girl vainly went at the glazed mess.

"What in the world are you doing?" said the widow. "Let it soak."

Stung, Emily stepped away from the basin. Two red streaks appeared on her cheeks. She stood with her back against the counter, hands braced behind her, shoulders hunched; it was the posture of a child trying to appear casual. In the resulting quiet, the widow sipped her soup and assessed this odd girl. She couldn't be more than fifteen, knowing nothing of life, and never allowed out in the world; a young woman mostly unchanged from the original child. Gradually, watching the girl's increasing discomfort, the widow deduced what the problem was: Zenta didn't believe in soaking. Zenta's way, which was the only way, was to scrub like mad while the water was at its hottest; never waste hot water. Zenta's hope was to scrub the skin off the world. The widow, on the other hand, had told Emily to stop, and for some reason, the foolish girl had obeyed. So, they were at an impasse. Sometime soon, Zenta's feet would thump across the floor and she would swing through the doors into the kitchen. And then what hell would rain down on Emily? The widow felt a deep pang of pity, maternal and therefore perilous.

"Well," the widow said brightly, "this splinter is a pest. Perhaps I should soak it a little in water." And with that she stepped off her stool and went to the washbasin and began scrubbing. Brownish matter

55

churned up in the water as drippings and spatters peeled off the pan like poker chips and rolled under her brush. She went at the corners with her fingernails. From the edge of her vision she could see the girl, frozen in disbelief.

When Zenta strode through the door, the widow heard the woman's booming voice: "Emily, why aren't you . . ." And then, seeing the widow at her task, in a quieter, more approving tone, "*Clever* girl."

The widow stood at the end of her bed, then fell sprawling across it. After the whooping of the bedsprings subsided, there was no sound at all, though both windows were open. No breeze carried the scents of night into her room. No dogs barking. A candle stood as if petrified on the bedside table. The old woman and her servants were asleep, and the widow had been at her nightly predations, wandering the empty rooms of the house, opening drawers and cupboards cautiously, silently, so contents would give warning before they shifted, a gentle half-sound before the sound came. Everything she touched was a sound first, or, if she was careful, no sound at all. The old house seemed to sleep as well, like some huge living thing. During the day it creaked and groaned in the way of old things. Now, in darkness, it stood on its foundations in absolute stillness. The widow lay on her bed, wakeful, ears ringing with silence. In her hand lay a wedding ring, not her own, filched from the cluttered back reaches of one of the old woman's desk drawers.

She had been lying with the ring in her hand for she knew not how long, the small warm hoop of gold resting in her palm, a thin almost sharp thing, light as a lock of hair after all the years of wear, ultimately discarded.

She looked at her own ring finger, which was bare. No indentation, no mark saying a ring had ever been there. She hadn't been married long enough for it to show.

And yet here she lay, clutching another woman's ring. Well, it was gold, and it would not be missed, not immediately. How long since the old woman had worn it last? What reasons had lined up against it so that the bird lady had wrung it from her finger and hidden it in a drawer? The widow had found it among bits of string and ruined pencils. *I loved my husband well enough.* Perhaps it wore on her, the perpetual grip of it. A needling reminder: This is what you used to be — what are you now? Or maybe it began to take on a peculiar weight that belied its actual mass, the solemnity and burden that comes at the end of things, just as joy and callowness come at the beginning. Do all widows remove the ring, eventually? Do they do it quickly, from self-protection, like a mountain climber struggling to cut the rope on a fallen companion before the weight also pulls him down?

Somewhere in the house a door thumped closed. She felt rather than heard it, a thud that came through the mattress. She waited. Another less sensible thud. Silence. Then, a sound she actually heard of footsteps on the stairs, quiet and furtive, but stepping quickly, two stairs at a time. By now she had rolled over on her back and was frozen in a crablike posture, half sitting up, motionless so she could better hear. The boots — yes they were boots, she could hear the heels — came along the hallway quickly, a determined march.

And then Jeffrey entered her room. He came right in, seized the door handle behind him, and backed the door closed till it clicked. The widow sprang off the bed and braced herself in the corner like a cat. The gold ring dropped unheard to the rug and rolled under the bed.

"I want you out of here," he hissed.

The candle next to her slowly stopped wavering. In its light her eyes were gold streaks. She knew what had happened, knew they had found her, could tell by the black outrage on his face.

"Was it them?" she whispered.

"Listen, you! Make your goodbyes tomorrow. She'll give you food and such, and then out you go. If you linger here, I'll let them have you."

The widow shook her head. "I don't know where to go," she said.

"I don't care." He glared at her for a long moment. "Take your problems somewhere else."

She nodded meekly.

"And don't you breathe a word to her what you did. Not a word. It'll break her heart. Unlike you, that old woman never hurt a living soul in her life." He backed out and shut the door on her.

The widow was alone in the barn. It was night, but she had not dared to light a lantern. She would not wait for morning. It wasn't safe. So she had brought with her a heap of pilfered items that lay now on the ground as she entered the uneasy mare's stall and tried to gain control of it. A fur coat was ground by a hoof into urine-blackened straw.

The other horse, a small gelded bay, would not even let the widow come near, but the roan was older and calmer and the widow was able to slip in and stand near the mare's neck and let it quail and veer and shoulder the walls of the narrow stall. Its head was reared up, round nostrils puffing at her face. She rubbed harshly at her scalp and pressed this hand to the mare's face and snout, not knowing why she did it, just figuring that all animals must learn one another's scent. She draped a halter around its neck. She slipped a thumb into the mare's mouth, along the gums, back where there were no teeth, and pressed down till the mouth opened and she could slip the bit in. The rest she pulled over the stiff ears and held the jerking head down and buckled the throat strap. As a girl, someone else had always done this for her, little Mary the master's daughter, a candy-eating child astride a hobby horse. She was surprised she remembered how, and she stood back and wondered at it. Would this be the first of many small retrievals, illuminations of a vast personal darkness, like the amnesiac wondering, "Can I play the piano?" and then playing?

From over the stall door she took a blanket and English saddle and laid these over the horse's back. The girth strap swung there, just out of reach. Fearful of bending her head down near unfamiliar hooves, she caught the girth strap with the toe of her boot, Zenta's boot, and brought it up and cinched it tight. She stood and looked at her handiwork. But then the mare exhaled, and the girth strap hung loose. If the widow were to try to mount now, the saddle would slither round and hang from the horse's belly. When she went to take up the slack, she found the horse had held its breath again and the strap was tight. This was a conundrum. Having been tricked, she wondered how to proceed. After several experiments, she remembered that repeated upward thumps with a knee into the mare's belly would cause it to puff, and the strap could be cinched tight. Finally, the widow mounted and stood the horse in its stall, speaking gently to it. In answer it nodded and jerked the reins, oddly passive now that it was saddled. She backed herself and the horse out of the stall and took a stroll through the barn, bending to avoid beams. At last, she brought the mare to the open barn door. Horse and human looked out at the night.

The house stood at some distance from the barn. A path of pale stones wound an ornamental route between the two buildings. A farm for aristocracy. She'd seen many just like it. Conservatory, library, drawing room, barn. A vegetable garden perhaps, where the lady of the house grows lettuce and carrots. She knew the architecture and the kind of lives lived in inherited houses like these. And she believed misfortune was the likely end of this house, of every great house. The children die or move away or refuse to have children themselves, someone marries unwisely, someone becomes sick, someone goes mad, the young wife is barren, the old man gambles unchecked, there are no more parties, the staff dwindles, ivy overgrows the windows and birds nest everywhere, rooms are closed off. When Mrs. Cawthra-Elliot eventually died, her staff would empty the house, keep what they wished, and close the doors.

The widow dismounted, tied the halter to one of the oversized barn-door hinges, and went searching for anything useful. A set of leather saddlebags lay in the corner of a tack room. They were old and frowsed with white rot that brushed away like salt. In another smaller room she found nothing but a broken horse-drawn sleigh, a child's carved wood sword, and a scorched fire screen with an urn painted on it. In the two days she had been here, she had seen no sign of children, grown or otherwise. She had found the deceased husband, or at least a massive formal portrait of him in his military uniform. He had sharp features but an oddly gentle eye gazing out upon what little was left of his life. Beneath the painting the old woman had set up a table on which she had gathered her departed husband's possessions, masculine flotsam, laid out as a shrine. A shrine relegated to the corner of an unused room. *I loved my husband well enough.*

On her first nightly exploration of the house, the widow had found this room and had filched a tiny lapel pin in the shape of a star. She found it pretty. She had put it on her shift and looked at herself in the glass. There had been a little tin containing a notebook and a pencil. She had taken several items that seemed useful to her, including the notebook and pencil, and also a short, lethal bayonet knife that came with its own sheath. Thinking of poultry, and her future needs, she now went in search of a pot.

All these things fit awkwardly into the mouldering saddlebags, the flaps of which were stiff with age. She tossed the stolen fur coat behind the saddle and hung a beaded silk handbag from her shoulder. She mounted again, hitched up her skirts, and proceeded from the barn, a mad silhouette in the night. From the direction of the house came a dog that barked at her once, short and high, a call of question. She listened to things moving in the dark. The dog came sideways, peering, and it circled in a strafing pattern while the blue roan stood its ground. Eventually, they went on, the dog making small yips. She walked the horse slowly over the gravel drive, holding the saddlebags tight to keep their contents from jingling. No light in the house, candle or gas. Its ivy walls went scrolling by and then were gone. They passed through a small field and came upon two looming trees the widow had seen from her window and thought to be stumpy. Instead they were enormous, with vast canopies. The leaves filtered the moonlight and, as they passed under, woman and horse were streaked, erased, reformed.

Soon, they came upon a fence and stood looking over it into another dark field. The widow circled the roan and took them back a short way, then brutally heeled it forward into a canter, and heeled again before the fence, as the dog ducked and veered. They took the jump, landed awkwardly, and trotted to a stop with goods rattling and the roan shuddering and sidestepping with surprise. The dog simply took off. The widow gripped the reins. Two hearts pounding. So, she remembered how to jump too.

They went on into the dark field and soon were gone from sight, leaving the house where they both had been kept and cared for.

The old woman stood at her doorstep before breakfast, her gnarled little hands wringing together and a look of fury on her face. Zenta and Emily cowered behind her. The three women regarded the red-bearded men who waited on the steps, rifles across their backs like hunters.

"I told you," she said, attempting a sternness she did not possess, "you have the wrong house." Under the chill of their flat stare, she slowly withered, the trembling lip now mute.

"You have two choices," said one man. "You can cooperate, or you can see what happens when you don't. Now, where is she?" His eye settled on Emily, clearly the weakest of the three.

CHAPTER
FIVE

The widow had given up guessing the time at around midnight. The moon came and went, its light erased by scudding cloud. She had cantered the horse when she could, along an open road or a clear path through the fields. Houses stood at a distance, flattened to two dimensions by the moon's light. Cattle watched and chewed, standing or reclining in pools of their own shadows. At what she judged to be the edge of this little burg, she passed a lonely bull segregated in a pen, who gazed over his fence and watched her go. She craned around to see the massive creature, the heavy head hung low, and the wide back gleaming under the stars.

But now a profound dark had fallen and she walked the mare slowly and stopped often to gauge her direction. Cocks crowed into the pitch black. Beside a fence she dismounted and tied the horse. She gathered her skirts about her hips, squatted, and urinated into the dry grass at her feet. Then she remounted and went on.

Toward dawn the sky cleared, and she realized she was on the foothills of the mountains she had seen three days ago, blue and shrouded, from the old lady's carriage window. These had been her target since her first sight of them. They stood like a monument in her path, promising freedom and camouflage. Pink suffused the horizon, but the sky directly above was all blue and stars. She heard the crack of a rabbit gun far off, and the mare stopped and listened as the sound ranged about them and the hills muttered back. From the direction of the sound the widow figured she had already begun her climb into the foothills and the town now lay some distance below her. She went on, listening, but there was no more gunfire.

They entered a thick stand of trees and once again were sunk in darkness and nearly blind. The widow dismounted, took the saddlebags down, and sat upon a bed of moss searching for something in the bags. Her hands were her eyes. Next to her the mare cropped grasses and chewed, a hollow and leisured grinding to her right. Soon she found a match and in its flare she glimpsed the forest floor, a strange and wicked-looking topography. She saw her own skirts and the horse gawping over at her, its pupils contracting, before the match stuttered and it was black again. Since her childhood, which had ended not so long ago, she had wondered about the existence of goblins and small, biting sprites. Her father had instilled this silliness in his girl, waking her sometimes when he came home late and drunk. Over the objections of her grandmother, they would go out into the dark garden as the child staggered and half-dreamed, and he would seize her and point, insisting some tiny creature hid there, just out of sight, standing motionless in the foliage. Incredible behaviour for a man of his nature and

65

training, a former Anglican minister, his collar now coiled and tucked away in a sock drawer.

Had the news of her crime reached him yet? She felt a wincing regret, for she knew she could not go home to her father and grandmother, not now. That house was no longer her home, and she would not be safe there. Even if she knew her way, the least public route home, they would never hide or protect her when she arrived.

The widow took up a pipe, which she had packed with tobacco, and drew the embers up and sat back smoking in the gloom. She had taken this pipe from the old man's shrine; it was an expensive and antique object. The bowl was out-sized and ornate, carved into the shape of a stag's head whose antlers came off in a hinged lid. She drew up a fragrant smoke and sighed it back out.

For two days, the widow and her mare climbed steaming foothills into mountains whose peaks were seamed with impossible snow. The punishing heat faded and the air became pleasantly warm. In the mornings heavy fog poured upward from the earth and drifted in ghostly forms through the trees. She stared: This one is a shepherd's pipes, that one a woman's hand reaching. She watched a gaggle of vaporous forms trouble the surface of a little forest slough, and it gave her a curious image of what her own mind endured. The voices. Furies born and soon dead with a simple breath of sun; but potent while they lasted, and terrible.

At dusk the first day she came upon a lean-to built of rotted timber and set against a mossy rock face. Slung across its open ends was canvas sacking that had been eaten at the bottom by mould. She called out but no answer came, and so she ventured close and threw back a flap to gaze upon decomposing blankets and a ratlike strewing of blackened newspaper. No occupant rose up to greet her, no sign of life anywhere. One folded wadge of newspaper in the corner had been underlined in black and the lines had bled into one another. The widow had not slept in two days, and before that never for more than a few hours. Here was a shelter, at dusk, a human sign among the trees. And yet she backed away from this burrow as if from a compost heap roiling with vermin. She wiped her hands on her own ragged dress. On the ground about the hovel she found more refuse. Spoons, an empty wallet, a glove, more newspaper, half-buried under pine needles and loam and none very far away from their source. Like an archaeologist she unearthed a pitiful human sphere. She deemed it to be male, though anyone following her and gazing at her rest spots might think the same of her. The widow mounted and went on.

She rested that dusk and woke later to find all light erased. The night was so dark she thought something stood between her eyes and the rest of the world. Blindness could not be this complete. Nothing but the sound of wind through trees. Somewhere to her left, the breathing horse. And high above, the slow funhouse creaking of pine branches. A blessing of her young life had been the fact that she remained more afraid of her

67

own mind than of the dark. In fact, she loved the night. Still, here among the trees there was the call of unknown things. Small scrounging sounds to the left . . . or in front? She had taken the saddle off the horse and now she lay with her head on it and listened. The horse puffed. She reasoned that the mare would alert her to news of a predator. She did not know that a horse's eyesight is far worse than even a man's. All it has is a sense of smell, and that depends on the wind. Throughout that long night, the widow listened to the movements of the mare, and tried to ignore the question of how she would catch it in the dark if indeed something came through the trees toward them.

Morning came in a fug of humidity, the sun a hot smudge above, the ground steaming. When the widow stood, she discovered her skirts were soaked. She bent and wrung them out, but they stayed damp and heavy, and the cloth lapped coldly at her calves as she mounted the horse and rode. They went on through groves of aspen, and the widow saw the clawmarks of bears on smoky trunks, impossibly high, near her waist as she rode. All about lay the papery shreds of torn bark.

The next morning, the air grew colder. She was climbing the range day by day. She sat in meditation on the saddle's rhythmic creak, the suck of hooves in the wet leaves. She was obliged to dismount from time to time and draw the mare from an impassible web of hemlock or a corral of dead and fallen pines. She worried she was going in circles or even retracing her steps.

They went on into hollows and draws, then up again, along ridges and across clearings that smelled of mint. The blue roan was fattening, since the widow stopped often to let it feed, and it seemed stronger by the day, stepping across alpine meadows so green and seemingly cultivated they spoke of heaven. White dots of mountain goats moved along vertical bluffs with tiny kids following in awkward dashes over the precipitous terrain. The widow watched their pinpoint hops.

She bathed quickly at the edge of a frigid mountain stream and the water stung and lacerated her nerves. A painful cleansing. Where possible she used her long hair to dry herself, for she dared not use her clothes, and the old lady's fur coat simply slithered coldly over her skin, absorbing nothing. She paced naked in the sun, teeth clenched, hugging herself, watching the mare as it wandered and grazed. She had forgotten completely about the saddle blanket. Oily and stiff as it was, it might have warmed her. She did not know how to properly hobble a horse, but by now had intuited how to tie the reins to one foreleg so the mare could bend and eat but could not gallop or even trot away from her when she came to collect it. She found stiff dried moss with which she tried in vain to curry the horse's coat, and she lifted the mare's hooves and dug pebbles from the frog with the old man's bayonet. This much she remembered to do.

She ate her mouldy bread and soggy fruit. The bushes were full of berries, but she dared not eat anything unless it was recognizable, and nothing was. She saw rabbits, which now looked like food on legs, but could not devise a way to catch them. She saw an eagle and several fat foxes, and at dusk, grey owls gliding silent on the night air with their enormous wings. She put on the fur coat and discovered just how small the old lady really was. She cut her skirt up the middle, front and back, and, shivering and naked with the needle in her hand, sewed it into wide black pants so that her knees would no longer be exposed as she rode. This was a good solution, except that now she had to remove her clothing entirely when she needed to relieve herself. In the cold night she was obliged to rise from her dozing and walk the mare to keep them both warm, while their common breath followed them in meaningless Braille.

On the fourth day, the mare scented the air wildly and stood electrified at the edge of a steep meadow. At first the widow did not know the object of its terror, and then she did. A massive old grizzly stood just clear of the far trees, but the roan's poor eyesight had not located it yet. The widow stared in terror at what stood across the meadow, swinging its head from side to side as if in similar disbelief. Light brown and sleek and fat, it was bigger than she had imagined any animal could be. The shadow of an entire cloud passed slowly between herself and the bear. Sun penetrated into the deep grasses and flowering weeds. She clung to her dancing mount as the mare puffed and trembled, unable to find the source of its dread. And then the bear was gone; it simply backed away into the darkness of the trees. The widow amended her trajectory and went on, praying. *The Lord roars from Zion. These are the words of the Lord.*

Trees, everywhere. And the sun above. A whispering of wind in the high branches and every pine needle and summer leaf moving. The widow rested atop a boulder in a clearing and removed her boots. The saddle was hung lopsided on a branch. She walked slowly around in the soft mud and rubbed her cheeks with the heels of her hands, clearing her head. All morning she had been assailed by memories, inappropriate, ironic ones. Not the usual phantoms but something else, some catalogue of places and things — and for each she suffered a transient yearning. A familiar street corner, a broken banister railing in her father's house, a wet newspaper full of potato peels in the kitchen. Unpopulated, these memories, but each one nonetheless saturated with human presence, like an unattended meal still steaming. Something was coming, some message — each memory sculpting its own silhouette. She fought them off, struggling the way a swimmer does who must not rest but does rest, only to return to the surface, sputtering. A gang of drab sparrows played tactical games among the deep indentations her feet had made in the mud. The mare shook itself like a dog, and they all flew away.

She had now spent six days and nights alone in the mountains, and still she didn't know where she was. Yet she wasn't frightened, merely attentive. The thing to be feared always came from within: exhaustion, unsound thoughts, ignorance, starvation. As a child she had been

71

dragged away from a panicking horse because she had failed to see that it might injure her, the hired man shaking her by the shoulders, shouting, "Do you want to get me fired?" And yet, she had been nearly demented with terror by a dream in which her hands fell off at the wrists. That summer, her bed had been set outside on the screened veranda where it was cool, and when she had wakened screaming, the caged birds by the door had volleyed about their little wicker palace. The sound of adult feet thumping down the hallway toward her, where she sat rigid and shrill, her arms out before her, staring at her hands, still seeing them gone. All the next day she had nursed a miasmic horror: she was unsound, dissipating, her body unable to hold together. And the blame for it lay in dreams. This was the locus of fear for her, a worm in the heart, where hope rotted in its dark whorls, where unwanted visions leaped out — the darkness of her own mind. And yet here she was alone in the wilderness, strangely content.

It was a bright, soft morning. In the sun, the air was warm enough for bare skin, while under the trees the mare's breath blew into vapour. An arctic chill crept the boundaries of each shadow and gusted from the deeps of the woods. The widow rested her feet in front of her and stared down at the white and blue toes. The mud soothed the soles of her feet and she shuffled them back and forth and clenched her toes into it. She eyed the sparrows glumly, imagining one cooked upon a fire, a meal no bigger than her thumb, crackling and hissing in its small supply of fat. There seemed to be no berries at this elevation, or if there were, they were wizened, white, and bitter. She had not been able to find a gun or rifle in the old woman's house. So how to kill a small animal? How to capture a bird? She had stopped the horse at every creek and stream to gaze into the clear water, looking for fish, minnows, anything alive. She saw nothing, ever.

Her will was strong enough, but she lacked the knowledge to help herself. She had been trained for another life, and her mind in its dulled state turned over and over in a mire of useless things: sonatas and études; the art of a good menu; trousseaux; dress improvers or bustles, so outdated now. Bedtime at nine. Toast cooling in its wire stand on the breakfast table. Alabaster skin and parasols. Weeping girls who did not get what they wanted at Christmas. One ate and drank and got fat. One worried about chills. Old women mistrusted the damp summer air. Death did not come this way, lingering in the trees. It came by apoplexy. By cancer. By public hanging. Her uncle, known to everyone as a wrathful man, had fallen to the rug in his drawing room clutching his throat, his death caused by an outrageous grocer's bill.

By noon she had wiped the mud from her feet and calves and put on her boots again. She went to the mare's left, stroked the long neck, and mounted. Horse and rider went on slowly. Steam rose from the mare's rolling shoulders and drifted past the widow's knees, but the widow shivered even as the puddles below her glared brightly in the sun. All through the trees ran paths made by animals big and small. The smaller the animal, and the more of them, the more deeply rutted the trails. The widow had discovered these natural highways at dusk one night, the patterns highlighted for her by the deepening shadows. The red of the sunset had imparted a hollowness to physical things, the evergreens silvered and flat in their sleekness, and suddenly the tousled grasses revealed these animal paths, itineraries, wandering lines of habit she had not perceived before. Rivulets and whorls where mice scurried round rocks and tree trunks. A squirrel's stitch of hops between pines and then with a leap, nothing. And wider, subtler erosions, where hooves and bellies had drifted and where soft lips had torn away leaves. In the absence of any human map, and wishing herself away from human danger, the widow turned her horse and followed these ghostly rivers, wandering deeper into a wilderness she knew nothing about.

At dusk the light became as thin and cold as the air. There was no sound, no echo, the mare's footfalls silent in the deep bed of cedar needles. There were no shadows; everything lay impossibly flat to the eye. *World without end.* The mare put its hoof on an old rotted log, and a muffled crack came from under seasons of flowing grass and blown leaves. The widow slumped in the saddle. Hunger or fatigue? She could no longer tell them apart. She dismounted, staggered briefly on her numbed feet, and plopped down heavily, cross-legged, still holding the reins. Pine cones. Could she eat pine cones?

Into the grey air there came a hint of blue, a rustling of leaves as the wind sighed goodnight. Soon she began to see unaccountable things. In amazement, she watched the silhouettes of dwarfs or perhaps children hurry behind trees or float with their arms aloft as if they lay in water. The mare, too, seemed to track some movement, its flecked eyes following some floating thing at its knees. Nothing there? The widow put a hand out. No, nothing there.

When night fell in earnest, she tied the horse to a branch, removed the saddle, and sat under a tree clutching her knees, listening to the sounds around her in the murmuring dark. Pines creaked in the wind, comically gothic. The wind hissing through the millions of needles. And there was a repeated sound, one she took a long time to identify: it was the mare pulling at the reins. All night, the mare pulled at its traces to reach down and eat the grass at its hooves, the widow awake and listening, unaware of the meaning of the struggle. The sun rose on both woman and horse, pitiful creatures, hanging their heads like exhausted convicts.

When they were mounted and moving again, the widow aimed them uphill. In her disordered mind, she wondered whether this was north. Was north up? In fact, the widow did not know which territory she might be in or whether she had passed into another world. So limited was her understanding of the land she stood in, she would not have been surprised to see the ocean soon. *No good woman knows too much about geography or politics.* Even her father had believed this. She tried to picture the map her husband had hung on the cabin wall, but it had no connection to the world she saw around her. Each American state had been

75

filled in with a different colour, all of them tidied together like a box of sweets. Canada itself was a broad emptiness of circumscribed territories each holding its own name and nothing more. Assiniboia. Keewatin. Alberta. Coloured pink, like all things British. One summer afternoon last year, the widow had stood, hand on hip, and gazed sadly at it, trying to divine the place of her birth, the place where her father slept, perhaps, or bent over his breakfast in his shirt sleeves. She scanned the strung nuggets of the lakes and thought she might know one of them. Without cities or borders, no line to indicate where she had come from or where she was, the widow had stared at Canada and seen it as others did. An attic. A vacancy. A hole in the world.

Who knew what lay there? Was it this perpetual forest, dripping and silent? The mare picked its way through knee-high fern and sprays of pale aspen sucker, its shoulder falling as rotted roots collapsed and thick moss slid. It tore at ferns and leaves as it went, slow and plodding. From time to time a trickling vein of icy water came down from the summits and ran through matted grassweeds. Little pools oozed up where the mare's hooves had been.

The widow looked about her with the ragged clarity of starvation. Clarity and a disastrous elation. This was what church aspired to, she realized: a greatness in the hollowing mind, brought on by dissolution. *My heart is distracted within me; I fade like a passing shadow.* Not a soul in the world knew where she was, and this knowledge gave her pleasure.

The widow leaned deeply to avoid a branch and nearly fell from her saddle. She snorted with false amusement, to fool herself into feeling amused. *Tired, tired, always tired.* She shivered in her blighted cloth while phantom snow fell and the stars above reeled. Her mind spun in its dark bowl, seeking in vain a better way to see. The trees heaved in the wind like reeds in a swift current, and her looping and sourceless thoughts stuttered to a stop to see them. The world was huge, endless, and the widow in her body was not. She was alone and lost, the weak crying of her own baby in her ears.

She rubbed her face hard with the heels of her hands and took the pipe from the pocket of her coat as she rode. Put it in her mouth and sucked a stale incense from it. She would not waste a match. This calmed her, and she let the endless forest part for her and swallow her trail. Night came on quickly as the shadows of mountains swept up along the range. The constellations came out in a gauzy crowd above, but the widow was slumped in her saddle beneath dripping boughs and saw nothing. *What?* she said. *Come over here,* she said.

With a start, she awoke to find it was finally dark. The mare, which had long ago stopped of its own accord, hung its head and slept where it stood. The widow dismounted stiffly and just stopped there, bent over by weakness, nearly unconscious. She felt nothing of her body except a complex of inflexible sinew across her back. A night wind hissed wildly through the upper boughs and yet no breath reached down to her. She stood erect, then twisted her torso this way and that and felt each string of muscle tremble. A little later she woke again and found herself rolling over on the ground, trying to find a more comfortable position, head on the saddle, legs tucked up to her chest.

Once starvation had begun, actual sleep became impossible. The widow's hands and feet burned, and the burning entered her dreams and destroyed them. She felt that no human soul was near her, no fish in the streams, no animals, no voice. The mare stood motionless as a clay statue. There was only water and sky-high wind. The widow felt the burden of her own existence, the endless labour of it. She had tried to eat grasses, the soft cores of pine cones, white cold roots she'd dug up with her bootheels. But each had caused her to sicken or vomit, and now her stomach was inactive, carved out. With no idea how to save herself, she lay motionless and febrile, while all about her edible ferns waved and the hard nubs of rosehips leaked perfume unknown. Abundance lay about her, but she starved.

Black shapes came wandering through the outer dark, huge creatures that stopped and bent their antlered heads to the ground. The widow sat upright, weak as a child, her mouth hung open. *Come here, horses*, she said, *come*. Clouds drifted along the ground and took her with them, her body catching on tree branches and dragging on the ground. She dreamed, did not dream. Covering her face, she imagined snow, falling needles of stars. *I am not in a storybook. You are no prince. I won't die for you.* She held something alive in her hand. It was her other hand.

The dark shapes moved away silently, quickly, as if pursued. And then swift monsters hurtled after them, keening, and their barks were dreadful. Cold wind ran through her like electricity. Hands and feet burning.

CHAPTER
SIX

By morning, the widow sat upright among fallen branches, the forest now motionless above her. She was some distance from the saddle and saddlebags. The mare was not in sight. She ventured outward in short spokes from her bed, but it was obvious to her that the mare was indeed gone. Had there been wolves? She had dreamed of running wolves. But she had also dreamed of her grandmother dragging her by the ankle across a lawn. She stood wherever light came through the trees in pools and shafts, and its warmth was pure pleasure. She rubbed her numb arms and face. No sound anywhere. Strange that her heart still beat and her breath came unbidden. She hung the saddle on a branch to dry, though there was no point — she would not use it again. The spattered grey hide and dark ears, shoulders rolling between her knees. Even the widow's unmoored mind could grasp the meaning of it. Without the horse, her meandering would be slower and she would lack even an animal's attention to progress. Survival was unlikely. She set the saddle up as a shrine, not to the lost animal, but to herself, to the fact that she had existed.

She left her belongings and wandered aimlessly. Spider webs brushed her face and she did not wipe them away but let spiders cling to her and ride a while and drop away. The sun came down in beams and shafts, and once, when she looked up, she saw the moon hung high and pale in the blue morning. Tricky thing, pretending to be gone when it wasn't. She was reduced to an idiot child lost in the woods. It was with an idiot's glee, then, that she came across the tracks of her horse, and bent to see the deep, scored prints where the animal had run and dodged and dodged again. Other horses had run with it and diverged through the trees, hounded by dogs. Not dogs, she reminded herself. Many wolves, harrying the horses.

The widow followed the tracks and came across a carcass. It was a big mule deer. The body lay with its hooves toward her. From ten yards away she could see blood pooling in paw prints in the mud, the throat and belly torn away, intestines dragged over the ground. One leg askew.

She turned immediately and fled, staggering, with a directional acumen that might have surprised her if she had still been capable of surprise. Dodging through the forest with her dark pants flapping, catching trees and clawing a path round them, slapping branches away, and falling finally upon her meagre belongings, snatching the bayonet from its sheath, turning, and stumbling back again.

A lone wolf awaited her when she returned to the carcass, this gasping human, gaunt latecomer to the feast, weapon in hand. She spoke to the wolf in

81

affectionate tones, but her stance and the hollow glitter of her eyes told the animal otherwise. Dun fur rose up on its shoulder as the horror of her scent reached it. The widow was a monster of nature, out of place, pale and stinking of humankind. The wolf fell back a few paces for comfort, then lifted its snout and scented again the wretched thing before it. The widow approached the carcass, every fibre in her body aligned by need. The wolf did not wait to see her cut into the deer's haunch but turned and loped away.

Sparrows flitterred right through bushes like immaterial sprites and shrilled to one another. The widow closed her eyes. Before her stood the little fire she had built and maintained for hours. With food in her belly, she drew again on her pipe and puffed a fragrant white smoke, raising a signal into the air that wandered among the hackled pines. The fire was her only concern. That, and going in search of dry wood and leaves, stoking the fire when it lagged, squatting like a golem by its warm perimeter and meditating on the flames. Fat hissed uncut from the deer meat and dropped onto the coals in pops of flame. When the wind changed, the widow would shift the spindly tent of green branches she had fashioned to support the meat. A greasy smoke billowed over her and she was all but lost in the clouds of it.

She had eaten some of the dark, purplish flesh raw, about a golf ball's worth. It was pliant and dense and rich, and it smelled vulgar. After the inevitable vomiting, she had turned immediately back to eating.

She felt as if she were working against a death that was mere hours away. All morning, her affronted belly seethed. She had expected this. But more strangely, transient pains came and went in her limbs, an oppressive ache bore down through her left shoulder as if some vulture stood there, grinding. The tendons of her jaw tautened, and pain spread out and upward across her skull before it subsided. Each distress came and passed, and none lasted more than a few minutes. The body fortifying itself, surveying the empty territories. The widow just sat and endured these events, gaunt and clinging to her pipe, with her knees up around her chin.

This, she thought ruefully, *this* is the bride, the mother in her apron, or sitting upright at the dinner table, full of bright conversation. These hands had held a hoe that worked a hobby garden, held a rifle and appalled her husband with her aim; these hands had held the bodies of pheasants up so she could look closely at them, their heads dangling like pendants, their wrinkled eyes half-closed. She shifted on her haunches and covered her grimy face. Go away, go away. Remembrance: a fly that won't leave but bites and bites in the same spot. She poked around in her saddlebags for the matches and busied herself with lighting another ration of tobacco.

She attempted to recline with her feet out before her, as she had done only days ago in a green and fairyish wood. At that time, her horse had been near her in the dark and there was no other threat than self-told ghost stories. But now her belly was so shrunken and taut she

83

could not comfortably recline, and so she was obliged to squat again.

Later, she rose feebly and went hunting firewood. There, among a clutch of lush underbrush, grew something she suddenly and with joy recognized as edible. Fiddleheads. Little curled greens that hid among the parent ferns and that, she knew, tasted buttery when charred along their frilly edges. The widow bent, trembling among the low vegetation, and picked every one she could see, clutching them to her like jewels and snatching back the dropped ones — until she straightened and looked about her at the endless sea of them. Why had she not noticed them before? Was it that good luck tends to bring more of itself, or had she finally found the energy to seek her own survival? The vast shadow of some bird floated by overhead, but when she looked for it, she saw only a ragged seam in the evergreens and, beyond that, a flat whiteness. The widow stood gazing upward, the pipe stem clenched between her molars.

Her father had smoked a tiny ebony pipe when she was a child. Black and polished and prone to extinguishing because of its narrowness. It was, she felt now, a slightly pretentious object. But he had had many affectations, her father. He would let her pack the bowl for him, using the wide end of a golf tee to tamp down the wadge of tobacco, and using its sharp point to dig out the resin and ash. He would glance about to see whether any women were likely to see him and then put his feet up on the antique fire screen, cross his legs at the ankles, and put on a pensive face.

84

He would explain to his daughter the properties of fire, the vile, vindictive nature of lightning, and the new theories of controlled electrical current.

"There is an exhibition in London," he had once told her, "where a thousand glass bulbs are illuminated together and the nighttime becomes as bright as day." People thought of electricity as a liquid, like water, he'd said. It might be prone to leaking. Women's hair would crackle with the excess discharge of energy, and horses could not be compelled to stand waiting on lighted avenues but ran away still harnessed to their empty carriages, eyes rolling with fear.

"Still," he had said, "when bustles replaced hoops, they claimed that this panicked horses too. Traffic accidents are an impediment to commerce, so will ladies *please* dress conventionally?"

Idiocy amused her father, and he saw idiocy everywhere. He was a man who affected an interest in science, and perhaps it was of some importance to him, but his gabbing was mainly intended to annoy the softheads around him, whom he considered to be besotted by religion. Because he was a former Anglican minister, his grasp of scripture far exceeded that of anyone who might want to take him on, even her churchy grandmother, who retired each night to read a page or two of the Bible before sleep — the gospels as soporific; Job's endless trials a stiff sleeping draught, his story left unresolved. Her father, on the other hand, would tap his own standard Bible where it still sat by his bed, never dusty but never moving its position on the table, and say, "Now, that's a grand tale." He would not follow his brothers or mother to church. He had never visited his wife's grave in the church-yard, as the rest of the family did once a month, to gaze down on the rose marble tablet. She remembered her grandmother bending to flick debris from its face. A small photograph had been embedded there at great cost, framed in tin. It was now completely faded away. This was the comedy of it. Mother, wife, daughter-in-law — now a signified blank.

She would stand at her mother's grave with the other grim-faced attendants, trying to blot out the memory of her father, who, in the drunken month after the funeral, one night summed up in frigid detail the most likely condition of his late wife's beautiful body. Not resting on the bosom of Christ. Oh, no. Not sleeping. But this other horrible process. One's passage through life, he'd said, was as involuntary as peristalsis, and life itself enacted a frightful digestion. For her father, the problem lay in life's enclosure; once started, it must stop. And no comfort at either end. No heaven, no saviour. Just cessation and decay.

"Why do you pretend there is more?" he'd asked his mother. She shook her head and announced that she pitied her own son, for pain was making him morbid.

"Oh, I see," he said, "we mustn't be morbid about death? How comforting it must be to have a bedtime story to tell yourself, Mother, how consoling to stand like idiots around a stone."

His faith, when it flew, had left nothing in its place, no opposite protesting view, no view at all.

86

Her grandmother whispered to her at bedtime, "Despair is a sin, Mary, and a minister in despair is the most pitiable creature on earth." The soft hands stroking her cheeks, charm bracelets jingling. "You must always have hope for your father, hope for his return," as if he, too, had passed over to some other place. She remembered her father years later, after the worst was over, sitting in the garden at night, visible only by the glow of his little pipe, the tiny caldera with its rouged lip. He was invisible in the dark with his mourning clothes and black hair. After his wife's death he never wore anything but black again.

The widow sat in her well of uninvited memory. One looks back in awe. Alone in a dim clearing with nothing but the flash of sparrows about her. No sound but wind. A dry white sky was stretched over her and seemed barely to move. It was cloud but not cloud — simply the lighted void. *Is not God in the heights? And behold the stars, they, too, look up in wonder.* These things came to her, these little bits of Sunday school prattle.

She rose with a pain in her gut and put away her tobacco pouch, wrapped the pipe in cloth and tucked it away too. She put the saddlebags and purse under the skirt of an evergreen tree and took the saddle and blanket from where they hung from a branch, stirrups dangling loose, and also laid these on the carpet of pine needles. Then she took her clothes off and went on pale and unsteady legs, bare-assed, into the trees, where she sat across a fallen rampike and expelled a painful, intermittent slurry from her body.

87

That evening she went sighing into the tent of branches and curled up with her belongings, the fur coat over her like a blanket. A lonely summer night, where snow fell in the alpine dark and lay dusty upon the leaves and grass. The meat frosted over near the dead fire; the surrounding ground was wet, ringed with snow. But the widow slept with her cheek on the stolen little silk purse, a sucked-on strand of hair in her open mouth.

This is how William Moreland found her. He had tracked what he recognized as the smoke from a pipe, expecting to find several men. He had approached cautiously, from upwind, in case there were dogs. He found nothing but a girl.

Moreland stood over the dreaming stranger for a long time, hands on his hips and a pistol at his waist.

CHAPTER
SEVEN

When she awoke, he was across the clearing, sitting on his haunches.

"You aren't with the Forest Service, are you?" he said.

The widow stared at him, half sitting up. He could not actually be there, that was obvious, and so she tried to avert her eyes, wash the illusion away. But he would not vanish. She coughed and ran a palm over her sleepy face. He was still there. And so she sat up and attempted to fathom the presence of this human, here in the wilderness. An agonizing mix of panic and gratitude filled her. Safe or not safe? She could not tell.

He was smallish, tidy, with a huge old-fashioned moustache, shirt sleeves rolled to his elbows even in the cold, and suspenders to keep his pants up. His hair had the same healthy oil you saw on Indian women, and it shone in places. A deep pink suffused his cheeks — like a child who has been running.

"You all by yourself?" he said. He had affected the tone of one speaking to an idiot. She did not move or speak. He approached her and she scrabbled away from him, but he kept coming. It wasn't until he touched her that a true clap of terror ran through her. This was real, it was happening, and she could not know where it would lead. He tried to raise her, but she was so weak her knees would not support her. The widow sank down heavily, her head spinning. Her hand was shaking in his. The man was looking up the mountain as if judging the grade. Then he assessed her belongings, which lay strewn all around her, a rude human debris. He seized her arm.

"Ally-oop!" he bellowed and threw her screaming over his shoulder.

The first night, she lay alone, febrile and tossing in his tent, while he sat outside by a fire and guarded her. At least that's what he told her, patting his pistol — that he would guard her against "intruders." Her head nodded and she panted shallowly with fatigue, but looking about the dark forest she wondered what intruders . . . what people? His camp was sparse, like the camp of a man on a short hunting trip, but everything was worn and rotting, many years old. A pair of snowshoes hung from one tree; from another, a shaving mirror. On a fallen log lay a hat so formless and marbled from sweat and rain that it might have been a large riverstone. He told her his name was William Moreland and that he had been living in the mountains for nine years. He didn't explain why.

He had fed her and washed her face with snow that he melted in a pot. The hot water and fusty washcloth made her skin tingle. He was extraordinarily gentle with her. She closed her eyes and tried not to weep. He explained that he'd thrown away her fiddleheads, for they were poison in great quantities; and the deer meat she'd been eating might be all right, but on the other hand it might kill her, depending on the animal and how sick it was. How else but from a sick animal could this skinny girl have got meat? He didn't know about the wolves.

"Did ya eat any raw?" he said loudly into her ragged, vacant face. But she could only watch his mouth moving. Sickness, fear, shock. She was on the edge of consciousness, at the horizon of it, a penumbra where the light sputters.

On the second night she woke to find him there in the tent with her, lying as formal as a mummy, his hands across his belly and his eyes open. All the blankets were laid over her. When she shifted to see his face more closely, he shot up and scrambled from the tent as if swarmed by bees. The widow lay listening to the wind in the trees and her benefactor's feet pacing the cold ground. They were at a high altitude, the air thin, few birds, the gurgle of mountain streams encased in ice. It was summer, but his camp was dusted with snow in the morning. It melted with the sun, but slowly built up in the shadows, dry frozen waves that crumbled like meringue under his boots. She spent most of her time inside the tent, staring out at him. She was awake now, and keenly aware of her position. Her grandmother would have thrilled to such a vivid disaster, like something from an oriental tale. She would have called it *peril*. And yet, the old woman would probably have condoned John's marital brusqueness, the way he impelled her urgently to the bed and drove himself into her with a force she could barely believe. His first furious go at her the worst, for it had been long-awaited, and she was utterly ignorant and unprepared for blood. Now she watched William Moreland with a worried eye as he stirred a pot of coffee. Smaller than John. He moved more quietly, though, his sleeves rolled up, immune to cold.

When he went out hunting, she roused herself and explored the tiny camp, inspecting everything he owned. She found her own belongings mixed in with his, and so she moved these into the tent and piled them together. The saddle of course had been left down the mountain's slope where she had hung it. She discovered a frying pan with Office of the National Park Warden burned into its wooden handle. No tobacco, no pipe. Worn socks so often darned that they were at least half thread. There were papers, and a notebook in which he had written his thoughts — nearly all of them, as far as she could make out, concerned the benefits of solitude or the grandeur of nature. These she struggled to decipher in her habitual way, word by word, forming the sentences and repeating them to commit them to memory, her mouth moving like a child's does. A strange picture of this man's life formed in her mind out of these glimpses.

He was soft of heart: "This evening I watched the thick mass of white fog as it slowly disappeared, revealing these beautiful green mountains surrounding the Canyon Station." He wrote humorously about God: "The Great Elementary Director has spent almost twenty-eight days amusing himself by way of creating misery for earthly humans. I for one would almost think he had created a switch that would alternate from rain to snow." And it seemed that he had lived lately in Idaho and Montana, where he made himself a regular at empty ranger stations and observation towers: "As one climbs the steps leading up to the little cabin, fifty feet above the ground on four tall cedar poles, the view becomes so impressive the observer feels as if they were becoming strangely intoxicated by the airy stimulants evaporating from such a beautiful nature-created scene."

Here was a man who suffered no loneliness, who spent his days as he wished, who believed he could so deeply commune with nature that deer would eat from his hand and allow him to scratch their heads. It also seemed Moreland was a chronic thief. The U.S. Forest Rangers had issued a warrant for his arrest after his incessant pilfering of their cabins. "Four men sleeping upstairs. I got a pair of good boots, the better part of a bag of oatmeal, lard, not so good rifle, and two pairs of pants." In other stations he got maps, binoculars, chewing tobacco, matches, sleeping bags — anything a woodsman might fancy and everything he needs. "I borrowed fifteen fire rations — mostly shotgun shells but some pistol too. Oil of clove for my tooth. What sainted relief came with that."

On one occasion, rangers had entered a cabin and found his abandoned meal upon the table, still warm. There were tales of pursuit, well-equipped men on snowshoes, on horse-back, pounding after their quarry in the moonlight, and Moreland far too swift for them,

93

disappearing into the woods like a djinn. His evasive techniques were out of boys' adventure books. He removed his shoes and, using long sticks, made tracks so his pursuers would think he had veered in another direction. He walked in reverse. He climbed trees. Always faster than the trackers, Moreland was a man chased through his own home, knowing its every corner and hiding place, accustomed as other men weren't to the subtler physiology of forests and rivers and snow, all for having been out in it, alone, without respite.

"I went to the river to cut down some trees, and afterwards I threw the logs in so the rangers would think I had fashioned a raft. Then I took my boots off and went straight up the mountain, stepping along a trickle of water no wider than my foot. In this way, I succeeded in losing them."

"Got a good handsaw and some coffee at Oakland River R.S. There is a poster up on the wall about me. They call me the Ridgerunner, which is a good name, since they could as easily call me 'that bastard.' I am a pain in their necks and they can't wait to get rid of me."

The widow closed the little notebook and stood thinking among the cedars and underbrush. She continued to think while stirring the fire back to life, her mouth dreaming the words over again. *These beautiful green mountains.* By the time the Ridgerunner returned, holding a limp and garrotted rabbit by its gangly hind legs, she was in the tent again, peering out at him like a badger in her cave.

"Ho," he grinned, "you still here?"

He slept during the afternoon, as the rabbit stew cooked, lying on a rain slicker in the sun with his arms behind his head. And at night, he guarded her.

On the third day, she saw a change in his demeanour. He kept glancing in her direction — a sly, determined glint there. She suffered a panicked certainty of what would come next. He would force himself on her. She reminded herself her husband had often done that, a voracious energy so overtaking him he was blind to her grunts and struggling, her attempts to rearrange him or push him off, his hard, heavy body laying down unintended bruises. Looking now at William Moreland, she gauged her chances of escape or rebuff, and slumped. She sank farther back into the dim of the tent.

Finally, he did stride across the clearing, but instead of entering the tent, he pulled an upright log to the open flaps and sat quietly with his hands on his knees, smiling. It was an unusually warm day. From his breast pocket he produced a little wadge of papers. They were newspaper clippings, and he riffled through them like playing cards, apparently looking for one in particular. When he found it, he began to read in the overly formal manner of a schoolboy. "Fire broke out at the university library building at Smithburg. It was totally destroyed. The fire is thought to be the work of incendiaries with a grudge against books."

He grinned widely at her, waiting.

The widow could not fathom the meaning of this prelude, if indeed it was a prelude. After a moment, he took out another clipping. "Patrons of Hoglund's

Barber Shop were obliged to rush into the street to stop two well-known church matrons, Miss Pike and Miss Case, who were administering a severe horsewhipping to the local mailman. The beating had been going on for some time before it was finally stopped. The victim, John P. Berry, refuses to lodge a complaint, as he admits to having slandered the ladies on numerous occasions."

The widow shuffled a little closer to him and made herself comfortable, still unsure what he was doing.

"I like that one," Moreland said. On the next clipping he stumbled on the word *professes*.

"Dr. Joquish, a well-known citizen of Turo, claims that his soul recently separated from his body and went up to the heavens where it met and talked with a goat. He . . . *professes* to remember the circumstances well. This story is alarming to his family and the faculty of the university where he teaches. But the doctor is a man of strong mind and he refuses to retract his statement." Moreland glanced at his audience, clearly amused. But the confused widow simply gaped at him. He tried another:

"Victoria Green, of Olander, was bound to the county courthouse for the sum of $500. She was charged with sending obscene matter through the mails. Miss Green sent her neighbour a letter of the filthiest description because she blamed him for destroying her rose bushes." Seeing that this had produced a half-smile on the widow's face, he quickly searched for another story, pulling at the folded clippings and refiling them until he found the one he wanted. This sheet was yellowed and badly worn, and he was obliged to hold it delicately before him.

"Jacob Neuhanssen, lately a farmer out of Durham Falls, was discovered by a local physician, J. M. Keeler, to be in the process of hanging himself from a tree in front of his house. Keeler rushed to cut the suicide down, but in dropping to the ground Neuhanssen broke his leg. As the farmer was now unable to move, the physician ran to get his wagon to take the unfortunate fellow to his surgery. But in his haste, Keeler backed the wagon over Neuhanssen, killing him. No charges are to be laid against the physician."

The widow burst out laughing. Moreland stuffed the papers back in his pocket, clearly pleased with his work. He rubbed his hands together heartily and stood to go.

"More later," he promised. And with that, he went to lie in the sun with his hat over his eyes. The widow sat stunned at the flap of the tent, an open-mouthed smile lingering on her lips. She studied the contours of Moreland's face in profile. A similar smile lingered there.

That night, the widow again found him lying next to her. She remained still, warm under her blankets. He lay with his hands on his belly, the picture of calm, but after a moment she saw his heart beating hugely under his shirt.

"William," she said. At the sound of her voice, he lurched up and made for the exit.

"Stay," she said, gripping the back of his shirt so it came out of his waistband, "stay here. Lie down and sleep. Don't argue." She removed a blanket and spread it over him. And so they both lay, fully clothed against the cold mountain air, neither sleeping, but then, after a time, sleeping lightly. When she woke, needing to pee, she saw their breath had formed ice on the inside of the tent. When she touched it, it tinkled like glass and fell away, almost evaporating as it touched her hand.

In the days to follow he would coax her from the tent to teach her how to use a rifle. It was something she already knew how to do, but she liked the sound of his voice. They worked without ammunition, for he could not waste it — even so, they could both tell how wild her aim was. The calibre of rifle he had was for larger game and would not do for rabbits, he said. "Unless you want scrappy pieces." He also showed her how to lay a proper snare. But the rabbits seemed to know an amateur job when they saw it and avoided her traps entirely.

He took her on a walk for her strength. Together they wandered the sloped ground below their camp, the canopy of the trees so thick above that the air was motionless and the bark sparkled with frost. They sat in a clearing where the mist was thick and cold. It moved in like cloud, and in fact might have been. A rivulet of icy water gurgled nearby. He snapped rosehips from a still-blooming bush and ate them. He told her about his life, some of which she already knew from her spying. He had been raised in the Idaho woods by a lenient and often absent father. He believed most people could benefit from solitude. Too much society, he argued, always left one anxious and depressed. He was thirty-five years old, or so he figured, but a life outdoors had aged him considerably. He had been employed once or twice, but the experiment had always ended in criminal charges. One summer he worked as a flumewalker for a Montana logging company. Every day he would check the long water trough that ran downhill past stumps and other logging rubbish, along which logs would be sent banging and leaping to the river. If there was a jam in the flume, he would clamber up, slam his hook into the offending log, and pull it free. He was expected to keep the trough clear of debris and daubed with tar so it didn't leak. He was happy in his work. But he had also made repeated romantic advances on a girl cook who already had a lover. The girl never actually rebuffed him, and so a kind of feud developed. Moreland's rival had friends while he himself had none, so everywhere he went in camp, he was unwelcome. He took to wearing a pistol. Eventually he was moved to use the pistol to blow a hole in his rival's bunkhouse door, and that was the end of his job. He knew when to disappear. He'd spent that winter in an empty and half-ruined company cabin ten miles north, but no one thought to look for him there.

Later, he worked for another logging company in Idaho, making dynamite sticks to blow stumps out of the ground, pouring TNT into paper sheaths and attaching the wicks. His fingers were stained black from the powder and they ached at night. The scent of it had stayed in his nostrils, prickling, and he carried the dust in his hair and clothes. He was extraordinarily careful around matches and fires. Soon he was promoted to "powder monkey" and was allowed to blast stumps from the ground. He learned to drill holes in the massive roots, below the flat, ringed surfaces as perfect as tabletops, angling the drill down through the roots and dropping the already hissing bombs into the dark.

"One fellow wasn't fast enough," he told the widow. "The ground jumped up and broke both his legs. But I'm pretty quick on my feet."

That job, too, ended when someone, not the Ridgerunner, blew the saw house up, dynamiting one supporting beam completely away so the building groaned over sideways and hung there like a poorly made wedding cake. With no work to do, and thus no money, the men fell to drunken conjecture, and of course the most likely culprit was William Moreland. Furtive, reclusive, prone to argument, and sporting a pistol, the Ridgerunner again tested the winds of human opinion and found reasons to vanish.

By mid-winter that year, the Ridgerunner was as close to bankrupt as a woodsman could be: his boots worn down to flaps, his supplies exhausted, no ammunition left. Nothing in his possession was dry, nor had it been for weeks. Rot had set into everything. That was the only reason he got caught, he told the widow — he was slowed down by misfortune. Two detectives, Horner and Roark, hired at great expense by the now enraged director of the Forest Service, found his footprints and followed them to their source. They had been tracking him without success for four weeks, his trail fading or simply ending without explanation, so the two trackers were almost convinced the Ridgerunner was not entirely real. And so they were momentarily amazed when they came over a rise and spotted him there. It was like seeing a real leprechaun. Moreland was camped down in a hollow, out of sight, huddled by a deliberately modest fire in the dusk. Had they not been looking for him, they might have passed right by, unaware of his presence. Rifles poised, they crept downhill toward him, one from the north, one from the south, and the Ridgerunner did not hear them coming. Not until Horner tripped on his own snowshoes and fell face first down the slope, shovelling up a mound of snow before him that eventually covered his head. Before the Ridgerunner could move, Roark was behind him with the rifle at his ear.

"Well," Moreland said, "I guess you sweethearts have been looking for me a long time."

"Yessir," said Roark.

"You wouldn't like to let me go, would you?"

"Not a chance."

They took him to a cabin, one he'd broken into the previous May. He chuckled as they struggled with the ruined padlock, and eventually they smiled too. He was given a meal and some new clothes. The Ridgerunner's socks were so rotten they could be put on from either end, and his captors held these artifacts up and marvelled at them. He was not what they had expected. Instead of the rude delinquent they had set out to capture, here was a polite, well-mannered man. They were also surprised at his modest stature, for in their minds the Ridgerunner had become a behemoth. He sat peaceably and ate hot oatmeal, dry venison, handfuls of nuts, and he drank coffee. He asked for bread fried in lard, and Roark made it for him. They found two odd boots for him — same make and size, different colours, but he pronounced them marvellous and strode about the station floor with his arms outstretched. "Boys," he said, "I'm a dandy!" He slept handcuffed to the very bunk he had slept in, months ago and alone, but this time, when he rose in the morning, he didn't make the bed, or tidy up, or take anything with him when he went out the door.

His lawyer told him it would be a hot debate. On the one hand, ranger stations were intended by the American government to be used as a refuge by lost travellers, they were to be properly stocked, they were not to be padlocked. On the other hand, had Moreland ever actually been lost? Twenty-seven times? In court, his lawyer painted him as an individualist — as all men are, or have the right to be. And he painted the Forest Service as a critical organ of the government that had been corrupted by a rot that seeped downhill from the director's office.

The prosecutor, on the other hand, may have regretted his position, or may himself have been an individualist at heart, for he chose to dwell on the cost of the manhunt. This forced him to bring out account books and ledgers and other soporifics, for which the jury began to hate him. In the end, it was the fact the rangers had resorted to padlocks that turned things in Moreland's favour. That, and the Ridgerunner's obvious charm when testifying on the stand. He was an amiable, well-fed, well-rested man. In small doses he even enjoyed human company. He was amazed at how much could change in a few years. He admired the dress styles of the women in the balcony, the way the judge wore his moustache. He told the jury that if he'd known jail was so nice he would have given himself up much sooner. Even the judge laughed.

But the trial went on for many days, and by the end of it, Moreland's equanimity had fled. A man becomes a hermit for a reason, he told the widow. Every time he was brought back to his cell, he paced like a dog and complained of a stifling lack of air. He could neither eat nor sleep, his gut was anxious, nothing would help. He attempted civility, joked with his keepers, but his eyes belied the attempt. It was like there was a hum coming from him that rose in pitch every hour, and it began to jangle the nerves of everyone concerned. In a stunning lack of correctional judgement, the Ridgerunner was let out of his cell to wander the halls of the courthouse, but soon returned as if pursued by the furies, saying he didn't see the point. He seemed unable to retreat within himself, as other men did, and find solitude there. He lacked the practice, perhaps, but the more horrible truth was that he knew of another, larger life.

"I can't shut the world out," he said to the widow, "any more than I can do without air." So he had paced his open-doored cell, clutching his last shreds of patience, and on the final day, when his keepers clapped him on the back and wished him luck, they did it as much for themselves as for Moreland.

The jury returned in ten minutes with an acquittal, and William Moreland was free. As soon as he was down the front steps of the courthouse building, the Ridgerunner was off again, walking in a straight line toward the edge of town. A wagon or two drifted along beside him, occupants curious to see the notable little outlander in new and oversized clothes, a pair of mismatched boots on his feet. Poorer than ever before, he now had only the clothes on his back, for everything else had been confiscated or thrown out. His lawyer had handed him two dollars, but the Ridgerunner had gazed at the bills in his hand as if staring at some childish trinket. The next afternoon, he was on a trail going along the Clearwater River, where two Forest Service workers were labouring on a firewall. He chatted with them and told them who he was, and they betrayed unguarded excitement, offered him their lunch, and asked him where he was headed.

"I came back to see if these mountains were as beautiful as I remember them," he said, "or if I just imagined it all. I'm not going to stay down here." He headed for the first ranger station he could find, stocked up, and headed north into Canada.

"They probably think I'm dead now," he said. "That was nine years ago. 1890."

The widow thought for a second. "That's thirteen years ago," she said.

"Thirteen?" William Moreland reared back. "What year is it now?"

"1903."

He sat for a second longer, then stood and put his hands in his pockets. A bunch of crows settled in the treetops above and argued hoarsely. It was a long time before he spoke.

"I missed the turn of the century."

CHAPTER
EIGHT

That afternoon, they picked their way down the talus, the Ridgerunner holding her elbow, then went along an alpine river and paused among the wild roses, a soft, warm breeze coming from the lowlands. The widow took a rosehip from the bush and ate it, as she had seen him do. It was dry and almost sweet. She bent to touch the blooms where they drooped, pale pink. Altitude changes everything, she thought.

After a while, they sat together quietly, he glancing at her from time to time expectantly, as if she, too, might offer her autobiography. What could she possibly tell him? What could she admit? Nothing. Her mind drifted down the mountain to where it must be warmer, past the foothills, down onto the plains and the farms, where men would be bent sweating over their work, and cows with dung-covered tails swatted away flies. Women fanning themselves. Her grandmother would be having her midday lie-down, a Bible open and ignored on her chest. And her father would be in his law office, sweating in his dark suit. On the wall, the twin diplomas: law and divinity. The widow knew, because she knew her father, that his feet would be up on his desk and he would be smoking a pipe. He did contracts, and few of those. No stirring courtroom polemics for him. There would be few clients, only the ones he liked, because he had married a rich and sickly girl, and employment was purely a caprice, a distraction, meant to keep his mind off his mourned wife, her name a hex against the remainder of his life, what he called "the interminable, pointless joke."

Had he heard yet? Did he know what his quiet daughter Mary had done? Well, that would shake him, she knew. He was now the father of a murderess. Divinity and law, people would say he had failed at both. She looked ruefully at the Ridgerunner and wondered whether she could tell him about herself. But how to tell him about a life she wasn't sure she remembered fully?

She recalled her mother only in glimpses: the long, slim fingers, the brow white and unmarked despite the woe it hid, white nightgown after white nightgown, medicine vials and a porcelain bowl, a closed door, silence in the house, a glimpse of blue-veined feet dangling above the floor, weak sighs and hanging head. It seemed that this was all her mother was or ever had been. Perhaps, long ago, she had risen from the bed occasionally or walked slowly in the garden. In an unimaginable past, the woman must have been strong enough to have a baby. But everything is remembered by its moment of greatest intensity. Dying was hers.

The invalid had to have rest; lupus took up all of her attention. So the little girl became a spy, peering into her mother's dim room where curtains moved like ghosts and nothing else did. The point of thin toes at the end of the sheet. Slippers on the mat, ready for a walk that would never happen. A withered voice sighed, murmured, beseeched no one: *I don't know what I've done wrong.* The sweet smell of sickness seeping into the hall where the girl stood still as a panther, watching the hand that had never touched her, never stroked her hair, floating about the sheets. *Oh,* the soft voice sighing, *this is depressing.*

Sometimes Mary would sit outside the sickroom with her hands in her lap, and it was as if they were together, the two of them — the girl silent, listening to her mother's despairing voice coming from the other room like a kind of confession, whispers meant only for her: *He's always so certain. How can he be sure?* Then a shallow half-sigh of fatigue.

And yet when anyone came into the room — the girl's grandmother, for instance, standing by the bed, her stout hips wrapped in white aprons, or her father sitting on the bed and kissing his wife's thin hands — there was no such display, not a hint of self-pity. Just attempts at bright talk, a theatrical wellness, the fiction that she would soon find her strength and get up. This, too, the little girl heard, waiting spectral in the shadows. And her grandmother would stride out to seize her, saying, "Off with you, now. Go and play."

The end came in silence. The clock in the invalid's room had been deliberately stopped to cease its chattering, syncopated war with the last laboured breaths. A maid sobbing down a long hallway. A hearse moving slowly down an avenue of trees under the heavy bell of summer sun, the mourners on foot behind it.

The widow stood slowly and brushed twigs off her wide black pantlegs. How fiercely these long-unremembered things rose from the darkness. It was impossible for her to shut them out, they came in floods, ringing in her ears. When she looked back up, she saw a smoke-coloured thing among the trees, moving leisurely along, head down, cropping.

"My horse!" she cried, pointing.

"Where?"

"Right there!"

"Where?" The Ridgerunner stood up now too. "What are you seeing?" he said.

The mare's heavy head swung up and gazed at her, the mouth chewing. Short blond sticks of hay fell from the churning jaw. Impossible; there was no hay in the mountains. The horse shook its mane and went back to cropping, tail swaying gently as it stepped forward. She heard the hooffalls, smelled its damp hide, the dream floating there, stunningly real. The widow sat down hard and could not speak. Tears ran down her cheeks. She was helpless to stop the ghosts.

William Moreland came and sat with her. She felt the warmth of his thigh next to hers. After a long moment he took her hand.

"It happens," he said. "I see things too."

"What things?" she said dubiously.

"Sometimes I see myself," he laughed. "It's true, my very own self. One time, I saw myself naked. I'll tell you now, that's the last thing on this earth I wanted to see." The widow managed an exhausted smile.

"Can you learn to put them out of your mind?" he asked. "Can you ignore them?"

"No," she said. Then, thinking about it, she murmured, "Maybe."

After that, he set about cheering her up. Lessons, he felt, were the way to merriness. He would not let the widow retreat into the tent. He cajoled her into putting on his snowshoes, and she clomped gracelessly about the camp. Zenta's boots, heavy as they were, barely filled the leather straps. And the snowshoes were impossible to manage. She found that she could proceed only in straight lines. When she attempted to turn in any direction, her balance abandoned her and she teetered and windmilled her arms until he was obliged to dash over and steady her. Incredible to think that this man could somehow run in snowshoes, in the dark, swift as a deer, and elude his pursuers. She looked at his smiling face and told herself he was just a normal person, not much different from her. She had done something similar — would he believe that she was able to outrun bloodhounds? Well, she wasn't likely to outrun anything in snowshoes. She stormed like a drunkard around the perimeter of the tent and finally collapsed against a tree, laughing.

"You're a vision," he said, "a nymph on her fairy wings."

"Be quiet!"

"The picture of grace and beauty."

"I'll make you be quiet!" She threw herself into the task again, lumbering after him.

110

★　★　★

By increments, they crept together in the tent. First, they rearranged the blankets so both bodies were covered. It was all very polite. Each watching the other's breath rise over them — his, hers, short white breaths. She was the first to roll over and look at him. Hers was the first hand to steal along under the rough blankets, where she found his leg, the worn outer seam of his pants. Her knuckles lightly brushed the long thigh muscle beneath the cloth. He rolled too, took her hand and pulled it up to his chest, where his heart raged. He kissed her fingers. They lay motionless, as if to go no further, but, heedless, the communion between them rushed invisibly forward. Wind hissed in the trees. His arm stole to her waist, hand tracing the contour of her back, exploring the rise of her shoulder. They came together and her mouth was pressed against his throat. She felt his sigh pass beneath her lips, the rough cloth of her widow's costume bunched up and tangled with the blankets.

He pressed himself, hard now, against the give of her thigh, shifted, then pressed again. The widow's blood racketed in her ears. She closed her eyes and held her breath. He lay her on her back and his knee crept between hers. She was a tiny floating thing, coming to the cataract's edge, gentle before the thundering drop.

"No!" she said suddenly, and struggled to get up.

Thinking he had been rebuffed, the Ridgerunner slid quickly away. She rose violently from the blankets and began pawing at her skirts, only to remember that she had sewn them into pants. She began unbuttoning her

111

bodice. Finally, he understood and began to help with trembling fingers, the two of them in a war with the multitude of tiny buttons. She pulled the clothing down, standing bent in the cramped enclosure, and wriggled from the legs of it, then fell on him with kisses, only to discover he was now pantless too.

The widow's head was swimming. How long had it taken them to get to this? Had she wanted this at the beginning? She didn't care, never would care, and so she touched him, his hardness leaping in answer, and began angling herself down onto him.

"Wait," he whispered and removed her hands from him. "This way. If it doesn't go in, you can't get knocked up." He did not enter her, but positioned her over him and pressed her down in her own wetness, slid her slowly back and forth, back and forth, along the length of him, his hands on her hips, guiding. She acquiesced, watching his eyes watching her. The flap of the tent's canvas, the strange kissing sound between them. And something in his face, some beautiful fury transpiring there. Her husband had never looked at her, never opened his eyes, but had buried his face in her hair and, to her view, he became only an advancing and retreating shoulder. Now, she could see this man's face, his pupils huge in the dark, see his joy, and it was contagious. All at once, she felt something.

"Slower," he whispered, but she would not slow. She moved back and forth, braced above him, amazed by the tug of pleasure.

"Wait," he said, "wait!" Still she rocked faster, pursuing a filament of something new, a voice on the wind, following as one does in a dream, hunting blindly, knowing somehow which way to turn, chasing a firefly into the dark.

He groaned and seized her knees as he jetted over his own belly, jetted and subsided. He subsided and lay still — but she was still floating helpless, disastrously unfinished. She rocked again, insistent, like a thwarted child, but it was gone. Silence hung in the tent's dim little universe. The warm liquid between them grew cool. She felt goosebumps spread along his thighs. Crouched darkly over him, steam rising from her shoulders, her hair hung over her breasts, the widow glowered down at William Moreland.

"Mary," he pleaded to her ghostly silhouette. "Now, Mary . . . I did ask you to slow down."

All that early morning they wrangled among the blankets, the widow kissing his face, and when the light came, they emerged sleepless and famished. They washed, and she set to cooking while he shaved. It was silent in the little camp, and the widow wore an easy smile on her face. She stole a look at him, watching his beautiful hands move, her metal spoon hanging above the pot, forgotten.

Later, in the manner of old duffers sitting before a fire, the two hermits fell to comparing storms they had seen. The Ridgerunner's stories were the more epic for his having been roofless during them. He remembered a blowy, restless summer evening when lightning had struck unexpectedly from a variegated sky, and there had been a single titanic roar, deafeningly close, that left him jabbering in surprise. Minutes later, he'd spotted a flickering glow in the trees to the north of his camp where a stricken tree, then several trees, had ignited. This clever escape artist had been at pains to decamp fast enough to outrun the advancing flames, scrambling to pack his bags with the glow behind him, then running like a mad Berber with chattels rattling on his back. There were nights when the aurora borealis seemed to seek him out, linger over him like a lover, a moaning rumble along its shores. He told her about deep summer on Idaho lakes when there came clouds of silverfish, mosquitoes, plagues of blackflies, waves of them, humming the air like eruptions from some infernal fissure. For him, the seasons passed like people on a road, each with its own character, its own thoughts and messages. There was the cold spell, he estimated it to be around Christmas, when wearing every stitch of his clothing was not enough, and so he carried his canvas tent round his shoulders and over his head like a massive monk's cloak. He had drifted south, but the cold weather followed him. Any animals he could shoot had to be skinned and cleaned where they fell or their bodies froze hard as hammers by the time he got back to camp. A snared rabbit, utterly stiff. The Ridgerunner dancing to stay warm, knocking the dull head against his knee, parrying the thrusts of an imagined fencing partner, the dead rabbit as his foil. He dreamed of killing something big so he could cut it open and put his numb hands inside and warm them, just once, but the deer and elk had drifted south off the mountain ranges. Finally, the cold abated and snow fell softly, day

114

and night, snow to his chest, twenty feet deep in the draws and gullies, windblown drifts that stood higher than his head and that he scaled in his snowshoes like an ant struggling up the toe of a boot. Snow in his lungs, on his blue lips, driven on furious night winds through the very fabric of his tent, and in the morning, crystals carried sparkling on the air. In this extreme cold he saw peril and beauty in measured balance, like a promise to him alone, silent confirmation of the divine.

The widow sat riveted as he talked. His tales were honed by the storyteller's art, and selective, but this girl was the perfect audience and her eyes shone darkly in the firelight. She wore an aspect of devotion.

"I think you're brave," she told him solemnly. "I wish I was like you."

"Oh hell," he said, delighted, "brave's got nothing to do with it."

In her turn, she told him a tale of green hailstones as big as a man's fist tearing through the trees and drumming on the cabin's roof. In a hissing melt they came down the chimney and expired in the fire, dousing it, so a river of sooty water ran the length of the building and the widow was frantic to sop it up. With a dirt floor, and nothing but an old wagon cover spread across the bedroom floor, she lived in fear of mud. Finally she and John had laid a bucket in the hearth and sat watching as it rang out, spittoon-like in the night. After the storm came an unearthly quiet, the yard littered with glistening debris, while far away, injured cattle bellowed. The cabin's only window had

115

been staved in that night and had never been repaired. John had simply blacked it out with hand-hewn boards hammered into place, and with that, all light, but for what peeped in through the front door, was excluded from the cabin's damp interior. Eventually John admitted he lacked the money to buy more glass. She gave him back her engagement ring so he could sell it, but no window came; the ring simply dropped into the well of his debts. She wondered whether she should ask for help from his brothers, Jude and Julian, for they owned the next parcel of land, but she saw them so rarely, and they had never been warm or helpful . . . Here the widow's tale ceased and she fell into tense silence.

"One thing about living up here," murmured the Ridgerunner, "there's no goddamn debt." The widow snorted, then sighed.

It was a mystery to her why he should need time between bouts of sex, for she needed no such interval. He could not make the coffee in the morning for her kissing him, and she would not let him leave the camp to check his snares but dragged him back to the tent. She fretted over his ratty socks, and told him she would sew him some new clothes, perhaps a coat made of hide. She asked him where they would go next, what kinds of places they would see, as if they were a genteel couple on holiday, they didn't mind where they went, and they would never part. The shadow of something fretful passed over his face and then was gone.

116

One warm afternoon they lay together, almost sleeping, arms and legs entwined, her thighs slaked with his semen, while the shadows of leaves trembled on the tent's screen. Outside, the shaving mirror rocked where it hung, victim to a gentle wind, and cast an oval of light swaying idly about the camp. A bright spot leaping, and a band of brightness within which motes and insects danced. His breath in her hair, his pulse visible along the inside of his elbows. She rolled and pushed him on his back and placed her head against his chest, so she could hear the thundering source. Untold months of sleeplessness evaporated in a sigh, a slack mouth, and this heartbeat.

Later, he sat naked at the foot of the tent and held her feet in his lap. He stroked the hair on her leg, running his palm along the nap. He cupped her calf in his hand, weighing the muscle against his palm.

"You could eat this," he said.

She poked his belly with her foot. "Have you done this before?" she asked.

"Do what?" he said. "Threaten to eat a girl?"

Her eyes were unreadable. "Who was she?" she said.

"Well, now, she had big, beautiful brown eyes and long lashes. And she was taller than me." His face had taken on a sly cast, so she knew he was not serious. "Not a big talker, of course. But a good listener."

"All right, who was she?"

"My old Jersey cow," he grinned.

She did not laugh at his joke but dismissed it with a sigh and sat up suddenly, her hands behind her, bracing. Her face was gloomy and she regarded him intently. His smile faded as her eyes bored into him, depthless and strange.

"John had others," she said. "Two that I know of. And I was his wife. It doesn't seem likely I'd know everything, does it?"

"John," he said, weighing the name.

"He could have had many of them. I'd never know."

"Some men do."

"Why? Why do they need to?"

"What do you mean, *why*?"

"I never denied him anything," her voice was harsh, for the giving had been at some cost and was regretted. "I worked hard for him. But nothing I did was right. Everything I put my hand to displeased him. Sometimes, I would imagine I was one of those girls. In my imagination they looked nothing like me, and I gave them names. I wondered whether he was different with them than he was with me."

"Men do it," he said thoughtfully, "because women let them."

"Maybe."

"Would he be angry about us?" he asked.

"No. Because he's dead."

The Ridgerunner's face registered surprise, but not at the news — she knew it was her flat tone that took him aback, the want of regret. They sat in silence, a strange unspoken conversation between them. His face questioning, and hers slowly answering. And then, in tiny increments, they both began to grin again. A dappling of light across the widow's gloom.

118

"All those women," she sighed, lying back down, "it never did him any good. He didn't have the slightest idea what to do."

The widow woke at dawn. She stretched and yawned and pulled her hair from her face. Above her was the soft canvas of the tent, through which a golden light flooded. The shapes of trees waving in streaks of sunlight . . . she smelled pipe tobacco. At this, she bolted upright, scrambled from the tent naked, and went striding across the clearing to where the Ridgerunner sat on a stump smoking her pipe. She swiped it from his mouth.

"*Bloody* . . ." she muttered, rubbing spit from the stem, "bloody *man!*"

"Now," he wheedled, "I thought we discussed this issue of ownership and the tyranny of . . ."

"No."

"Darling . . ."

"I said no, I meant no." She poked solicitously at the bowl, checking the way he'd packed it, then bit down on the stem, saying through gritted teeth, "This pipe is mine." She turned and paced back to the tent, her ass pink with cold, her feet storming the frosted mud.

"You know," he said, "if I was ever to disappear, I'd be sure to take that pipe with me." She stopped and turned around, a stricken look on her face.

"Would you ever leave?" she asked.

"Never," he said.

Two days later, the Ridgerunner was gone.

★ ★ ★

They came diagonally across the dusty street, shoulder by shoulder, and stepped up onto the boardwalk, their long legs swinging. A second later, the brothers entered the telegraph office. One or two of the girls gaped at them while the others tapped. The elderly manager got up laboriously from his seat, shaky, his eyes shifty, as if these customers were about to rob the place.

"Order forms are over there, gentlemen."

The brothers turned to the counter against the wall.

Gradually the office fell silent, the remaining telegraphists pausing over their keys, while a soft electric hum came from the generator in the middle of the room. A muted pattern of motion echoed between the men. One head inclined, the other followed. Making out the transfer form, turning in unison, approaching the front desk. The manager smiled dryly, presenting a false, mercantile goodwill. The brothers ignored him and assessed the price list.

Finally, one of them put down a large finger on the price list. "This one," he said, and his brother lay a single coin on the counter with a snap.

The old man smiled and bowed and took up the paper message and the coin. "Thank you, gentlemen. Come again." He continued to nod and smile. "We'll send this off right away."

But the two men did not move to the door — they were waiting to see the message sent. Suddenly, one of the telegraphs erupted with a spatter of coded clicks, the metallic voice of an unknown operator. With a start, the old man beetled over to the youngest girl.

"No mistakes, please," he said fiercely and put down a transfer form. It was addressed to a magistrate in Toronto.

Father,

found and lost her stop Mountain range impassable stop

Will hire guide.

The telegraphist put her fingers to the hammer and began.

CHAPTER
NINE

A lone eagle drifted in lazy circles, studying some unseen curiosity. The widow stood shivering at the edge of the camp. An inch of wet snow covered everything. Her boots were wet. The air so clear she could see through the trees to the range beyond, white-capped and running in a palisade away to nothing. The eagle was floating overhead now, its wings black, the pale head angled to watch her. Then it vanished in a green blur of trees, followed in a moment by specks of sparrows, shooting after the monster, peeping in triumph, as if they themselves had driven it off. A vigilance committee that lets the thief simply pass through town and be gone. The widow followed their progress, hollow-eyed and pale. She watched until all that was left was a flat white sky.

That morning, she had returned from checking her empty snares to find the camp not only empty but vacated. She had stood at the perimeter, blinking in disbelief, more shocked by William Moreland's absence than she had been by the sudden sight of him, standing there over her as she expired, his hands on his hips. This was more unreal. Her small pile of belongings had been collected on a fallen log to keep them dry. He had left her the pipe after all. The tent was gone, the fire cold, nothing was hung on the trees or strung from ropes between them. She discovered that he had left her food, some rabbit meat, a handful of coffee grounds, and a letter explaining his inevitable flight. The letter was so filled with expressions of love that she wondered for a moment whether he had meant it for someone else.

Now she sat alone as the sun set, rain settling on her hair, and read each word again in stunned disbelief. This time her mouth didn't move. It was like he was whispering in her ear, but meaninglessly: *Love . . . adore . . . union of our spirits*. Then, at the end: *I cannot stay. It is too much for a solitary man to change.*

Too much, yes, it was too much. There was no sign of him, and yet, when she looked, he was everywhere. Their footprints, both sets, had mackled the uneven ground, hers on his, his on hers.

How cruel now that she had really seen him, touched him. That he had been real, not another phantasm drifting greyly among the trees, a little gasp of loneliness from her afflicted mind. But a beautiful face, and a voice not merely familiar but in her bones. The Ridgerunner was gone, and she could still smell him on her hands.

She turned the paper over. There were two words there: *Head west.*

Which way was west? She knew, at least, the sun rises in the east and sets in the west. She looked up: no sun. Trees hove into a dark spiral above her, and beyond

123

that, black needles of rain were coming in from heaven. There was no west, no north, no earth beneath her feet. Her face streamed, upturned, her eyes pressed shut. An enormous sob shook her. She folded his letter and slipped it beneath her clothes to keep it dry, though the paper had been folded in rain, and brought rain with it, slowly foxing as it lay against her breast. The widow staggered to their recent bed, the pressed concavity where their tent had been. She did not make a fire, but lay on the carpet of needles, cocooned again in her fur coat.

The air grew cold and still. Snow fell through the cedars and covered her, covered everything else, until the whole night world was only snow, and she but a ripple in it.

All the next afternoon the widow followed a stream downhill, stepping from rock to bank along its meandering edge. For two days she had been sneezing, and now her lungs were congested. She moved slowly and her back ached. From time to time she was obliged to hold her saddlebags close and lean out to spit, though she looked about her before doing so, as if some scandalized neighbour might be watching. Moss clung to the pates of riverstones, water droplets suspended among the green fibres, gleaming even in the shade. It was a steep incline and sometimes the widow went slewing on the loose earth, wheeling her free arm. The hiss of a waterfall reached her long before she found it, water curving over the final brow, beyond which rock and earth and grass dropped off in a sheer cliff. She peered over the edge to see the white stream drill off several shelves below. A pale rainbow was blown over the sloped and craggy rock face, and she looked beyond to see a meadow far below. Streaks of some purple flower ran through the distant green surface.

The widow would have to find another way down to the meadow. So she went back upstream a little, where she sat abruptly and wept, face in her hands. And when she was done, she sat in silence with her nose completely blocked and her eyes unfocused and downcast. She crouched like a dog and drank from the stream, kissing the surface and sucking the icy water up. Then she took off her boots and put her feet in. A strange burning sensation at her toes . . . and yet the water felt icy at her ankles. Curious, she pulled out her left foot to inspect it. The skin of the heel was yellow and appeared thickened, and there was a red rim around it. The toenails were dark. Her right foot was just as bad. Were her feet frostbitten? Or partially so? She rubbed gently at the sallow skin. It was like rubbing sand into her flesh. And yet when she stood and walked, even in bare feet, they felt no worse than the rest of her. Some muscles hurt, her lungs ached. The widow's slim shoulders were especially sore from carrying all her things. As she went back upstream, she bent from time to time to snap wild roseships from their stems and collect them in her pocket, for the rabbit meat was getting high, and she didn't know how long it would last.

Halfway down the incline she paused to lower her bags so she could wave the dark cloth of her pants and cool herself. As she descended, the scent of the meadow below came to her in gusts and hints. Her knees trembled from exertion. She had stopped sneezing but still coughed and spat great gouts of yellow phlegm. It was as she bent to do this that she looked down to the meadow and saw a figure far below. The figure wore a light, wide-brimmed hat and sat mounted on horseback, holding another horse by the reins. He was looking up. Was he looking at her? Had he seen her? A wheeze came and went deep in her lungs, but there was no other sound. The figure remained motionless. She thought perhaps one of the horses was kicking at flies on its belly, but they were so far away she couldn't tell for certain.

Without knowing why, the widow ducked down suddenly and crouched like a spider on the ground. Her breath came fast, and it puffed up the dirt near her face. A rock outcropping stood between her and the watcher in the meadow. For many minutes, she didn't dare peek over it, but when she did, the figure was gone. The widow sat up, white-eyed. She hadn't decided what she would do when she found herself near people again. Suddenly it came in at her in a rush: People going out to church, streets, houses, carriages, the crack of rabbit hunters' guns in the fields. Police.

She pressed her face against her grimy palms. She knew she could no more retreat back into the mountains than she could go back home — not to her father, and surely not to the cabin. She froze, her fingers pressed to her eyes, and saw again the open door of her cabin, the laundry hanging from the line as if everything were all right. At twilight, the trees utterly still. Herself looking back through the open door into her own dark house. She had stood alone in the clearing, to all appearances a woman waiting to hear a sound from within the house, perhaps to hear someone calling for her. But she knew no sound would ever come.

The widow gathered up her things now and hurried along the path on trembling legs, choosing any fork that would take her away from the man on horseback.

No more than half an hour later she found herself in a clearing in the trees, the expanse of purple meadow flowers ahead of her, and the man on horseback regarding her from his mount. She took a step backward, as if she could withdraw before he saw her. But it was hopeless. He'd followed her progress down the rock face and come to wait at the place where he knew she would emerge. He was Indian, and sat on a very basic saddle atop a massive, scarred bay. Two braids came down over his green shirt front, and his face was shaded by the wide, uneven brim of a felt hat. His expression was one of amused curiosity, and the widow suddenly knew what kind of figure she must cut: a girl with wild hair, grimy face, fusted saddlebags, muddy silk purse, and torn boots. She held the fur coat against her hip like a load of laundry. The man's other horse was being led by its halter and it nickered at her. The widow's mouth fell open.

"That's *my* horse!" she croaked, her voice ragged with disuse. And indeed, it was the little roan, starved

127

and sway-backed, far less beautiful than its ghostly imagined counterpart, now watching the widow with strange, flecked eyes. She had never noticed before that its eyes were flecked.

The man said nothing and his expression didn't change. He turned both horses and started across the meadow.

"Wait!" she said. But he didn't wait for her. "You! Do you speak English? Let go of my horse!"

The little ensemble went on through the sunny grasses, the horses' tails swishing tiny insects up from the heads of flowers. The widow staggered after them.

"Thief!" she squawked. "Come back!"

She was quickly falling behind. "Let go of those reins!" she called out in desperation.

And to her surprise, he did let go of them. But the mare continued following him, nudging the rump of the animal before it, only occasionally looking back, reins dangling, to see the widow far behind, struggling along through waist-high grass.

By evening the man had started a fire and made himself some coffee and was frying meat in a pan. The widow sat at some remove, glowering, the delicious smell killing her. He did not look at her or speak, but she noticed that no matter where she went around the little camp, he never turned his back to her. She had collected her mare with only a little difficulty. Around its forelegs the man had affixed a hobble. As she approached, the mare kept backing up, moving just out of reach and jerking its head away. But finally it allowed itself to be captured, and she stroked its head and cooed into its face. She curried it with moss and twigs, but the experiment failed; it only made the grey hide streaked and dirty. She looked over at the man's bay horse. Its coat gleamed. He must have taken the horses to a river and run them through it.

At last light, she found herself inching closer to the fire. He now lay with his head propped on his saddle, fingers laced across his belly. She could see his eyes under the hat. They were watching her now, not as amused as before. Something about her worried him. Had he seen her coughing and spitting? Of course he had. It was likely he'd seen her long before that, standing atop the waterfall. A strange shame filled her and she could not meet his eyes. The idea that she had been wandering like a troll above the waterfall, while someone gazed up at her — it was a horrible thought. She began to retreat into the dark when his voice came to her.

"How'd you get separated from your horse?"

To her astonishment, she understood him. He had no accent she could detect. In fact, his voice was much like her father's, a nice voice. She didn't reply at first. She would not tell this stranger that she had lost her mind before she had lost the horse. Finally, she settled on the most transparent answer.

"Wolves," she said.

He nodded under his hat. "Truth is," he said, "I don't know why I was waiting for you to come down out of there. I should have been home days ago. I guess I was curious. And I thought it'd be a man." The fire hissed and glowed at his feet. The soles of his boots were lit by firelight and she could see the crisp stitching in them. "Did you come from Frank?" he asked.

She stayed silent.

"Sparwood?"

She shook her head.

"All right, then. Where?" He propped himself up on an elbow. Unfortunately, she now had his attention. The widow's addled mind stuttered away from the truth. Could an Indian get her put in jail? Probably. Would this man want to put her in jail? Impossible to tell. She lied and gave him the name of the next biggest town to hers. Strangely, this seemed to shock him.

"Are you saying you came through that pass?!" he pointed into the dark trees behind her.

"What pass?" she said.

"Those mountains there. You came right through them?"

She nodded.

"Well, that's something." His grin was huge. "When I tell my wife that a stupid white girl just wandered through that pass . . ." He chuckled and lay back down again.

She sat cross-legged, elbows on knees, her cheeks burning with fury. He didn't care one bit about her. She was a funny story he could tell people. He hadn't offered her any of the fried meat. And she would be damned if she'd ask him for some now. The fire settled suddenly and a corona of infernal fireflies exploded upward. The widow tossed another branch across the glowing mass of it and glowered at the man as the green bark steamed. The warmth was gorgeous, and her withered lungs ached with each breath.

When he spoke again, his voice was already slurred with sleep. "She won't believe it," he said.

The wind picked up in the trees above them. The heat from the fire tormented her feet, even through the soggy boots, and so she angled her legs out into the dark. A rank smell came to her on the breeze, and she recognized it as the rabbit meat in her bags. As repulsive as it was, her stomach growled. It was warmer down on this plateau, even among the trees, even as the damp earth soaked into her clothing. Down here it was summer. She felt a pleasant fatigue invade her body as she lay wheezing in the dark.

When the widow awoke, she found she had rolled in her sleep some distance from the fire, which was now going full strength. A coffee pot sat tilted among the coals at the fire's edge, and steam issued from the sharp little spout. She was alone in the clearing. She sat looking at the fire for some time before she dug into her saddlebags for the tin cup and poured herself some coffee. She stirred it with a twig and blew on the still boiling liquid until it was drinkable. When he returned, she saw that he had been bathing. His dark hair was twisted into a rope that hung down his back. He wore no shirt, and the water that ran down his back darkened the waistband of his pants. She turned away, for she had always disliked it when men paraded around with their shirts off. Even when her own husband had removed his shirt to cut wood or work on

131

the roof, she'd considered it prideful, vain, a kind of taunt. *You can't do this, woman — but I can.* She remembered her father's amusement when she had abused a hired boy.

"Why don't you take off your drawers too?" she'd cried. "Why not hop around like a dirty old monkey?" And her father had laughed while the boy flushed with shame.

The widow put her cup on the ground and began to walk away into the trees.

"River's the other way," he said, and she amended her direction.

It was a wide, shallow creek of mountain runoff, thick with riverstones, meandering among glacial humps in the ground. Meadow grasses grew right to the edge and tipped over and waved in the current as if drowned. She washed her face and feet. A high white cloud floated thinly over the mountain peaks. Dark pines stood in perfect alignment to the heavens. The widow coughed a deep bubbling cough, then spat. She squatted among tufts of water grass, her feet braced on uneven rock, and she peed. Afterwards, she washed herself, wincing, for it was agonizingly cold. She stood by the swift-moving river and looked out across the meadow to the mountains. William Moreland was up there somewhere, hidden in mist.

She had thought she was alone, but he had come upon her when she slept. How easily he could have tiptoed past, let her lie there sleeping, dying. Instead he had waited. He had admitted to watching her sleeping face all that first night. "You had this little strand of hair in your mouth," he'd said. A wincing tightness in her heart, just to think of it. Unbearable. She could still smell him, still hear his soft voice in her ear. The tent where they lay entwined together, her mouth against his arm . . . The widow's eyes welled with angry tears and she began sobbing. *Turn your back, just as he did.*

But how to do that? How had he done it?

When she returned, red-eyed, the man was properly dressed and his hair was braided. He gave her some hard little lumps of cooked dough. She bit into one and discovered that, while she had to chew endlessly, it contained dried berries and was delicious.

"May I have some meat . . . please?" she asked. He pointed to a rock on which he had laid out for her a blackened chunk of meat, already marauded by ants. His face said he had put it out some time ago, why hadn't she noticed it yet? She pounced on it, blew the insects away.

"I'm taking you to Frank," he said.

"Who?"

"It's a town. From there you can go back to your home." He watched her gobble the last of the meat so fast it left her hiccupping. "Or not. It's your choice."

They packed up their gear and she hung her saddlebags over the roan's shoulders. There was no saddle now, nothing to strap the bags to, so she would be forced to hold them in front of her to ensure they didn't work their way sideways and fall off as she rode. Without the saddle too, she could not mount the horse, no matter how she hopped and struggled. The man watched bleakly for a while, and eventually was obliged to dismount and come over to help her. Once she was up, he stood back and assessed her posture on the horse, but what he saw seemed to worry him. "Is that really your horse?" he asked and put a finger possessively around one of the reins.

"Of course. I told you that."

"You don't ride her very well."

She glared at him and yanked the rein away. This seemed to displease him even more; his face darkened. He snatched at the halter and dragged the roan toward a beech tree that stood alone at the edge of the clearing. "You see that?" he said, pointing to a scratch in its bark. He seemed to be pointing out one of a multitude of scars.

"What?"

"That, you stupid woman. *That!*" His finger pecked at the little slice. It might have been made by a knife, she could see that now. A wide Y shape, or maybe a T?

"That is a Peigan sign. And our campfire over there? I made that on top of their old one."

"And you're not Peigan, I assume?"

"Lucky for you."

She understood him, finally. He didn't trust her, didn't think she could ride with him out of trouble, he was afraid that she would drag him down and get him killed. As if in answer, he said, "Keep up, or I'll leave you flat." Then he turned and mounted his horse and together they rode out into the bright meadow. Saddleless, the roan's spine ground into the widow's pelvis in a way she knew would soon become painful. Her belly struggled with the first solid food she'd had

134

in days. And yet she felt well rested. She looked at this Indian's back, gazed at the rump of his horse with its swinging tail — it had finger-waves in it like a girl's hair. It occurred to her that this man could have taken her horse, taken all her things, left her in the mountains. But he hadn't, and that was something. She was clearly a burden to him, and nothing more than curiosity had got him into this. She felt sure she could veer off and go a different direction and he would not try to stop her. The widow wanted to repair things somehow, but didn't know where to start.

"What's your name?" she called to him. He was silent. They went up over a hillock, the horses rocking their necks with each step of the incline, and lightly trotted down.

"Do you mind my asking what kind of Indian you are?" The roan strained to tug at grasses as it went and she hauled up on its reins. "You can at least tell me your name, can't you?"

"What's yours?" he countered.

"Justine," she said, choosing the name of a girl she once knew. So, silence on one hand and a lie on the other; he had outdone her again. She ran her fingers through her hair in consternation. They continued along the edge of the creek together. Swallows skimmed over the grass and darted above the surface of the water catching flying bugs, and everywhere was the hum of bees. He relented a little and slowed his horse so that they were only a little off-parallel, but he radiated impatience, as if even walking the horse was something she did poorly.

"You know I'm from Cooperstown," she said. "You know where I'm from. Why can't you tell me about yourself?"

"Crow." He shook his head in its mottled hat. "I'm Crow Indian. We say Absarokeh. My mother was born on the other side of that hill, right there."

She waited for him to elaborate, but his face remained closed.

"And where were you born?"

"Baltimore," he said.

And with that he heeled the bay into a trot so he was ahead again. The interview was over.

The Ridgerunner crouched at midday in the lee of a massive cedar and waited and watched with his hunter's patience as all around him the wind blew. Grasses swam, trees bowed and creaked, and there was a hissing in the canopy above. He was the only still thing on this mountainside.

From his vantage point he could see the clearing, his own former camp, and the cold ring of stones where once there had been a fire. Movement everywhere. It promised a glimpse of human life, maybe even some small thing blowing across the ground, and her chasing after it . . . but no. No scent but cold and pine, no voice. Here he remained, hands squeezing the leather straps of his pack. He was whispering, his lips forming half-words and the shadows of explanations, excuses passing in sequence over his face.

After many minutes, he rose and eased the enormous weight from his shoulders and rested it against the tree.

And then, as if heading onstage, his face brightened falsely, and he hiked up his pants and strode into the clearing. William Moreland stood alone, hands dangling at his sides. Of course she was gone, everything was gone, every useful or comfortable thing. He had taken his things, she had taken hers. All that remained was the evidence of a camp.

So very unlike him to leave such a wreckage, for any following ranger to find. He had left too quickly. And there was too much evidence to conceal. The countless footprints, bed of pine needles in the shape of a tent's floor, a nail hole in a cedar where he had hung his mirror and then later removed the nail and packed it, the rope burns halfway up a trunk from the tent's guy line, the small puddles of coffee and rain, now frozen . . . and one of her bare feet expressed in mud, perfectly preserved.

He bent over this fossil, the small toes blurred by movement, but the lines of the foot intimately clear and frosted. He knew the weight of that foot in his hand. Faultless and warm. He closed his eyes, fighting an unnameable thing in himself. Then he seized the fire-blackened stones one by one and flung them two-handed into the trees.

He would erase it. All of it.

CHAPTER
TEN

That afternoon the widow followed her companion through a grove of scraggy, ivy-tented apple trees on an abandoned farm. She looked for buildings but there were none. No house, no barn. No shadow of human presence. Nothing left of the enterprise but this orchard in its decayed, marching lines. The mare tramped along heavily and the widow slumped on its bare back. A perfume in the air, the ground around them poxed with fallen fruit that lay in layers of years, squelching beneath the horses' hooves. The rotting apples seethed with drunken wasps.

The country passed with a comforting sense of procession now, and the widow was pleased at the way forest and rock-fall and pilings of scree seemed to sweep along majestically, not so wheeling and vertiginous any more. Here she was, wandering behind a man again, his purpose having become hers, just as she had gone with her husband into the wilderness on their rumbling ox cart. She recalled his white shirt sleeves, his clean black suit coat draped over his thighs.

How easily it had happened. Without understanding that she had agreed to anything, she had simply followed John Boulton into a new life. Behind the newlyweds rode several men on horseback and another cart pulled by heavy horses, and the drivers, mounted on crates and bins that rocked wildly with every tilt of the ground, were old and rough. They swore, then apologized to her, swore and apologized. At night they camped, and she would retire alone to their large tent and immediately put out the lantern to preserve oil, then lie in the dark and listen to the men talk. She had to listen to what they actually said to know they were arguing, since no one ever raised his voice. The fiercest accusation she heard was, "There's been a lot of that going on 'round here," which had been met with a long, fuming silence. But no one denied it, whatever *it* was.

Sometimes one or another of them would sing, often without accompaniment. One favourite was a teary song about a child left alone by his wicked parents and finally devoured by wolves, the mawkish chorus of which always provoked laughter. Later, she could hear the men snoring, murmuring in their sleep. When she rose in the morning, the oldest man was already up and had cooked breakfast, and he brought her food and fussed over how much she ate just like she were his own child. Nurture was not in her experience, and she hadn't known how to answer it, coming as it did from such a weathered old coot.

It was incredible how quickly an entire camp could be packed away onto the cart and strapped to the backs of horses. The oxen stamped as the yokes were put back on. The men whistled. Then they all moved on in a rambling, creaking train. At times the path they followed would spread out and fade, like spilled water, and the wagons would stop, and her husband would drop from his seat while everyone waited and walk ahead to look at things, trying to remember the way back to his property. At those moments, she would gaze in dismay at the trackless territory where they stood, dressed in their travel clothes, wondering what mote of memory or logic drifted there in her husband's mind, what in the world was telling him the way to go? Where was he taking her, and what did all this emptiness look like to him?

He had promised her a "well-appointed house" with hundreds of acres of land. But when they arrived at the spot, there was no house. All that yet existed was a small square foundation on which more workmen had erected their tent. The newlyweds set up their tent in the trees, and it took two months before they had a roof, or privacy, or anything resembling a bed.

And here she was again. The same solemn procession through wilderness into an unknown future, only now she was widowed, childless, abandoned by her lover, ghostly thin in her clothes and stolen boots, following a stranger. Together, they stepped their mounts over windfallen trees, with the river to their left and far ahead, the balding rock faces cut deep by the river that had forged the pass. Presently she saw signs of human society: they passed trails of desiccated horse turds only a few days old and mined already by burrowing insects. She saw the impressions of shoeless hooves, several trails through the grass where previous riders had gone, and finally the gnawed corpse of a ground squirrel flung in the dirt by some dog and forgotten.

People. The widow pulled the mare up and sat among these signs, worrying.

Then she saw to her right a stand of beech trees, ghostly against the dark alpine forest. And there among the trees, as white as if they were made of bark themselves, a loose congregation of teepees. Muted forms walked in and out of the shade cast by the tents. A pack of dogs milled about, yipping. Wild lines ran through the grass away from the encampment, like spokes from a hub. The widow could discern footpaths and wider trails where carts could be dragged. Most led to the river where it tucked in close before swinging away again toward the mountain valley.

"Stay here," her companion said.

"No, I'll come with you."

"I said, stay here." He dismounted and brought his saddlebags over to her and laid them by the mare's hooves. The mare bent to puff at the flap as he dug into them and removed another lump of hard bread. This he handed to her as her horse craned and sidestepped, hoping to get some too.

"You see where those dogs are?"

"Yes."

"You don't go any closer than that."

"Well, why in the world not?" He didn't answer but mounted and swung his horse round.

"What's wrong with you?" she huffed. She dismounted, slithering weakly to the ground with bowed and trembling legs, and watched as he rode quickly to the river and walked his horse through the shallows, soaking it to the knees. Then he turned the horse and, together, they exploded toward the village in a fan of water, thundering a wide berth around her. She stood with the reins in her hand, holding her breath with alarm.

She understood then that he considered her to be terrible luck. Clearly, he had washed his horse's hooves in the river before entering the camp as a gesture against contagion.

The wind ran visibly over the grass, the hand of some indifferent force passing through her and her little story without opinion. Bad luck, or something else? She thought of her father who, even when he was no longer a minister, would nonetheless let his hand linger in the shallow, lukewarm bird bath that stood in the side chapel of any church and that held water he himself said was not holy.

"Why do you do that, then, if it's not holy?" she had asked.

"Habit," he had said and grinned at her so that she knew he had lied. But there was indeed something deep-rooted in it. His hand stole out and slipped into the water almost lovingly, hesitating to withdraw. He had imbued this gesture with something more than its Episcopal purpose, though what exactly it was, she could not guess. Her grandmother had no trouble guessing.

"You're hedging your bets," she'd said, "in case you've been wrong — which you have been. You hope you're lucky."

Her father had just laughed. "Nonsense," he had said. "Luck is the entertainment of gamblers and mystical old ladies."

"Mystical, am I? Because I don't follow your miserable view of things? All right, that's fine."

Her grandmother thought there was nothing so alluring as the unknown, a world revealed in seances, in art, and in the inscrutable code of the palm. It was written in tea leaves and cards — all of it infused with Christian hope, because these things belonged to God, and He could always be appealed to. Her father, however, felt the mistake lay in the asking, in the infantile need for answers when there were none.

Mary hadn't known who was right then, and she didn't know now. Everyone had been inclined to think her father's complaints were too much, his pain out of proportion to his injury. But now, as she stood alone among the long grasses, attending the sorrow in her own heart, she wondered.

Eventually, the widow saw a figure coming toward her, an Indian girl in short dress and pants, walking in a slow, indirect path. Wind blew her hair about her face and she chose her steps carefully. Her face was round and her skin smooth, and on her feet she wore soft leather wrappings embroidered with beads and other small, shiny things. She stood regarding the widow for a moment in undisguised critique. Then she began to talk. She put her hand out, gesturing. When the widow did not respond, the girl stepped forward and touched the dusty fabric of her black suit. She spoke again, earnestly. The widow listened, understanding nothing.

143

Finally the girl began to tug at the ratty clothing until the widow shrieked and clutched her collar and let go the reins. The mare immediately moved away, cropping grass as if repelled by natural magnetism from its owner. The two women stared uncertainly at each other, neither speaking. The Indian girl's face slowly drained of intention; whatever the plan had been, it had failed. Nothing could be done.

By noon, the widow was asleep in the sedge at the river's bank. The girl sat at a small distance, up to her shoulders in the long grasses, bored, a languorous curve to her neck, and her back not quite turned to her charge.

A little while later, the widow was awakened by a gentle whisper far above her head. It seemed to come from memory, a matriarchal tone of authority in it. She opened her eyes — and recoiled to see a white woman gazing down at her. She was suddenly aware of herself, lying moist and tangled in her funeral suit. The woman had a square, handsome face. She was covered from head to toe in what appeared to be deerhide, and carried in her hand a bundle of something wrapped in white cloth. A strand of blond hair escaped its leather binding and flew about her head in the breeze.

"Hello," the woman said. "I'm Helen, Henry's wife." The widow scrambled up and straightened her clothes.

"Henry?" the widow stammered.

"He brought you here. Didn't he tell you his name?"

"No."

"Oh, hell! He is the *most* suspicious man. Never tell anyone your name. Never keep all your money in one place. Never sit under a dead pine. The list goes on." She smiled at the widow. "What's your name?"

"Justine," she lied.

"Are you hungry?"

"He . . . Henry, gave me some bread. But I've been a while in those mountains."

"So he said. I didn't believe him. But looking at you now, I guess I do. How long did it take you?"

"I . . . I think I lost count of time."

"Sure, you would. With no idea how to feed yourself. No idea where you were going. Am I right?" The widow nodded. For it was true. Take away William Moreland, take away the dream of him, and she knew she would not be alive.

"Were you running away?" the woman's voice was soft.

"Yes," the widow said, suffering the bright-eyed scrutiny of her interrogator.

Helen took in her dark widow's clothing and did not inquire further. They might have been of a piece, these two women in rough-stitched clothing. But one was not like the other, and both knew it.

"Well," said Helen, rousing herself, "here's a little food. It isn't much, but I guess you'll choke it down." They sat together in the grass and Helen unwrapped what the widow could now see was the kind of bonnet maids often wore to do their chores. A simple white cap, now used only as a rag. Inside were chunks of apple, smoked meat, more bread, and a handful of tiny dried berries. The meat was so tough it required the widow to tug and saw at it with her teeth, like a dog, until it tore away. It had a habit of sticking to her teeth like old taffy. Together they ate, passing food between them.

"Are you married?" Helen asked.

"I was."

"I'm sorry," she shook her head sadly. "You're all alone now."

Helen had beautiful golden skin and long fingers. Across the joint of one finger was a thick white scar. She chewed loudly and smacked her lips. The widow was absurdly affronted by this fact. She decided that her benefactor had lost her civilization. "Where are you from?" the widow asked.

"Baltimore, originally. My father was a breeder. Well," Helen laughed, "he *is* a breeder. I don't guess he's dead yet."

"Is that where you met Henry?"

"Yes. I fancied myself a real horsewoman, and he came onto the ranch, and he had the most peachy horse. I'd never seen the like."

"That old bay?" the widow said dubiously.

"Oh, no! You'd have noticed this horse if you'd seen her. She was stolen two years ago. I was in a state about it." Helen fiddled with some grass and sucked her teeth rudely. "Henry knows where she is, but it would be . . . unwise to steal her back."

The widow swallowed with difficulty, sighed, "This is delicious!" and immediately set upon the food again.

Helen tried not to smile. "Well now, if you don't mind, can I give you a piece of advice?"

The widow was still working earnestly on a mouthful of pulpy bread. She raised her eyebrows.

"If you're going to Frank, to the town? When you get there, make a beeline for Mr. Bonnycastle. They call him the Reverend, or if they're being cute, they call him Bonny. He's a minister of some sort, among other things. He's the only man in that vile town you can trust. It is not a nice place, Frank. I was there only a little while. Henry was away, and I was not very . . . it was tough for me because of his sister, who was angry about me. His mother was no enthusiast, either. In any case, that's all I know about Frank."

The widow nodded. "Bonnycastle," she said, committing the name to memory. She had eaten by far the most of the bread and meat. "Why did you come out here in the first place?" she asked her companion.

"Because God wanted me to be here."

This statement confounded the widow. It was as if some important bit of meaning had been withheld from her and she had no hope of understanding anything without it. Her face must have registered her bewilderment, because Helen tried again.

"I loved him right away," she said. "Almost on sight. Some things are so obvious when you look at them. And when that happens there isn't any choice. Babies, for instance. You can't help wanting to hold a baby, can you?"

"No," said the widow. Her throat constricted. Dried berries ran round and round in her mouth in a sweet paste. She hadn't known how to hold her own baby, the boy wrinkled and fusty, raging feebly. The midwife had watched balefully as she tried to breastfeed. "You're bad at that," the woman had said but offered nothing further. She merely sat scowling as the infant's thin cries pierced the air like knives.

The widow's companion chattered happily on. "You know what I mean; it was simply undeniable. Like the weather, or a cut, or . . . or rain," Helen continued. "You can't pretend it's not raining."

The widow nodded. She had spent nights tucked round a pine's narrow trunk, trying to ignore the drippings and hissing of rain through millions of needles, the damp earth seeping through her clothes. No, out here you knew it was raining. There was no escaping it. No chesterfield before a roaring fire. No baked stone slipped between linen sheets to warm your feet at bedtime. Her grandmother had refused to let anyone take a bath during a lightning storm, or wash dishes, or touch doorknobs, or polish silver, in case water or metal should conduct. It had seemed to Mary then that anything she wanted to do was forbidden, and for her own good. She and her father would complain of boredom.

"Go to bed," the old woman would say, thinking herself clever.

"I would," her father retorted, "but there are metal *springs* in my bed!" Finally, her grandmother would relent and ask someone to go make her some tea — but please stand *back* from the stove. How little anyone really knew about the elements then. Standing at a rain-smeared window watching the massive oaks toss their heads. Drawing a fire to rid the room of dampness. Girls complaining: See how unruly my hair gets?

And now here she was, cross-legged in long grass with the sun overhead, a strange woman regarding her with undisguised curiosity. It occurred to the widow that she may have spoken out loud. Talked to herself! Perhaps her memory had leaked out, as conversation does through an open window. And yet Helen seemed as comfortable with the widow as she would be with a playing child, babbling to itself. Her smile was genuine, devoid of anything except curiosity when she asked, "And how did you meet your husband, if you don't mind my asking?"

Here was something the widow could answer, for it seemed like a story she had heard — as if John had been a different man, and she a different girl, which perhaps was truer than it sounded. And so she told this other girl's story, a tale no more than two years old. Her dark hair whipped about her face and Helen's about hers, as if the two women were underwater plants waving in a river's anxious current.

Mary had met John at a party she had attended with her grandmother. The irony was that neither she nor John had really been part of the gathering. Other girls stood on the lawn and threw horseshoes while the boys jeered or shouted advice. Meanwhile, Mary hid indoors and tried to make herself invisible. Her grandmother had ordered her outside, away from the clutch of spinsters and grannies, and when the directive had been ignored long enough, she had dragged her into the hall

149

and hissed in her face, "You get your little self out there and mingle with those young people!"

"I don't like them. Any of them!"

"You'll pay particular attention to the Cartwrights, if you have any sense."

"Grandmama!" Mary protested but found herself propelled out the side entrance onto the lawn, where she lingered a while in the shadows with her hands clasped. She drifted along to the fence to gaze out at the road and dream of being somewhere else. She didn't "do well" at parties, and her grandmother was nearly wild with embarrassment and frustration. She would hear the old woman complaining to her father after dinner as they sat on the dark forecourt and her father smoked his pipe.

"She's the prettiest one at every party," she said one night. "I don't know what's wrong with her. Or with you. You encourage her, I think."

"Mother, you always force her to those wretched over-populated things. She does better with smaller groups. Or hadn't you noticed?"

"There are much better chances at garden parties, more young people, better families. She stands a better chance."

"Not if she clams up, she doesn't."

"Well, you're no help at all. Even if she didn't say a word, it might work out in the end. I wonder if she isn't wilfully unpleasant to those boys. Sometimes the look on her face would etch glass. Just like you."

"Me?" Her father laughed.

"She treats boys the way she'd treat a filthy dog — no, she treats dogs better — and I know where she got that."

"You must admit, there is a similarity."

"I do not agree. And neither would you if you'd had a son. Her mother wasn't nearly as pretty as Mary is now. And her mother married well enough."

"Thank you."

"Oh, it'll be a curse on me if I let her become an old maid and ruin her own life! Why can't she smile and be a delight like the other girls?"

"She will, when she sees the point."

"She's eighteen already. The point will become all too clear if she waits much longer."

It went on like that. Mary became the subject of discussion, the project of the moment. She grew accustomed to hearing herself discussed in the most candid terms, and gradually, it had the effect of making her think of herself as a story, a tale still in the telling, and she became curious about what would happen to this misanthropic girl. The idea of a life of spinsterhood seemed to fill her grandmother with an elemental terror, and gradually this fear became contagious. Her father, too, lost his equanimity. That year they had hired a maid who was marrying age, and the little brooches and posies her "beau" gave her began to irritate everyone.

"Who is that supposed to be?" her father had asked the girl, staring closely at a pendant she wore round her neck. A goat-faced figure in the oval, its hand raised in benediction.

151

"Saint Anthony, sir."

Her father had guffawed. "Wonderful! Would that be Anthony the saint of barren women or Anthony the hermit?"

The machinations of courtship seemed to annoy him as much as they bored his daughter.

So, broochless and miserable, Mary had allowed herself to be dragged to another party, where she had been scolded like a child and sent out to make nice. In this sullen mood, she had hung over the fence like a tomboy to stare at the fields beyond, where horses wandered together slowly and cropped grasses and pawed at unseen things. Girls shrieked and giggled behind her and she pressed against the fence as if driven away by the noise. And that was when the light-suited man had walked up the road toward her. When he came level with her, she saw that he was tall, well dressed in suit and summer hat, and his face was solemn and handsome. There was a slightly reddish hue to his hair. He stopped in the road, pale dust drifting past his shoes in a memory of walking, and he took his hat off and bowed deeply. It was an exaggerated, theatrical gesture, almost sassy, and she didn't know how to take it.

"Ma'am," he said.

She nodded, a half-scowl on her face.

"John Boulton," he said and replaced his hat.

Mary's scowl abated somewhat. "Pleased to meet you," she said automatically.

"You haven't told me your name."

152

"My mother wouldn't like it if she knew I was talking to you." She startled herself with the fib. Why had she said that? John Boulton's eyes went past her and scanned the wide lawn, all the girls and all the boys. He seemed to inventory them and, when he came back to her, seemed happier to know her than before. As if he, too, preferred open space and was himself a straggler at heart.

Later, she would wonder how much her solitary stance had attracted him. In fact she suspected it had played a part. Here was a girl who could stand the quiet and isolation, a girl who didn't need a social life, didn't want it. How much better she would be in a lonely log cabin than would these happy, playful girls who ran about the lawn holding hands, or stood in clutches whispering gossip, or ran to their mothers crying with overexcitement.

In time, the widow knew, as surely as she knew her husband, that he might well have made the decision at that moment, settled on her as his best and only choice. Like all gamblers, and to his peril, he trusted such moments of intuition. It may have been his only reason for being at church the next day, seated ahead and to the left of Mary and her grandmother. He was beautifully dressed, his face was tanned from outdoor work, and a gold watch fob of high quality hung at his waist. Later, on the steps outside, he approached and smiled knowingly at Mary before introducing himself to her grandmother as a businessman and landowner. His father was a magistrate and had staked him a large claim, and he was on his way out to see it. Her grandmother had nearly staggered with surprise at her good luck.

And so the courtship began. For Mary, it was like slipping into water and letting the current carry her, faster and faster, toward an unseen, roaring drop, out and away from her father, her childhood home, everything she had ever known. When John asked her if she would marry him, she said she would think about it, but they both knew what her answer would be. If she left, she might be free to change, to be something and someone else. Often, at night, she would press her face into her blankets and cry wildly, but she could not have explained why she was crying, for there was a delight in it also, an unaccustomed passion.

She continued to "think about it" and John's impatience with the wait quickly became palpable. Maids advised her, in roundabout and polite ways, to stop fooling around and accept. When she expressed her doubts, saying there were things she disliked about him, her grandmother had said, "You'll grow to love your husband, don't worry, just as I did mine, and as your mother did. Nothing starts off right."

The next time they walked together, when John pressed her again, she said yes. He clapped his hands together heartily and said, "Good girl!" Then he kissed her, and the memory of that contact tingled on her lips for a long, stunned moment. The wedding was held in her father's former church, performed by another minister, her father sitting small and inconspicuous near the aisle, watching his usurper do an efficient job — a quick, simple ceremony attended by anyone interested enough to come, and no reception afterwards. There would be no more dawdling. John was in a hurry to get on.

Later in the day, as the train idled by the platform, Mary hugged her father and grandmother. She cried as they stood among her many trunks and leather bags and wooden boxes and crates. The expression on her father's face was uneasy, almost guilty. Perhaps it said that he was not ready for the change, or that she was not ready. She was nineteen, her husband thirty-five. But there was no stopping it now.

"Will there be room for it all?" she asked, looking at her life as it was slung up into the baggage car.

"Where we're going, there's nothing but room," John had said. "Wait till you see it."

As the train pulled away, Mary was unaccountably blissful, as if drunk with the promise of transformation. This stranger, this landowner whose confidence was infectious, was now her husband. He was hers. She alone was allowed to kiss him, to touch his hair with her hand. Other girls had sat in the pews during the wedding with acid expressions, and they all flirted with him afterwards, wasting their charms in an effort to diminish hers. Or so she suspected. All her grandmother's mysterious womanly advice about sex, nearly inscrutable in its refusal to be direct, had worked its magic, so that every time she looked at her husband, she found it hard to breathe. Eagerness or terror, it didn't matter.

On her honeymoon night, the bride lay in her clothes on the bunk while the train rocked gently from side to side, and she waited for him. The groom never came to her. He spent the entire night at cards, and lost fifty dollars and his watch.

CHAPTER
ELEVEN

Henry appeared before nightfall, leading his horse by one hand and hefting a second saddle against his opposite hip. Helen seized the widow's hand and said, "You will remember what I said about the Reverend Bonnycastle, won't you? Stick to that man like glue."

"Yes, ma'am."

Helen went to her husband and they stood close and spoke for a few moments. Then she turned without a goodbye and headed back toward the village.

Henry said nothing to the widow but merely nodded. The mare let him approach, and it craned round to watch, walleyed, as he laid over its back first a thin blanket, then the saddle with rough stirrups dangling off twisted rawhide thongs. He thumped the animal's neck and the mare nodded and blew its lips.

Henry and the widow mounted and rode along a path by the river for an hour, two hours, until that path faded out to nothing, and then they cut laterally through the trees, brushes of pine and hemlock stroking them as they passed. Almost immediately there was the smell of smoke in the air, and the horses began to walk alert, their ears scissoring with curiosity.

The widow heard the first whiz. And then, without warning, a whistling rain of arrows fell around them. One small, singing thing went past, then many, the air hissing with them. So alien was this event to the widow that she imagined birds had begun to fall from the sky, embedding themselves like tiny suicides in the ground, in the trunks of trees. Henry was bent low, cocking his rifle, as the widow's horse wheeled in confusion. It stood sideways to the assault, stamping its forelegs in terror. The widow screamed and hid her head behind the neck of her mare. There was silence, then a thud, and the widow felt something slap her calf just below the knee. A frigid twang went down clear to her foot.

When she looked down, she saw something pale protruding from her calf. The little mare sidestepped and swung around as the crack of the rifle racketed and swung off the hills. Mary reached down for the object sunk into her leg, but it began to bend and shimmer, and then she was slumped in a half-faint, flopping loosely as the mare, finally choosing flight, trotted aimlessly toward the river.

A minute later, Henry came back, trotting his huge bay horse and leading a second, saddleless young stallion. It bucked and reared away from his mollifying hand. He spoke softly to it, but it would not take the offer. It must have been a newly broken animal, for there was a thin strap of hide that hung from its lower jaw, looped into a hackamore, and the stallion pulled and tore at it in a panic until Henry let go, and the animal trotted away into the trees. He sighed as he watched it go. Then, wearily, he dismounted and came to look at the widow's injured leg.

He folded back the black fabric and inspected the place where the arrow had gone in. The widow leaned vertiginously out so she could see too. A short, vaneless shaft protruded from a pucker of skin that was growing bluish. There was no blood on one side of her calf, but the metal arrowhead had passed through the far side and stood out scarlet. At the point's edges were little shreds of matter like wet wool. Her head bounced once on its neck as consciousness flickered. He seized her by the upper arm and dragged her from the mare, ignoring her shriek of pain. She sat panting, glaring at him, her pupils dilated so her eyes appeared to be nearly black.

"Don't touch me!" she hissed.

"I won't," he said.

"They tried to kill us!"

"No. They want us to take another route, that's all. So that's what we're going to do."

He sat down facing her and looked closely at the shaft of the arrow, blew on it where the wood had snapped.

"This hit something and broke before it hit you, bounced off a tree maybe," he said, and there was something like relief in his voice. He leaned way down and peered at the underside of her calf. He sat up and fixed her with a look she couldn't translate, a slightly dim-witted look, as if he was clowning with her.

"You want to know why you're lucky?" he said. She was about to open her mouth and say "why," but before she could, he grabbed the arrowhead and swiftly drew the length of the shaft through her calf and out. The slender tube came out with a squeak, like a finger on glass. She began to scream, but there was a rushing sound in her ears and suddenly the world swam away. She slumped into a faint, chin on her chest, and then drifted sideways to the ground.

She woke to pain. Henry was pulling her by the front of her collar, hauling her back into a sitting position. Her head lolled a little, and then she was awake again, looking around in confusion.

"Stay up," he ordered. Then he focused his attention on the arrowhead, whose side points had sunk into his palm when he'd seized it. Carefully, he began to extract the points, wincing, his fingers trembling. When it was out, he flung it into the weeds and pressed the little cuts to his mouth

She lifted her skirt to check the leg, her head bonging horribly. A thin dribble of blood issued from the obscene little hole, like sap from a maple trunk.

"Oh God," she sighed.

"Your leg's not bad enough for us to turn back," he said. And then he went off to the river to get water.

Later, after a rest and a cup of water, Henry frogmarched her to her horse and impelled her into the saddle, and they went on. He took them on a path along the river through deepening dusk. Bats came out above them, darting low over the water and skirting the treeline. And the riders, too, avoided the trees. Then the bats vanished, as if puffed away, replaced minutes later by nighthawks, swooping like acrobats in the miserly light. A breath of snow on the air. They stood their horses in the frigid shallows and let them drink, the mare like a toy next to the bigger horse, her homely head raised, listening. Then they went on, the widow listing in her saddle like a drunkard. He'd told her to let go of the reins and hold the saddle horn to keep from falling. After a long interval, she did as he said. The mare followed like a pack horse, and the widow was the burden.

Finally, all light fled. Henry halted, and they no longer heard the hooves below them on the scree shoreline. The horses' breath sounded hollow and small in the night. The widow felt Henry's hands about her waist, pulling, and she slid to the ground. With only one good leg, she sat heavily and yelped with pain, and she remained sitting, blind, as he took the horses away. Small dots of cold hit her cheeks, motes of snow falling from the empty heights. He was removing the tack. She heard the whup of leather cinches being undone, stirrups clacking against river stones at a little distance. The horses shaking like dogs, blowing, glad to get the saddles off. The sound of him currying the animals down with the blankets, then flapping the blankets out, one by one, near her.

"Yours," he said and stamped his foot. The nearest one. She rolled over onto it, her arms across her chest, and slept on rocks. Slept despite the howling of her wound. In the middle of the night, she dragged the blanket round her and cocooned. Her face covered. Her breath like a furnace.

"Wake up." His voice came in the dark. A thin edge of a question in it — in her dream, he thought she was dead, that she'd died during the night. A body wrapped in its shroud ready for the river, while inside, a sly, dreaming ghost awaits. Her mind drifted off again. Then a boot, nudging her. "Up now."

They had bannock and coffee in the pre-dawn, two figures crouched round the fire. Then they saddled up, the widow doing her slow part. They mounted and went on uphill, moving laterally along the higher range, the mare's shod hooves sparking as she slipped and scrabbled on the loose stones. Overhead, the morning sky glowed, cut sharp by the inky edge of mountain ranges all around them like a bowl, and everything in it was black and they were invisible. The widow gazed at the rock faces and tried to recognize something, anything. The pass she had traversed, or even a familiar peak. But all was strange and black. As the light grew, the air warmed quickly. This brought forth from the trees a thin mist that ran in tributaries along the pebbled ground like a grey river. The horses' forelegs waded through it.

By noon it was raining and they were going straight up, Henry sometimes on foot, leading the horses by the reins on the switchbacks, then mounting again and continuing uphill, both riders leaning forward in their saddles. The rain was fine and light, hardly falling, blowing on the wind. It blew under Henry's hat and his face streamed and shone.

They reached the town of Frank in the afternoon and went down the empty main street followed by

162

amiable dogs. It was hardly a town at all, just a federation of camps separated by mounds and fissures in the ground, and by messes of cut lumber stacked high and stained nearly black by the weather. Buildings stood next to tents that stood next to hybrids of the two, unlighted and unpainted, made of hand-hewn boards, some caulked with mud or moss so their listing walls were corduroyed and tufted. Few or none had windows. Outside one tent, a pair of coveralls had been hung out to dry, pointless in the drizzle, and a deep red mud dripped from its cuffs.

"This is a town?" the widow asked, incredulous. "Where are all the people?"

"People?" Henry craned round in his saddle. "The *men* are underground. In the mine."

They came upon a strange low doorway cut in the side of the mountain. An air shaft, no taller than a playhouse door. The widow looked uphill and saw two others, cut discreetly into white rock, framed carefully in thick black wood, and standing no taller than four feet, as if some dandified gnome might soon step from his front door and greet the day. There were three shaft entrances in sight, but all were empty and there was no sign of men anywhere. Just then the horses crested a seam of rock like a great deep root of the mountain, and the travellers saw in the distance the grey and looming mine head, at the dark mouth of which human figures moved, stooped and hurrying. It seemed to the widow that they had moved from wilderness to wasteland.

163

The mine head looked almost like a grain elevator, a tall, boxlike structure with smaller boxes attached. The widow gazed about her in horror. Barrenness and ruin lay all about it, the building forming an epicentre of destruction. The ground was trampled and muddied and streaming, hatched with cart tracks, strewn with debris. Mounds of grey culm lay here and there, the chaff of coal mining, silvery rubble tipped out by the carts, through which ran negligible seams and chips of coal. Several of these knolls were smouldering, the coal on a slow burn, thin rills of smoke corkscrewing into the rain. The smell of it on the air. And pine and rain and mud. The horses stepped carefully over a narrow-gauge track for mine carts that ran from the head, heading downhill into the trees to some unseen destination.

But this vast ugliness seemed to flash and be gone, like a contained blight, a comet's small impact. Then they were riding among the trees again, and even the dogs were silent, as if it had affected them too, and made them thoughtful about the ravages of man. If not for the simple footpath along which they rode, the widow might have thought herself miles from any town again.

When they found him, the Reverend Mr. Angus Lorne Bonnycastle was standing on the roof of the skeletal frame of the church he was building, a pencil drawing of a stick cathedral with a dark little man on it. He had been working alone, down on one knee, hammering away, but he stood when he heard the horses' hooves. Seeing Henry, he waved eagerly, dropped his hammer, lost his footing, and fell on his back, nearly toppling from the apex. The widow let out a little yelp, and Henry put a hand to his mouth in unguarded dread. Eventually, the figure in black regained its balance, clambered up again and waved. Through his fingers, Henry said, "Jesus Christ!"

The Ridgerunner went on, shouldering his rucksack high, yearning into the wilderness. A deserter amid the green, near blind with confusion, having not slept yet, for every breath in the trees seemed to promise her arrival. The movement of sunlight, a crack in the underbrush, woke him. He sat up round-eyed, a sorry grin on his face, a lie forming in his mouth. And then nothing. She did not come. How could she? So he rose and went on, looking back as a thief does. He had stolen something, and he knew it.

And now, as shadows skated long over the ground, he stopped dead in his tracks and held his breath. An irregular thing lay on the ground a few paces back. Here was a fingerless hand. A mummified shoulder. He had stumbled upon a fellow traveller. The shape of the fallen man expressed clearly on the ground, upholstered with grass. And five feet away, the upturned, jawless cranium with its little amphitheatre of teeth. The Ridgerunner stood motionless, his eyes mere slits, a hand to his face as if there might still be a lingering stench. But there was none, and his leathery companion was as indigenous now as any fallen tree.

It was a cruel joke — not on this other man, for that was obvious enough, but on Moreland himself. Even

165

here, solitude was impossible, as if the world were a nerve-jangling carnival where grotesqueries might swing out on springs and cackle at him — lost and wild girls beckoning, dead men aping his own likely future. He stepped wide around the shallow lump, wide and quiet, and went on quietly, as if some unseen spirit hung in the trees, watching. Then he started toward higher ground. Moving not north or west, but up, higher, toward the peaks. Away from man and woman. Away from life itself.

PART TWO

FIREFLY IN THE DARK

CHAPTER
TWELVE

Mornings found the widow making the Reverend his breakfast on an old, spraddled stove that stoked hot as a forge and smoked at its poorly welded seams. It stood on pale bricks, and the sooted pipe went straight up through a hole in the ceiling, heating the single room above, and from there ran through the roof to end in a blackened and smoking funnel. She made bread and biscuits, coffee, salt pork, beef jerky, oatmeal with blueberries in it.

It had been a week or so, and now she had taken on the Reverend's habit of rising when daylight was still hours off. Sitting up with the heavy blankets to her breast and the forest's cold breath at her naked back, she could smell his pipe from where he sat on a stump outside in the dark. Smoke. It reminded her of William Moreland, his mouth speaking, sweetness puffing in wisps of smoke with each word, his hand holding the pipe stem, and his sleeves rolled to the elbows. The widow would close her eyes, sigh, and breathe in the scent.

The Reverend slept on one side of the upstairs room and she on the other, a curtain strung between them. Her bed was of oddly naval design, foreshortened, with high headboard and footboard and low walls to keep the sleeper in. The wood was expertly lacquered and inlaid with a queer petal design where flowers ran into flowers and fractured and blew tears all about. She followed the garlands with her finger. It was a queen's bed, weighed down by striations of blankets and hides, on the top of which lay a tattered silk chinoiserie, a black bedspread on which birds hopped from impossible branches, every feather gratuitously real, every beak like a yellow seed sewn into the cloth. Touching this finery, pressing its smoothness to her cheek, she remembered her grandmother's quiet bedroom, the wide, soft bed and the old lady drowsing there. Next to the widow's new bed was a window, perhaps pilfered from some railway car, pried out whole and set into the wall, held in its scored metal frame by a line of rusted rivets. This was where she slept. The Reverend himself slept on a simple straw tick. When the widow realized she had been given the only real bed, she tried to refuse it, but he said simply, "It was never mine anyway." He hammered nails into the walls for her to hang her clothes. Smiling apologetically, he said, "Luxury, for a woman accustomed to sleeping in the woods."

His house was like his church: vaguely cockeyed, sketched in, made by hand by himself alone, without a level, without proper tools, without one hour's training in the carpenter's art. Every line in it was askew. It stood drunk against the plumb of the surrounding cedars, with hammocked floors and rude walls listing, everything held in place by a mad excess of nails. As the widow clumped lamely down the stairs on her aching leg, the staircase wowed like a suspension bridge. Unless she went very carefully, she was announced by the squalling of ill-fitted joints.

The Reverend Bonnycastle spent much of every day working on his church, whanging gamely away with a hammer, using the warped and blackened boards from the town's abandoned pile, which he said dated from when Frank was a lumber camp. As yet, his church had no walls or roof, but was simply framed in. Up close, the composition was anarchic, fascinating, joints meeting at organic angles. From a distance, however, it was nearly comic. Miners would stop on their way uphill and stand with hands in pockets, just looking. Of all the men in town, the Reverend may well have had the least aptitude for building.

After breakfast, at the widow's request, they sat across the table from each other and read from the Bible, just as she had done at home with her father. It gave her a childish pleasure to read to the Reverend, for it felt so familiar.

"The Lord roars from Zion and thunders from Jerusalem; the shepherd's pastures are scorched and the top of Carmel is dried up." The Reverend Bonnycastle sat merry and polite as the widow recited, but a furtive boredom crept the edges of his attention, so after a few days these events ceased.

She tended to prefer some sections to others, queer things such as Amos, and she returned to these often. She would not read from his Bible, only from her own, and he didn't question this. He told her he'd been

171

pleased enough to see that, given her meagre possessions, she still carried a Bible. He had taken it up from the table where it lay and opened the stained leather binding. Inscribed to an infant daughter from her father. On many a worn page, in the margins, she had made tiny, inscrutable drawings and symbols. Some were impossible ciphers. Others seemed to have recognizable shapes. He ran a fingertip over a tiny rain cloud, a door, two women bending over a star. He flipped the page. A fist inside a heart. When he closed the book again, his eyes canted curiously at her, but he said nothing.

The Reverend was dark of complexion and deeply tanned. His eyes and hair were almost black, and he wore a full black suit with a long coat over it. She noticed he wore no collar and seemed not to own a cassock. Her father, by contrast, had often worn a cassock with thirty-three buttons, one for each year of Christ's life. But the widow could see how trousers might be more appropriate here. The Reverend's hair was roughly cut, probably with shears, to one blunt length, and he sported a totally unchecked chin beard, something that had not been fashionable during either of their lifetimes. The index finger of his left hand was missing completely, the knuckle like a burl under the skin.

He was exceedingly formal with her, almost prudish, even on the first day as he had cleaned and dressed her wound. He had worked carefully, with no more of her leg exposed than was necessary, just the bloody and swollen calf muscle. He coaxed dozens of splinters from the skin, pressed a whisky-soaked rag to the wound, and held her hand as she huffed and wept in pain.

"What's your name?" he had said, peering minutely at his work, as if speaking to the arrow hole.

"Mrs. Boulton," she hissed. "Mary Boulton."

"You can call me Bonny," he said.

She had looked down at their clasped hands, and she slumped, leaning her clammy forehead against her knee. In her pain, her weakened state, she'd told the truth. Her married name. What hell would come of it?

At that altitude the nights were cold — late summer snow fell from the stars and blew among the trees. On her first night, she had hung a heavy sack across her window for warmth and tucked the edges in. The Reverend talked in his sleep, his prattle coming and going, the dry shift of the straw in his tick. The widow lay under her blankets and listened as the cedars outside her window waved in the night wind. She did not sleep but lay listening to her mind's ramblings. Given enough distance from their crimes, even the wicked may eventually sleep as others do. Or so she hoped. Memories, gestures, her husband's indifferent voice. She suffered the echo of her baby's fussing, his shallow breathing. She wrapped her hands round herself, rolled to her side, and closed her welling eyes. Wait, wait, and they will pass, and perhaps nothing will rise in you.

Long before dawn, a muffled cough outside her window startled her. She sat up, woozy, and saw men, a dozen of them, bent and silent shapes walking along in

173

twos and threes under the moon. Miners on their way to the mine. They went along slouching, coughing, the occasional voice mumbling, but they fell silent as they passed the Reverend's house. Here and there among them a lit carbide headlamp bobbed or the ember of a cigarette swung at the end of an unseen arm. They carried tools over their shoulders, picks and drills, their silhouettes tottered past, monstrous in the wan moonlight, looking to the addled widow like trolls in a children's shadow play. And when the players had passed she saw only the dark road, the empty stage, waiting for the next scene, where soon a devil or perhaps a witch would bolt up before the lamp's hokey flare and dance away after them.

She had spent two days slipping birdlike in and out of naps. Pulling back the covers to bend double and pick at the gluey cloth wrappings on her calf, peel back the thin wool to see the ghastly hole, a pucker of skin round a black and glassy bung. She washed her leg, wincing, and laundered the wrappings. And she limped around the house while the Reverend was out working on his church.

His kitchen was tidy and marvellously full of implements, efficiently feminine, as if the woman of the house had recently stepped out for an overnight trip. A bread board stood upright by the large tin soup kettle. The widow applied her thumbnail and scratched up a flaky dust. A rolling pin, pans of varying size, a cigar box full of knives and spoons and ladles, galvanized canisters of flour, cream of tartar, salt, cinnamon.

Cinnamon! She opened the little glass jar of powder, held it to her nose, and breathed in the deep, almost ecclesiastical perfume. She was suddenly in her father's house, in the kitchen, following the old cook around while she worked, sitting on the counter by the sink licking a spatula thinly covered in gingerbread batter. She remembered flour sifted into a wide ceramic bowl in perfect peaks, salt and sugar denting the summit, and finally a tiny spoonful of cinnamon dropped in, a small thrill among the whiteness. She put the package back on its shelf and went on, full of admiration. By the back door were four pairs of scissors, one a heavy set of shears hung by their thumbs, and next to these was a new rabbit gun. There were several oil lamps, one elderly storm lantern full of cracks.

In a trunk by the Reverend's bed she found a silk bag full of treasures: thread in many colours, embroidery silk, three hair combs of varying fineness, thimbles, a little paper strip of hooks and eyes, and cloth in many colours. She stared — several blond hairs twinkled amid the jumble. Digging deeper, she found a dress, almost fashionable and made for a tall woman. The widow reached in and fingered the baby's breath lace at the collar, saw expertise in the work, a wealthy past. She tugged at this curiosity a little and lay the bodice across the box's rough lip. An ink stain at the right wrist, dust condensed in the fabric, the dress so well used that the body of the departed woman was present in its wear. A paleness was impressed on the dark nap, and round the breastbone the sagged impression of a heavy necklace. A cross, no doubt.

In the mid-morning Mary would stop and listen, hearing a faint soprano wail she could not identify. She would cock her head, thinking it came from the north . . . no, perhaps from the east. Sometimes she would go to the foot of the stairs and look up. Eventually she thought to ask him about it, and he told her it was the train coming along the pass, far downhill by the river, coming to pick up the coal.

Before the light failed completely there was always a gust of wind through the trees. She remembered this from the cabin too, as if the world blew itself out before settling into the dead stillness of night. Unnerving and falsely portentous. Or perhaps it *was* portentous, for that had often been when her husband came home, a dim shape in the half-light. A shadow, slouching, reluctant to be home. By contrast, the Reverend came home early, lit the lamps, talked happily, yawned and yawned and yawned, and fought sleep. And when they were both in their separate beds, he would call goodnight several times, forgetting each time that he had already done so, his voice slurred with sleep.

"Goodnight, Mrs. Boulton."

And she would call "Goodnight, Bonny" and lie for a long time watching the shadows.

One morning, the widow woke to the sound of a scuffle outside on the dusty path that ran through the trees outside the house. The air was dry and cool. Her leg panged terribly. She probed it gently with her fingers and found the swollen hardness of it had subsided a little, although it was no less painful. She fought her way up through the blankets weakly, walking her arms crabwise behind her, and finally peered through the window. Out on the road stood the Reverend Bonnycastle in shirt sleeves looking down on a young man who sat on the ground beside his hat.

"Come on," said the Reverend, "get up."

"You'll just hit me again."

"Come on." He extended an arm down to the boy, who took it cautiously, and together they levered the boy up so he stood. Then they both stepped away and assumed a boxing pose. The widow blinked in amazement. The two figures circled each other on a soft path. The Reverend came at the boy, and they swung and ducked and feinted, they wrestled standing up, like bears, grunting, their boots fetching up pale dust from the road. The younger man pushed his opponent away and offered up a haymaker, which missed, nearly throwing him off his feet.

"Good boy!" the Reverend said heartily and knocked him down again. With that, it was over, and the Reverend turned and went back to the house. The widow struggled from the bed and hurried down the rickety staircase. Every inch of her body ached, and her swollen leg was unbearable. Still, she made the bottom of the stairs just as the Reverend strode through the open front door. He was rolling down his sleeves.

"Bible lesson," he grinned and went on into the kitchen.

Through the open door she saw the boy. He was standing now, knocking the dust from his hat. He levered it onto his head and gave the house, and perhaps the widow too, if he could see that far, a repenting look, and went on down the road.

Cooking was problematic for the widow. They had no fresh beef because a carcass would attract bears, even if you buried it. Chickens wouldn't last long before martins or foxes or the cold killed them. And so it was game meat they ate — deer or squirrel stewed for hours with mealy potatoes and wild onions, hares baked or cooked over a spit, the occasional mountain goat that required tireless chawing. Any beef tended to be clammy, salted, or smoked, always barrelled, with a watery swill in the bottom. Biscuits and porridge with salt. Blueberries, raspberries, strawberries, all wizened and made potent by altitude. The only true comfort was baked bread, emerging perfect from the wood oven, golden streaks on each fragrant loaf. But no butter.

She cooked lunch for the Reverend every day and brought it to the church in a bowl, tucked steaming inside her coats.

"Mrs. Boulton!" he would call in joy when he saw her coming.

One bright day, she came hobbling slowly over fallen rock, went round massive cedar stumps and branchfall and mounds of long-rotted sawdust and needles in her trousered getup and his buffalo coat, looking like a shambling, pin-headed troll. He perched on the skeleton of his bizarre church and waved wildly, as if she might be about to give the lunch to someone else, then clambered down the outmost corner beam with his logging spurs on, nimble as a monkey. He greeted each meal like a prize at a fair.

"All the steam's gone," she said, flapping the lapels of the buffalo coat.

"Not a bit of it!" he said and set upon the stew with theatrical greed. They sat together on the promontory that soon would hold the altar.

"Where are the pews?" she said.

"I'll attend to the inside when I've done the roof and walls."

The widow sat demurely, her wrists between her knees, and looked about her at the uneven flooring, the handmade mallet at her foot. She listened to the Reverend's chewing. She could smell him, the scent of wood and sweat and something else, something more complex in her nostrils. She looked quickly at his face, at the muscle working in his cheek. He smiled, without looking at her. Above them, clouds roamed along to the west, the tall cedars bent after them.

"People might come to services," she said, "if you only had some pews."

He stopped chewing. Looked about him. The two of them sat mapping out imaginary pews in rows. He craned his head round to where the altar would go. A service open to the air, nothing above but rafters and the heavens.

"I believe you're right," he said, then went back to eating. Dry leaves chased across the church floor. Later that afternoon, he set about making pews, rough unsanded benches for the men to sit on.

179

When she got back to the cabin, the stove had gone out. It was cold, and it would take ages to get going again. She was not expert at dealing with stoves. In her father's house there had always been girls to do the work — a cook, maids, and then later, when her mother was at her worst, nurses. Later still, John had tried to teach her to tend a fire. He'd had his method, his preferences regarding kindling, a guaranteed approach. Everyone had their own method. The widow could keep a fire going while she cooked, but later she would forget. Turning her mind to another task, she would ignore the sound of wood collapsing inside the stove, the heat fading away, and before too long, the stove was cold again. Her husband had been deeply annoyed at the waste of good kindling.

"You are a wretched housewife, Mary," he had told her. It was one of his many criticisms but patently true. She stood in this new kitchen, delicious-smelling but growing clammy with the cold, and she booted the stove's hollow side and swore at it like a man would.

In the early morning, amid the trembling of mountain aspen, three horsemen came. They crested a rise one by one, the horses blowing, for they were heavily packed, and their riders were large. One man was some distance ahead, and he was the tracker, an old coot in a crisp hat and long oilskin, who stopped often to look down, or dismounted with arthritic languor to stand over some invisible clue or sign and kick at it with his toe. Then he would struggle back up and go on. For two days they had traced a drunken path over the mountain's flank,

180

following the widow's peculiar trajectory into the wild. The route like a skittering mouse, light-footed and almost aimless, and in this the old man silently read the signs of her dissolution: exhaustion, confusion, the rest stops in exposed or wet places, the stupid choices.

And now here was a body imprint scuffed into the needles beneath a pine bough, like a snow angel, proof she had slept here. A few feet away her horse had stood, a band of worn-away bark where the reins had been tied too high, and the horse had tugged and tugged to reach the grass at its feet. All this the old tracker took in, moustache twitching thoughtfully.

The two redheads arrived beside him, their horses nudging his affectionately, for all three animals belonged to the tracker. Only these two men were strangers here. They looked down for signs of their quarry but saw nothing; looked about them at the forest and saw nothing. The old man adjusted his hat.

"What're you boys gonna do with this lady when I find her?"

"Leave that to us," said one of them.

"You just do your job," said the other.

The tracker regarded them a moment more. He wasn't fearful of them, but he saw why others might be. There was an animal quality to them, the way one was dominant — his eyes were steady, his voice was steady, he always spoke first. By now, the old man could tell the difference between them at a distance, simply by watching their movements. That was no problem. But which was Julian and which Jude? He just called them "boys." Mostly because they didn't like it.

"You realize we're gonna find her dead, don't you?" he said.

Neither man replied. But he saw it in their faces — one brother didn't give a damn, and the other did.

The tracker chuckled and swung his horse around, and they all went on.

CHAPTER
THIRTEEN

The air grew warmer by the hour and sun came through the trees in filtered shafts, soft and indistinct. Mary sat with the Reverend outside while he smoked his pipe, she on the stoop with her knees up to her chest. She rubbed her sore leg. He tamped down the tobacco with a ruined galvanized nail, and when he was done, he wiggled the nail into a well-worn hole in the side of the stump he was sitting on. The smoke hung in the still air and drifted about his face. She knew the brand — Orford, a poor tobacco prone to mould and bitterness. She remembered her father saying about a man he disliked, "He's an Orford man," a sly smile suffusing his face. "He believes in moderation in all things, including sense."

A distant rumble crawled the hills, and man and girl looked up through the trees. The sky above them was clear, the storm having moved on down the pass. The widow got up awkwardly with her sore leg and clumped back into the house. When she emerged, she had her own tobacco pouch and her pipe. She set to work packing the bowl, pressing it down firmly with her thumb, testing the suction.

The Reverend watched this procedure with veiled admiration, taking in the curved stem, the ornate stag's head bowl, the antlers that came off in a hinged lid. "That is a mighty fine pipe," he said.

"I stole it," Mary said bluntly. She lit the pipe and handed him the pouch and glanced obliquely up at him, daring him to say something. But he said nothing, and his expression pretended that she had not spoken. Together they sat in silence and smoked. The Reverend brought the weathered pouch to his face and sniffed the fragrant compost within.

"Much better than your Orford," she said.

"Quite," he said.

"Go on, Bonny," she waved her hand at the pouch. He smiled eagerly and knocked out his own pipe, put his boot heel on it to snuff it out, and began fixing a new pipe with her tobacco.

She put an arm round her knees, gazed out into the cedars, and reflected on the Reverend Bonnycastle. His friend Henry had found her staggering out of a mountain pass without her horse, and with no idea where she was. He had taken her into his house without a word, fed her, cared for her. Over the weeks, Mary had seen many private questions pass over the Reverend face, and though she had braced herself for the predictable prying, it never came. He simply didn't ask. She was allowed to keep her secrets. It began to dawn on her that she could trust this man. She was suddenly, intensely grateful to him. And that came with a stab of regret, for who else had ever done that for her?

★   ★   ★

Sometimes discontent is unknown to the sufferer, a shadowed thing that creeps up from behind. It had been that way for Mary. Of course, she knew there were reasons for her unhappiness, there are always reasons. One thinks, I am unhappy, I am discontent, because of this or that. But such thoughts are like a painting of sorrow, not sorrow itself. Then one day it comes, hushed and ferocious, and reasons don't matter any more.

Her husband had trudged into the cabin, bringing new snow on his boots. It was not even dark yet. She had turned slowly, waddling with her pregnant belly, a spoon in her hand, surprised by an unexpected guest barging into her house — and discovered it was her own husband.

"You're home," she said stupidly.

"I'm home indeed," John answered.

She saw immediately that his demeanour was different; he seemed cheerful, smiling almost coyly. The spoon hovered and she blinked at him.

"What is it?" she said bluntly.

"What do you mean?"

"Why are you smiling, John?"

"Goodness," he laughed. "Can't a man smile? I'm just happy to be home."

She'd never heard him say anything like that before. He said it lightly, but his eyes were not on her and he was giddy. He looked taller, more robust than he had in months. Happiness made him beautiful — she remembered that John had looked that way when she had first met him. Slowly, a thankful smile crept over her face and she went back to stirring the pot, swaying a little with fatigue.

"Dinner won't be ready for a while," she said. "I'm not used to you being home so early."

"No hurry," he said, rubbing his hands on his thighs. She followed him with her eyes as he went into the bedroom and lay on the bed with his coveralls still on, arms behind his head. He looked at the ceiling and smiled. A contented man come home to the wrong house.

"Mary, would your father let that old silk chesterfield go if we sent for it?"

"What?"

"That long green one."

"I . . . I don't know. Why do you ask?"

"I think it was big enough that we could lie together on it, don't you? There's nowhere else for us to lie but here," he said, bouncing his hands on the sprung old bed. She did not say anything, for there was no money for anything, let alone to ship an old piece of furniture hundreds of miles. She bent to peer inside the dark oven at the biscuits baking, and as she did, she heard his humming coming through the stove's wall, through the iron belly, a muted thrum she could feel in her cheeks. His presence was resonating everywhere.

During dinner he talked and talked and never looked at her once. It seemed to her that he was careful not to. He was full of ideas and plans, things they could not afford and therefore would not happen. She was accustomed to having nearly silent meals with her husband, so this was a surprise. Almost immediately

186

her heart began to lighten. His joy was contagious, and she found herself laughing, agreeing to ridiculous things.

That night John seized her the way he always had done, pregnant or not. But after a time, he became unusually gentle and yearning; he seemed to be trying to please her. He was usually a silent lover, but that night he had sighed, "A" — a single non-word that alarmed her with its incongruity. It was as if he were play-acting — not for her benefit, but for some watcher, as if he imagined someone else in the room with them and he wished this audience to think he was happy.

In the morning, a profound melancholy had come over him. He was like a man who had been drinking and merry, but was now sober and sorry for it. Mary was stricken by this reversion and did not know what to do. Austere and silent, he finally put both elbows on the table and regarded her while she hurried his breakfast to the table. She found this peculiarly calming, for it was so much their usual habit: him watching her struggle to do the most basic things a wife must do, dissatisfaction written all over him. Her grandmother would have blamed her. She was a poor domestic student — in her ineptitude, Mary brought censure upon herself. Never mind that she was barely nineteen, or that all her training had been for a different kind of life. There was, she believed, something about her, or in her, that bred dissatisfaction. She remembered her grandmother saying to her, "You must stop being such a gloomy child. Can you not be pretty inside as well?"

These things went through her mind as she stumbled and clattered the dishes to the table.

Once John had gone out the door, a fretful energy overtook her and she could not remain still. She forced herself through the morning's chores with the patience of an ox, stopping only to lean on the broom and close her eyes and hold her enormous belly with one hand. She found the bedroom a mess, the drawers in disorder. On the chest stood a little box in which she kept what remained of her jewellery and comforts. She looked at it: the box stood open, its contents jumbled. Her heart sank at the possibility that she had done this herself and now did not remember, for that was becoming common, and she did not know what to do about it. Such lapses were brief but profound, like waking disoriented from sleep. It did not occur to her that John could have gone through the box — not until she discovered a comb missing. She scrounged again through the box and then she searched the cabin. The comb was gone. Slowly, she realized that John had taken it. A simple inlaid comb, worth nothing.

Of course, at first, she could not fathom why John might want a comb of no value, a pretty little thing only a girl would value. And then, she did. After that, it was a process of seeing things again: his ebullience, his gentleness. In bed, he had imagined not his exhausted and pregnant wife, but another girl, and he clasped her more gently than the wife, sighed upon her, his imagination filling the gaps.

This was the first shift, for Mary, the painful little kink in the flow that forced all thought to adjust to the truth. These were the seeds of her despair and madness.

Thinking about it now, the widow decided it was also the first step of many that had brought her here.

That day, once they had finished their pipes, the Reverend did not go to work on his church as usual. Instead, they went off together through the trees to the centre of town, heading for the trading post. He carried a burlap sack over his shoulder, and she followed behind with her saddlebags held against her stomach like a muffle. They stepped in unison, like grim twins in long black pantaloons, the Reverend's dark hat on his head, dust and weather worn deeply into the felt. Stepping gingerly along on humps of moss the size of sleeping men among the trees and the rotting logs, the wild mushrooms fanning tiny staircases up the cedar trunks while a fairy rain shook loose from the branches above.

The widow followed her keeper, hurrying along with her strange lame gait, placing her boots where his had been, feeling the spongy give of forest floor. He pressed it far down, and she pressed less deeply. And when they had passed, their trail faded away again as moss and needles and leaves slowly uncompressed and tiny filaments stood upright.

"Fox!" he said sharply. "Brown fox." But when she looked there was nothing but the gentle waving of underbrush. They waited. Not a sound from the departing animal, as if it, too, was standing its ground, curious, listening or watching from its secret station. The Reverend shifted the burlap sack to his other hand. She could hear his breath, the strange catch in it.

"You're good luck," he said. "A fox is a good omen, and I never see them. Everyone else does, but never me." He smiled cheerfully at her, turned, and went on. The widow allowed herself to believe him — he actually thought she brought him good luck.

Finally they emerged from the forest and ventured out over the mine's debris. Deep runnels of cold rainwater still gurgled downhill across their path, fetching up mud and sucking brightly in the hollows. He took her hand to steady her, and one after the other they hopped from bolder to rock, keeping to the dry ground. Then he let her hand go. The widow shambled on behind him, a dreamy smile on her lips.

The trading post was no more than a large wood foundation on which had been erected an oiled canvas tent, the kind seen at sideshows. The sides were squared off at the height of a man, to approximate walls, and there was a vent in the roof surmounted by a little cap with a red flag on it. Thin blue smoke issued from the vent. The flag, an arcane and never official Red Ensign, drooped permanently, weighed down by weather to form a kind of tongue that was unmoving thanks to fusted rot years old. Above the door was a board that must have once said *McEcherns* in red-and-gold lettering. Wood borers had been lustily at the sign and now it seemed to say *MEEEherns*.

The foundation of the building came up to their knees, and there were no stairs, so the Reverend and the widow clomped up onto it. They went past overturned chairs and a cluster of rain-filled booze bottles. The air inside the tent was dim and smelled thickly of smoked hides. The Reverend said, "Mac?" No sound came from the dark corners.

"Mac!" he bellowed, and there was a distant halloo from outside.

By the door was a pile of hides that rose above the widow's head. She went to it and discovered they were mostly buffalo, thick unwieldy things folded like blankets. Next to that, she found the hides of cattle: black, ginger, the colour of coffee, some with winter hair, others smooth as a hunting dog's back. Almost hidden was a small collection of cured deerhides and soft chamois, rolled into tubes and stacked like cord wood. She saw a bundle of rabbit skins packed into a wooden box, little things you could fashion mittens from, or use to line the hood of a coat. She pondered these for a moment. She stroked the thick shoulder ruff of a wolf, ran an empty foreleg through her fingers to the cropped end where the paw had been removed. The stiffened edges of eye holes, the jagged W of the mouth. She flipped it over and found an enormous bullet hole. Inappropriate calibre for a wolf. Someone had gone hunting for bear and run up on a wolf. The widow figured the impact must have knocked it off its feet. She poked two fingers through to the fur and wiggled them in the softness.

"Someone sure killed him," the Reverend said over her shoulder.

They heard footsteps, and a moment later a tiny man beetled through the back flap of the tent. He was buttoning up his pants.

"Pardon me!" he said. "Had to see a man about a dog."

McEchern had a strangely soprano voice, and in the gloom of the tent, his body seemed impossibly foreshortened, as if he were walking in a trough and visible only from the knees up. The widow ventured closer to get a look at him. She stood by the Reverend, who was already leaning one elbow on the long wooden plank that served as desk, bar, and counter. She saw then that the man was a dwarf, no more than four feet tall, stylishly bearded, wearing a bowler hat, and that he had pale blue eyes. He grinned smartly at her but did not remove his hat. Behind him stood a pile of moulding books, an old rifle hung on a nail by its trigger guard, and another bunch of empty bottles, arranged in a line — evidence perhaps of what had been consumed on the premises, or maybe advertisements for what McEchern could supply.

"How long have you been lurking?" he asked them.

"Hours," said the Reverend. "I've grown roots."

"You haven't either," McEchern grinned.

"Don't you worry about someone robbing you?" the Reverend said, smiling in turn.

"Piss on that. I'd know exactly who'd done it, and I'd go skin 'em . . ."

"How could you possibly know?"

"Easy. How do you know what kind of animal's been in your pantry? By what it took. I know the smokers, the drinkers. I know the dope fiends. I know who has a sweet tooth. And most of these boys wouldn't steal a stick of wood if you put a gun to their heads. So that kind of narrows it down."

"Well, what if they took, let's say, a saw?"

"Then I'd know it was you. Now dry up, will you. Who's this?"

With what seemed to the widow to be genuine solemnity, the Reverend introduced her. "Mary Boulton, I'm pleased to introduce Charles McEchern, merchant, entertainer . . ."

"Gentleman," the dwarf postured.

"Oh, I think not. Mac is, among other things, the local drug peddler." McEchern put a hand to his chest and affected speechlessness. Then: "Apothecary," he corrected. The little man's amused face peered out over the desk at her, the eyes betraying nothing.

"I got anything you need for what ails you. Or I can get it. Might take a month, though." And then, as if a switch had been snapped off, he spoke to the Reverend. "What about the Americans? When are they due?"

"Very soon. A few days, perhaps."

"How many horses have they got?"

"I'm not sure. Twelve maybe. Can you handle . . ."

"Look. I can take as many as you get. There's more buyers this time, Indians mostly. So they'll go north directly." This seemed to satisfy the Reverend, and he smiled happily and slapped the dwarf on the shoulder.

"Will ya take a drink?" McEchern offered. But the Reverend was apparently doing calculations in his head, and he walked away into the gloom of the tent,

193

his lips moving. If the widow had ever wondered what possible economy had kept the most Reverend Mr. Bonnycastle afloat — and she had — there was now the shadow of an answer: The Americans were purveyors of stolen horses.

Under the dwarf's elbow lay a pane of thick glass, and under this lay a small cabinet filled with unusual objects. A pocket watch, a monogrammed silver shoehorn, a leather Bible with gold corner reinforcements, and a gun. The widow gazed at the pistol's weathered butt where the letters COLT were calligraphed in ropy italics. The heavy cylinder, the long, cannonlike barrel.

McEchern regarded her sagely, and affected a posture of keen estimation. "I'll wager, Madam, that you are a reader of the Good Book," he said. Obviously, he'd misidentified the object of her interest.

"Oh, she's that," came a voice from the corner. "You should hear her."

The widow blushed furiously. Praise was dangerous, unwelcome. It might bring demands for a performance, something she could not manage without her own hieroglyphic Bible. The round, clear eyes of the proprietor did not leave her face. He was a clever little man, she could see that, for he had registered her discomfort and was considering various possible explanations for it. She hurried away and busied herself among the shelves of salt and baking powder and baskets of dried apples. Great fat bags of flour at her feet, and battered tins of tea.

194

CHAPTER
FOURTEEN

It was a windy day when the lunatic came through town. His horse was moving fast and he wore a faded uniform — North West Mounted Police. He was sitting forward in the saddle, coming in from the same direction as the widow had, along the pass, out of the depths of Indian country. He came on at a gallop, the horse scrambling over the stones, its hide white with dried sweat, its sunken flanks marked with long smears of dried blood from the spurs. Horse and rider barrelled past the mine head where workers were bent sullenly over their lunch bowls. The men looked up in dumb surprise. Then he was gone. One or two miners wandered after him.

At a gallop the madman bore down on McEchern's store till the horse balked in a wide spray of gravel and scrambled lamely sideways, suddenly choosing a different direction, though all directions were the same to them. The dwarf had been tidying bottles from his front stoop when he saw them coming, and his jaw went slack. The animal's weeping eyes and crusted hide, and the rider fraught forward in his seat, elbows held high as if riding down the banks of hell to trample the devil. He was black-eyed and clearly mad, his rotted

195

uniform a mere shadow on him now, staved-in helmet corralling the man's clogged hair. He made no sound, though his mouth worked horribly as if he would chew the air. Unlike the miners, McEchern did not freeze but moved with surprising speed, laterally, back into the darkness of his tent. When he emerged again, rifle raised, the bizarre mirage was gone.

On they went, horse and man, dashing in uncertain bursts uphill, past tents and over laundry, kicking up pebbles against the walls of half-finished cabins, bringing out a stunned audience that followed them on foot. In the end, it was the church that caused the rider to haul back on the reins, and the disbelieving horse understood that they were to finally come to a stop. Perhaps it was the building itself that did the trick, a hollow and cockeyed impediment; or perhaps it was the sight of a man in black, with a black hat, holding a huge and splayed hammer, standing on the church's unfinished roof looking down on them, one hand extended in divine insistence: *Stop*. Those who ran uphill following the circus witnessed it: the Reverend simply put out his hand, ending the madman's rampage.

In fact, the Reverend admitted later, he had fully believed the lunatic would not stop, that his horse would not preserve itself but would instead hurl them both against one of the building's questionable support beams and bring the whole edifice down about them. The truth of it was, he had put out his hand to ready himself for the fall.

196

Now the lunatic held his wreck of a horse among a gathering crowd and swivelled his head on its scrawny neck in wild paranoia, like a man beset by wolves. The horse's breath came ragged, with the deep, hollow-chested cough of the near-dead. Gently, men stepped forward to take the reins and calm the dancing animal.

"Settle down now," said one fellow, speaking to the man, not the horse. A wordless howl from the lunatic, fists trembling at his throat. He was looking up at the trees, the tips of the pines where wind hissed among the needles. Poplar leaves flashed — light dark light dark — in secret insinuation.

"What's wrong with him?"

"Look at that horse. He's nearly killed it."

The widow hobbled up and stood among the crowd. The Reverend clambered down an outside beam in his claw-footed boots to stand at the gasping animal's neck. He put his hand on the disintegrating leather of the police boot. It was a strangely tender gesture, the hand with its missing index finger, as if the Reverend were saying, "Trust me, we are comrades in ruin." He shook the thin leg, and slowly the rider dragged his terrified attention away from whatever the trees were telling him. His huge eyes settled on the Reverend's kindly face. He let out a sob.

"Arthur," said the Reverend. "Get off that poor horse and come with me."

The lunatic had been cajoled into dismounting his horse, and the two of them stood together with trembling, withered shanks and swimming eyes. The

197

Reverend turned toward home and the lunatic followed, mild as a lamb.

The horse was corralled in the empty church, not hitched, but standing with its head hanging among the rough pews, tidemarks of sweat on its hide and dry froth at its lips, eyes dull as granite. A congregation of worriers stood about, hands on chins, considering its chances. Food was a bad idea. Horses can neither belch nor vomit, so anything that goes bad inside might stay inside. A simple kink in an intestine can be fatal. Water was all right, but should it be warm? Cold? Finally the horse was given a wet rag to suck. A tentative hand pushed the wad into its cheek, but the animal would not suck, and eventually the rag fell to the floor. Finally, one bright fellow exclaimed: "A blanket!" And they all ran in different directions to find one.

Arthur Elwell — for that was the lunatic's name, as the widow soon discovered — was not faring much better. He sat in the Reverend's kitchen, a hollow-eyed cadaver, his razorous shoulder blades showing through the fabric of his uniform, hands knotted up under his chin like an old lady with the panics. His jaw worked constantly, and somewhere inside, the lunatic was speaking, for with each breath, barely audible words floated out and others were drawn back. The widow stood by the door and made not a sound.

"Give me your boots," said the Reverend, kneeling before the man, and the thin leg came up, knee bone creaking, and hung trembling as the Reverend gently twisted it, toe and heel, and the boot slid off with a hollow sucking sound. The sockless yellow foot slowly

198

lowered to the floorboards and lay there, as bloodless as a dead thing on a beach. The second boot came up.

"Bonny . . ." the voice croaked and then subsided. The madman's head drooped and he shook it sadly. Unmistakably, it was an apology. The hands wringing in the lap now, and the eyes canted sadly to the steamed window, beyond which the wind continued to blow.

"Tell Mrs. Boulton about yourself, Arthur," said the Reverend. "She's never met you."

"Mrs. Boulton?" Arthur repeated, then swallowed dryly.

"There," the Reverend inclined his head sideways toward the terrified widow.

The widow fought an urge to run out the door. How hazardous it was to be fixed by those terrible eyes. To watch the white and red mouth open and the roiling tongue work within. To allow this madman to speak to her — the shame of it! — to share his infected thoughts, the illness spreading. The man sat there, an indictment of herself, of her own madness, a leper in his cave, warning, *Touch me not. It will bloom in you.*

The Reverend put Arthur's sagging boots by the door. Then he turned, smiling, and took the widow by her rigid shoulders — the second time he had ever touched her — and guided her to a chair.

"Sit," he ordered. "It'll be good for him. And it's a fair story." He went to the stove to make tea. There was silence. Wind creaked among the shingles and moaned along every uncaulked seam in the place. The widow barely breathed. She and Arthur sat in mutual terror.

"I'm sorry, miss," the lunatic said.

"It's all right," she lied. "Go on. I'd like to hear." And without further encouragement, Arthur started talking, the words coming out smoothly and with uncharacteristic calm, as if rehearsed, or perhaps like a psalm, something to stave off the darkness. At first, he would stop, waiting for a comment from his audience, but neither of his listeners spoke. The Reverend didn't even turn his head, and so the madman went on talking, the story after a while coming out unbidden, in a dry, quiet voice, like he was telling himself who he was.

He had grown up in an enormous suite of rooms in a hotel among eight bright, happy siblings and a phalanx of keepers who scurried after them, tidying. His mother was head of the women's auxiliary, so she was always out visiting hospitals in her furs and silk stockings, wandering the wards with other ladies, worrying over the lumps in the beds. His father was a political man who spent much time in his library arguing points of policy with colleagues, while bouncing one or another child on his knee. There were parties during which Arthur affected the role of a butler. Guests chuckled and ruffled his hair. There were endless toys and trips out for tea and cakes and skating on the river. At one such skating party, the ice had broken suddenly and four young couples had drowned. And though Arthur had been there with everyone else and had watched the doomed struggling and crying out at the crumbling, frozen edge, he could remember none of it. A maid had dragged him stiff as a doll from the ice and set him in a sleigh, his hands pressed to his face, and for hours he could not be compelled to speak. It became a family story — Arthur's lost day. His sister, playing the maid, would seize him round the middle: "Poor mite," she'd say, squeezing him, "Poor little weaklin'!"

At fifteen, Arthur realized others did not hear voices the way he did, that others' heads were mostly silent. This he puzzled out slowly, over a long period of time, watching the face of the cook as she rooted in cupboards, seeing no distraction there, nothing calling her out of her thoughts, no demands on her patience. He took to reading books because, for some reason, he heard nothing when he read. He became pale from lack of sleep. His father, in the way of all bright and active men, began to push the boy harder. Calisthenics, running, and finally military training. Arthur was sent to an academy to train as an officer. A small, strange, troubled boy, he had found only one friendly face at the academy, and it happened to be Angus Lorne Bonnycastle. It didn't hurt that his new friend could fight.

"I stuck to Bonny — I knew where my bread was buttered," he said, and the Reverend chuckled.

At semester breaks, he returned home, a little taller, a little worse in the head, and, to counterbalance, a little more self-controlled. He ate with his clamouring family at the dinner table and recounted tales of other boys' exploits. When asked about his own, Arthur would affect an enigmatic air, as if he himself might be the ringleader, which he was not. When he was old enough, his father decided he would go west and join the North West Mounted Police. It was what he did with all his sons — this boy will go to architecture school, that boy into business. So, at the age of eighteen, with an officer's commission, Arthur found himself on an afternoon train heading into the sun. Black billows of engine smoke blew past his window while the other recruits slept or played cards. He was alone again among men.

The train stopped at Maple Creek and Fort Macleod, and a few boys got off at each. Arthur Elwell was stationed with the rest in a small outpost called Strike Him on the Back, close to the disaster of Batoche. He found himself on a windy plain with a trunk full of books, a notepad or two, regular exercise and duties, and all this punctuated by brief clashes with whisky runners and the occasional small band of Indians. Many people in the area were glad to see the police, but some were not. They came in futile war parties of two or three men at a time. Usually the dead lay where they fell for a day or more before someone came to claim them, a splash of colour in the dry and antic grasses, the wind ceaseless and disquieting, weather brooding on the horizon.

One lingering twilight, Arthur stood watch by the gate, rifle at his shoulder, gazing at two bodies — one of them a man Arthur himself had killed — their shirts riffling in the wind. As he watched, he discerned movement, a jerky flailing, and incredibly the man rose up. This spectre stood, bent at the waist, hands held to his fatal wound, and staggered toward the trees — he was neither dead nor alive. At the last moment, he turned his terrible face toward Arthur. It was ashen and streaked with tears.

Arthur's madness kicked into overdrive. In the morning, the bodies were gone, and so was Arthur Elwell. He was a deserter.

But his father was a member of Parliament and wealthy, and he had some influence. It would do no one any good, he explained, to have Arthur executed, would it? Arthur had been a fine officer, a quiet man, and a very good shot. It was difficult to get recruits in the first place, to convince young men to leave everything behind and become police officers in a country so wild and empty it was unfathomable to those who had never seen it. So the NWMP tolerated his frequent absences and always took him back.

The widow sat back in her chair. Her aversion forgotten, she pondered this sad chronicle.

"So, you just light out? Where do you go?"

"Sometimes I visit Bonny. Other times, I . . . don't know where I am."

"Why don't you go home, Arthur?" she said gently. Such a fine, warm family. It seemed a glorious thing to her. Arthur's eyes skated over her knees and shot away again.

"They wouldn't know me any more."

Behind Arthur, the Reverend shook his head at the widow.

And suddenly Mary's heart withered to think of it. Of course they would not. Look at him: a restless ghost. Arthur could not return home any more than she could.

203

★ ★ ★

Two days later, it was a bright afternoon, and Mary came sliding down the mountain's talus. Above her stood hard white peaks, clouds of snow caught there, blowing curlicues. She held her rifle high and waded through the loose pebbles as if she were coming down a waterfall. Boulders the size of horses lay among the smaller rocks, but mostly rivers of pebbles and sand flowed downhill in a hiss. She could feel dissolution with every footfall. Her leg was healing nicely now, and she had grown accustomed to the tug of stiffness in the ruined muscle. She turned and headed for the trees. The air crisp and dry, snow above, the sun pinwheeling through the cold, crystalline mist. A few summer flowers poked from rotted logs, but she knew that when evening shadow passed over them, they would grow filaments of ice along their edges. At the first touch of sun the next morning, the petals would melt to colourful slime.

The thick dark buffalo coat weighed heavy as a yoke on her shoulders, so she took it off, hung it on a branch, and sighed. She took up the rifle again and ventured through the trees, going laterally along the slope, which was carpeted by seasons of needles. Her footfalls were quiet. Her boots fit loosely, and so she slid continually downhill inside them and was glad they laced high up on her ankle or she might have slid right out of them. Birds whirred from branch to branch before her. After a short distance, she sat on her haunches and listened, elbows on her knees and the riflebutt on her boot.

Her little horse would have been no use to her now, she reflected. The ground was too sloped and awkward. In any case, the Reverend had sold her.

"To whom?!" she had burst out when he told her.

"Henry, in fact. And, uh" — he fiddled with his buttons — "I sold her for nothing. But, Mrs. Boulton, Henry *did* do you a wonderful service. Searching you out, bringing you here to me. I thought we owed him something."

She'd thought about that for a long time afterwards. The word *we*.

So her hunting was done on foot, as it would have been anyway, and she was cognizant every morning when she rose that she did not have to feed and water the horse as well as the Reverend. There was some good in that.

She had washed and repaired her clothes, tidying the seams of her wide pantlegs, hemming up the shredded cuffs. Her original stitching had been utterly wild. She had sat by the Reverend's homey stove and peered in disbelief at the pinched and buckled inseam, the inexplicable gaps. It was as if someone else had done the work. She remembered telling the bird lady she wasn't mad — but perhaps she had been. She recalled sitting naked on a rock, bent to the work of making pants from her skirts, intent on dressing as a man, a mermaid wishing herself legs. Was she any better now? She held a palm up and looked intently at it, but she saw nothing in the lines of her hands, no patterns, no intimations of anything.

205

Now the Reverend had two of them — lunatics — and he seemed quite content with it. Arthur followed him to his church every day, and she had taken up the rifle to find them all something to eat. Incredible to think it, but having Arthur in the house was almost a happiness for her — he was so unutterably mad, a chattering, trembling wreck of a man, and yet so benign in his character, his real self. Sleepless, he wandered the lower floor of the house at night, whispering, tidying. The widow would lie upstairs in her bed, listening intently, pacing the floor with him in her mind, her own head mostly silent, struck dumb by pure curiosity about the man. And she would wake in the morning to find him asleep in a chair, bony and slack-jawed as a corpse. His quiet thank-yous to her, his attempts to help at the stove, the alarming sight of him at the chopping block wielding an axe with badly palsied hands. She had begun to see what the Reverend saw in him. And that made her wonder what the Reverend saw in her . . .

A muffled boom came. The widow felt it through the soles of her boots. And then, from all directions, she heard the rattle of loosened rock seeking lower ground. She jumped up, wild-eyed, expecting the mountain to come down upon her. But after a moment, the world was quiet again. Eight feet away, a sparrow sat on a thread-thin branch and balanced itself with silly jerks of its tail, undisturbed by the noise. It bent and wiped its beak on the branch. So, after a wary moment, the widow took up her rifle and went on.

Cresting a rise in the land, she came upon a little door cut in the mountainside. An opening into the mine. Like the others she had seen, this one had been expertly framed and supported with rough wood beams; masses of cut rock had been cleared away from its mouth by hand. But how did the men get in there? A child would have trouble fitting in. She approached it and bent to peer inside. The floor and walls were uneven and jagged, cut without care, and it went in only a short way before angling sharply down. She leaned closer and listened. A discernable suck of air came from the hole, and when she leaned even farther into it, strands of her dark hair flowed forward against her cheeks. It was an airshaft meant to ventilate the mine. The air was going in, downward, sucking constantly. And then she felt a boom again, and the airshaft's damp breath puffed in her face like a hollow cough. Pebbles bounced downhill again. She stepped back, tasted rock dust on her lips. The miners were using dynamite.

Hurrying back to find her coat and collect her game, the widow chased a porcupine from its fetid hollow log. The animal set off downhill with a rolling, stump-legged gait she could barely believe — quills rattling. She'd never seen a porcupine move that fast. In the lowlands, where her husband had taught her to hunt, they merely waddled grumpily to the nearest tree, climbed ten feet, and hung there, stinking. John had never bothered to kill one. But now the widow pitched herself downhill after the beast, stopping to take aim, losing her target, then scrambling on. It began to dawn on her that she was not a wily hunter, and she was now lame as well. How different it was, this slalom through

207

the trees, from standing by the cabin, shouldering a rifle on a hostage tree trunk with her husband behind her correcting her aim. Or walking with her father and a stable boy out into high grasses, a dog flushing game birds up into the air like cards in a shooting gallery. The widow lost her quarry at the same moment she began to realize she'd lost her bearings. The porcupine was somewhere nearby, hidden. She stood panting.

The sound of a waterfall. Wind in the trees. The scent of water on the air. She went a little farther, and the trees began to thin and then fell away completely into a deep gorge blurred by mist, across which stretched a strange contraption she could not identify. She ventured down the slope a little to look more closely. The thing in question seemed to be an assemblage of trees and saplings and rope spanning the gorge. Exceptionally slender, it swayed like a spine. It was, in fact, a suspension bridge made from two fallen cedars, one on each side, reaching across the drop, constructed without the aid of metal or milled wood, nothing but trees, branches, and rope. Something of it spoke of Indians, some whisper of flexibility and utility. A rough elegance in the sway of its back. It was a shortcut for hunters, perhaps. Impossible to know how old the thing was or who had built it. She ventured out onto it a little way and discovered that, despite its spindly construction, it felt solid underfoot, possessing a strange elastic strength. She ventured a little farther. She could see the edge of the drop, the river below, misty and green. The widow bounced experimentally and, a moment later, received an alarming series of motions in return, fluid and uneven, as if something powerful stood at the other end trying to shake her off her feet. She backed cautiously off the bridge and stood watching it swell and heave. Then she went on her way, heading back uphill toward the spot where she had left her coat.

Twenty minutes later, she found herself standing above the front yard of the mine. Below her lay a wreckage of lumbered trees, various paths webbed across open ground, wheel tracks dug in deep, and here and there, mine cars, a few rusting or tipped over or missing a wheel. A gaggle of silent miners knelt at a long, stained trough, bent over it, separating the good rock from the bad, piles of discarded culm about them, their hunched bodies silver-black and spidery, their arms moving ceaselessly. A few mine carts stood lined up at the edge of the hill, ready to be wheeled down, perhaps to the train platform. To the widow's left stood the towering mine-head, shrouded in trees. She wandered to the edge of the curiously flat overhang on which she stood. She leaned incautiously far out and saw she was standing directly on top of the upper frame of a large entranceway, the gaping mouth of the mine. All paths across the scarred ground converged here. Two men sat eating their lunch. One big, the other small, both black in the face and white round the neck and forehead, wearing the common markings of miners. The widow heard their spoons clacking on metal plates as they ate. The men's voices came out suddenly, and she could hear every word. One man said, "You ought to said something, Ronnie."

"Huh?"

"I said you oughta told me about that goddamn hole."

"Sorry, Jim."

"Sorry hell."

They ate a little more in silence before one of them spoke again.

"It wasn't there yesterday."

"I know it."

"That whole north seam is a fucking bag of tricks. Nothing's holding it up is why. We got no business laying charges."

"That's not your say so, nor mine. So just shut up about it."

"That big fella, you know, the . . . Italian or whatever?"

"Norwegian."

"He dropped a match down the north end, where Flynn fell, and you should have seen how far down it went. It just fluttered down there and kept getting smaller and smaller."

"Don't tell me, goddammit! And don't say his name. What's wrong with you?"

"Sorry, Jim . . . You get that smell yet?"

The other man put a blackened hand to his forehead and sighed. There was a long silence.

"Yeah. Water," he said.

"Does it smell fresh to you?"

"I dunno."

"It's coming in on that seam."

There was a short pause, then the same man's voice came quiet, "You think he's still alive?"

"Drop it, Ronnie."

"You think it's possible?"

"No, I don't. And you step one foot in that mine and mention his name, you'll be sweeping up your teeth. I swear to Christ, Ronnie, you're worse luck than a woman."

"Hold on. You don't have to . . ."

"I coulda dropped a hundred feet before I hit something."

The two sat in silence for a moment.

"Next time," Jim said, "open your trap and say something."

The reverend and the widow gazed upon the object before them on the table. A massive bloodied porcupine lay supine, its brown teeth bared and its forefeet curled as if begging. The Reverend reached out his thumb and forefinger and waggled a stiffening leg. The animal's odour was lavish.

Arthur cowered behind them, looking from human to animal. "Can we eat it?" he asked.

"*Eat* it?" the Reverend said. "In theory."

"I could make a stew," Mary grinned, "maybe even a pie."

"Good grief."

"I've never heard of it . . . eating a porcupine," Arthur reflected.

"A soup might work," she mused, "or maybe smoke the meat and lay it up?"

Despite himself, the Reverend had begun backing away from the table, averting his face from the spectacle.

"This is the best way to skin it, Bonny," she said, pointing along the corpse's soft belly. "Start here . . . then cut along the legs like that." The variegated quills on its back were almost a foot long, and they collapsed dryly together as the animal was rolled. Smaller barbs grew at its sides; even among the soft belly hairs were suspiciously stiff-looking fibres. The Reverend was breathing through his mouth.

"Well," she said finally, "are you going to skin it or not?"

"Me!?" he protested.

"Oh, Bonny," she said fondly and went off to find the whetstone and a knife.

A week later, Arthur was waiting for the train. He sat outside McEchern's store clutching a mug of steaming coffee, much subdued, his eyes fixed deep into the forest where the trees seemed to fade into an infinite number of vertical lines. Whatever his affliction — and the Reverend would not conjecture, though everyone else did — its engine had choked and died. He was now able to eat, sit still, even smile. But he looked no less otherworldly. Here was the same long, pale cheek, the same staring eyes. His smile was ghastly. Arthur was an illustration of the transforming habit of madness; his face had become a mask, the patina of dread laid over it so often that it stayed.

His horse was not so badly used as it had at first appeared. Fright and dehydration had been the worst of its afflictions. After a day its legs ceased shaking; after two, its appetite returned. It was a surprisingly robust horse, and unwisely fond of its owner, wandering with bobbing head toward Arthur when he came down to the store. Even from a distance, Arthur's gait was bizarre — a wooden toy man dancing on his string.

That morning, he had arrived dressed in his ratted uniform, holding a little package of food made for him by Mary. She had even put her hand on his arm, in a motherly way, though they were much the same age, and patted his scrawny bicep.

"You'll eat this soon, won't you, Arthur?" she'd said. "Not wait till it goes off?"

"I will," he said. The Reverend was behind her, and the two of them fretted like worried parents around a schoolboy.

A clutch of miners had been standing around considering the horse. They now turned their attention to Arthur. One man took up the ruined police helmet, its crown staved in, the metal torn away as if some massive can opener had been at work on it.

"You have an accident?"

"No. I did it myself," Arthur said into his steaming cup. The men assessed the lunatic with renewed interest, some suspiciously, some with affection — a good story is always collectible.

"Why'd you do that?" another man said. But the lunatic had no story for them. His hand came up slowly and gestured limply in circles about his head, like a man shooing flies away from his ears.

McEchern appeared at the flapdoor of his store, a cute smile on his lips. "Tell 'em about the wind," he said, "like you told me." And immediately, Arthur did, launching into the recitation the way a child tells a joke, breathless and in a rush.

"North wind is safe. It keeps everything in place. West wind is no problem either. But a south wind is bad. You fall apart in a south wind if you don't keep moving. You don't dare stay still. And this is proved by science. In countries that have lepers, there's always a south wind. It makes you slow and sick and, sooner or later, everything falls apart."

"It's scientific," McEchern said, standing behind him.

"You don't say," murmured a bearded face, while others grinned. The widow stood sadly by Arthur and watched as he took in the mirth he had caused. When it wasn't frightening, she observed, madness was funny.

A long, mournful wail could be heard far away along the valley: a train coming up the pass. Arthur put down his cup and gathered his things, took the reins of his horse, and said his goodbyes, his manners formal and remote. Then he and the horse turned and together walked away.

They rode when they could, and when the trees became too thick the tracker made them dismount and walk on in a line, man, horse, man, horse, leading the animals by the reins through impassable areas. Dry branches caught at their sleeves, knees, and stirrups, and the animals staggered and slid on exposed roots. Eventually, the tracker stopped with a stamp of his foot and a frustrated bellow: "This is bullshit!" His horse jerked its head in surprise.

The tracker turned to his clients with a scrunched face and sputtered, "Just . . . just wait here. I'll find where she came out." He hiked up his trousers and went off at a bow-legged trot, stepping around tree trunks, his dark oilskin congealing into the forest.

A second later, his voice came echoing, "Don't make a fire, boys. It's too thick in here. You'll barbecue us."

The two men stood uncertainly, reins in hand, alone in the huge silence. A few tiny birds blew past them and settled on trees, hopping in spirals up the trunks, stabbing at insects. Then one by one they blew away again.

"She came through here?" said one, disbelieving.

The other shrugged.

"Does he know what he's doing?"

His brother thought a minute, then said, "Yes."

Half a day later they were on their way in a different direction. The old man had explained that it was one of only two possible ways she could have gone. He had simply guessed. And almost right away, he picked up her trail again.

At dusk he called to them and pointed into the trees, and together they walked their horses toward a dark, lumpen thing that hung among the branches. It was an English saddle — bizarre relic, now rain-soaked and speckled with fallen leaves. The tracker dismounted and

215

approached the object, hefted it and brushed the debris from it, smelled the underside for mould and checked under the flaps. He brought it back to his horse.

"Mind if I keep this?" he said amiably, already strapping it behind his own saddle.

"For God's sake, man. Is she here?"

"She was."

The old man continued to pack the awkward object properly, and the brothers waited, for he had a habit of lecturing on the finicky ways of pack horses and the rituals of constructing a fair and balanced burden. In fact, it was the only subject on which he ever strung together more than a few words, and he could be as dull as a schoolmarm on it.

"That's a fine saddle," he said, stroking the tooling along its edges. The brothers glanced at each other, helpless.

Finally, he set to work reading the signs the widow had left. He wandered cautiously through the fiddleheads and found what he was looking for. The evidence of a little fire, grease deposits in its charred centre. Even the brothers could see it. A few formerly green twigs she had used in some way to cook meat. The underbrush beaten down and many footprints . . . some of them leading uphill. In fact, that path had been used several times, perhaps ferrying goods to some drier, better spot uphill. The old man ruminated over one deep boot impression, and slowly his expression became sourly skeptical — as if the ground was telling him something preposterous, like a child making up a silly story.

216

"All right. Leave the horses," he said heading uphill. "Come with me."

Ten minutes later they all stood at the perimeter of the Ridgerunner's vacated camp, considerably camouflaged by him. He had scuffed away evidence, tossed it into the trees, covered as much of the pockmarked ground as possible with loose branches and needles. But all three men could see the beaten-down ground, footprints everywhere, the exact imprint of a tent in dead grass — obviously a tent from the shape of it, and not a tepee. The old man nodded his head. "Your girl's got herself a boyfriend."

His customers looked at him with dawning awareness, for even they could make out the obvious signs.

"It's a pretty good cleanup. I'd say a woodsman, white, most probably. They ate together, the girl and him, always over there. They slept together, is my guess. It gets kinda cold." He stood, nodding, a moment. For the tale was telling itself, in pine needles and dead grass. The couple had lingered here for some time in cohabitation. And until they had stumbled upon each other, manifestly, they had been total strangers. A smile crept over the old man's face.

"Can't say as I was expecting this," he said.

CHAPTER
FIFTEEN

Thunder rolled along the mountain ranges toward morning. The widow lay awake, her eyes closed and a woollen hat on her head against the frost. It itched and felt suddenly hot, so she clawed it off and lay sweating. Her leg ached badly, though it had been good for days. She reached down to finger the scar like a dimple, a thumbprint in her calf. She pressed hard, but the muscle hurt no more or less than before. A rumble came from the west, cruising the clouds and heading east. She rolled over and tossed the covers off her leg. It cooled her and so she slept, dreaming of a city full of canals. It was a dull dream and she felt she had dreamt it before. Things were brought to her on the canal and she stood on a dock and watched flotsam drift on the surface. Eventually, she peed into the canal. The widow woke up suddenly, her bladder painfully full.

She slipped silently from the covers and pulled the bedpan from under her little bed. She squatted naked over the bowl and tried to make as little noise as possible. The air was warmer than it had been. She closed her eyes in pure thankfulness. On past nights, her breath had blown snowflake patterns on the window glass, and when she was absolutely forced to crawl out and pee, her urine had steamed as she hunkered over the bowl with her teeth chattering. In the mornings, when she took the pan to the trees and flung it out, a solid block of ice flew end over end and landed with a thud on the ground. But today the air was almost pleasantly warm. In the faint morning light that came through the curtain, she remained squatting and slid the bowl away and wiped herself with a little rag kept for that purpose. She heard the Reverend breathing, the catch in his lungs. And then she heard a padding sound, like someone drumming fingers on a table. In the semi-darkness she saw a small red squirrel watching her. It advanced a few steps, braced on all fours like a miniature, tawny bear. Its eyes were black and strange and emotionless.

"Bonny," she whispered. At the sound of her voice the squirrel dashed in an arc to her left.

"*Bonny!*" she cried, clambering back to the safety of her bed.

"What? What is it?" She could hear his voice go from groggy to alarmed.

"There's a squirrel!"

She heard the sound of his mattress as he shifted under his covers, and then the dry scritching of his knuckles rubbing on his bristled jaws. He sighed.

"Go back to sleep, Mary."

"It's staring at me."

"No, she's just confused. Go back to sleep."

The widow crawled back under the covers and lay glaring at the rodent. Indeed it did seem confused. It stood awkwardly, like a toy, then ran without warning from corner to corner, then sat upright with its black eyes unmoving, as if thinking.

"How do you know it's confused?"

"Her nest was in the chimney, so I moved it. She's been looking for it for hours."

The widow lay back reluctantly, still watchful, listening to the light patter of the squirrel's feet.

"What if she doesn't find it?"

"She'll find it."

The squirrel spraddle-walked along the floorboards with its head down, sniffing, then leaped onto the wall and hung there, tail whipping.

"How do you know it's a she?"

"Oh, go back to sleep!"

For the next three nights, Mary was unable to sleep. She sat undressed in her queenly bed and endured the night. The irony of insomnia, she reflected finally, is that sleep does indeed visit briefly, but it surely will be interrupted — this time by chittering raccoons trying to enter the house. At least the squirrel was gone. The widow put her face close to the window and craned to see below to where the hunched bodies circled and waddled, calling irritably to one another. Silver backs. She searched the sky for signs of daylight, but there were none.

She lay back down and sighed. She felt hot and kicked the covers off. Then the cold air chilled her and she rolled over irritably, sweeping the covers up to her chin. She scrubbed her feet against the linen sheets. They needed laundering again — damn them. Damn the laundry and the stove too. Her mind ran off on a series of grievances, which were halted suddenly by the sound of the Reverend's voice.

"What are you doing?"

"Nothing."

"You're flopping around and grumping."

"I can't sleep."

"Well, you're keeping me from sleeping."

"Sorry." Mary heard him shift his position on the dry straw mattress and scrub his knuckles against his jaw the way he often did.

The Reverend yawned and said, "Would it help you if I told you a story? Do you think I might bore you to sleep if I tried?"

She snorted. "I think so. What story?"

He was silent for a long time, too long, and finally she said, "Bonny?"

"What?"

"What story did you want to tell me?"

"How about the story of my life?"

"Oh!" Mary said, amazed. "I'd love to hear it." She snuggled down and pulled the covers to her chin and waited. And after an interval he did tell her.

His childhood home had been a family estate, cold and too large and filled with mismatched paintings and foreign *objets d'art*, an unwanted inheritance. When money was needed, his father sold a painting. It was that simple. But the house itself was unsaleable and a burden. His own room when he was a boy had been lined with shelves that ran twenty feet up to the filigreed ceiling. Every shelf was empty except for a dozen or so mechanical toys bought for him by cousins and aunts. They were all placed far too high for any child to reach — they were decorative.

His mother did not live with them, though she would arrive from time to time with many trunks. She was greeted as a guest, and when she left, the house was unchanged. The maids disapproved of her fashions, and when the boy sat with these girls in their rooms after dinner, they aped his mother's hairstyle and manners in the mirror, and he laughed.

When the boy was twelve, his father decided it was time for his son to see the world. Japan, Indonesia, India, Egypt. Unaccustomed to proximity to his own father, he now had plenty of it. On steamships, in the lobbies of foreign hotels, in carriages, waiting in train stations, sitting on the steps of temples while his father smoked. In Cairo, he even sat in his father's arms atop a camel as they drifted along the reeking streets, the camel's roaring setting the boy rigid with fear, while hawkers and touts ran alongside reaching up with their wares — a brass bell, talismans of shell and horn, clay statuettes of unknown deities and demons. One round-faced and smiling man proffered various mummified human body parts cadged from pyramids and crypts. A linen-wrapped hand, a foot, a jawbone; all snapped away from their source like kindling, leaving jaw sockets empty, the dry pipes of bones whistling. His father admired the hand most of all, and bought it. When they unwrapped it in the hotel room, the boy recoiled. It looked so plausible — fingernails perfect and desiccated, the colour of coffee. Wrinkles along each knuckle, a palm whose lines were almost readable. It was hard and weightless. His father slipped it up his own sleeve, gesticulating with it: *Be a good boy, Angus, or else.* And then he held it lightly in his own moist palm and said, "This cost less than a glass of beer."

In Japan, Angus had stood in any number of ornamental gardens with his hands in his pockets, waiting for his father to finish with the girls, watching whiskered fish slumber in the cold winter water. He remembered monkey forests, waterfalls, walled compounds with wide latticed doors through which could be seen laundry hanging.

His father fancied himself a storyteller, though Angus saw him as a liar. Kindly but venal. He insisted he'd seen an eagle unable to fly away because its shadow was bogged down in mud, and that he himself had kicked the shadow free. It was the kind of lie even a small boy sees through. But his father would affect a wide-eyed amazement and tell these same whoppers to strangers, especially women, who, to the boy's disgust, always found it charming.

It was on this trip that his father took up the habit of opium smoking. On the steamship home, he rarely came to dinner, but lay constantly in his rooms, dreaming with open eyes. Angus was reduced to making his pipe for him, for he could not manage it himself after the first one, and he would rage feebly from the bed till the boy obeyed. Back at home, his father ran through his enormous stash, and though he harried every Chinese person he could find, he could procure no more. He became distant and melancholy.

223

Before too long, he booked a passage to Indochina, and his son was sent away to officer's college and told to do well by the family name.

The school had the ridiculous name of Aspiration Academy, and this was where Angus met Arthur Elwell. There were no classes on history, strategy, or even mathematics. There was no library. All the boys' books were confiscated at the beginning of the year and returned, dog-eared, at the end. All any officer-in-training needed, apparently, was a day of endless athletics punctuated by chapel. They were taught to run, ride, shoot, and box, and it was in this latter sport that Angus excelled. Small students were often matched with large ones — for hadn't it happened so with David and Goliath? With no taste for pain, Angus Bonnycastle quickly learned the art of ducking. He also learned to follow his opponent's eyes. He discovered the soft spots under the ribs; if he hit hard enough, the defending gloves would slide away from the face to expose the tip of the chin. Within a year he had worked his way to top boy and was a minor celebrity. Weaker boys flocked to him, the way one finds a tree in a hailstorm.

And that's when the headmaster challenged him. It was a howling error on this man's part, and everybody knew it. If he beat the boy, he would look like an ass. But he *had* to beat him, or where was the natural order? The match was long and miserable, and it was very close, but it ended with the headmaster in his trunks on the floor. That night, Angus was called to the headmaster's rooms and flogged until he bled. Several days later, a rematch was declared.

"I remember very well the announcement at the end of chapel. One of the teachers made it, and he was grinning. He said God would defend the righteous man. 'His hand will come down and stay the devil.' I thought about that for a while. And I decided he was right."

That night, a few other boys, Arthur among them, snuck into Angus's room and urged him to knock the old fart's block off. And in the morning, he did.

Of course, he was flogged again. It went on to a third match with the same result, the headmaster limping down the hall with a baboon's purple and furious face, and the boy lying in his bloodstained sheets at night, thanking God.

"Bonny," the widow said in a low voice, "what was wrong with that man?"

"The real question, Mary, is why didn't I just lose?" He chuckled a little, and in his voice she heard unrepentant pride. "In any case, the semester was over soon after that. The old bastard actually shook my hand goodbye. I packed my bags and went home an officer. You didn't know I was an officer, did you?"

"No."

They lay in silence for a long time, the air so still and cool the widow closed her eyes.

"Funny how life goes," the Reverend said and yawned. A raccoon keened outside the window to its mate, then went grunting away round the side of the house.

"What happened then?" she said sleepily. But he said nothing. "How did you become a minister?"

She waited. And soon she heard his sleeping breath.

★   ★   ★

That night, the widow actually slept. She lay dreaming in her bed, her mouth open like a child's. And in this dream her father stood to his waist in rushing water, fishing rod held high above his head. The sun was sharp on the corded water, dancing like pennies on a blanket. She saw his thick black shirt, the stiff collar glinting like metal, and his gaze was fixed on the river. He took a step deeper into the cold water, gave the rod a gentle tug, another tug. The unseen fish fought ferociously, the line of its life leading to his hand.

Look at him, Mary! he shouted. *Look at him!*

She couldn't see it at first, then suddenly there it was: the long refracted shadow raging sidelong, fighting the thing that held it fast. Her father let out some slack, and the thread chased away along the surface, ravelling free, a harmless cobweb. She tried to call out but she could not, her voice was frozen in her throat. He braced in the riverbed and gave the rod one quick, savage yank. The singing line cut the river's nap with a ripping sound, and slowly the burdened line went slack in dying increments. She sank to her knees and wept, *Lost, all is lost.* Small drops came up in the wind, the sound of many women singing. The water began to rain upward, slowly, like a woman's hair rising in the wind. A glitter on the air. The widow lay rigid on her bed with fists at her side, and tears crept back to her temples, but she kept dreaming. Her father stood in the rising water, the rod in his raised hand like a sword.

226

CHAPTER
SIXTEEN

The widow stood by the stove and, keeping as far away from the scorching metal side as she could, reached with a long spoon into the pot of rags she was stirring. Each patch of cloth had been folded into a rectangle that could be pinned to a belt and worn between her legs. She had placed them in boiling water along with a good handful of precious salt — for purity. She did not need the pads yet. What her grandmother called her glad tidings had not yet returned, though it had been . . . she tried to calculate how long. Nine months, then the baby lived for ten days, then spring came, then . . . but how long had she been running? How long had she been here, with the Reverend?

She had scrounged upstairs through the trunk under the Reverend's bed and the various boxes against the wall, finally finding a small drawstring bag full of bits of cotton cloth, some cut at angles into diamond shapes, some torn into strips, with various patterns and colours, intended certainly for some future quilt. She had sorted out the largest pieces, ones that could be folded into the right shape, and laid them across her knee. She scrutinized the tiny floral pattern of one swatch, the pink daisies, the wandering green vine. On another, an implausible golden urn, badly drawn, and twisted braid — what a monstrous dress this would make. Where had this textile come from? What had this woman been planning?

The widow held this cloth in her hand, an artifact from some other woman's life, some other woman's secret trove of useful things. A mother? A sister? All the Reverend had said was, "That's another story." Mary put the textile to her nose and inhaled, but got nothing more personal than the sharp scent of wood, forests, rain. Whoever this woman was, she was gone. Just as the widow kept her little Bible, perhaps he kept these things not for themselves but to remember someone, to carry her with him.

She had put the rest of the cloth pieces away, careful to fold and replace everything the way it had been, even wrapping the drawstring round the bag and tucking the end under as she had found it.

When the rags were done, she started water for a bath. She poured two more buckets of icy mountain water into the pan and watched as tiny bubbles formed at the metal walls. A thin, resonant hiss issued from it and she blew across the water's surface to see the wisps of steam dance away. She ran her fingers through her ropy hair in anticipation. When the water was boiling, she took the pan by its handles and, bracing her feet well, poured it into the bath. Then she set up chairs about the bath and hung blankets between and over them to create a small bathing tent, with one open flap where she could add buckets of water as they boiled.

She ventured outside in her undergarments and big black boots to a patch of wintergreen that grew near the house, gathered a handful of the small dark green leaves, brought them to her face, and breathed in the sharp, almost medicinal scent. Then she went inside, crushing and rolling them between her hands, and dropped the fragrant leaves into the bath. Her grandmother had always counselled that winter-green chased away consumption and brain ailments. Her father's opinion of this was predictable, of course: "Your grandmother gets a lot of bunk from advertisements in the newspaper. If they sell sheep dung to cure rickets, she thinks it cures rickets. Otherwise, why would they sell it? That's the curse of a generous heart."

In the months after the worst of his despair, her father would lie sleeping in the small ceramic tub, his head lolling back over the edge and a sheet laid over everything up to his chest so that the young maids wouldn't be scandalized when they warmed his water. They went away with the buckets, shaking their heads. It was the kind of shameful thing one expected of the dissolute and wealthy. Her grandmother accused him of flirting with contagion, for bathing too often would make anyone sick. She followed a speedy regimen involving a cloth and a bowl of water, morning and night, and she applied powders and slept in a hairnet.

These memories came back to the widow now with a pitiless candour. She suspected that her grandmother's best efforts — with both son and granddaughter — had fallen far short of the mark. Even as her son fell apart at the seams, all the old woman could do was scold. Inadequate in her skills, antique in her attitudes, besotted by the opinions of others, other women especially, she had turned to endless scolding and censure of her only son, and was blind to the unhappy child who stood before her. Not her child, but someone else's; not her duty, but she would do it anyway, after a fashion. Mary had been sent off with the first man who would have her. Her father fretting on the train platform, as if he suspected where it all would lead.

The widow sighed and looked about her at the Reverend's home, her new home, and slowly the pall began to lift. Here was a man who wore his scars on the outside and held a merry heart within. How much better that was than its opposite.

The widow added pot after pot of hot water, steam exploding from her little tent. Then she crept naked under the blankets and dipped first one foot and then the other into the bath. Slowly, she lowered her buttocks in, pulled the last flap closed, and finally sat rigid and upright with her knees raised to her chest. The water came halfway up her hip, covered her ankle bones, but that was all. She dangled a metal cup from her hand, carefully dipping it in and ladling a little hot water over her shins. Only after a long interval was she able to lean back against the scalding metal side of the bath, put her head back, and sigh.

The scent of the green leaves in the water, the steam, her breath. Through a tiny space in the blankets she could see sunlight, the rafters, lines of nails in the wood, hammered in place by the Reverend. She pictured him on one of his cock-eyed ladders, fishing a nail from his pocket. The whole place looked like him, had his mark. The widow slid down into the bath and let the scalding water touch her chin. It was dark and quiet in her tent; bands of sunlight came through the steam. The heat was penetrating her shoulders, and she felt her muscles let go.

Am I happy? she thought. *Is this happy?*

It was a question she used to ask herself as a girl, lying alone in bed and wondering about the future. She would close her eyes and think ecstatically: *I am so happy!* and let the words float inside her, testing the truth of them, until, slowly, inevitably, the feeling became hollow and sank away to nothing. Certainly she had often been glad — glad of a Christmas present, glad to see her father coming down the lane, glad to sit down after a long day of chores. Had it been a happy life so far? Not particularly. Not for anyone. The question seemed remote now, like something in a Bible lesson, the voice of some marm asking: "And what did the children do when they reached Jerusalem? They . . . *rejoiced.*"

She ran a palm over her belly and tried to feel something there, some remembrance of pain or fullness, of life or the lack of it, of her own blood even, an intimation of her former self, travelling like a muffled voice from skin to skin. But there was nothing. She was as empty and unchanged as if none of it had ever happened. She put a hand to her forehead, breathed deeply in the damp air. A hot tear ran back across her cheek. What she felt now was simple relief. In the Reverend's house she had found a kind of amnesty. It wasn't happiness, not damned happiness.

She'd been properly happy on her wedding day, gaily waving goodbye on the train, embracing her husband when he finally came to her in bed. Happy as expected. Then the happy duped wife, the happy inept housekeeper left constantly alone, with winter roaring outside the cabin and the voices roaring inside her. The happy mother of a sick and dying baby . . .

The midwife and her companions had arrived long after dark. John had known they were coming when the owls stopped calling. There were three of them — the night woman and two men, all on horseback, one man holding a lantern. The old woman trailed John into the cabin, following his candle, while the two men stood in silence by the trees and held the horses by the reins. The animals' coats steamed in the snow-blown air.

Mary lay barely conscious near the bed, a candle on the wet wood floor next to her. The baby trembled weakly between her legs. Though she did not know who was speaking, Mary heard the woman's voice.

"Oh God," it said, from a long way off, "have you two no sense at all?"

"Can you help?" John said.

"Heat!" she hissed. "Get the goddamn stove on! It's cold as hell in here."

And then Mary heard a soft voice, "My dear, oh my dear . . ." drifting in the darkness and knew it to be the midwife talking to the baby.

Morning came and the men were gone, all of them, John having departed with more easy company. The midwife sat hard-faced by the bed, her arms crossed. Mary lay like a shrivelled queen under the blankets, the baby on her chest, her hands limp at her sides. She opened one eye.

"So," the midwife said. It seemed to Mary that she had been waiting.

"Is it . . . did I?" she croaked.

"Yes." The midwife tapped Mary on her collarbone, by the baby's cheek. "Here."

The new mother looked down, almost cross-eyed, like a drunk eyeing the buttons of his vest. She saw the top of a small, pale head. Her hand drifted up to it. The baby barely moved, but its breath came fiercely, a tiny, panting thing against her breast.

"A boy," the midwife said and got up and left the room.

Mary lay her head back. She held the boy, the warm crown. She felt around for a hand and discovered one, small as a nut, unmoving. They lay there together while morning light came through the window. She turned her head to see the light, motes of dust floating in on the sun, some rising, others falling, a strange traffic of specks. But she paid them little mind as her hand held the marvellous tiny fist.

The midwife returned with a cup of melted snow and, dipping her fingers into it, baptized the baby. "Name of the father son holy ghost amen." When she was done, she sat with her hands in her lap, looking at the young mother.

"He won't last," she said.

Each day, the baby faded a little more. Mary whispered to him, urged him into life the way one urges a runner in a race. She gave him names, tried them out in sequence, and then suffered the conviction that if she finally chose one, the job would be finished, and he would depart. After a week, he could no longer nurse, his mouth open against her breast, and he rarely cried. She lay him in her bed and fanned his face, trying not to see the calm, almost indifferent eyes. She put her ear to the baby's chest just to hear the birdlike flutter. He grew less responsive by the day, and every subtle sign of his drifting away pierced her. Unslept, starved, still bleeding, she had to be careful not to faint when rising from the bed or from a chair, her hands on her knees and her spinning head held downward, the cabin thumping, and her ears going briefly hollow. As the baby slept and sank deeper, she forced herself to rise, to walk, to pace. She was afraid to sleep lest he leave her, or spend his last moments alone. Day became just like night to her, there was no distinction and no break in wakefulness. Everything was burning, she was on fire. She put her forefinger into his hand, but he could not grip any more, so she carefully pressed the tiny fingers in place and watched them fade open again. The sun rose cruelly pink and soft on what would clearly be his final day. She could not breathe, could not blink, but watched helplessly as the room suffused with light. She stayed with him to the end, and long after.

Her husband had been gone for a week. When he returned, his son was dead but not yet buried, and his wife had gone mad.

John had been obliged to light a fire over the spot for most of a day before he could get a shovel into the frozen earth to dig even a shallow grave. When it was dug, the walls of it steamed, and cinders fell rolling down the sides into it. Mary had no recollection of how the boy was put in it — her mind was a savage blank on that — but she did remember the hollow *clank* of the shovel as John tamped the mound down and the wisps of steam still rising in a ring about it.

Spring had come in a gush of muddy water through the bare trees. Grey jays swept from branch to branch, calling to one another in their fluty voices, and water lay in sparkling pools about the cabin. Mary had taken to her bed and barely moved from it. She watched the light crawl the rafters above her, and her mouth constantly whispered. Everything in her mind came forth, mouthed senselessly, repeating and circling back on each thought.

John's voice penetrated the air, and she turned her head to see him standing there. "Can you not do something, Mary? Can you not get up?"

235

At first, John was always somewhere in the cabin, the quiet husband, his smell of leather and cattle following him. She had no idea how he fed himself for she didn't feed him, and she herself could not eat.

"There should be a woman here," he'd said. It took her some time to realize he meant some other woman who might look after them both. He stood by the door and glared at the world. He sat at the end of their bed. Sometimes she thought she could hear the men in the fields — their voices, laughter — but she was never sure whether it was real.

Then one afternoon she became hungry, and she sat up, the body on its phantom climb upward, swimming away from death. She began to walk again, and as she regained her footing, John began to leave her alone for longer each day. Back to work. Sometimes he went on the long trip to town. Gone again for the week.

So that was that; she could not die after all.

She rose and wandered the house like a stranger, finding it terribly messed, plates unwashed and bread left out to go hard. The canvas floor cover was bunched and filthy, and there were drifts of leaves in the corners of the cabin. John had knocked his pipe out into the washtub. His new boots were set side by side on the table, and his hat had fallen from its peg to the floor. These things were like omens, dire warnings she alone understood. She bent to sweep, several minutes at a time, then sat on the bed, her head reeling and tears in her raw eyes. She waited, but she did not know what she was waiting for. A rainbow cut through the trees, and the air was heavy with white mist. At night, she could hear a strange booming, far away, as if the sky itself had woken from an angry dream. She sat on a chair, her trembling hands in her lap.

One morning she saw a young bear standing over the grave where the child was hidden. It had already pawed out a shallow hole but had found nothing. As if nothing had ever been there, as if the boy had been a dream. The bear's eyes were small and uncertain. It swayed slightly, gaunt and spring-hungry, its skin hanging loosely at its belly. She watched it wander off, following a scent perhaps, smelling something green pushing through the snow that lay preserved in the shadows and gullies. She went out and, with gentle hands, swept the earth back into place.

John went off to the fields during the day. Men and a few boys came with him, hired to turn the thawed fields, but when they arrived in the morning or returned at dusk, they always stood outside the cabin door with their hats in their hands, as if everyone knew that crossing her threshold brought misfortune. They left without food or coffee. She was not strong enough yet to cook for so many, and when they were gone she put her face in her hands with shame. At night, he lay with her in the bed and slept. He allowed her to curl up behind him, her chin on his spine. He was warm, almost hot, extraordinarily alive.

She had been out behind the cabin, hanging John's laundry in the early summer breeze, the human debris of their small homestead strewn about the yard, when she looked up and saw herself. Standing in the shadow was a girl so similar to her that Mary's mouth fell open. The girl came forward into the sun, sidling the way a cat does, her eyes coldly assessing. They stood in mutual regard, waiting amid the curling rivulets of mist that a chinook had blown through the trees.

"Where is he?" said the girl.

"My husband isn't home . . ." Mary's voice faded away. She stared, fascinated by the girl's long dark hair, pale skin, pregnant belly.

"I don't want *him*. Where's the baby?"

Unable to speak, Mary simply gaped. The girl licked her lips, her eyes taking in everything. Then she turned and went into the cabin, cute as a daylight thief, her ankles showing and her short skirts speckled with bits of weed. She lifted a work hat from its perch on a chairback, then dropped it onto the seat. She went to the kitchen and ran her finger over the bread board. She entered the bedroom and stood looking at the photographs on the dresser while Mary lingered at the door.

"I imagined this place different," the girl said. "It's smaller. You keep it a mess."

Mary realized her heart was leaping. Every move the girl made promised disaster, as if by a gesture she could sew flames along the floorboards. The girl put her hand to the swell of her belly, not kindly, not solicitously the way women do, but as if to hold it back, hold it in, her face no longer merely unfriendly but infused with rage. She turned to leave the bedroom and Mary dashed out

238

of her way, backing along the kitchen wall, her eyes tracking the unwanted guest. The girl paused by the table panting under her burden. "You're a lucky person," she said bitterly, looking not at Mary but at everything else. "I wish I was lucky as you."

"Who are you?"

"You could ask him. But you don't even know where he is, do you?"

Mary's hand came slowly to her mouth, her eyes welling.

The girl gave her a rueful smile and nodded. "Now you see," she said, exiting. "But I don't know where he is either. And I don't care."

It was then that the girl spotted the little grave marker. She went to it and stood over it for a long time, hands loose at her sides, and after a while she put her foot out and poked at the cross to right it, but it drooped again, lopsided. Then she turned away into the trees and was gone.

Mary remembered what happened next only in dull flashes. The *click* of her wedding ring as it hit the sandy earth — thrown in like a pebble or a spent match or any other substanceless thing. The glint of it in the dark hole — then shovelfuls of earth raining down over it. Damp air, damp clothes, warm drafts of wind coming through the trees. The cross slumped in its hole. Marking the place, at the boy's head. Marking the death of it all. Her wedding ring buried, as if she were already a widow and her husband already dead, the clock running backward and forward at the same time. Everything had been taken from her — her father, her birthplace, any money she had ever possessed, her engagement ring, her only child, and now her husband. The girl had looked around at nothing, and had seen everything.

CHAPTER
SEVENTEEN

The widow sat to one side of the leaf-strewn altar and watched the men come, one or two among them with their helmets lit, and the others following. They came in small groups, some murmuring among themselves, clearly amiable, others silent as if nothing more than chance had brought them together. It was the first service to be held in the church — the widow gathered they were infrequent anyway, impromptu. She wasn't sure what form they usually took. But since the pews were finished, and since it was Sunday, the Reverend had called a service at dawn, at the end of a night shift. A thin, bluish sunrise frosted the tips of the cedars. A massive aspen that stood by what would someday be the front door of the church reached high above its peers and spread its trembling, dislike leaves in the growing light. But down below all was dark, and when the men sat down on the pews and blew out their head-lamps, the church fell into gloom, a vague whiff of sulphur from the carbide lamps. The assembly waited for the Reverend, who was late. He had dashed home quickly to retrieve his bible. Around the widow sat moving shapes and their voices.

". . . used to be open range, mostly. We fenced in our gardens to keep cows *out*. Now they got fences everywhere. Like a man'd build a fence just to be polite."

"Wo ist der ficken Pastor? Ich bin so müde," said a sleepy voice.

"Who's that girl?"

"I said I dunno."

". . . they look like a black snake only they got these, well not rattles, more like plats, maybe two or three of them, five inches long. And they sling those plats at you, and if they hit you, it'll just rip you up, like someone went at your leg with a knife."

"Shut up about snakes in church."

"Coachwhips. I've seen 'em down south. They aren't so bad. You take them joint snakes, now. That's not one of God's works. You hit one, he breaks into pieces, layin' on the ground like a broken icicle, not moving at all. And during the night . . ."

"Can't say as I believe that."

". . . during the night they grow back together. Ask him if you don't believe me."

"Will you both shut up? This is a church, and there's a woman present."

". . . but he jumped down on this feller and went at him, and I'm shouting, 'Don't let 'im go!' I was too scared to go help. Sorry, but it's true. Then this old fat boy runs up to me and says, 'What're ye shouting at?' So I say, 'If you're so curious, go on down there and take a look.'"

"Haw haw!"

"No way. Nothing grows back together."

"Earthworms do."

"Ronnie. I swear, you'd believe any old bunk someone told you."

"I thought they did too. Shows what I know."

"Stop asking me. I got no idea where she's from. Go ask her yourself."

Slowly, the sunrise began to rain down through the trees into the unwalled church so that the shapes of the men became clearer. The parishioners sat huddled together after a long shift underground. The Reverend had laughingly told the widow it was the only time to catch them when they weren't either drunk or asleep — directly after a shift. Their breath was visible, vapour rising from their unhelmeted heads and damp clothes and soaked boots. They waited so long that eventually some slept, leaning together, heads on shoulders. Their faces were black and white, one common pattern shared by all of them — the eyes white, the forehead white, the face and temples black. Mouth blackest of all. The widow could not tell even the approximate age of any man, not by the sooted and theatrical faces, nor by the ruined hands or the filthy and corduroyed necks, nor by the unearthly eyes. She noted a strange but not altogether unpleasant scent that wafted from them. Rainwater, gunpowder, sweat.

"Here he is!" someone shouted, and everyone stood. The Reverend strode through them, stepping among those who had been seated on the floor of the nave. He handed his Bible to the widow and turned to face his flock. He wore his long black coat, held his wide-brimmed hat in his hand, and stood with his hands on his hips, like a proud pirate on the deck of his ship.

"I am late. My apologies to you men, some of whom" — he made a solicitous gesture to one withered and sagging fellow in the front row — "are tired and want nothing more than to fall into your bunks."

"No worries, Father. We're here." The shout came from the back.

"Well, shall we get on with it?" the Reverend said.

"Let's go!" several voices replied. There was a true eagerness in the crowd, as if they were attending a sporting event, and a look of pride spread over the Reverend's face.

The widow was confused. This wasn't the way her father had ever started a service, nor any other minister she'd seen. But then, nothing was the same any more, or even familiar, nor had it been for a long time. She took a look around her at the unfinished church, the wowed flooring, the leaves drifted up against the pews, and above everyone's heads, the trees standing tall and silent. And then there was the flock itself: all men, some still holding their axes and shovels, men with ghostly faces, exhausted and odorous and moulding in their seats, like something dank had floated up from hell to see what the Reverend was up to. Devils on holiday. But the Reverend seemed so pleased. Mary told herself he was doing his best.

"The righteous man," he began, "has nothing to fear. He knows not worry nor fear nor uncertainty, and his days are filled with light." There was a shifting and shuffling among the miners. Several of the Reverend's poorly made benches squalled with the movement of their bodies. The widow could not tell what they were thinking for they sat poker-faced, waiting.

"The righteous man is the most blessed of all God's creatures because he has made his own place on earth. He has forged it with his own hands, his heart, the sweat of his brow. *Resolve*," he presented them his fists, "is the engine of righteousness."

"Amen," someone said.

"Who said that?" The Reverend stepped forward eagerly and craned his neck. There was silence. It was unclear to the widow why he was so keen to know who had spoken; she could find no likely source among the eerie blackened faces, many of whom were staring at her.

"*Resolve* is the simple key to happiness. Resolve is in every man, every one of you, no matter how rotten your heart or black your deeds. Whatever you have done, you may undo over time — if your heart is strong. True, in certain unusual circumstances there is no escape. Certain men bear so deep a stain on their corrupted hearts that nothing, not even the love of God, can erase it. I shall illustrate."

The Reverend removed his coat and lay it over the altar. Scandalized, the widow retrieved it and draped it over her arm.

"Thank you," the Reverend whispered, barely moving his lips so no one else but she knew he had spoken.

245

"I shall show you the work of a man . . ." he unbuttoned his shirt and, to her dismay, removed it, "who called himself a teacher. A teacher to me and other boys." At this, he unbuttoned his long johns and stood naked to the waist. The widow wanted to avert her gaze from the sight of a man half naked in church, but what she saw stunned her. He was a normal man, normally built, with strong arms and torso. But across his chest were many diagonal marks, raised white scars, and across his shoulders lay dozens more — deep, indelible signs of some weapon, a whip or a cane. He turned to display his back. More marks, intersecting and parallel, one over another, some deep, some light, like the surface of a butcher's chopping block.

The widow put a hand to her mouth but made no sound. None of the men spoke or even moved, but she knew somehow that many had seen this before. The damage was incredible, the marks repetitive and precise. None seemed to stray toward the edges of his frame, there were no sloppy sideways cuts, nothing under his arms or near the waistband of his dark pants. The widow had a vision of a boy not even trying to evade the bite of the whip, and refusing to flinch.

"We resolve to endure the burdens of this world," the Reverend said into the silence. "What more can we do? We cannot know from which hand will come comfort, from which hand punishment. How much in your life has been a surprise to you? And you? We cannot save ourselves from injury, because it will surely come. Life itself is injury, the way bread is made of flour. We can only strive, with a merry heart, to do the right thing.

Effort is your salvation. Of course, there is no effort without error and shortcoming. But give yourself over to resolve. To courage! Be a man! Which of you wishes to be among those timid and cold souls who have known neither victory nor defeat?"

There was a murmuring of assent and a nodding of heads.

"Now," he said, stepping off the raised platform down onto the floor with the men, "who's first?" There was a movement at the back, and several hands shoved a young man out into the aisle.

"Ricky's the only one today, Father."

"Only one? Are there not more of you?"

"Father," appealed one fellow at the back, "you've whupped the rest of us. Ricky's the only one left."

There were a few chuckles from the front row. The Reverend stood a long minute considering the issue. "Well, Ricky," he said finally, "I suppose you'll have to do."

The boy came to the front on shaking legs, and slowly, reluctantly removed his coats and vests and sweaters, and finally peeled the filthy upper portion of his long johns down over his waistband. With a few shamed glances at the widow, he tied the grimy arms round his waist. When he was ready, the boy stood uncertainly, waiting. It was then that the widow realized she was about to witness another Bible lesson. Pugilism . . . in a church! She was holding the Reverend's clothing, and she clutched it to her chest. What should she do? How could she stop it?

247

"Shake hands," urged someone, and the two half-naked figures did. And then the boy and the Reverend stepped away from one another, composed themselves, and assumed boxing poses. The boy was disastrously huge, muscled and sinewy from carrying rock, swinging a sledgehammer, pushing groaning carts on metal tracks in the mine. The boy looked like a man, and next to him, the Reverend looked like a boy. Even the widow could tell the fight wouldn't be a fair one.

"Who's gonna count three minutes?" a voice whispered.

"Never mind counting, it's first man down, is all."

"You have to count. You gotta have rounds."

But the fighters were already at it, the boy striking first with a long, slow-armed swing and receiving a walloping counterpunch in return.

"There's no rounds and there's no betting. This is a church, for Chri . . . Anyway, you don't need it."

"'Course you do."

"No, you don't."

"Well, what if it's a tie? What then?"

"There won't be a tie."

"No man wins every time, I don't care who he is. Think about it! You don't expect a coin to always come up heads, do you?"

"I would if the Rev was on the coin!" This remark produced an approving roar of laughter from the men, who were now standing to get a look at the progress of the fight. The widow was gritting her teeth, her eyes riveted on the fighters.

248

"If the Rev was on the coin he'd beat the knickers off the Queen!" roared a young fellow. With that, there was laughter and a stomping of feet. The thundering sound alarmed the widow, and she felt suddenly certain that the place was about to fall apart around her ears.

"Stop it!" she barked at no one. They all sat down again, grins fading on their rueful faces.

"'Scuse us, ma'am."

There was a hollow *thump* and Ricky emitted a grunt. The Reverend was stepping back and sideways, back and sideways, his head dodging Ricky's blows. Then they came together in a staggering clinch, the floorboards sagging under them, and exchanged rabbit punches. Finally, the widow couldn't watch any longer and she buried her face in the Reverend's coat.

"Go, Ricky boy! Give it to him!"

"He ain't about to win. Don't waste your breath."

"Sure he is, just look at him! He's bigger than all of us put together. He's gonna win just from sheer size . . . Aw, dammit."

"Woah!"

"All right, what'd'ya think of that?"

"Oh! I can't watch."

"He's finished. The boy's done."

"No, no, no. Give him a second. He'll recover."

"He hasn't got a second. The Rev's coming . . . Woah!!"

"There goes your boy. Lookit him."

"Told ya so."

"Oh, hell."

The widow uncovered her eyes in time to see a
tremor go through the boy's legs from feet to hip, as if
he were trying to keep his balance while standing on a
galloping horse. He pawed at the air with numb hands
and his eyes rode upward, momentarily giving him the
aspect of a man recalling the past, perhaps fondly. Then
he fell backward and hit the floorboards with a mighty
thump, and there he lay at the feet of his colleagues in
the front row, barely conscious.

There was silence for a long moment, and only the
Reverend's breathing.

"God almighty," said one miner. "The man never
loses."

"You wouldn't believe it if you didn't see it yourself."

"Resolve," said the Reverend, panting, "is the way to
the Lord. The way . . . to righteousness. God favours
hope, and He favours the righteous. That's . . . all for
today." He spread Ricky's coat over him where he slept.
"Watch over this boy tomorrow, Stan. Make sure he
doesn't fall into any holes."

That night the widow woke to the sound of her father's
voice, very close, his mouth nearly at her face,
bellowing — a terrible wordless cry of surprise or
shock. She sat erect, breathless, with the clatter of her
terror running through her body. She was alone in
her room, the house quiet and dark, but she knew her
father was there with her, an angry male presence. She
could feel him — his breath, his heart hammering. The
pure essence of him seemed to gel slowly before her,
like a filament of cold air running through warm. She

saw nothing, and yet she reached out to him. There was nothing before her, and yet she knew he had opened his terrible mouth. All was lost. He knew of her crimes, her madness. A roar like a lion woke her again, really woke her, and the widow sat up in bed and saw the real moonlight. She heard the Reverend drawing his laboured breath. The sound was so familiar and rhythmic, she closed her eyes and attended it closely, grateful to him, as if this were his way of comforting her.

But all was not well, and she knew it. John's brothers were looking for her still. It could not be otherwise. Might they follow her, all the way through that pass — could they, when she herself didn't know the way she had come?

After a while she lay back down again and held the blankets to her chin.

CHAPTER
EIGHTEEN

At least three nights a week McEchern held what he called a soiree, pronouncing it with mock hauteur. Swah-ree. He knew better, but the little man liked to amuse himself. The aim was to sell whisky and rum to the men, and the men in turn would sit with him outside the store and complain about the mine, or debate current events, especially anything involving the rebellion in China, or make as if wise about women, or speak of God, the latter usually done by one or two unhappy and unpopular fellows and suffered in silence by the others. Even the Reverend seemed unwilling to invoke heaven at these events, but chose instead to sit quietly, tending his pipe.

On these evenings, the widow always sat by the Reverend, off to one side and away from the men. She remembered Helen, Henry's wife, saying, "Frank is a vile town." Looking now at McEchern, acutely drunk, and the rest of the inebriates congregated on the store's front landing, anyone could see her point. The widow pulled her hat farther down over her brow and held her shawl tight around herself.

Some weeks ago, the Reverend had introduced her as his "ward," but that ruse was met with derision. So he'd said, "Think of her as my beloved sister," which seemed too vigorous a mental exercise for the men. Finally, he'd simply told them to put her out of their minds.

"Come on, Father," said one fellow, "you're not using her, after all."

The Reverend had looked around at the assembled negotiators, his face as unfriendly as a judge's. There was strained silence for a moment. "The first of you gentlemen to get out of hand will be sorry. Am I clear?"

After that, the widow was able to sit in relative peace by her benefactor's side, suffering nothing worse than constant staring and the occasional comment.

"Do you let your beloved sister smoke a pipe, Father? Isn't that the way to perdition?"

"Not the brand she smokes."

It was on an evening like this, with the sunset long past, the heavy incense of rot and smoked hides wafting from the tent's door flaps, and the demure movements of small animals in the trees, that the assembled heard something large coming toward them. No mere twigs were breaking, but whole branches. The revellers fell silent, listening to the lumbering footfalls. A bear? No cougar would make such a noise. Finally, with a crash and a grunt, an enormous man emerged from the night trees like some steaming mountain giant. Several voices cheered at once.

"Giovanni!"

"Un saluto a tutti gli ignoranti!" the giant said in a rumbling voice.

The widow gaped in disbelief — she had seen this creature before. One morning, weeks ago, she had been

out alone setting snares, kneeling among tree roots and
low alpine junipers where the rabbits hid, intent on her
task, a length of wire in her hands. She was bending
and rebending the wire in order to snap it. As she
struggled with the problem there came a sound to her
left. At first, the widow thought she was seeing some
bizarre chimera conjured up by her unslept brain. A
colossal, hump-shouldered creature with a heavy head
that seemed to have compressed his neck was standing
among the trees watching her. She gasped, and his sly,
goatlike face broke into a grin. He wore a coat made
from the many pelts of a local variety of tabby, patched
together into a misshapen quilt that draped his
incredible shoulders. In some places, the fur had worn
away, leaving a troutish pattern on the thin hides. Being
an artist, perhaps, he had reserved a little ginger for
each cuff. He spoke to her in a language she didn't
know.

"Poverina. Calmati, calmati."

The widow had stood frozen on the carpet of cedar
needles and fixed him with a look of undisguised
mistrust, and yet he seemed to speak gently to her, or
as gently as a monster could manage. She made as if to
run past him but immediately balked. He towered over
her, even as he stepped aside with an absurdly courtly
gesture to make way. His strange mouth seemed to hold
an overcomplement of teeth. Yes, she saw far too many
in there. She took a step back. Ghoulish children's tales
from her nursery came back to her. In the woods there
were ogres, trolls, wolves that stood on their hind legs
and dressed as men, spirits that came up out of the

254

ground in the form of snow and smoke and foul odours. And this man smelled *bad*; she could tell from where she stood.

"Stai tranquilla," he had growled, waving his hand as if to woo her to him. "Basta cosi!" The widow, thinking herself slandered, had gasped in shock, turned on her heel and ran, the dark cloth of her skirts flying up behind her. And all she had heard behind her was the low rumble of his laughter.

Now here was this creature, stepping amiably among the other men. Incredibly, they made room for him. He sat his massive bulk down on an upturned stump, slapped his thighs — each kneebone as wide as a man's head — and sighed deeply.

"Hell," said his nearest companion, "he's worse than ever."

A loud fragrance floated on the air, the sweet hammer of carrion, damp charcoal, and some kind of acrid chemical. "Mi dispiace," said the cat skinner, "puzzolente."

The Reverend turned to the widow. "The thing to know about Giovanni is that he understands everything we say, but we understand nothing he says."

"Not true," said one man. "We got two Italians on my shift. They can talk to him."

"He don't talk back, though," said another man.

Giovanni chuckled.

"The other thing to know is, *he makes whisky*," said McEchern, rubbing his hands together. "Take the black off a train engine. Eh, Giovanni?" He raised his voice. "You gonna bring me some soon?"

"Primo o poi." The huge man's hand drifted languidly in the air, promising nothing.

"Anyone get that?" The dwarf was clearly worried that this gesture meant bad news for his whisky. McEchern's head, on which was always perched his bowler hat, didn't even reach the cat skinner's shoulder. He looked like a child at his father's knee.

"I think he means hold yer piss, Mac. Anyway, it ain't the end of the month yet. He always brings it round at the end of the month."

"So he does," said the dwarf, subsiding, "so he does." He patted the monster's ratty sleeve and raised a cloud of dust. "Good man, Giovanni."

"Ya," said one inebriate, "and his whisky don't freeze, like some others I know." The dwarf was about to take the bait, his eye lemony and his finger pointed in accusation, when the giant spoke.

"Avete finiti con queste stronzate? Voglio da bere."

"What'd he say?"

"Who knows? Give the man a drink."

As the night wore on, a few exhausted celebrants wandered home. They would get a few hours' sleep, perhaps in a tent or bunkhouse with other men, and then get back up before the sun rose, helmets alight. They would trudge to the mine and disappear down the sloping tunnels and drifts where the air was thin and the darkness profound, where wisps of gas floated and water trickled, where they laboured like winking souls in the airless dark. The younger ones, the unlucky, the unwise, would volunteer to step off the drift into the tiny metal miner's cage and from there be lowered into the void, down to a lower bowel. In McEchern's view — and he repeated it often enough — these men were fools hanging by their nuts in the dark. In his opinion, above-ground commerce was the way to go.

"Look," he would say, "even Jesus couldn't wait to get out of the cave. God knows what you'll find down there."

"God sees you everywhere," said one drunk, rousing himself. "He sees everything."

"Don't you start! Go back to sleep."

"Talk about spooks," offered one bent and wizened fellow, "I been seeing things down there. And hearing them too. Something awful."

"You have not."

"Yesterday I saw — now, you shut up — I saw something all lit up, floating along the drift, down a ways from me. Looked like a bunch of fireflies. Ten, twelve little floaty lights. Made a sort of crackling noise. But when I went to go see, they kinda flew backward away from me. Like they were afraid."

"Fairies."

"Sparks," said a sober old voice. "Coal dust sparking up."

"You'd better hope you don't have sparks down there," said the Reverend. "We'd all better hope that."

"Huh-ho." A rueful laugh. "We got worse than that, Father."

"He means nothing by that."

"Naw, he's a ninny."

"Shut up. A fact's a fact. We got ground tremors now. She shakes all on her own. We don't even have to set

257

charges much any more. She shifts a little every day, and down comes rock."

"It's pretty helpful, really," a young man laughed. "Sometimes all we have to do is shovel it up and dump it in the cart."

"They *all* do that once you open them up."

"Sure?"

"Of course. She's just settling, is all. A mine's got to settle. Part of the business. And you, seeing fairies and such." The old fellow spat over the edge of the platform into the dark. "Bunch of women, flapping yer skirts."

They sat in silence for a few moments, pondering the ground beneath their feet, the porous earth spinning slowly in its dark socket.

"I seen a ghost once," said the young miner. He pointed to the widow. "Just as clear as I can see her."

"I never saw one, but I heard a few."

"Ghosts don't exist. It's gas and white dogs and . . ."

"Whisky."

"Anyway," the boy continued, gazing earnestly at the widow, "this ghost I saw was all in white. I saw her walking along the railroad tracks. But I didn't think anything of it at first. Thought it was a man. I was out checking the back of the station house to make sure it was locked. My dad was the station master, but, but he was . . . well, he was drunk a lot. I always helped him out. And I looked over and saw it wasn't a man, it was a girl, dressed all in white. And she wasn't walking, she was gliding along the tracks . . ."

"Maybe she had rollerskates."

"Leave him alone."

"... and then she vanished. Just like that, she was gone. I mean, it was like you sitting there, ma'am, and then suddenly you're gone. I saw her one more time too. She was coming toward me outta the dark. Moving without moving her feet. And this long hair she had. Spread her arms out wide and opened her mouth, like to scream. And then she was gone again. I could never figure out an explanation for it, nothing that made sense. I never told anyone about that. Not even my mother. Don't know why I told you."

"Neither do we." There was laughter from the men.

"Okay," came a gruff voice. "I got one." The speaker was moustachioed, and he talked round his cigar. "Guy told me he knew a fellow who had a haunted tree."

"Did he say tree?"

"Ma, arresto."

"And this guy said that every night around midnight there was something, couldn't tell what it was, hanging from that tree. It was dark, and it was in the woods, so he couldn't tell for sure, but it looked a lot like ..."

"His dick."

"There's a woman present, you flathead."

"... like a hanging man. It looked like somebody hanging there from the tree. Every night this happens. So one day, he tells his buddies all about it, but they don't believe him. They're smartarses, like this one here. So he tells them, he says, 'If I show you this terrifying, ghostly, abominable sight, will you believe me?' They say yeah, and on top of that they'll buy him drinks for a week, which *they* think they're not gonna do because it can't be true. So the next night the guy is waiting."

"Which guy?"

"Guy with the ghost. He's waiting there, and waiting, and waiting. It's near midnight. Still no ghost. He starts to figure that if he doesn't come up with a body hanging in his tree, he's not going to get any drinks. Never mind looking like an idiot. So, like the bright fellow he is, he climbs on up into his tree and hangs there himself."

"He hangs himself?"

"No, he just . . . I don't know! He just hangs there somehow! Anyway, soon enough, along come the boys. And they stop dead in their tracks. They turn white. They start to shake. 'Well,' says one, 'he told us the truth. There, by God, it is.' 'Yeah,' said another, 'but he said there was only one of them. I see *two*.' And sure as shit, the guy turns his head around, and there's a body hanging right next to him!"

There was general groaning.

"That's a true story."

The Reverend handed his glass of rum to the widow. She took a sip and coughed and took another sip. She had a sudden memory of telling the bird lady that she didn't drink. She handed the glass back to the Reverend and wiped her lips.

After a long interval, McEchern roused himself in his chair, little feet dangling. He leaned out and fixed the Reverend with a grin. "I saw a ghost once," he said.

"Did you, now?" said the Reverend.

"Why, yes, thank you for asking."

"You'll tell us about it?"

"Well, I wasn't going to. But now that you all seem so eager." He smacked his lips and leaned back in his chair. "One night," he said solemnly, "I approached a farmhouse . . ."

"Oh no, please," said the smartarse, "not this one again."

But McEchern continued unfazed. "I knocked upon the door. Rap, rap. Door opens, and there before me is the farmer. 'Hello,' says I. 'It is very late at night and I am far from home. Can you help a traveller who is lost?' 'Well,' says the old farmer, 'all I have is that old house yonder. You can stay there as long as you want to. No one ever stays long, though — it's haunted . . .'"

"Golly. You don't say."

"Well, being as I am a stout and brave fellow, I go off to the house and settle in. I build myself a nice fire. There is food in the kitchen and a bookshelf by the door. I take down a book and sit in a chair to read. After a while, I hear a creaking on the second floor. Then, down the staircase, walking slowly, comes a big angora cat."

"A cat?"

"Biggest thing you ever saw, huge green eyes. It gives me a cunning look, then it goes over to the fire, and, by God, it just steps right in. Starts scratching the coals around. Now, I am surprised by this, as you can imagine. Never seen a cat crawl around in a fire before. But I figure the world is full of strange things and this is one of them. Just when I'm starting to get used to the idea, the cat up and talks to me. Says, 'I don't know

261

what to do about attacking you. Maybe I'll wait for Martin.' I can see your face, ma'am, but this is the nickle-plated truth. Anyways, after a second, there's more noise upstairs, and then down comes another angora cat. This one is even bigger than the first one. And it has mean, red eyes. It, too, goes up to the fireplace. But instead of getting in, this old boy backs up and pisses in it, only instead of piss, out comes a stream of flames."

"Pissed in the what?"

"*Fireplace*. Sit up and listen."

"Well, I'm trying to hold my book steady, but that's proving to be a difficult task. This cat looks over at the first one and says, 'Shall we commence on him now or wait till Martin gets here?' Well, gentlemen, you can imagine the effect that had on me. I drop the book and I'm standing there with my knees knocking and my hat rattling on top of my head like a pot lid. I don't know whether to piss or play pinochle. But just then" — the dwarf paused and fixed first one and then another of his listeners with a wide-eyed stare — "from upstairs, I hear a loud shuffling sound. Something pretty big is up there. And it's heading for the stairs. I mean, this is one big old boy, and he's comin' for me. 'Ladies,' says I on my way out the door, 'I gotta go! When Martin gets here, you just give him my regards.'"

"Haw haw!" bellowed the smartarse. "That's a good one, Mac. I thought you were gonna tell that old thing about the three holes in the barn door again. I can't stand to hear that one."

"Three holes?" prompted the Reverend.

262

There was an embarrassed shuffling among the revellers.

"Not with a lady present," McEchern said flatly. "Nor with you here either, Reverend."

Suddenly, the lantern at his feet guttered and leaped, then winked out altogether. Darkness settled over the men. Some looked up, waiting for the stars to reveal themselves. Here or there burned the orange glow of a cigarette. Two pipes floated side by side; the widow's was the more fragrant. Movements in the underbrush, a thrum as a night bird blew past. On the widow's skin, the damp trace of mountain air. She was almost asleep under her hat when a voice came.

"Bene," growled the cat skinner, and everyone jumped. "C'era una volta, una ragazza bella chi ha mangiato un'arachide velenosa . . ." And thus he began a long, senseless story told in the dire tones of a fairy tale, a narrative that drifted happily into the night, and no one interrupted at all.

The Ridgerunner hunched hollow-eyed before a dim and scrawny fire. Nothing stood above him but the bare peaks of the mountain range. He waited like a guard in his panopticon, watching the wilderness. Below lay the forests. He was used to turning his back to the hills, watching the downhill slope. But there was nowhere to turn his back to any more, for it was all below him now.

Where the moon fell, it was bright, and where it did not, there was nothing, blackness, a liquid wash of empty space. Alone in the bitter cold, he gazed into the fire's antic dream. His altitude was so high now that flame and man alike struggled to breathe. The very meat on his bones was cold, his breath no longer vaporous; only his urine emerged hot from his body, steaming lavishly.

The Ridgerunner had watched day fade quickly into a wash of stars, a bristling darkness. It had always been his habit to remain awake at night, to travel in the dark, letting nocturnal animals alert him to the presence of rangers, grizzlies, or anything else he'd rather avoid. He often slept during the warm midday hours. But at this height, sunlight carried no warmth, and so there would be no sleep. The forest had thinned out. Rock jutted through the topsoil like bone through decaying hide. Dwarf evergreens clung to the fissured rock with grey limbs and exposed roots and stunted pine cones the colours of a spent match. He began scrambling, using his hands, standing for long moments assessing the vertiginous plain above, carving his own switchbacks. Resting against trees as he climbed, he panted short and shallow. For the first time in his life, his scant belongings had become a burden to him, the damp tent rarely unravelled now, the cooking pot unused for lack of game. There were no deer, no rabbits, no mice, few bugs. As the air had thinned, food had become scarce, the trees had shrivelled, and he himself moved ever more slowly — the very engine of life was on the verge of stalling.

He began to starve. It was clear why he was starving, and the remedy was obvious: to descend. But he went up, pressing into solitude, a hermit in flight. On distant slopes, the cotton boles of mountain sheep stood watching his slow progress, arrested by the strange sight of a man. Cold sun lay on every lifeless surface; sometimes there was pale lichen, sometimes nothing at all, just clean rock and empty air, a hawk floating over the void. He came upon entire fields of virgin snow, prehistoric and immaculate, blinding to the eye, crusted with a glassine layer so ancient and dense the Ridgerunner could only shuffle-skate over it, and when he stamped his boot, it would not give way. Soon the only evergreen life consisted of strange low shrubs that spread over the rocks like vast lilies, their twisted roots running in venous forks away to scorched points. He no longer camped, but merely stopped, paced, built a fire to watch it burn. He refolded things, packed and repacked, held small objects in his hand, doubting their utility. Checked his empty pockets.

And now, here he was, hunched before a fire, starving. Where the moon fell, it was bright. He put his hand out and gazed at the thing, pale and insubstantial. This hand on her breast, a gorgeous terror echoing between their two bodies, her face coming down to meet his, her dark hair in curtains to his left and right.

He had simply abandoned her, the way a man flees a small, unchecked fire in his house, knowing that it will grow, leap from curtain to ceiling, consume every supporting beam. Thirteen years alone in the woods, no change except the seasons wagging. And then there she was on the ground, demented, half-starved. Change came roaring in. Her warm body in his tent like a salacious dream, her beautiful voice, that unnerving gaze.

265

The hermit had run to the top of the world, or nearly there. Above him lay only blizzard and rock. Fissures obscured by the thinnest membrane of ice, shelves of wind-blown snow cantilevered over caverns of air. Nothing lived here. Except William Moreland, his flame sputtering.

CHAPTER
NINETEEN

The deep days of late summer reached with forgiving fingers into the cold mountains. For a week the nights were cool, the days soft and warm, and the breaches between them seemed to go on uninterrupted — not twilight exactly but a bright, aimless drifting for several hours. Foxes came blinking into it, furtive as cats, night creatures exposed by lingering light, their blackened snouts raised to test the air. In the mornings, the widow rose early. She made the Reverend his breakfast; pork, dried-apple bread, coffee. Most times pork was available, but at other times there was deer and, in dire times, bear. There was jerky about, but she had none. She bought cornmeal when McEchern stocked it, and molasses, chicory, dried beans hung together on a string. Soap was rarely available, so she made her own, as her husband had taught her, stirring the vile mess for hours as it thickened. She had instructed the Reverend on how to make a hopper for the ashes, where the corrosive lye would drip out, and as he built the object she hung over him in endless fretting and criticism.

"I *know* how to build a simple box, Mrs. Boulton," he said. He always chose her formal name, as if she had no other.

"Is that so?" She tilted her head in obvious mirth and pointed at the house they lived in together, with its listing walls and the windows bunged in at angles and collecting rot in their downhill seams. It was his pride, and his indictment.

"What?" he protested, fighting a smile.

John had not built their hopper himself, but had had one of his boys do it — Mary had never known which one. The object had simply arrived, solid, leakproof, a wonder of cabinetry, twice lined with heavy canvas so it dripped slow and clear. The lye had eaten through it within a year. All hoppers disintegrate, she knew; there is no remedy.

Now, three cakes of soap lay drying on the dining table, their funk palpable. Mary pressed a cautious finger into one mushroom-coloured block and it resisted her coldly.

And there it was — her own hand.

A pale scar across one knuckle, from what accident she could not recall. The skin dry, swollen, the knuckles as bulbed as a boxer's and stained with calluses. She brought her hand up closer to her face and inspected it. Her thumb was the worst: the nail looked like a white; lifeless thing driven into the flesh so hard it must remain there. She took in the signs of ruin. All the scrubbing, the lye, the rough axe handles, sewing needles, dirt, glass, the sweating nub of a thimble, metal slivers from tin bathtubs, wood slivers from everything she touched, shards of broken dishes clawed up by hand, blunted knives slipping, the many boots polished, the innumerable woollen long johns wrung till her hands ached, and the gaping black mouths of ovens. All these had left their mark. What would her hands have looked like in another life, one in which she had not married John, but instead had stayed with her father?

Life written on the body. And yet, no mark was left where William Moreland had brought this very hand to his mouth and kissed it. His lips running along her wrist. His, among all these wounds, was invisible. Mary put her hands behind her back and went to stand by the open door.

She wasn't sure what her face looked like any more. She had not once looked at herself in William Moreland's shaving mirror. It had hung from a tree for all those days, and the sun had been reflected in it so that a bright spot wandered the camp. He had used the mirror to shave, or just to inspect himself, stroking his moustache with uncommon pride. But she herself had never glanced into it.

The mirrors in her father's house had long been covered. For two years after the death of his wife, he'd draped them in black cloth, hung a black wreath on the door, wore a mourning ring on his finger with black enamelling that repeated *her* initials infinitely round its polished curve. For two years, any correspondence from the house was written on cream paper with a thick black border round its edges, formal and traditional, grandiose in its grief. Mary's grandmother wrote voluminously to merchants and the lawyer and her own cronies, all on this morbid paper, but her father wrote nothing. He spoke little, but stormed from room to room, glaring at the trappings of his defeat. He threw

269

out the sickbed with his own hands, destroyed his wife's vanity stick by stick, staved in the mirror with his heel, and then sat holding her hair-brush in his hand, weeping to see the few strands it held, while Mary's grandmother stood in the doorway white-faced. He got drunk and remained drunk. It was a ferocious self-erasure, and with it came a sudden hush in the house. He had lately been a quiet man, but he was now completely silent. His silence was terrible and angry, and he wore it like an engulfing flame.

In those days, Mary slept even less than usual. And when she did manage to sleep, she often woke to see both of them at her bedside, her grandmother's terrified face hovering over her. She was made to understand that she had been screaming in her sleep, racketing out the dream's disaster.

"What did I say?" she asked.

"Nothing," her grandmother had sighed. "You don't say a blessed thing. You just shriek like a banshee."

Her father looked down at her through his miasma of sorrow. "Was it her?" he asked. "Did she speak to you?"

One night an elderly maid had slipped into her room, placed a dry, light hand on the girl's forehead. "Who putteth her trust in thee," the maid had whispered, "and evermore mightily defend her, nor let the wicked approach to hurt her . . ." Mary had looked up in bewilderment. When the old lady left the room, she had put her finger to her lips.

Her father, too, was sleepless in those days. And staggering. Rum was his drink, and so a sweet reek followed him about the house, burnt toffee cut with piss, and his breath was rank. He would go whole days without responding to anyone; he would not even meet his daughter's eye, but stared dully ahead, too deep in the smoking ruin of his heart to see the world. In increments, the engine of his anger began to fail. He took to his bed, sometimes for days, reclining in his rumpled clothes and barking at the maids, accomplishing nothing, for nothing was the point. His mother kept up a constant harangue — to him, to the kitchen girl, to the walls. "Does he think she'd be proud of him? Does he believe the world stops? When is enough for this man?"

Gradually, there were signs of repair. Mornings he sat watching sparrows on the forecourt and held a bottle of milk to his chest. He found a book, *Lives of the Caesars*, and began reading about the outrages and intrigues, the scheming women, armies lost in the darkness. On one of her birthdays, he had actually smiled at the cake, charmed by its little candles, perhaps ten of them. But when his eyes wandered back to his daughter, the smile faded, and it was just his face again — solemn, tired, patient. He gave the impression of a man who was waiting for something that never came.

How long ago it all seemed to her now. If she had ever hoped that once the emergency of her mother's life had ended her father might turn to her, she now knew the truth — she had been invisible to both her parents. For her father, there had only ever been one *her*, and once she was gone, so was his connection to everything else. He drifted. He had never taken off his wedding ring. It was there still, Mary knew, a cold, pointless thing warmed by his hand. This widower had not cut the rope, even to save himself.

She, too, had lost everything, she, too, had drifted. But then, were the facts of her case not worse than her father's? Was he not, then, weaker than she? His wife, at least, had loved him back; at least he had a living child. How might he have fared in her place? Alone, paupered, betrayed. Where would his extravagant grief have taken him? Would he have done what she did?

She stood by the front door of the Reverend's house, looking out into the trees, filled with gratitude. Everything was the same and yet wholly different. Like a woman rising from the damp sheets after a fever, the widow looked about her at a new life.

All that was left now was her crime.

At the sound of her husband's footsteps, she had put down the black cloth and poked the needle into it. She rose to meet him.

John came through the door, knocking clods of dirt off his boots. He handed her his rifle, which was his habit, and watched while she checked the breech, removed both the shells, blew on the smooth brass casings, then reloaded them, and closed the breech. Just as he had taught her and as she had done each time he returned home. He had been her tutor in almost everything. He removed his hat. A robin was calling outside and he was prying off his boot. She pointed the rifle at him and pulled the trigger, blowing a hole in his thigh so the bone came out the back. A pink mist

272

suffused the air and she was abruptly deaf. She watched him crumple doll-like to the floor.

Widowed by her own hand — or perhaps, since he lay struggling, soon to be widowed — she had sat down to wait. Eventually, she took up her sewing.

A steady rain had fallen during the night. It was quiet in the cabin, though in her head there was ceaseless clamour, this time like wordless shouting. In the morning, water lay in bright pools about the cabin while the sun shone merrily. Among these puddles the widow went naked, holding a shovel. Pale and trembling, her young body like a nymph's. She had hurried to a certain spot by the trees. The grave there was nothing more than a shallow indentation, barely visible under normal circumstances, now betrayed by a wide pool of water, and the listing cross. On this spot she had buried her child . . . and the only thing of value left to her: the ring. She put the shovel's edge down, but she could not bring herself to push. Knuckles white on the handle, her face terrible, frozen in a silent beseeching of the motionless water, or what lay beneath. Again she braced, and the blade sank a little deeper into unresisting mud. Wind shook rain from the branches above that landed on her back in little taps, an unseen hand recalling her to herself. She shivered among the hackled trees, then dropped the shovel and went back inside.

Sewing in the evening, by the light of a candle. Because the cloth was black, she had had to do it almost by feel.

There was boundless silence except when the waxed thread snapped between her front teeth. She tied a knot with one hand. Her husband had taught her so many things, but this was the one and only thing she had taught him to do, to tie a knot with one hand. When it was nearly morning she rose and went in search of something to eat, finding only a loaf of bread that was damp and tainted by a species of mould that tasted of grass. She held it to her nose. It did not smell like grass. She held it to her nose again, then began smelling the air around her. Something fusty in the air of the cabin. She ate the bread anyway, naked, her long hair running down her back like weeds. She was cold, still cold, and so she put on his coat, which hung by the door, stepping carefully past . . . not him any more but *it*.

Warmer now, she sat with white knees protruding, finishing the sewing of her widow's dress.

Of course, she knew the sound when she heard it: the crackle of boots outside. A slow, steady gait along the recently dried ground — a boy, sent by the others on the long trek to fetch the boss. The widow sat fully dressed on the bed and waited, shawl across her shoulders, hands in her lap. The boy called out, standing at a polite distance from the house, looking at the open door. A fly hummed in the other room, searching for the blood that had called it in. She didn't so much hear the insect hum as became aware that she had been hearing it all along — all the long night before, and into the brightness of morning. Her husband's leg was visible to her, strangely torqued within the pantleg, foot pointing the wrong way.

The boy was standing out there, a question forming in his mind. It was only a matter of time.

She closed her eyes and felt a strange intimation — herself and the fly and the air of the cabin and all its contents were a simple, uncorrupted thing, a gesture still in process, something predictable, with a catalyst that long ago had started them on their forward motion, all heading to the end, and the end was ruin.

Well, here it was.

The boy called a few times more. And then he stepped in.

CHAPTER
TWENTY

Packed expertly into his sagged and weather-stained tent were the things McEchern judged to be the necessities of life in a mining camp. These were numerous and eccentric. Ropes, wooden buckets, tin buckets and baths, tobacco, knives of various degrees of nastiness and in various stages of rust, paraffin, blankets, sewing notions, snuff boxes, two rifles, a box full of mismatched door hinges, dubbin, grease, lantern oil, salt pork, flour, coffee, delousing remedies, raisins, stove piping, a pickle jar of lenses from eyeglasses, a Colt revolver with a walnut grip full of slivers, corn flour, rifle shells in four calibres, headache powder now aged into a solid block from which he was obliged to hack pieces for sale, nails (all used), pegs, hammers and pickaxes, two bowler hats (worn by him on alternate days, but still for sale), a child's windup tin horse, a cigarette box filled with buttons, barrels of whisky, jugs and jars of rum, a watchmaker's kit with loupe, ink, handsaws, two ten-foot logging saws, various planes and files, metal plates, spoons, knives, forks, and cups, and four small vials of laudanum.

One of these he presented to the widow when she came shopping on a late summer day. She was on her own, free of the Reverend's paternal care. Laudanum, he said, was the very thing for what ailed her, the pain of the world would fade, and no more sorrow would mark her brow. He held up one little bottle and joggled its contents. The widow, thinking he was promising a cessation of womanly pain (and in a way he was), was appalled at his brazenness but amazed at the progress of modern medicine. With scarlet cheeks she scrounged in her purse for some of her carefully hoarded coins from Mrs. Cawthra-Elliot's and purchased a bottle. She popped the top, took a sniff. The scent was sharp and arresting, much like a poultice. She put the bottle in her purse and went about the tent to finish her shopping.

McEchern followed her with his eyes but didn't bother to step down from his stool.

From the shadows of the tent, the widow considered the enigma of Charlie McEchern. He wasn't a very old man, and so it seemed unlikely that he had amassed all these oddments himself. The wormed sign over the store must be older than he was; even the stove that heated the place was weirdly antique, poxed with cherubs. There he sat, the little man, the dwarf proprietor, his child's hands spread out on the counter and his shoes swinging. It was like he had broken into someone else's abandoned shop and, faced with customers at the door, had simply opened up and amused himself by playing the part of merchant.

The store's canvas door flap swept back and in came two malodorous miners. With their racoon faces and their helmets hung from their belts, they stepped heavily on the wood floorboards, awkward now that they were in a world not made of rock. The shorter of the two was white-eyed with some private anxiety.

"Where's the little man?" he said, and the widow assessed his height wryly for a second before she stood aside to allow them a view of McEchern, sitting baleful and quiet at his counter.

"Mac," the miner said. It was almost a question.

"Boys. Go on. The place is yours." The small miner led the way, while the taller one followed. Shy as farmers they went about collecting their goods. The shorter one's hands were shaking. Together they collected matches, two canvas sheets, a hatchet, twelve metal tent pegs, blankets, and a camp kettle. When they shambled to the counter McEchern regarded them with a fond, weary expression, a face that said, *What now?* "Aren't you two usually below ground this time of day, Jim?"

The two men were silent, their eyes not meeting McEchern's. A porcine scent of unwashed human wafted from their clothes.

"On your way somewhere?"

"Yeah. Away from here," said the big one.

"No, we ain't. Shut up, Ronnie!"

"Well, well," McEchern's grin was wide. "You two don't know if you're coming or going." Their grimy faces coloured — it was obvious to Mary from the scarlet of their foreheads.

"What do you need with all this stuff, Ronnie? Heading out of the mountains, are you? Find better work elsewhere? I hear the CPR is hiring men if they can swing a hammer." The big man's eyes were nearly popping with his desire to speak, and his jaw began to work silently, but Jim cut him off.

"Lay off, Mac. Now how much do you want for it?"

"I *want* a hundred dollars. But I'll take . . . four eighty-five."

"What!?"

"All right, four twenty — and that includes a parting gift from me." McEchern felt around under the counter and eventually produced a bottle of liquor. He held it up, a bottle of cloudy swill with a swollen wood stopper. The contents of the bottle was the colour and consistency of saliva. The widow guessed it to be Giovanni's moonshine. Ronnie's face was the picture of surprised admiration, and he reached for it like a toddler, but McEchern swiped the bottle out of reach. "You're in a sharing mood," he told them.

They passed the booze from hand to hand, the small man's share rudely chugged away in one upturn of the bottle with a gurgling rush down his throat. He handed the liquor on and winced in silent agony, veins ropy in his throat.

The widow was the last to partake. She brought the bottle to her lip and took a gulp before the smell actually hit her. She let out a strangled gasp. The booze went on a leisured clawing down her windpipe, with a disastrous burn thereafter.

"Diabolical!" McEchern wheezed happily.

Jim was gathering up his and Ronnie's purchases, stuffing what he could into the kettle and eyeing the change he'd left on the counter, counting again to make sure he hadn't left too much. If he had, there was no way McEchern would mention it.

The widow was swallowing repeatedly, a hand to her agonized throat. She still hadn't recovered her breath.

Out of nowhere Ronnie said, "We got blown over."

With that, Jim stopped moving; he seemed to sag in his ripe and sweat-lacquered clothes. There was silence for a moment, the fire crackling in the stove.

"Blown over?" McEchern looked from one to the other of them. "By what?"

"Blast of air," Jim said, his voice like that of a mourner in a chapel, afraid the dead might hear. "Blew me halfway down the drift, took Ronnie off his feet." The widow and the dwarf looked at Ronnie, took in the size of the man, and tried to imagine a wind strong enough to make even him stagger.

"Knocked me over," Ronnie repeated.

But now that Jim had started talking, he seemed unable to stop. "It come up the sump hole with a bang, Mac, the most awful sound you ever heard. Suddenly I'm on my ass, two yards away from my helmet. Shit raining down around us like someone set a charge right over our heads. Some moron down the drift was just laughing away. Probably the seam he'd been working on just fell out right at his feet. But it ain't funny. There's some as don't care. Say you're a ninny and the like. Some think they're immortal, just cause they haven't died *yet*. Well, I know when bad's coming, and it's by God coming. We been smelling fresh water for weeks. Smelled it but never saw any. Sure enough, yesterday here it comes, filling up the sump hole, and bringing . . . *things* with it."

"Things," said Ronnie stupidly.

"Like what?" said the dwarf.

Jim just shook his head in answer. "Tell you one thing, Mac. I ain't about to leave this boy here," he indicated Ronnie, the world's most enormous boy, "just on account of some jackasses think God gilded their balls." He didn't even apologize to the widow. "Nope, we're out of here." He gathered up his goods and, seizing Ronnie's sleeve, dragged him from the tent.

The widow stood swaying, the alcohol still boiling her brain. Diabolical it was, and, she could see now, habit-forming. She eyed what was left in the bottle that hung in the little man's hand.

McEchern chuckled and shook his head. "Poor old Jim," he said. "He's always been a bit soft. Thinks witches exist. Can you believe that? Thinks you can cure warts by burying your hair. And he scolds poor Ronnie like a wife. Some boys are just not cut out for mining work. Myself, for example. I wonder what 'things' he was talking about."

"Flynn," Mary said simply.

"Oh." McEchern tipped his hat back with a little thumb. "I wondered where he'd got to. Nobody tells me anything."

The dwarf pondered her face for an unguarded moment, and she let him. It gave her a chance to scrutinize him. Despite the disorder of his misshaped parts, the abbreviated legs, the infantile hands, the knobbed shoulders, a strange handsomeness had assembled in McEchern. His face was untouched by the disaster, the blue watching eyes more human for where they were set.

"Jim might be right," he said, "about bad coming. Maybe if you look for something long enough, it comes to look for you. Maybe you call the joke on yourself. I'm afraid of bears, for instance. Have nightmares about them. Go out of my way to avoid the bastards. And you wouldn't believe how many I've run smack into. One old boy, in the pitch black, he was right by the path, just outside there, he woofed directly in my face. Ruffled my shirt collars he was that close. And then he turns and runs into the trees, making the biggest racket you ever heard. I would have pissed my pants, but I was too scared. They say you can smell 'em coming, but I never did. I guess I only run into clean bears. Hey, you seem like a clever girl. Want to see my new venture?"

"Whisky?" she said.

"Nope. Baths."

He took her outside to the back of his store, where he had erected another, smaller tent — a tall, simple rectangle in which maybe eight cots could be arranged. It was crisp and as yet unweathered, the canvas almost white. McEchern had strung it up tautly with guy ropes and drawn the door flaps back cutely like the curtains in a lady's window. Inside, there was a stove for boiling water, four deep tin baths, various small tables and benches set about so bathers could undress, and at the foot of each bath stood a rough clothes tree so a bather could keep an eye on his pockets. Considering the condition of the two recently departed miners, the widow saw the point in a venture like this.

"The way I figure it," said McEchern, "a man will pay for a good bath if you don't charge too much. I'll keep to two days a week so I know when to get the stove on." The widow, towering next to him, had contracted the hiccups. He waited patiently for her to get them under control, for it seemed she wished to ask him something.

"How are you going to get the water from there," — she pointed into the trees where there ran a thin mountain rill — "to here?" She pointed into the tent. "What if you get three customers at a time? You'll be run off your feet."

"All right. Yes. A few kinks to work out." The dwarf's face went lemony. "Now, what I'm going to do is . . . I'll, uh . . ."

"Well, do you know how to barber?"

"What?"

"Give a man a shave, trim his moustache?"

"Can't say as I do. I trim my own. What do you think of it?"

"It's a very fine moustache."

"It is, isn't it?" McEchern stroked it proudly with his child's hand. He had lost the train of the discussion, derailed perhaps by whisky.

"Well, I only ask because . . . because I *do* know how."

"To what?"

"To barber! I used to do it for my father, and my . . . for another man."

"Did you now?" His face was suddenly serious, almost comically so, the hand poised at dragging down the long whiskers, the brow furrowed with thought.

"In fact," she said, "I'm quite good at it."

McEchern glanced around the little marshalling area, assessing the logistics. A bath. Then a shave. Who couldn't find a few coins for that? And the fact that the shaving would be done by a girl — not some seasoned old dame with her face done up like a mortuary photograph, but a pretty young girl. Her hand on your cheek, her face bending close to yours in concentration . . .

"You know," the widow said finally, "men might haul their own water to the stove if you give them a free drink."

McEchern's mouth fell open in surprise at such a good idea. And then he gazed at her with such depthless affection that the widow couldn't help smiling.

A few days later, the Americans arrived. They came in from the west, having taken the long route overland, through Indian country, the better to avoid cities and police. They came up the footpath toward town driving four stolen horses before them, a slow rooster tail of dust rising in their wake. There were eight men, all brothers from a family of horse thieves, sun-blistered, nearly asleep in their saddles, their hats hard with age. They looked like they were fashioned out of mud, all eight washed to the same matte shade of nothing, the same colour as the ground they passed over. Even their eyes seemed to have faded away. The saddle horses on which they sat were slat-ribbed and surly, their rumps badly wasted, nervous as cats among the tents and buildings. They crowded together as they walked, clannish, and the men who rode them seemed to draw up too, to hide within their coats. In stark contrast were the four quarter horses that preceded them, captives run together, tied halter to tail, led by one man who rode in front. These animals were robust, sleek despite the dust, and they stepped high.

The widow saw them coming, and she ran back into the house calling, "Bonny!" He hurried out the door, still chewing his supper, wiping his hands on his pants, and showering them with greetings.

The oldest brother came closer and calmed his uneasy horse. Late summer butterflies about his hat. He opened his mouth to speak and nothing came out. He cleared his throat.

"Bonny," he croaked to the Reverend. "Been a while."

"It's been a year, Gerry. How are you?"

The man was swallowing hard now.

"Gerry? Are you not well?"

"Just been a while . . . since I talked to anyone."

The Reverend glanced at the seven brothers behind the man, seven mud men on mud horses. "You talk to them, don't you?"

"Not much point." Gerry grinned. He noticed the widow where she hid in the doorway, and his eyes grew wide. "Pardon me, ma'am," he said and removed his hat. Under it seemed to be another hat, this one white.

And then all the brothers did the same, seven hats coming off to show various white brows on which sat bouquets of stiff and matted hair. A murmuring of ma'ams.

Mary delighted at the preposterous sight of them — like creatures risen from the grave, doffing their rotten hats. Gerry turned and pointed at the four quarter horses, now nipping at one another like colts. "We got these for you to look at. A kind of sample, I guess. They're no better or worse than the others. We got twenty-three more penned up out of town a ways. We'll need some feed soon, and salt. We've run out of salt."

"Are you serious?"

"What?"

"You drove twenty-seven horses?"

"We had over thirty. Lost a few on the way. A couple got away, and we just couldn't run 'em down. One got taken off in a river, thanks to Jamie." A boy in the back glowered and set his jaw. Clearly he did not agree it had been his fault.

"Excellent!" said the Reverend, beaming. "You boys really did it this time. Now, can we offer you anything to drink? Mrs. Boulton, do we have food?"

"Well," Mary thought for a moment. "I made bread. We have plenty of coffee. And I have all that stew . . ." She smiled politely and pointedly at the Reverend. His face fell, for she referred to porcupine stew — not the first batch but, incredibly, the second. The widow, it seemed, was totally incapable of snaring a rabbit, or killing a bird, or shooting a deer, but had easily bagged her second porcupine. A large mass of pungent stew sat

286

congealing in a pot on the cold stove. Neither of them had had the courage to eat it yet. The two hosts assessed the bedraggled men before them, the hollow cheeks, the stave-chested horses they sat on. These men would eat grass if they had to.

"Heat it up," the Reverend said, forcing a grin. "Nice and hot."

The next morning, the widow was outside McEchern's store, bent over one of the American boys, carefully shaving the difficult terrain of his Adam's apple. He was nervous and kept swallowing, so the object would leap and sink without warning. She halted and huffed with annoyance. Of all the parts of a man's body, the widow found this the most bizarre, the most unnecessary. The tiny knob in its centre, with a hollow divot just above. Impossible to shave! She seized the boy's jaw and pressed his head against her shoulder, which caused him to freeze in terrified pleasure. She looked like she was about to slit his throat. On the other hand, he was reclining on her breast. He didn't know whether to fight or faint.

McEchern strutted in and out of the bathing tent, where several other brothers lounged in tin bathtubs with their heads laid back against the sides. They all had bleeding knuckles and some were smoking cigars. Most of them were still drunk. A light rain fell, cold as snow.

The widow called for McEchern, and the dwarf hurried out and handed her a lavishly steaming rag that had been sitting in water on the stove. This she wrapped quickly about her customer's face. A muffled cry came from under the rag and the boy's arms and legs flailed. Then he sat still, clutching the chair seat, mouth in a pained O, a diaphragm of cloth blowing in and out with his breath.

"There you go, Jamie," the widow said. "You just sit there for a minute. That is your name, isn't it?" The boy moaned something and jawed his cloth like a puppet. It was not a bad haircut, now that she looked at it. The boy had wanted his sideburns cut like mutton chops, an outrageous fashion seen mostly on the covers of lurid books, and he preferred his hair to touch his collar. She ran a hand over the crown and pulled down on the nape hairs to check they were all the same length, and slowly the boy went all woozy and relaxed, and his legs went wide. McEchern stood watching her, a sly smile on his face. His pockets newly full of coins. Her apron jingling too.

The name was Cregan and they all hailed from Bozeman, Montana, though they hadn't returned to that town in so long a time the youngest ones couldn't claim to remember it at all. They came from a family of fifteen boys, an incredible assault on the laws of probability. The mother dead of exhaustion when the youngest was two — lucky for her, the family wisdom went, otherwise she would have just gone on having boys. How many could she bear? As with any family of more than four children, the older ones looked after the younger ones. Most of the boys knew how to sew and change a diaper, and they all knew how to cook, though badly.

A few of the fifteen had made the mistake of staying in Bozeman and becoming respectable. They'd fought their way into law schools or opened legitimate businesses. But their name, at least in Bozeman, was forever in shadow thanks to the remaining eight. The Cregans were invoked wherever the discussion turned to the puzzling nature of the criminal mind, or the eternal ineptitude of the law. And the Cregans were indeed felons, cattle rustlers, horse thieves, arsonists, though they had never been caught at, let alone convicted of, anything halfway serious. Just drunkenness and brawling, which they seemed to enjoy the way some men enjoy sports. They came into any room as a group and went out the same way, often backward, holding broken chair legs aloft. In jail, having been nicked for one or another minor infraction requiring a short stay, they ate together, were bunked in groups to keep fights down, mumbled to one another in a queer familial shorthand, and acknowledged no one else. The oldest walked like a general with his own private army. When they were released, now properly fed and rested — refreshed, even — they went straight back to work. They, too, considered themselves businessmen, purveyors of a valuable product at a reasonable price — it was just that, most often, the product belonged legally to someone else.

Their own horses, the ones they owned and had names for, followed them around like lapdogs. The widow had noticed this the previous day as the boys stood attending to the tack or bending to untie their rain-bleached bags and panniers. The horses nudged them with soft noses or hung curious heads over their shoulders. Once the animals had been washed and curried down, they didn't look so badly used. And you could see their types: bay, roan, sorrel. Points of white on this one's ears. Flaxen forelegs on another. They were the kind of animals that grew not merely hairy in winter but shaggy, their necks ropy with muscle, with big homely heads. As the men washed them, the horses bent to the buckets of water at their feet and sucked loudly with parched lips. One massive gelding with the mackled hide of an Indian horse had wandered right into the Reverend's house seeking its owner, who was sitting at the table, happily eating the abominable stew. Everyone heard the soft clop of unshod hooves and the warning cracks of the floorboards. The boy jumped up from the table, bellowed, "Sorry, folks!" and, putting his arms round the creature's neck and pressing his shoulder to its chest, impelled it backwards out the door, knocking its head on the lintel. When he came back inside and sat down, the gelding stood uncertainly on the threshold. Then it wandered round the side of the house and waited by a window, like a governess peering into a playhouse.

A few miners drifted up to the house as the news of the Cregans spread, and, like the horses, these men waited outside, sitting on stumps or crouching on their own haunches, smoking, waiting for the Reverend to come out and talk business. Two Indians came along later and hovered about the periphery, perpetual outsiders. The widow wasn't sure whether they were Crow, like Henry — she couldn't tell from the way they dressed. Plain pants held up with sashes, coats made of blankets, and under those what looked like pyjama tops.

Finally, the Reverend emerged from his front door to a cacophony of queried and offered prices. The crowd headed out together to McEchern's, the Reverend and the Indians in earnest debate in front, a mass of miners following, and the eight boys lagging behind, walking with that stiff-legged strut common to constant riders whose feet rarely touch the ground. The widow had been left with mud everywhere inside the house, spur marks in the table legs, and every last scrap of the stew gobbled up.

Now, a day later, here she was, a hand on the shoulder of a Cregan boy, who was freshly shaved and drowsing under a hot towel. She gauged the size of him. Six feet at least, and probably not yet fully grown. Fifteen boys. She shuddered in silent sympathy with the doomed mother. Strangely, they all looked different, not like brothers at all, each unique enough that it almost called their paternity into question. Faces no more similar than those of an audience at a show, and their temperaments just as varied.

By contrast, how similar were the widow's own husband and his brothers, three men who, despite their different colouring, shared a common face, as if their features had been pressed from the same living mask. The original had been their father, certainly. There had been a picture of this man perched on her dresser in the cabin — no picture of the mother; perhaps none had ever existed. The father was standing alone before a photographer's fanciful backdrop, his face so mirthless and severe that one felt sorry for the photographer. Behind this black figure, in the watercoloured distance, stood a pastoral little bridge, a wide, soft river, and a rowboat with two figures in it. Gaunt and impatient, he was an indictment of this prettiness, as if he had walked in from some more sober place and stood deliberately in its way. Here, then, was the progenitor, the father-in-law, Pater. She had never met him, but she knew him well nonetheless. As the winter had come and darkness had descended upon her — or, rather, as it had ascended upward out of her — she had been alone in the cabin and seen that frozen and brutal face more often than her husband's. Slowly, the resemblance had done its work. First she saw John's father in him, then the two were no different, and finally John was his father. One day, when she looked at the photograph, there was John. In that empty cabin, she had met no face but theirs.

The widow realized her heart was pounding. She breathed deeply. Dropped her shoulders. How different things were now. How surely life had crept back into life. The bed she slept in now was surely her own, the roof over her head somehow more secure. The Reverend in his kindness and routine was like a blessing she didn't deserve.

She rubbed her damp cheeks. The pines above her were a natural canopy protecting them from the misty rain that floated down. Sometime soon McEchern would have to put up a tarp to keep off the rain and snow while she barbered . . . or perhaps, not so much to keep the rain off, for not much of it blew laterally through the trees, but to mark the place where she stood. She knew that in McEchern's mind, she was now a fixture, belonging to him as much as did the stove that heated the water and the tubs that held the bathers. And like these other things, he worried about her and was protective, as if some sly bastard might steal her away from him. She smiled a little at that — he was a peculiarly likeable little man.

Now McEchern himself came around the north side of the store hauling a wheelbarrow in which a four-gallon barrel of rum rolled and bonged and leaked at its seams. The two handles of the wheelbarrow were on the dwarf's shoulders, and he pulled like a dray horse. At the sound of booze coming, one of the brothers twisted round in his bathtub, cigar in his mouth, and craned back to look out through the tent's flap. This brother was tall and fair-haired, named Sean, and as the widow gauged it, born somewhere middle of the pack. He saw the widow standing there, her hand on the shoulder of one of his many brothers. McEchern rumbled past him into the tent, met by whoops of joy, but Sean kept looking. By now they all understood that Mary was not the Reverend's wife. His was a feral and lovely face, dark from weather, the eyes by comparison startling white. A wide, knowing grin broke across it. He winked at her.

The Ridgerunner squatted by his little fire, for there was nothing dry to sit on, and he held skewers of meat over the fire and twisted them slowly, his mouth

293

watering. The moon was on its way down for morning. Four gnarled twigs soaked in a puddle extended from his hand like arthritic fingers and at the tip of each a barbecued mouse. Tails and feet cindered away, heads mere nubs, but a mouthful of meat at the centre, and it smelled good.

How many days had he paused here, under this rock overhang, watching the valley, unable to bring himself to descend farther and follow the river? Once he gathered his courage and went down, he might hunt or get some supplies, ask around . . . ask about Mary. She must be down there somewhere, probably with the Indians or farther on in the little mining town. He sighed deeply and closed his eyes. The warmth seemed a miracle to him, the drizzling rain a consolation. If he could find a dry spot, a crag or an overhang, he might even be able to sleep.

For days he had been watching. There would be nothing for hours, just forest, the river, cloud. Once or twice he could spot a pale body moving by the river, Indians bathing and splashing, so tiny as to be almost imaginary. And then a train would come along the valley floor, its long wail both vulgar and cheery. A sign of life.

What was the town like? How big was it? There might be fences, roads. There might be signs, simple wood planks announcing a name. Property. He might find himself trespassing the outer reaches of some private habitation — and always, on farms, there is an affronted figure in the distance watching. And of course, in any town, a poor stranger like himself could not loiter on the grocer's steps as others did. An outsider must keep moving, appear harmless and temporary. Curious eyes might follow him as he made his way past. Even in the bars, among drunks, there was no standing here, or there, for this was someone else's plot of floorboards; there's the owner's hat, his drink, the invisible, ineffable stain of tenure that develops over time and use and selfishness and belligerence . . . William Moreland's hands sweated and he wiped them on his thighs.

This was where he was about to go. This was the pit into which he must crawl in order to find her. He could not bring himself to consider the possibility that she might rebuff him. Neither could he backtrack and leave. There was only one way to go. Down.

CHAPTER
TWENTY-ONE

It was still dark when the widow sat up abruptly, put a hand to her forehead, and groaned with annoyance. The headache had arrived during the afternoon and settled in for the night. It would pass, she knew, but until it did, sleep was impossible. She put her cheek to the cold window and closed her eyes. Her breath slowly blew a fan of vapour on the glass that remained long after she had lain back down.

Before dawn, the Reverend came down his staircase, heralded by the creaking proof of his poor carpentry. He found the kitchen empty, the coffee not made, the doors still shut against the night. The emptiness of the room surprised him, her absence like an affront. And it was chilly — as it used to be before the widow had arrived. He told her later, "I thought you'd left me."

Then he heard her upstairs, shifting heavily in her bed.

"Mrs. Boulton?" He went to the foot of the stairs. She did not answer.

"Will you get up, Mrs. Boulton?"

She made a peeved sound, a kind of half-moan, said, "No," and shifted irritably in her bed. More silence. He called a few more times, to no effect. Over the next few minutes, the Reverend earnestly meditated on his faults, for it must be that some act on his part had caused her to go on strike. Had he been rude? Had he been unfair to her? But he could remember no moment of inavertent rudeness, no shadow of annoyance crossing her face, no little huff of frustration. Quite the reverse. She had recently seemed to become quite happy — he thought she was growing content with him, just as he was with her.

Sadly, he made his own breakfast. Sour coffee, burnt oatmeal with too much salt. He couldn't find the dried blueberries, for it was now Mary's kitchen and he was a stranger in it. The Reverend Bonnycastle grumped his way out the door and headed off, not to his church this time, but to the mine. It was a new tack he had decided to try. Attendance at church had recently dropped off to nothing. Perhaps because there were no new volunteers for a "Bible lesson," and anyone who'd already had one wasn't keen on a rematch. The previous Sunday he had spent waiting in his empty church, then later in solitary work, planing boards for the walls.

"If they won't come to you, why don't you go to them?" the widow had said.

"Where?" he'd asked.

"In the mine, Bonny. They must rest sometimes. They must eat lunch."

"I suppose."

"And," she had said, casually scooping a few bread crumbs off the table into her palm, "you might offer a little variation in your sermons. A different subject . . ."

"Variation?" he said uncertainly. The idea had bewildered him at first, but gradually he saw the sense in it. No one wants to see the same show repeatedly. He could go to them, he could change his tack. So, that morning, he went sadly out the door, walked to his church and right past it, and went on to the mine.

Meanwhile, the widow lay in a deep fog of laudanum. Hours of ceaseless thumping in her head had finally caused her to remember McEchern's remedy, which still lay in the bird lady's opera purse. She had unstoppered the bottle ready to swig, but realized she didn't know the dose, or how often to take it. In the end, she had tippled a little of the bitter syrup and brought the bottle back to bed with her. At first, she felt nothing but a vague desire to sleep. She took another little sip, and then one more. By the time she took her fourth sip, the widow realized in a visceral and dully alarmed way that the first one was only just beginning to bloom, huge and gorgeous, the drug in a belated rampage through her blood. If this was what one sip felt like . . . The widow would have panicked if she'd been capable, but she was no longer capable of anything. There was nothing to do but close her eyes and wait.

McEchern was right. There was suddenly no pain, none at all. It wasn't simply that the headache was gone, nor that the chronic ache in her leg had vanished, nor that her cold, stinging feet had warmed, nor that the stiff knuckles of her work-worn hands had loosened. The release was total, *all* of it was gone, from every muscle, every drop of her blood. She slipped unresisting into nirvana. And when the Reverend called out to her, his voice barely penetrated the first layers of an infinite covering that lay over her and protected her, and beneath which she slumbered.

She saw things. For a time, there were cavalcades of dark sunbursts, discs of light pocked with inclusions, something resembling faces in those burning stars. The closed eye sees itself, bright halo round the depthless, staring hole. Later, a ragged thing struggled its way up through a heaped mass of bodies, while overhead the red sky wrinkled. Arms parting limply to let it pass. The widow's small body struggling up through heavy bedclothes. No worry. No pain. The room full of figures; they simply jollied forth, meaningless, harmless. And so this relief came to her as well, a release from fear.

She found herself at the stove, sleepy-eyed, stirring a pot of water. A gentle sluicing sound as the long wooden handle cut the surface. She yawned. A dream. No? . . . All right, not a dream. She looked down at herself and saw her thighs, pale and bisected by a bunched pair of bloomers. She was only half-dressed.

This set off an alarm in her, a bark that shook her, and she was suddenly much more awake. What followed was a series of careful steps. She bent to see that the stove was properly stoked; that there was actually water in the pot; that her feet were in boots; that she was indeed bare-legged; that the Reverend wasn't there to see her thus, wasn't upstairs, wasn't outside; that his coffee pot was still warm on the stove; that it was filled with a liquid so sour-smelling he could only have had made it himself; and that his empty bowl lay daubed with dried oatmeal, hard as buckshot. Last, she went to the window and winced up at the sun to gauge the time of day. Her mind wandering its austere routines, unworried, like a beetle marching through a forest of grass, looking down.

Two hours later she was washed and dressed, carrying the buffalo-skin coat, walking along the path under the trees to the church, bringing the Reverend his lunch as usual. Floating along, smiling, the laudanum bottle tucked into a coat pocket, the bitter taste again on her tongue. Give the taste a name. Things must have names, mustn't they? Strange sentiments came and went through her unburdened mind: that trees were possibly friendly; that her footsteps might count out to some important number; that her father was thinking of her that very moment. As she sauntered, she flushed up ground squirrels that shot to the high branches and glared down on her, chittering. She passed a Cregan — who knew which one? — and nodded to him, like any civil lady on her way to the shops. But something about her made the boy turn and watch her go. A rhythm in her step more of the dance hall than the shops, and her head canted cutely to one side. Hips swinging. He went on his way again with an occasional glance back at her.

The church was almost finished, or so it looked from the front. She came up the path toward the high frontage, the new surmounting cross. The warped wall boards had only worsened the queerness of the edifice since they had been whanged into place with an organic sense of the vertical. Wedges of empty space admitted the elements. It was much worse than the house, as if the Reverend was actually regressing in his work. She hauled open the heavy door only to find the place empty. Stupidly she called for him, then sat down on a pew. The rear wall of the church was not yet erected, and a palisade of tree trunks stood behind the altar. There was a slow stirring in her addled mind, a sense that things were not as they should be. She had told him to go somewhere, hadn't she? Where was it? She got up and went out to look for him.

By the time she got to McEchern's store, she had forgotten why she had come. She had forgotten why she needed to see the Reverend, and now there was only the rootless desire to find him. This dwindling spark of purpose was finally extinguished when she saw the dwarf hurrying uphill toward her, his face livid under the bowler, making admirable progress on his condensed legs.

"Where in the Sam Hill have you been?" he hissed.

The widow smiled beneficently down at him. "Me?"

"Yes you, goddammit! I've got two of 'em lined up waiting for you, and one in the bath. Now get your ass down there."

"Two what?"

McEchern's face closed in an effort to find patience, and he made a goatlike noise of annoyance. Without a word, he seized Mary's cuff and dragged her downhill to the bathing tents. There were two men on the store's platform, sitting together smoking and swinging their feet. From the smaller tent came sounds of splashing and humming.

"Gentlemen!" the dwarf bellowed. "If you didn't have beards like Methuselah before, I guess you do now. But your wait is over."

"I go first," said one massive fellow, his accent Norse. He flicked the ember off his cigarette and pocketed the butt. Then he came forward and sat on the chair, his weight punishing the wooden frame, leaned back with a perilous creak, and waited to be shaved. Slowly, the widow set down her coat, pulled up her dark sleeves, and went about her work, an unworried automaton. She stropped the razor on a length of leather tied to the chair, watching the long, slow strokes come and go, her slackened face all dreamy. She carefully lathered the man's face, patting the brush at his cheeks. The razor moved languidly, heavily, in a leisured rasping of his weathered skin, the blade fetching up two distinct colours of hair, black and white. She paused to squint at them. The Norseman sat with his chin in her palm and stared ahead, a blissful and slightly cross-eyed cast to his gaze. The widow was in her private study, and he was in his.

McEchern, by contrast, was now keenly aware he had a problem. He knew something was badly wrong with her; he had even deduced what it might be. He had also reasoned that, as purveyor of the laudanum, he would be in no small part responsible should her razor somehow find the Norseman's jugular. What was worse, the other waiting miner had realized something was wrong, or maybe he had caught the look of alarm in McEchern's eye, and was now beginning to shrink into himself.

"Well, young fella," the dwarf said, "can I front you for a drink?"

"No."

Neither of them took his eyes from the rapturous scene of the widow nearly hugging the chin of her customer, his imperilled throat exposed.

In the end there was no bloodletting, though the Norseman was unusually closely shaved. Then came the steaming towel, wrapped round the face and coming to a peak on the nose, like a dollop of whipped cream, the miner's leathery face barely registering the heat. Once he was done, the widow brushed off the threadbare knitted sweater that covered his shoulders, and he stood, stroking his cheeks and sighing, "Åh, vad du är verkligen duktig!"

The dwarf hurried toward them. "That's all for today, gentlemen. Shove off, now. That's right." The second miner paused for only a moment before allowing himself to be ushered away.

Small fissures of steam escaped from the flaps of the bathing tent and rose into the air. Mud was everywhere — on Mary's boots, built up in crusts round the feet of the barbering chair, around the tent, a deep puddle directly outside the door flap. Some mornings this puddle was solid ice, and men would emerge from their bath, faces florid and shining, and go skating on one leg, wheeling their arms, jerking to a stop when they hit the crusted, frozen dirt. But today it was soft and smooth. Edible-looking. The widow scuffed her boot heel back and forth and trowelled some up. The dirt was almost red up here in the mountains. A deep red-brown, like a fox's ruff.

Suddenly a soprano voice was at the widow's ear.

"How much of the stuff did you take?"

She discovered she had sat herself down on the barbering chair. McEchern was at her side, his face inches from hers, eyes a pale, wolfish blue.

"How much?" he said again.

"I don't know."

"One sip? Two? More than that?"

"Five, maybe."

"Shitfire, he'll kill me! Where is it? Give it to me."

"No."

"Give it to me, dammit!"

"Why don't you try taking it and see what happens?" Mary showed him the straight razor. It hovered in the air between them. The dwarf returned her a baleful, fatigued look — it was an expression she'd seen on many a piqued old woman. She couldn't help it; she bent over giggling.

"Very funny. Ho, ho."

Unconsciously, her hand strayed to the pocket of her buffalo coat, where the little vial hid. It was barely a twitch, but he saw it, and swift as a magician, the dwarf's little hand shot out and snatched it away.

She struggled out of her chair and stood swaying. "Mac! That's mine!"

"Not any more it ain't." He ran with it over to the store and hopped up onto the platform.

"You give it back."

"Listen to me, Mary," he said, turning and fixing her with a fiery glare. "Your doping days are over. Get used to it." The bottle disappeared with McEchern into the darkness of the store.

Meekly, the widow sat back down. Her mind tramped slowly around the problem, gazing into its hot centre. *Want more. Can't get more. If I steal it back, he'll know.* In her simple-minded state, it didn't occur to her that the dwarf had not refunded her money.

The mine's headframe clung to the sloped ground, its small black mouth open. Tracks for mining carts streamed in all directions, seemingly aimless until they converged and ran as one downhill to a loading platform by the railway tracks. A black stain seemed to erupt from the mine's mouth and spread out, ever wider, over the ground, like the scorch marks round a stove's door. As the widow walked, or rather ambled unevenly in her drugged state, her boots scraped up a heavy grey dust that fell as quickly as it rose. She could taste it on her lips.

A mine cart stood outside, heaped with slag. The widow called out, "Hello?" Called again. No answer came. A chilly breeze blew constantly out of the tunnel. She had expected to see one or another raccoon-faced miner who'd help her find the Reverend, but the entrance was deserted.

She had sat with some of these men at McEchern's store, cut their hair, shaved a few of them, marvelling at the mackling of their cheeks; the beards hid pallid skin, but wherever the black dust rested, its stain was as deep and permanent as the colouring on a cow's hide. She remembered the name of every man she had barbered. She had sussed out their likes and dislikes, ages and religions, their propensity for gossip, their feuds. She had even learned some of their superstitions, and these were numerous. Never say a dead man's name aloud. Never boast about a lack of injuries. Never refuse help to another miner, though above ground you might be murdering one another. Watch your footing at midnight, because the earth is upside down. Say a prayer to St. Barbara each time you descend: *Keep me from Him, for I liketh not to rush unbidden to Him.* All these things stood as talismans against disaster, ways to avoid provoking the living mass around you or annoying it with your bravado. But the greatest transgression was to allow a woman into the mine. This was the terror of them all. No one could say for sure what devastation might await, because no miner could remember seeing a woman even standing near the mine — a collusion, perhaps, of superstition and women's utility elsewhere.

If the widow had been sober, had this been another day, she might have remembered this. She might have waited for the Reverend outside or turned back and gone home. But on this day, her brain still boiling with laudanum, she stepped into the mine, oblivious to the hazard she brought with her.

The tunnel was low and wide, banked slightly downhill into the mountain, and went fading away from the light of day, straight into the dark. At her feet lay the narrow-gauge tracks for the ore carts, like twin veins, shining dully in the poor light. On the damp air, the smell of something familiar, something alive. Slowly, as she went forward, she made out the prints of some hoofed animal, first one and then many of them, small hooves, sunk into the dust.

Deer? she thought stupidly. She stopped, bent down to see the U of horseshoes, each dotted with nailheads. That was the familiar smell — the sharp and consoling scent of a stall. She remembered, then: pit ponies, working shifts like the men, pulling the heavy mine carts along the sloped drifts, living their lives below ground, growing old, retiring only when they went blind.

A small rivulet of water ran down the wall by the widow's shoulder. It travelled with her for a few steps and then disappeared into a fissure at her feet. Soon she saw dimly a metal cage, with gate open. Like a mouse trap, waiting for her. The widow in her buffalo coat held the little bowl of food close to her chest, the disorder of her mind stirring in its laudanum drowse. To go on or to retreat?

When she stepped into the cage her weight caused it to sink and then jounce lightly over the void. Her boots rested on criss-crossed steel bars, and the stale breath of the mine blew steadily upward, billowing her pant legs. A voice could be heard, carried on the hollow air, overlapping in echoes, the source far away and droning.

She froze and listened. The Reverend's voice was vaulting along the tunnels to her. Eagerly she studied the cage for a way to make it work. There was a chain made of wide, flat links. One end ran up into the shadows while the other ran down through the mesh flooring, extending a pale finger into the pit. This was attached to a contraption of pulleys and weights that allowed the miners to move themselves up and down. She put the metal bowl of food at her feet, woozy now as the cage bounced and swung, weightless. There was a giddy moment of holding her breath and looking straight ahead. She stared hard at the wall of uneven stone, infinite shades of grey foxed with brilliant black inclusions. There were white spots too, like thumb-prints. The widow went from vertigo to earnest study of the rock face before her, a comical transition, made as quickly as a child stops crying when handed a toy. It was a minute or so before she was moved to reach out her hand and touch the chain. Almost warm. With a slight pull downward, she rose a little. A pull upward, she sank. With halting progress, she ferried herself deeper into the mine.

The Reverend stood before a crowd of miners, each man seated on his helmet. They had gathered in a cavernous central stope, off which ran several tunnels like spokes. In the roof above them, two air shafts had been drilled, holes the width of a man's trunk that went vertically into the rock and ended in a speck of light. A constant dust rained down from the vault. The Reverend Bonnycastle paced back and forth before the men, intoning a standard Christian sermon; it would seem he was comfortable adapting to change. Unlike his customary pugilistic performance, this sermon was larded with Biblical stories, quotes read out by the light of a borrowed headlamp, questions asked and waited upon, though no answer was necessary, everything leading to a moral conclusion that was inescapable and broadly true. The subject for today was unity.

"Though one man may overpower another, two can withstand him. And a cord with three strands is not quickly broken."

Some men were clearly satisfied with this turn of events, enjoying a day at worship without a fist fight, while others seemed a little dejected. An old fellow started up a hymn on his accordion, an ancient and shabby instrument, its wheezing and rhythmic squeaking like old bedsprings in the throes.

And then, quite suddenly, it stopped.

At first, the Reverend didn't hear the murmuring at the back. He kept talking, but the murmur became louder. Men were looking over their shoulders. The disturbance went through the crowd in a ripple. Those closer to the Reverend began to twist round to look.

"What is that?" One fellow stood up and squinted curiously into the stope's darkness. There were a few aggrieved murmurs from his colleagues nearby, translating into a request for him to shut up. But then he pointed, his voice sharp. "What in Jesus is it?"

All the men turned, some with hands to their brows as if to shade their eyes from an invisible sun that bore down on them in this echoing excavation. Before them stood what at first looked like an animal at the tunnel's mouth, a furred and pinheaded form standing upright, like a bear scenting the stale air — as if any animal, no matter how demented or conniving, could have taken the elevator down to that level. There was silence among the men. The Bible in the Reverend's hand slowly sunk till it hung at his side. A look of resignation spread across his features, for he knew what stood there.

The creature swayed a little, drunkenly, and then it stepped forward and spoke. "Don't let me disturb you," the widow said.

Pandemonium.

CHAPTER
TWENTY-TWO

The widow had dragged the table outside into the sunshine and she and the Reverend sat playing gin, he constantly shuffling and re-shuffling, dissatisfaction radiating from him, the widow watching him with interest. Many things in his life came easily, but cards was not one of them. It was as if some curse drove bad cards into his hand, and even if he got good cards, he didn't know what to do with them.

"There!" he said triumphantly and put down a card.

The widow snapped down one of her own and took his. He frowned. The trees overhead shook in a breeze, and tiny drops of watery resin rained down on the card players, the scent of pine pungent on the air. The widow leaned back in her seat and sighed happily. He began to put down a card, then brought it slowly back to his chest, giving her a suspicious look. Eventually, he put it down. An eight. The widow snapped down a ten and took his card. The game went on like that until she had won.

"You must give me a chance to get you back," he said.

"All right," Mary said. "You deal."

As they played, and as he slowly lost again, there came through the trees gusts of warmth that spoke of summer. She took off one of her boots and set her foot upon it, then slowly worked the other one off.

"Bonny," she started, "do you think I dare go shopping?"

"Why not?"

"You know why." She had a blurred memory of one old miner seizing her by the coat collar and shouting in her face. She wasn't even sure how she had got out of the mine.

"If you want to go out, go out."

"But what if . . ."

"They know they'd have to deal with me. That's your card."

She took up his card.

"By the way, where is the stuff now?" he said.

"Stuff?"

"Whatever drug Mac gave you."

Her heart leaped with surprise. But of course she should have known he'd guess what had happened, and he would know immediately where she had got the dope. She hung her head and could not meet his eye.

"He took it back."

"All of it?"

"Oh, Bonny, I'm sorry —"

"How in the world could it be your fault? I'll speak to Mac later."

She put down a six.

He put down a jack. His hand hovered over it in disbelief for a moment, and then he took them both up. "You hear voices, don't you?"

This stopped the widow cold. Her cards dropped to her lap and she covered her face.

"There's nothing shameful in it," he said.

"Yes, there is."

"*Not* to me." He said it quietly but firmly.

"Did I say something, did I speak out loud?"

"No."

"Well," she huffed, "how did you guess, then?"

"I saw it on your face."

Slowly she retrieved her cards and organized them with trembling hands, for the surprise had made her clumsy. She couldn't believe it — she had almost convinced herself that she was free of these poisons, these terrible visits. There had been no voices for so long now, no visions . . . all right, there had been one in the kitchen. But no more than a shape in the corner of her eye, and she was pretty sure she had neither started nor turned to look nor given it the slightest attention. Just as the Ridgerunner had suggested, she now ignored them. So perhaps it wasn't that she didn't have them any more, but that she put them out of her mind, concentrating instead, with patient meditation, on the real. Or rather, what she guessed to be real. How to know? How to tell?

The Reverend reached out and took her hand in his own, warm and solid.

"I'm not crazy," she said.

"I know you're not."

★　★　★

During the night there was gunfire, unmistakable small cracks that sawed back and forth along the pass.

"Bonny!" Mary groaned. "What is that?"

"Nothing."

"Sounds like guns."

The Reverend shifted violently on his tick and cleared his throat. "One of those boys," he said, "probably shooting at a bear."

"What boys?" She waited for him to answer. Her eyes closed. Soon, she was just as asleep as he was.

The next morning, the Reverend arrived downstairs to find his breakfast set out on the table and the widow once again nowhere to be found. He went outside and peered around. Nothing. He sat at the table and touched his metal plate — warm, the porridge still steaming. Finally, she came through the back door and the Reverend suppressed a surge of gladness.

"I was just sick out behind the house," she said.

"What? Why?"

"It's the funniest thing. The feeling just came over me."

"How do you feel now?" he asked.

"Oh, fine, just fine."

He grinned at her and shook his head.

"What?" she said.

"You're not a complainer, are you?"

"Oh, you should hear me," she said, smiling. But she was pleased. It was the closest thing to a compliment she'd heard since . . . she thought for a moment. John had once told her her hair was soft. A maid had exclaimed at the quality of her needlework, but that girl had gushed at nearly everything, even common sparrows on the windowsill. A neighbour girl had said she looked lovely in her wedding dress. Not a word from her father about the dress or the wedding or anything. And her grandmother had merely been at pains to keep her from smearing the rouge on her lips. "It's simply got *everywhere*, darling," the old woman said, bending close with a damp handkerchief. "You look like a mad dog."

Well, compliments did not come often to her. She was surprised at how delicious it felt. She went to the stove and took up the pot and spooned a little extra oatmeal out for the Reverend.

After coffee and a pipe, they set off together for the open grassland to the west, a single wide alpine meadow rimmed by trees and streaked with purple flowers, in the middle of which stood a small corral for horses, surrounded by a crowd of men, some of them sitting atop the fence, others leaning and gazing between the rails at the beauty that stamped and nodded and blew within.

"Here he comes!" cried one of the men, and the Reverend raised his hand and went among them. The Cregans were everywhere, four of them in the paddock with the horses, ropes over their shoulders. They stepped among the milling animals, amid the eddying dust, skilfully separating one or another individual should a buyer wish a closer look. Many of the horses now wore hackamores, but they wore the lashings awkwardly and seemed affronted by them. In truth, these animals were long broken, but they had been so recently liberated and run together like a pack of wild ponies that the chill of freedom had blown through them already, and they were now an obstinate lot.

The widow clambered up the fence and gazed at the mess within. Men and horses churning together, the hats bobbing up and down, lost among the moving shoulders and rumps.

She'd never seen that many horses together. Her father had never kept more than two old ones, though the stable was large enough for more. Her grandmother could remember when all six stalls had been full, and buggies were backed into the barn one after another till the last one's traces stuck out the doors into the rain. Everyone had their own horse, and they were given names like Little Boy and Marathon. Her great-grandfather had been a horse-hater. He beat his animals and enjoyed it; his dying words to his sons included the hope that they would no longer have to deal with "goddamned horses," and within ten years he had his wish. Some of the animals were lost in a blizzard; a few were sold; many fell sick with unknown maladies, defied the vet's efforts, and died. These tales had had a melancholy effect on Mary as a child, and she'd wandered the barn, filled with existential gloom. The bridle of each departed horse hung rotting on the slat walls, and the stalls seemed imprinted with absence.

Until she was married, she'd never ridden anything but a "girl's horse" — gentle animals, usually old and slothful by temperament. Once married, she was introduced to a wholly different species: massive, powerful monsters with hairy forelegs and broad backs, stupid beasts with ferocious tempers. No one ever risked walking behind them. She remembered one such horse, annoyed by something, kicking the broadside of a wagon without warning, a mighty wallop that rocked the thing and sent goods flying off both sides. It took the men a day to repair the bent axle.

"That one," said a voice. It was Sean Cregan, standing close to her where she hung over the fence. "She's the best of the lot."

He pointed to a nondescript quarter horse pacing the far side of the paddock. It stepped low, watchful, its head down as if ducking from view. It was a stocky mare, almost homely, and it seemed to vanish and then reappear, the least noticeable animal among the others.

"Look," he said. "Just watch her."

One of the older Cregans was bearing down on another young horse, a beautiful chestnut-coloured animal that balked and hopped, swinging from side to side, exposed by the bodies of the others. The man held his rope shoulder high, the lasso set to snap out into the air. As if on cue, the little mare darted forward, almost invisible among high-held heads and stale dust and the whistles of men. She cut laterally across them all, and in response the group of horses moved organically, reconstituting like mixing dough. The quarry fell back and was obscured by others. The boy checked his toss and the rope fell short. Annoyed, he reeled the lasso back in. The mare was gone.

"That's a smart animal," Sean said. "She'll be the last to sell, but she's the best one. You get her on your side, you can really do some work."

"Who did you steal her from?" the widow asked.

"God," he said.

"You're smart, aren't you?" she said, grinning.

"I don't mean to be."

He reached up and took two of the widow's fingers, held them in a gentle grasp. She let him do it. His dark skin, her slim fingers disappearing into his loose fist, hidden among the folds, the scars, the lines, the astonishing wear of his hand. It wasn't a salacious gesture, but neither was it tender. It was covetous. *Why am I letting him?* she thought. She looked into his feral face, saw the sly question there, hooded but brazen, and felt a stab of yearning and regret. It welled up in her, disastrously raw. Disastrous because she desired not this man, but another. Oh to kiss the face, to find the tongue, to give her breast to him and look down and watch. And the rest, the taut, agonizing joy. As helpless as water to the pull of gravity, the widow's heart ran to William Moreland. Pooling there, wasted, unwanted. And so, wrath followed desire. How foolish it was to allow a man in, how terrible his power once you did.

The Cregan boy watched the riot of emotion pass over her, trying to read its meaning.

Behind them, a voice rose above the others, loud and exasperated, and the widow yanked her hand away and clambered down the rungs of the fence. In a moment, the Cregan boy was lost among the horses.

318

"How come I pay full price and he doesn't? How come an Indian doesn't pay?"

"He's paying, don't you worry," said the Reverend.

"Look at him! He can't buy shit. Where's his money?"

The Reverend gestured to the man in question. "Tell him what you'll pay me with." The man said something in Crow.

"There," said the Reverend. There were a few chuckles from the crowd.

"In other words," said a third voice, "mind your own business."

"Fuck that. It is my business — I want that horse he's got!" It was a good horse, anyone could see that.

"Pick another one."

"I don't *want* another one."

"Can we get on with this? I don't have all week."

The Indian turned and drew his horse around by the reins and the two of them headed slowly away to the north, the animal's tail swishing through the flowers and the Indian's hat hung down his back on a string. Indeed, he did not look like a wealthy man. He wore breeches too short for him and a collarless shirt, and these were weathered and drab, and he seemed to have nothing else to his name but his horse. Perhaps he had a camp somewhere, perhaps he just travelled light. His sour competitor stood, hands on hips, watching the horse go.

"Well isn't that just . . . *Fuck!*" he said. The rest of the men ignored him and the fury of negotiation resumed.

Most horses sold for money, and quite a bit of it. But a few buyers would pay for their horses by barter, bringing the Reverend meat, fur, medicine, ammunition. These were not just Indians either, but backwoodsmen, loners, solitaries living in the mountains. The widow had seen their instalments. The gifts might come for years, the Reverend had said, regularly and without salutation. A frozen side of deer stacked up beside the door in winter. A small amount of tincture swilling around the bottom of an old crockery bottle — medicine, but who knew what for. Footsteps in a straight line through the snow up to the door and away again. Only one or two would even linger long enough to smoke a pipe or chew tobacco. Indians didn't spend too much time in Frank. The common wisdom was that they were superstitious about the mountain and believed it was alive — a view that was much ridiculed in Frank. In Frank, there was ridicule of pretty much everything.

By mid-afternoon, half the horses had been sold and the rest were in the paddock, silent and tranquil, the strings on their hackamores dangling. A defeated calm had come over them; or perhaps they were stunned by how quickly the group had broken and left them divided, mere individuals again. The dust had settled and the noise abated, and the Cregans now clambered out of the paddock with stiff loops of rope over their shoulders. Two horses had been hobbled and let loose to graze among the own horses, and it was assumed these now belonged to the brothers unless pretty good money could be found. A fire was set up downwind from the paddock where stragglers sat and sipped coffee and conversed about the weather. The tents were erected as a kind of windbreak for the fire; but as the late afternoon came and the mountain's shadow crept, the tents began to flap in a cold wind. The widow sat close to the heat and endured the pangs of an empty stomach, a veil of nausea laid over the world. The Reverend came and sat by her, putting his hat on his knee, and he spoke merrily to the other men, joking and yawning.

Near nightfall they headed home, a loose string of human figures wandering toward town, the black-clad figure of the Reverend among them. They made their unlighted way over the mountain meadows among mile-long shadows, attended by a hunting grey owl. One by one they stopped to watch it, looking up unguarded, as children watch stars. The widow's dark pants riffled in the breeze.

The great owl descended the mountain face and passed soundlessly over them. It rode a thermal down, floating with its wings outstretched, its eerie face turned to watch something hidden in the grass until finally it cut left and flared wide, its incredible talons held forward, and dropped out of sight into the long grass. It did not rise again, and there was no sound, no cry before the kill. After a long moment, the audience went on, quieter now.

A fire crackled merrily in the dark. The tracker gobbled his dinner while his two customers hung over their food in silent anger. It was a stomach-churning meal of

321

smoked venison jerky, thrice-boiled coffee grounds, and for each hand a little soggy sourdough. As good a tracker as he was, the old coot was a horrendous cook, and he mostly pleased himself. As well, he had informed the brothers that their quarry was most likely long gone by now, spirited away by whichever lucky woodsman had found her and kept her. It was a lost cause, he told them.

"No," was the reply. "We hired you to find this woman. Do your job."

The old man spread his hands out wide, not remotely disturbed by their anger and evincing not a breath of apology.

"Listen. This fella knows exactly what he's doing. I can follow a trail all right. But he leaves nothing to follow. It's over, boys. She's gone."

Something in his complacency said he could have followed their quarry if he had wanted to, pressing on across the mountain ranges, finding the meagre evidence this couple left behind. No one moves over the land, hunts, eats, sleeps without leaving a single sign. There is always something to follow. All this other woodsman could do was to conceal the obvious. But an Easter egg is easily found, because one knows to look. The old tracker could have kept going, but he was growing weary of his companions, and they sensed it. But what could they do?

"You can go and look for yourselves," he joked. "But I don't guess you boys know where you are. Do you?"

He had let them storm and rage, demand obedience at first, then reason with him; he watched as they stood together in hushed debate and glared murderously at him. There was nothing for it, and they began to understand that. He told them he would take them on to the next town, the mining town of Frank, and from there they could stock up, settle in, or take a train . . . do whatever they wanted.

So here they were, hung over their wretched meal in the firelight, their red beards grown long and thick, their faces closed and gaunt, piqued by the old man's smacking and gustatory delight. They fixed him with sorrowing, heartsick eyes.

"We told you what she's done?" said one.

The tracker glanced quickly — the hind twin had spoken first.

"Yup," he said.

"Does it make no difference to you at all?"

The old man didn't look up, but he became thoughtful. He tossed his cold coffee across a carpet of soft moss and was about to reply.

At that moment, there came a crack. It came out of the dark, from the north. A clean explosion like the sound of a cannon. They might have thought it was a large rifle, perhaps someone hunting close by. But the sound was far too loud, too distant; it rolled up the range and came back down, like thunder riding the air.

A second later they felt the impact in their feet. Like a heavy footfall, close by. The tracker squinted into the dark. The far range stood angled before him, washed in moonlight. Something pale moved on it . . . The whole thing was moving.

He stood up and walked into the dark, to put the fire at his back so he could see more clearly. He blinked his eyes once and stared hard. The brothers wandered up behind him like curious dogs. In this way, they became the only living souls to witness the landslide in its entirety. The north face of the mountain was flowing downward, much the way a curtain waves in a gentle breeze. This was no mere avalanche; the entire cap of the mountain was coming down toward the town of Frank. The old man cried out in helpless anxiety.

For a full minute, the mountain seemed to billow, then slowly collapse, floating downward, lit palely from within. It luminesced from pure friction, so the shadows of individual boulders, incredible in size, could be seen hopping and bouncing. And then it hit the treeline. In streaks and lines the dark stubble of the forest was sheared away, the avalanche coming down in long, pale fingers, while the wide mass of a palm followed, erasing everything. As the longest finger reached the railway track and crossed it and entered the moonlit line of the river and spread across it, the landslide simply stopped. Down in the valley an immense wave of thick dust rose over the river, crested, and hung there, slowly rolling. A long moment later, well after everything had stopped moving, the roaring ended.

The old man could see no movement across the now concave mountain face. Only the moon hanging high and white over this terrible new landscape. And the river like a pinched vein slowly bulging. He still stood in simian pose, hands on his head, panting. Slowly, his hands sank to his sides.

There was no going to Frank now. Frank was gone.

PART THREE

WORLD WITHOUT END

CHAPTER
TWENTY-THREE

It had been a dream full of noise, a voiceless, howling wind. But now all was quiet. The widow opened her eyes and after a moment sat up. There was a tree directly in front of her. Seams of fine moss ran along the bark's nap. She leaned over and saw another tree, several more, and then nothing but night. Protruding from her forearm was a cedar twig, complete with needle tufts. None of this interested her, so she lay her head back down on the ground, hearing a faraway hiss and rattle coming through the dense earth, a sound like pebbles shaken in a metal pan. Her brain was ringing.

A little later, perhaps a long time later, the widow found herself in the process of standing up. With great difficulty, she staggered into an upright position. At her feet were smashed branches and twigs. She looked up at the tree that stood in her way. In the weak morning light she saw the broken top of it leaning into a grey sky. She understood somehow the immense height from which she had fallen. She could see where she had hit the tree, and where her body had barrel-rolled downward. The twig in her arm ached, and so she pulled at it, extracting an inch of swollen wood from the hole, while her fingers cramped and danced, and then went limp. She looked vacantly at the thing for a moment, the fibres of wood waterlogged with blood, then she dropped it and staggered forward on bare feet, heading for home, though she didn't know where she was or which direction she was going.

At first it appeared as if someone had rolled white rocks here and there to mark something out. Small boulders lay among the trees like dead comets at the end of their trajectories, each one with a tail of destruction behind it, all of them aligned in the same direction. These the widow stepped around, limping.

It was unearthly still. No wind. No sounds of animals. She could hear her own breathing, dull and hollow. On the air, a faint taste of dust. She passed a boulder the size of an outhouse, trees strewn under it like a straw bed, and she went on without amazement. It was simply in her way.

Something funny about the air — she stopped and listened; the trees above moved soundlessly. She shuffled her bare feet, to no effect. *So*, she thought, *I'm deaf again*, though she could not remember when she had lost her hearing before. At her feet, an old, scorched pot, lying upturned. No lid. She poked it with her naked toe and it rolled over. Ancient volcanic residue all around its sides, as individual as a face — it was her own pot or, rather, the Reverend's. She leaned down to touch it, and everything went black.

She woke again walking, looking for him. She tried calling his name but the effort made her sob, and so she went on in silence.

The smell of smoke. Here was a little lean-to, crouched against a shallow rock drop. A half-tent, with some ash-grey timber set vertically as a wall, and at its mouth a bent old coot in long johns and a hat, tending his fire. His cheek was pale as new porcelain, the grey-blue undercoat of shock.

"Queer, isn't it?" he said, but she could barely hear him. His voice was muffled, as if she were eavesdropping through a thick door.

"What?" she said, swallowing.

"You mean you ain't seen it?"

"I don't know . . ."

"All of that. Out there." His gesture was meant to take in much of the world.

Then the man shifted on his little stool and looked at her, the fire crackling merrily before him. He saw her bare feet, the blood running down her arm and thickening into viscid strings at her fingertips. He looked at the shreds of dark cloth, exposing her legs and much of her right hip, the half-buttoned bodice.

"D'ye think ye could sit down?"

She didn't answer. Didn't seem to have heard. Her eyes were strangely unfocused. So he looked away in a sudden spasm of embarrassment, shamed by the intimacy of injury.

"I was here," he said quietly, apologetically. "Just sleeping. All I was doing was sleeping." When he looked up again, she was gone.

The widow moved amid the trimmings of a nightmare forest. Blown debris was piled up everywhere. Branches

331

and stones. Trees leaned drunkenly, many broken halfway up their tall shafts, heavy heads tilted crazily. On everything was a pale dust, giving the dark green vegetation a leprous air. Small, colourful bodies were strewn on the ground like Easter eggs, bright fallen birds, killed by the first blast of hot wind. Finches, chickadees, grey jays with their velvet breasts exposed. Farther on, a young lynx lay bloodied on its side, eyes still moist, open mouth still moist, and on its motionless fur a growing dusting of chalk. She weaved away from it. Now there were bits of cloth and torn chunks of mattress and a kettle and crushed chairs. A door stood bizarrely upright, having spun through the darkness like a playing card to land there. A hat was dangling from a high branch. Through the curtain of bent trees she could see that she was approaching something wide and pale.

When she reached the verge of the trees and stepped out onto the moonscape itself, the widow finally stopped to gape. She sought a landmark, something to tell her where she was. Nothing was familiar, even the mountain was a different shape — an ashen, treeless concavity, strewn with rubble, some of it still moving, everything shrouded in strange clouds. The widow registered this the way one would in a dream. It was information, nothing more. She simply struggled on across the rock in bare feet, driven by her one thought: to go home.

A bloated red sun crept the far ranges. Even two hours after the avalanche, rocks still bounded downhill, beaming red as they went, deflecting, colliding with larger boulders and coming to an abrupt halt in a spray of shards.

The widow picked her way over the sharp ground. A boulder leaped ahead of her, another fell behind her, but she tottered on, charmed. Distantly, she could hear a sound, a human voice, shrill and insistent, coming closer. And then McEchern was seizing her round the wrist, his childlike shouting horrible to her ears.

"What in shit's name are you doing?"

Because she wasn't moving fast enough, he dashed behind her and pushed her rump, impelled her into a trot, hurrying her along, her bare feet leaving bloody smears on the rocks as she went. Finally he stopped pushing. All of a sudden it was cool and quiet. Together they stood in the shadow of a massive boulder, several storeys high. He seized her tattered, open collar and dragged her down to face him.

"You stay here," he said fiercely, his pudgy finger nearly on her nose. "*Stay put*, d'you hear?" She nodded meekly. Then he was gone, running away over the stones as nimble as a goat, one hand raised to keep the bowler on his head.

The widow sat down heavily and began to inspect her bloodied feet.

"I'm damned sure not dead," said a voice beside her.

She looked, and there sat a dirty boy she had never seen before. He was blond, his features rabbity, a wild and crooked grin on his face. His mouth hung open in near glee as he gazed about him at the desolation. The boy's right arm was laid across a flat rock beside him. The hand was thickened and blue and there was a dark line across the forearm where he had broken both bones. When he moved, the hand and wrist dragged a little. His lips were blue.

"You're not either," he exhorted her. "Are ya?"

She watched his mouth move and did not understand him.

"I'll tell ya a secret." He leaned toward her, teeth chattering, the hinge in his wrist ghastly. "Walter is sure as shit dead. I know that much."

"Who?"

"Walter. He's dead."

"I don't know you," she said.

"*Holee*," he cackled, "they dug me out from under I don't know how much. I was half out of the tent, and all tangled up in it, with this tree trunk laid acrost me. I was calling for ages. And when they started pulling me out I felt something soft under me. I said, 'Hey, fellas, I think there's someone else down there.'" The boy started hooting. "It was Walter!" He laughed so hard his nose began to run. But when he looked down at his swollen and flaccid fingers, the laughing subsided.

A spray of small stones exploded in a fan off the thing they sheltered behind. After an interval they both winced and ducked away, comically slow, two injured people in slow motion.

They sat listening to the crack and hiss of falling rock. And then the boy lost consciousness. He opened his mouth as if to speak, then his head lolled and he slumped back against the rock. The widow rose and stood over him, looking. The damaged arm with its extra joint lay dangling, the flesh bent like a sausage.

This curiosity held her for a moment. And then she headed downhill again, still searching. Intent as she was, she didn't notice the broken birds rising from the ground at her feet, popping like fleas over the shattered rocks.

What used to be a river was now a shallow lake, swelling upward along the fissures and runnels that wandered up the mountainside. Water spread wide and flat and muddy along the valley bottom. Dust suffused the atmosphere, erasing the far side of the valley, the flooded river endless now, a sea extending into cloud. Dust rained on the congested cedars, drifted over the empty railway tracks, and swirled about with the antic movements of several figures down by the water. A maddened horse dashed insanely up and down the new shoreline while bloodied, injured men tried in vain to catch it. The men had kerchiefs to their faces against the dust and the animal bellowed and coughed.

One of them, a big Swede, had a rope and was in the process of fashioning a lasso when the widow emerged over a hump of rubble. He strode out toward the lapping waterline to face down the galloping black yearling, palming the rope low, the slack gathered into loops in his other hand. He had tied the far end to a tree.

"No, no!" another man hurried toward him. "You'll break the bastard's neck!"

The yearling charged, then balked and dashed around them, its tail wild and high, darting into the water in a rooster tail of spray. It ran and bucked wildly, frightened into madness, then slipped and sank hindwise into the river, the unstable scree beneath its hooves giving way. A few more futile lurches and the horse slid in up to its neck. It began paddling away from the shoreline, confused, circling back, and then suddenly, without warning, disappeared altogether, as if yanked downward. The men ran forward to stand at the edge of the opaque river, its water the colour of milky tea.

"Shit!" said the Swede. There was silence after the suck of its going, then, horribly, a quiet churning from somewhere below. Bubbles rose in a curved line.

Then the animal rocketed upward, gasping and coughing, now turning instinctively to shore, eyes huge and rolling. It saw the men there, lasso dangling from the Swede's hand. Hooves pounded the surface in twin explosions, as if the yearling was galloping, and it pawed at the sludgy shoreline, long black legs finding purchase only to lose it, the body surging upward with great deep groans only to drop away again.

"Shit," said the Swede again, "he will drown," and indeed it did seem inevitable. Too late, the men backed away from the shoreline, but the animal swam in ever-weakening circles, afraid now of the shore, of the invisible and slithering thing beneath. Soon only the head swam along, and the huge round nostrils blew a beige mist along the surface. In the wan morning light, the surface of the water was glassy, motionless but for the turbulence of this foolish young horse. Finally, the animal found a more manageable slope. Streaming and glossy as a newborn, it humped and dragged its sorry way back onto dry land, then circled dully to face its pursuers, coughing like a bellows, its legs buckling. It fixed the two men with a look of sullen defeat.

"I go get him now," said the Swede, but it was a question.

"Fuck it," said a scrawny man. "Leave him be." They stood side by side, the lasso forgotten.

The widow sat and attended to her shredded feet, which didn't hurt too badly and had for the most part stopped bleeding. She turned her head uphill and saw curtains of dust hanging motionless over the landslide. Slowly, a veiled anxiety had begun to grow in her. Familiar. Like hunger. The emergency had begun to dawn on her, and the Reverend was at its heart. She stood up and turned back uphill.

McEchern's store had collapsed. The tent's centre pole had snapped halfway up and the jagged stump jutted sword-like through the heavy white canvas, beneath which the outlines of piles of goods could be discerned. The topography of the establishment was now implied in humps and sags, like sleepers under a blanket. The widow arrived to find the place crowded with miners — in this town filled with men, she had never seen so many at one time. Some had been bandaged with torn shirts and handkerchiefs, and they sat quietly on the store's raised platform. A few were moaning and writhing. All along one side, a number of bodies had been laid out in a row along the planks, each pair of boots in a slack V. The widow approached and leaned half-swooning against a tree, the thrum of birdwings above her, her eyes in unwilling study on these many boots. Toes risen up, a palisade against life, and beyond them, the faces of the dead. Among them was a pair of bare feet, the hooked toes intimately white and still. Farther away, dragged under the canopy of a spreading cedar so that he was almost invisible, lay another man, or what was left of him. One foot and calf was missing entirely, his crushed upper body merely reminiscent of a human shape, the knot of exploded viscera bluish and soupy. A wide smear ran along the planks where he had been dragged, and this alone announced the man's hiding place. The widow gaped, the sight so unreal that her mind could give it no meaning. After a moment, she simply turned and wandered away.

The dwarf was standing with another man, the two of them worrying over a third who seemed desperate to lie down and sleep. Several onlookers stood about, offering suggestions. Stand him up. Lie him down. Give him whisky. Give him salt. The man in question was the Norseman, now entirely red. His face was slashed in a dozen places, his neck and chest were streaming blood, his shirt was torn and deeply punctured, and blood had soaked the waistband of his pants. McEchern and the other man's hands and shirts were scarlet from handling him. Together they sat him upright and shook him to force his attention, and McEchern was plying him with water, which the drooping miner treated like poison. His trembling hand, sticky with blood, kept coming up to push the metal cup away. But when they managed to get the cup to his lips, he drank.

The environs of the store had become an impromptu hospital. Men rushed by with steaming buckets of hot water, with shovels and rope. They moved the injured along on stretchers made of blankets, fallen branches strapped together with rope, blasted sections of walls from fallen houses. Debris lay everywhere and they scavenged through it for what they needed. A crushed pair of boots had laces that could be used as a tourniquet. Wind-blown clothes could keep the injured warm. Among this industry there were dazed men, some of whom wandered anxiously and aimlessly while others simply waited, talking under their breath, or not talking, rolling cigarettes with cold and palsied fingers.

"Where is he?" she said to herself, fretful as a child, scouting among these strangers. At the sound of her voice, McEchern looked up, and his face wowed.

"C'mere, honey," he called as sweetly as if she were a tame bird. His fingers beckoned. "Come on now. I told you not to wander."

The widow remained where she was, her eyes on the fainting red man. Suddenly she was streaming with tears.

"You!" The dwarf thwacked his companion on the shoulder and pointed. "Go get her."

The big man settled the widow on an upturned tin bathtub to inspect her wounds, and there she sat, unable to stop sobbing, the tears running down her face and neck and into the shredded collar of her widow's costume.

"Look at this knot," he said with some admiration. He shuffled from side to side, probing with his thumbs at a massive swelling behind her ear. At some point, blood had flowed lavishly, hidden by her hair, but now it had stanched and coagulated, and where his finger pressed it was sticky and hot and almost numb. The widow suffered these ministrations the way a child suffers a washing. She could see the Norseman had finally been left alone to sleep, lying on the wooden planks with his legs dangling. She saw the swell of his chest, the torn knees of his pants, his legs hanging down in their loose boots, one leg bouncing very slightly with the pulse of his heart, slowly, like a contented man, keeping time with the music in his head.

Vaguely, the widow became aware of a grinding next to her skull. The big man was working something out of the wound. She reached up to touch it and her hand was slapped away. Then a sharp pain, and the man said, "Hello."

His grimy face appeared before her, exultant, holding between thumb and forefinger a small thing the size and shape of a tooth. A shard of granite perhaps. He flicked it away, patted her cheek and said, "You got your bell rung all right." She scowled at him, and probed the wound with her fingers, proprietorially. She felt the renewed warm tickle of blood crawling down her shoulder blade and into the small of her back.

McEchern's condensed shape could been seen searching around under the tent's heavy canvas, roaming from lump to lump, keeping up a consternated and muffled discourse with himself. She listened intently, following his voice as it floated among the other men's voices and shouts and moans, tracking him the way one tracks movement in the underbrush or a

340

chirruping among blowing trees and high wind. There was something in McEchern's voice that calmed her, and she, too, stepped into the vestibule, where suddenly everything seemed very quiet and there was only movement. She was at the verge of consciousness, waiting.

The big man was gone and she was alone. She looked about her for a familiar face, but the men were all camouflaged with dust, with blood, and something else, a distortion common to those in a disaster, a huge-eyed infantility brought on by surprise. On a few of the faces was something approaching exhilaration, gratitude, pride. How glad we are not to be dead. How clever to avoid it.

The poor red Norseman lay like a reveller in one of McEchern's drunken soirees. He was unearthly still. His foot had ceased bobbing. Beneath him, urine dripped between the planks into the shadows under the store.

She remembered it now. The noise so percussive and sharp she had felt it in her chest, like the nearby discharge of a cannon. An impact that came from no particular place, but out of the very air. Still silly from sleep, she had leaped from the bed and was dressing in the dark. Moonlight came through the window and she could see everything with perfect clarity. An unearthly rumbling everywhere, and the floor on which she hopped and struggled into her clothes was shimmying madly. She saw the Reverend groggy on his pallet, propped up on one elbow, his hair in a scruff on his head. His face silvery in the darkness, the glint of his eye. The look on his face was fear — he knew what was happening. He was speaking, but she couldn't hear the words. Something huge and white flashed by on a thunderous trajectory, puncturing the air and blowing her hair about her face, sucking the breath momentarily out of her lungs. The boulder blew past almost unseen, a curious flare amid the roaring dark.

She would never know why she'd run after it, stumbling on the leaping floorboards, the sound of other smaller impacts against the walls of the house behind her, like uneven gunfire, but she'd followed like a dog to the jagged, stove-sized hole near the eaves where the thing had escaped. Here she stood, the Reverend somewhere behind her in the dark, when a shadow cut across the moon and the screaming wall of rock hit the side of the house. The building flattened like a bellows, and blew her out into the night. She remembered the wind and the cold, her body tumbling through space, a body among many, all travelling together.

She was drinking now from a whisky bottle — mid-sip. She held the bottle at eye level, uncertain where it had come from, then lowered it to her knee.

"Have another." McEchern stood before her, his solemn face a foot from her own.

"He's dead," she said, unbelieving.

"I know."

"He didn't move. He didn't get up out of bed."

"No one had time to do anything. It happened too fast. Take a drink."

"But," she sobbed, "look at me!"

The dwarf's eyes left her face and skated aimlessly; indeed, how was it that she was there, alive and intact? He retrieved the bottle and took a swig, held it in his hand and pressed his wrist to his mouth. His face was dusty and washed out, the exhausted eyes small and dull and red-rimmed. Behind him, the hubbub of the makeshift infirmary, men shouting. He gazed at his collapsed establishment, burst like a balloon, the wormed sign pitched up at a woozy angle, the lettering shaded by drifts of dust, now saying only *erns*. Strange that in its collapse the little man's store had never been so popular. Given a moment to think, every man who was still able to walk had come here.

"That pole broke," he said, "and came down one foot from my head. Then the tent came down after it, sort of floating. I know an avalanche when I hear it. I just waited for the rest of it to hit. It never did. See over there, and over there? It came down both sides. Missed the store completely." He shook his head. "You and me got an extra dose of luck."

"How do we know he's dead, Mac?" she said, her voice weak and empty.

"Drop it, Mary," he said.

"But how do we know? Maybe . . . maybe he's all right." She had been plucked from the path of the disaster — why not him? McEchern was silent for a long time, and she waited, unblinking, as a wife awaits explanation from a wayward husband.

"That whole side of the mountain is gone," he said finally. His eyes grew moist and two livid streaks

343

appeared high on his cheeks. "The Rev's gone, too. Under a hundred feet of rock."

He stayed with her a while longer, the two of them sunk into silence, seated side by side on the tin bathtub, the widow in her tatters and bare feet, the dwarf's beard caked with dust and his bowler dirty and flattened on one side. They remained like that until McEchern roused himself to shout at an old fellow working his way under the folds of the tent into the store.

"Get out of there!" he piped, leaping from his seat. "You heard me, get out of there!" The miner only mumbled something and turned back to his struggles. As the dwarf walked forward he extracted from the waistband of his trousers the old Colt revolver and fired it once into the air. A unified jolt of surprise ran through the assembly of men. A few of the injured actually sat up to see what new calamity was coming.

"That's right," McEchern said as the jabbering man backed away from the collapsed door flaps. "No one goes in there but me. You hear that?" His voice was shredding with emotion. "I catch any of you fuckers helping yourselves, I'll make you sorry."

Darkness fell early that night, the sun setting cold and shrunken in the dusty air. The widow moved slowly in the fading light, wandering the face of the slide. Her hands were grimed with blood from nursing the injured and dressing the dead. A cavalcade of horrors paraded before her eyes still. She now knew intimately the colour of exposed bone, the silver sheaths on muscle, the whiff of intestine.

All that day, she had gone barefoot among the barnyard racket of moans and coughs and begging, helping where she could, and there was dried blood on her from a dozen different sources. Those in terror would hold her hand and bless her for her kindness; some of them called her by names that weren't her own.

But before long, one man had sat up and pointed at the widow, shouting, "It's her. She done it!" until someone told him to shut up. And eventually he did shut up, but there was strained silence afterwards, and there followed behind the widow something like a bitter wind, some men actually pondering the issue, the possibility that this bedraggled creature in her torn clothes had somehow brought destruction upon them. Men brought up on God and superstition in equal measure, labouring in dark mines, where no woman had ever stepped, its darkness full of ghosts. And now here she went among them, the living and the dead, in her witch's garb and bare feet, scuffing up pale dust as if it were an infernal smoke billowing from her skirts.

She had ministered to a young man with most of his hair singed off and cuts to his face, washing carefully the jagged wound along his jawline, within which an intact artery throbbed visibly.

"I don't blame you," he had said. "You can't blame something like this on a lady, no matter what she did." The wet rag had trembled in her hand.

She took up a needle and thread and willed her fingers still to sew the boy's wound closed, while he winced and whined like a dog, the skin rolling grossly away from the dull needle, like a worm from a hook, until punctured with an audible pop. This, she thought, is what the embroidery lessons were for.

"The place was unstable," another angry, quivering voice was saying. "What'd ya think all that rockfall was about? Fun and games?"

"I'm not saying it's her fault, just her doing." And all around the widow, in *sotto voce*, there sprang up impromptu debates on issues occult, with the widow as the question to be answered. Where does misfortune come from? What hand brings it? Are the wicked among us? Does disaster find them in the end? *Jonah fled from the Lord and hid among sailors, but He found him and brought to them all a terrible storm.* McEchern stood by Mary's side, his expression sour, and his eyes watchful of the men and full of warning. Pistol at his waist.

Now, walking up the slope of the landslide at dusk, the widow paused. She pressed these images away with the heels of her hands and went on, stumbling uphill. Incredible that mere men, tiny as burrowing ants, could cause such geological transformation. All the miners buried deep in the mine, their graves already dug. The men sleeping in tents, rolled under tons of rock and spread thinly about, no more sacred than a tree or a clump of grass or an entire meadow. And the pointless industry of the living — pulling dead men from the mess, sometimes just to recognize them, only to bury them again under the selfsame rock. There was no sound, not even the tinkle of falling rock any more, no animal sound, no wind. The world was hollow and dead, as closed and ghostly as the mine below. No moon. She simply clambered upward as the light failed, holding a buffalo hide about her shoulders, her breath chuffing, drifting behind her in the damp air. In her mind, she was heading for her buried home.

On her feet she wore a pair of McEchern's boots, another borrowing. At first, he had tried to find boots among the upturned feet of the dead, pulling off first one then another boot to test it against her foot, but they were all too big. Finally, he tried a pair of his own boots. When she had slipped the first one on her foot, she grinned. It fit perfectly. This seemed to her a terrible joke.

"What?" he'd said, but his face said he knew what. The dwarf and the woman, lucky miscreants, outlanders, errors that should not exist but lived on anyway.

She went on following a path more imagination than memory. Though she could not know it, she had been moving laterally across the slope, toward the mine, away from her buried home. Tumbled rock lay in her way alongside shattered trees, their branches torn loose or tufted into bouquets. The silhouettes of old root systems reared up before her like warnings, something brainlike in their clogged, venous gnarls, and dangling there amid the damp earth like Christmas ornaments were pebbles and shards. Soon, all was black, and she stood in weighty silence, uncertain how to go on. So

347

she huddled with her back against some large upright thing, waiting, although she knew not for what.

She remembered the Reverend's face in the moonlight. His mouth had been moving, so she knew he was speaking, but his words had been drowned out by the roar of the approaching avalanche. What had he been saying? She tried to remember the shape of the words. But it was impossible. The floorboards had been bucking under her feet. She remembered the tuft of hair on his head, the way it had looked every morning, and a wave of tenderness pierced her heart. Not her fault, but her doing. If not her, then who? The widow put her face in her hands and wept herself into an exhausted sleep, wrapped in the rough winter hide, her cheek on the cold rock. *Tired, tired, always tired.* Even in sleep, she listened for him somewhere down in the earth.

She dreamed and did not dream. The sound was like a little tin spoon clacking against a table. She felt it in her teeth. The rhythmic tapping was telling her something important, and in her half-sleep, she attended the lesson patiently. A clicking. Then a scrape. The sound of several voices, indistinct but very close. The widow sat bolt upright, letting the buffalo blanket fall, suddenly fearful in the pitch-black.

At first, there was a dim glow somewhere to her left. Like a match had been dropped between the fissures of rock and was guttering there. She heard a few more clicks, and then a small stone rolled away downhill, pushed by a human hand. The hand felt about, clawlike, and dragged a few rocks into the glowing breach. The widow screamed once and then clapped her hand to her mouth. In response came muffled shouts from below. There was a barrage of hammering, and eventually a hole the size of a pie pan opened in the ground, eroding and ever widening as the widow watched in disbelief. The light of several lamps could be seen, now flickering with the unseen struggle below. Then a lone miner emerged onto the surface of the slide, shoulders first and then sitting, like a man hoisting himself through an attic trapdoor, bringing with him a whiff of stale and gassy air. He did not see the widow there, for she sat sprawled in the darkness not moving, so he crawled like a newborn devil a few feet from his infernal fissure and stood upright on unsteady legs. He removed his helmet and put his face upward and took a deep, swooning breath of fresh air. And then he bent at the waist and bellowed, "Fuck me!" collapsing again to his hands and knees. Behind him, coming from the bright hole, could be heard hoots and whistling, the voices of men, raw and weak and full of joy.

CHAPTER
TWENTY-FOUR

The widow sat sewing atop a pile of buffalo hides with her legs crossed and her tongue working at the corner of her mouth in concentration. McEchern's store now had a new central mast made from a fallen Jack pine, with the bark still on it but most of the branches sawn off. The wood was green and flexible, so the pole swayed with the breeze, the canvas flapped and bowed and there was a nautical air to the establishment. Across the widow's lap lay several pieces of deerskin. She had begun to copy the clothing she had seen on Henry's wife, Helen — the simple trousers and overdress. Her skill at sewing being what it was, she was reproducing the garment exactly.

The widow had been a good seamstress, unusually skilled when she concentrated, a fact that had only ever impressed other women. Her father had once called her "manually dexterous," which she had correctly interpreted as a kind of slight. He valued only the mental skills, as men often did. He had no idea what hours of careful work had gone into the very shirt on his back, the sheets he slept on, the tablecloth on which he had his dinner — never mind the complex dresses and frocks on the women around him. Depending on the skill of the dressmaker, it might be an unutterable disaster to spill anything on a dress and stain it. There was no telling whether the garment, expensive as it was, would even survive washing. Fading was certain if you dried it in the sun, rot possible if you didn't. Mary had seen very elderly women move with athletic speed away from an inkwell or soup bowl in the process of spilling. And always, in the background, were the peeved faces and bent backs and ruined hands of the washerwomen. The stench of lye. The solemn and impressive lines of laundry hung in the basement.

Normally, the widow would have sat back and relaxed into her work, the way a woman might do petit point by a fire, with a cup of tea at her elbow. But the deerskin was nothing like cloth. Extraordinarily spongy and elastic, it rolled away from the needle's point in an organic way, and she was obliged to bend over it and fight with the seams. Much like sewing up a man's injured face, only not wet, not squirming in pain.

The widow sighed and cricked her neck. She was not happy, exactly, but content. This was nearly a miracle of the heart. Three days earlier she had returned from a futile search for her home and the Reverend, her pockets empty, not even the little Bible to her name, and she had entered the tent, and lain on this very pile of hides, her eyes dully open. For three days she had neither spoken nor eaten, but lay as if dead. *He is gone, he is gone.* Crumpled and tattered in her ruined clothes, she was like any other cargo in the store,

351

insensible to her surroundings, sunk into the black and miasmic horrors within. Tears streamed from her face into the rank hides. In little sinking moments of abandon, she dozed, dreaming repeatedly of the Ridgerunner, that he was among the dead now too, and that he hated her. The hours and days crawled by in procession, pointless, monstrously slow. From time to time the dwarf would wander by and pat her wrist or perhaps ply her with water.

Only hunger could penetrate the fog. In the end, it was the idea of cinnamon that drew her back. Porridge. She could make some hot porridge and put cinnamon on it . . . if she got up. Twenty years old and she had already reached the border of her heart's endurance twice. When she rose, she felt like another woman, one direly accustomed to loss. With nothing to her name, she had simply let go, let go of everything. The widow rose and clumped around the store, rooting listlessly among the fallen goods and coming up with a cooking pot. She boiled some oatmeal, sprinkled it with sugar and cinnamon, and sat by McEchern's stove and ate it slowly. Then she went about the place looking for scissors, a sewing kit. She flipped through the piles of hides, sorting out ones she could use. And here she had been for a day, bent over her work.

From his perch behind the counter, McEchern held forth on matters of current interest.

"It doesn't matter what you do, they get in anyway."

"I know," she said soothingly.

"Stand here with a Gatling gun, they'll sneak in and take what they want."

"You're right."

"Two barrels, two goddamn barrels, Mary! Gone. We have three bottles of whisky left and that's all. Can you believe that?"

"I can."

"Well, good for you. That's just wonderful."

The thread snapped between the widow's teeth and the dwarf winced to watch the procedure.

"Do you have to do that?"

"Do what?"

He watched her put the thread in her mouth, press the end with her lips to flatten it, and thread the needle. "I know who did it too," he said. "It's those two fat-faced boys. I'll shoot the little bastards when I find them."

"They're long gone, Mac," she said, "along with your barrels."

"And rope. And all the knives. And my other hat!"

"Have a drink to calm your nerves."

"Don't you get cute."

The dwarf thought sadly about the state of things for a moment, then hopped lightly up onto his stool and sat leaning on the cracked display case, his cheeks in his hands, the picture of sullen defeat. "Pricks," he said. "Sons-of-bitches."

In the days following the landslide, nearly all the miners had left town. The CPR had sent a massive rail-clearer that chugged up the valley in a cataclysm of acrid smoke and mournful whistling, a few boxcars in tow. It came ploughing through the flooded river waters, each set of wheels casting off a wake in which

353

infinite numbers of V-shaped wings ran off across the glassy surface. The cowcatcher in front forced a perpetual fountain of brown water before it, in which drowned animals bobbed and rolled. In the wan morning light, the engineer slowed his engine at the curve, slowed almost to a stop, coming on languidly, hesitant to enter the disaster and become part of it, and so the train crawled and chuffed, bawling repeatedly. Men came running downhill in a panic, waving madly, as if they actually sensed this reluctance and were afraid the train might reverse its course and leave them in the valley.

They crowded at the tipple, waving their hats like men on a pier, and a few waded along beside the vicious black metal sides of the boxcars, banging hollowly on the doors, grinning like madmen. The engineer stopped when the first car came level with the tipple, where in better times ore cars were tipped and coal was dumped into open railway cars. That day, bound and shrouded bodies lay on the platform, and ropes lowered them stiffly down into the boxcars, where they were lined up and counted, like cigars in a box. Forty bodies — one-quarter of the number missing. There was silence among the living men who stood around and inside these eerie cars, their minds still boggling at such potent disaster. With no work, no hope of pay, foremen and headmen dead, the counters gone and buried, the survivors had crowded in a mass aboard the idling train, some huddling on the roof, preferring that to the charnel house below. Only a few men, those who looked like they had grown up in the wilderness, remained behind.

A reporter had come to do a story on the slide, but since the men were mostly leaving, he remained on board, interviewing anyone who spoke English, while a photographer hopped about from rock to rock, trying to get a good shot of the now collapsed mountain. The photographer bent over his large camera box, leaned to adjust the jointed tripod legs. He rummaged in his bags for new plates. Of the photos he would take, some were of people standing on the tipple platform, people milling and curious, some unaware of the photographer, others not sure what he was doing or even what purpose his little wooden box might have. McEchern in his bowler hat and the widow in her torn weeds had been there among the crowd. The photographer put fingers to his mouth and whistled. He asked them to stand together, the woman in the middle, please, and slowly the group obeyed. He snapped the photo, satisfied. But on the final print he would later see a blur of movement as the men closest to the woman shifted away, stepped back, turned their heads away from her. In the centre, the widow, clear as a bell.

She bent now and snapped the thread with her teeth, tied a knot with one hand. She held up the new costume, a strange admixture of the parlour and the wilds. Though in outward style the dress was Indian, the widow had added a high collar, a profusion of tiny buttons held by loops of twisted thread, and an attempt at a ruffle across the breast that, in deerskin, lacked

355

refinement. Finally she tossed the garment aside and began tacking together the panels that would make up the pants. She hopped from the pile of buffalo hides and held this object against her, testing the length of the legs, kicking her feet out and marching around the store, holding the waist to her own.

The flaps of McEchern's tent were drawn back and the door went dark. Giovanni had stooped to enter the store. The cat skinner seemed even bigger indoors. His impacted neck bent with difficulty as he tried to avoid goods strung from ropes above. His body gave the impression of being accordioned, and should he ever stand up straight, he would rise into something truly massive.

"Salutare, nano," he growled.

McEchern gagged speechlessly for a moment, then rocketed off his stool.

"The very man himself!" he cried, his legs and arms askuttle as he hurried to the giant's side, gabbling and welcoming like a court jester round the king.

"Dov'è il padre?"

McEchern, thinking he meant something about moonshine, nodded and gesticulated, "If you've got it, I'll take it. By God, you got timing!"

Giovanni solemnly leaned over, hands on his knees, as if to address a child. "Eh, vive il padre?"

The widow froze in her dark corner, for all of a sudden she understood him. "Giovanni."

He turned.

She shook her head.

The giant sagged and his eyes drifted away. He sat his bulk down on a creaking box. He brought a badly burned hand to his face and wiped the whole homely surface of it, as a swimmer does when rising from water. There grew a familiar smell in the closed confines of the tent: burnt whisky, burnt fur, burnt skin. McEchern stepped up and took the massive injured hand in his own and hefted it like a dinner plate. The widow hopped down from her roost. All three inspected the seared and blistered fingers where the creases shone with a clear liquid and the palms were caked with blackened dead skin. Clearly, Giovanni's still had been incinerated and he had tried to save it.

"That must smart," McEchern said.

The giant shrugged.

Twenty minutes later, the widow was stirring a rabbit stew completely devoid of vegetables. They had plenty of meat, but not much else. It was the Cregans who had wandered about collecting fallen animals, dressing them, and salting or smoking the meat. They reasoned that there wasn't much time left for the meat. Another week and nothing would be edible, every carcass rotting, though much of it might still be unmarauded from lack of living scavengers. So stew was the everyday meal. She made masses of it available to anyone who came by.

McEchern applied to the giant's hands his recipe for burns, a grey-green glutinous sludge made from the simmered contents of a glass bottle on one of his shelves, full of what looked like loam — dried and powdered plants. He wrapped the hands finally in boiled rags and tied a medic's knot. He kept up a happy one-sided conversation with Giovanni, who sat pale and silent within his barrel of a body, his head turned sideways to stare unseeing at the floor.

The widow watched them over her cooking. There had been much of this lately. One man tending to another's wounds; sometimes the injured one rising and going to a worse-off fellow. Goodwill flowing downhill.

McEchern hefted the bowl of salve and shoved it at Giovanni's face. The stink of it roused him immediately. "Ma, che puzza!" he said, and the dwarf laughed.

"I learned this from an Indian lady few years back, calls herself He Walks. I always thought that was a funny name for a woman. She comes in here every now and then. Has all kinds of tricks; like she can cure a toothache by blowing on the tooth. Anyway, she showed me how to fix a burn." He rolled up his sleeve to expose his little muscular shoulder.

"See there? Lantern fell on me and got my sleeve. The skin burned before I could get the shirt off. Hurt like the very shit. I thought I was going to die. Wanted to chew my own arm off like an animal. Someone sent her round. Look at this. Where's the scar?" he said. "You can't see it 'cause it's not there."

The giant seemed not to hear. Rousing himself he turned to the widow and said, "Lady? When is ready, this food?"

His companions stood stunned, as if unable to understand him once he actually spoke English.

"Mary," said McEchern eventually, "this man's hungry."

The widow hurried over a bowl, and the giant held it in his lap and bent over it, spooning the hot muck into his mouth with affected good manners, the spoon like children's cutlery in his massive hand. He said nothing more but breathed with his bear's lungs and ate more slowly than anyone the widow had ever seen.

After a few minutes she went back to her corner, backed up against the pile of buffalo hides, hopped up, crossed her legs, and rethreaded the needle. From time to time she looked up at the scene surrounding her. To someone else it might be a sideshow: Her torn costume in almost lascivious tatters; the dwarf wandering aimlessly in his ridiculous bowler, strangely intact for all the devastation around him; the giant slumped and drowsing by an empty bowl, hands bound in strips like a leper, shrouded in his gruesome patchwork coat. The widow felt a surging gladness in her breast. She was suddenly grateful that she was alive, relieved at how simple things were — an ascetic happy with her lot.

Afternoon light fell through the tent's top hole and gilded the wood floor, fell glinting off lanterns and pots and pans. Buoyed by the moonshiner's appearance, McEchern bustled about the place tidying among floating dust and late summer insects. A Cregan, possibly the youngest, came in from outside. He stood at the counter with McEchern, and together they inspected the handle on a lantern he had been repairing.

"I think that's done it," said the dwarf.

"Give me the other one."

McEchern rooted under the counter and dragged another lantern out, this one with no bottom and so no place to keep the oil. The boy went out with it. Outside, the Cregans had erected a kind of forge and were busy repairing or recycling anything that came to hand. All eight had survived the disaster, camped as they had been outside town and half off the mountain, their prodigious familial luck holding. Their own horses had been hobbled for the night, so even when the landslide came, their animals did not run, but hopped and reared and fell harmlessly to the grass. The brothers had leaped up from their bedrolls and staggered about on the bouncing ground in the moonlight, bellowing to one another while their terrorized horses squealed. Finally, the fence had collapsed or was kicked down, and hundreds of dollars galloped off into the night. Of the eleven runaways, three survived. A few were found dead of exhaustion or injury, or floating bloated in the river like obscene rafts.

Now the Cregans were scavenging what could be found among the wreckage, their industry imparting a meagre cheer to the former town. The metallic sound of hammering issued from the yard, and a yelp of annoyance as someone hit his thumb or, perhaps, from the tone of the voice, a brother's thumb. After a while,

Giovanni raised himself slowly from his box and shambled out to help.

"Don't talk much, do they?" said the old doctor.

"Not so far," said his son.

They had been watching the two enormous redheads for ten minutes now, where they sat on the other side of the hotel restaurant. It was a small, pretty town, with a view of the mountains. In fact, the doctor and his son had seen these men several times around the hotel — they were hard to miss. The two brothers were always together, and never had any other companions. They exuded the air of men with nothing to do and nowhere to go. It didn't sit well on them.

The doctor's wife put out a hand and plucked at her son's sleeve. "Darlings, you're staring."

"Sorry, Mum."

The redheads had caused a stir when they came in together, two identical gentlemen filling the doorway. There was a hush from the breakfast crowd, followed by innumerable comments, some of them indiscreet. And yet these men had ignored the hubbub — they seemed immune to the excitement of others, the way one ignores the upheaval of pigeons. The harried waiter had come beetling along through a sea of tables to seat them, only to find himself following, invisible as a dog, as they strode to a table of their choosing.

"Coffee," said one, speaking to the tablecloth.

"Steak and bread," said the other.

Now the brothers just sat there and ate their breakfast without a nod to the waiter or a glance round

361

at the rest of the patrons of the hotel, or even out the window, beyond which stood two beautiful young women, talking and laughing. Of course they could hear the laughter, but it failed to interest them, even enough for one to turn his head. When they'd finished eating, one took up a newspaper, separated out a section for the other, and they both set to reading.

The doctor, too, held a newspaper on the table in front of him, but he'd already read it. And neither he nor his son could tear his eyes away from these strangers.

"It suggests mild gigantism, doesn't it?" he ventured.

"But they look proportionate. No elongation of the face or limbs, no hypertrophy of the bones."

"And then there's the ginger hair," said the old man.

"What? It's not that uncommon."

"Red hair and fair skin, tanned quite deeply in fact, but I can see no freckles. Can you?"

"Dad, it's impossible to see this far away."

"And, now that I think of it, look at the clothes. See the . . ."

"Boys, *really!*" his wife whispered, and they fell silent. The old man shook his paper and straightened in his chair, but he and his son continued to stare.

The doctor could see impeccable manners on men who clearly had spent much of their time outdoors. Fine black boots, manifestly expensive to begin with, now ruined by overuse. A life of privilege, now gone, or perhaps abandoned. Their coats and breeches were tailor-made to accommodate their great size, and yet these men had chosen a design of deliberate simplicity, an aggressive kind of modesty in its lines, achieving in the end only the homeliness common to all oversized clothing. The coats were also worn and needing repair.

"Heavy-footed too. I'd guess they each weigh a lot."

"I disagree, Dad. I think they are almost graceful. Good posture — another proof against gigantism."

The doctor's wife sighed with afflicted patience. And she started to talk brightly. "Well, since we're talking *incessantly* about twins, I knew one once. What was her name? Darby. No . . . Darcy? Maybe Darcy was the other one." The doctor's eyes drifted to his wife's face and stared through it for an interval, then wandered back to the giant men again.

"They disliked each other, isn't that funny? But you know, it struck me as perfectly understandable. Why would you love a copy of yourself? Why does everyone else get to be themselves, but you don't?"

The waiter swanned by and ignored the old doctor's wave.

"Bloody," he sighed and looked sadly at his coffee cup.

He took up his newspaper, passing disinterested eyes over the minute grey print.

"Diphtheria epidemic." "Delays in the postal service — why can't we be more like Britain?" "Worst landslide in mining history — superstitious miners predicted it." He sighed and turned to local news where he saw a promising headline: "Church Group Ran Dog Fighting Club — Popular Parson Bookmaker." He began to read that one.

There was a sharp laugh from the table. One of the men was shifting violently in his chair. The doctor glanced up and saw him holding out his section of the newspaper for his brother to see, folded neatly into four, and he was pointing at a photograph The landslide at Frank. And the widow, the lone woman among the survivors.

CHAPTER
TWENTY-FIVE

The train's whistle echoed as it departed down the valley. The track had been cleared finally, and the first regular train had come and gone. Curious survivors had wandered down to see it. The widow scrubbed the darkened wood along the platform of McEchern's store, a bucket at her side, the vague bawdy smell of old meat rising to her nostrils, legacy of spilt blood.

"Hey, girlie!" shouted a bent old fellow. The widow turned a fatigued face to him, rag in her hand.

"You got company on that train."

"What do you mean?"

The man grinned widely, a gap-toothed smile. "Couple of gents asking about you down there. Could be your lucky day." He chuckled and went on mumbling.

They came up the hill with rifles across their backs, following a newborn trail that went in gentle switchbacks through avalanche debris. Here and there the trunks of fallen trees were cut away, allowing a man to walk without bending or crawling; boulders were dragged aside or levered downhill to clear a path. Otherwise, human traffic acquiesced to the natural flow of the land, now jagged and white, and mostly motionless.

One brother touched the other's shoulder.

"Smoke." They'd been told to look for the trading post, the only place standing, the only place with a stove. And indeed, a thin ribbon of smoke rose into the air. But then they saw another, and two more, rising from the very earth. The whole landscape seemed to be smoking, smouldering. Someone passed them, striding quickly along, a barrel on his back, saying, "That's the coal burning. Come back in twenty years and it'll still be burning." And then he was gone.

So amazed were the brothers at this that they began to wander among the burning culm, gawking at the ghastly place they had come to. Perhaps this was why they didn't react to the first gunshot, but stood looking at where the bullet had pinged off and left a pale chip in the limestone. They heard the second shot, but failed to give it meaning. It seemed like the burning landscape was popping, like some hard-shelled, infernal oatmeal. It wasn't until they looked up and finally saw the widow standing on the deck of a huge, cockeyed tent, struggling to reload a rifle, shells dropping from her shaking fingers, that they understood themselves to be under fire.

Immediately the twins split up, scuttling low and fast as rabbits, eyes white, pawing at their own rifles as they ran. On her perch, the widow slammed the breach closed and drew the stock to her jaw, choosing the leftmost man. She led him — aiming slightly ahead of the rushing, stumbling form — and squeezed down hard and fired. The roar and kick of the gun blinding her for an instant so that when she righted herself she saw only the mad wheeling of his arms as he dove, coattails tossed up arsewise, and then he was gone behind a rock. Cursing, she swung right to sight the other man, but he was gone too. Behind which tree? Which rock? Again she swung left, drifted to centre, her vision wide and unfocused, keyed on motion, on sound, the gun's stock trembling against her cheek.

She'd missed them both. Three shots, all gone wide. The disaster of it was palpable. There was silence but for a voice or two from uphill, miners calling in question, curious at the unaccustomed sound. She stood outside the store, exposed, motionless, while somewhere out there her unseen brothers-in-law were loading up. Horribly, unbidden, the memory came to her of her husband cheering when out of sheer luck she had killed her first guinea fowl: "You hit meat!" Her mind stuttered and went blank; she didn't know what to do.

McEchern, for his part, was crouched behind his counter, covering his head, after having given her the gun and the shells, then hurriedly removing himself from the impending show.

The world was unearthly still. And then the widow turned on her heel and dashed through the tent, dodging goods and the jutting counter, and ran out the rear flap. Without pause, she flew off the platform. Her boots hit the ground together, and she went crashing and leaping through the trees in her peculiar, hobbling gait.

She ran downhill and out into a massive clearing, cutting laterally across the farthest extent of the landslide, her back wincing against the expected gunshot. Then she was back into the thick of the trees, throwing herself in long strides down the draw, grabbing saplings with her free hand and sliding on the loose groundcover, ploughing up huge drifts of pine needles with her boots. Nothing moved but she; no sound but her panting. She didn't dare look behind, but ran, keeping to the lower ground, till she scrambled up a small rise and plunged over the other side.

Her husband's flat voice in her ear, *That's how you find and kill something. Skylight it — wait till it runs over a hill, look for the silhouette.* The slam of a door. The roar of the shotgun, whistling rain of arrows, the sound of laboured breathing. A crack like a cannon in the dark. Nightmare piled upon nightmare. Her breath came in ragged and helpless sobs from her aching chest. She was a brash and racketing thing, alerting her pursuers to her exact position, nearly shouting to them in her terror, and leaving a trail of broken branches and scuffs that anyone but the blind could follow.

She hadn't fully believed it when she'd seen them. And clearly, they couldn't believe what they were seeing. Their faces, white and staring as she sighted down on them, the too familiar eyes, the wide, hard jaws. His jaw, his face, twinned, staring up at her in astonishment, and she, yearning to murder him again. His mouth falling open in surprise. A pink mist floating on the air, its dull taste on her lips, droplets on her hands, chin, forehead. His soundless open mouth as he fell. His mouth, saying, "You can have another," saying, "They come and go, like calves."

She ran hard, tall cedars stuttering past her, pickets in an endless fence, lines everywhere, flying depthless, her boots in syncopated beat along the ground, breath now regular and deep. She came over a shallow rise and immediately tumbled into the draw, falling into a stumbling chaos, the gun held aloft until she hit the thin trickle of water in a splash and thrashed through it, turned and followed the creek downhill like an animal. Boulders along the rill's edge festooned with moss and white flowers. Not so far away, the whisper of a waterfall.

And then she realized she'd reached it, the Indian bridge. The widow stood gasping among the callow greenery while somewhere uphill voices echoed. For a moment, she did not move. Behind her stood the bridge, spidery and delicate. She was frozen, willing herself to drop the rifle, to open her fingers and let it go. In her mind she was assessing the sagging bridge, the slick wet bark that waited for her boots, the loose and half-rotted handropes. The fallen aspens sagged over the gorge, roots exposed. Could it take her weight? Could it bear theirs? She knew she could not make it across with the rifle in her hand.

Then she heard them, their footfalls, sounds of progress through water. She dropped the rifle.

The widow reached the sloped face of the chasm and hopped lamely down to where the nearest aspen cantilevered out over the void. She threw herself onto it in a hurried clip-clop, her hands snatching at the ropes.

369

She was five feet out when the first swinging movement hit her, the organic response to her weight, ripping along the length of it in a tugging, heaving motion. She groaned and forced herself on, goat-footed, hunched, willing her feet to hold the slithering deck, which was no more than a single aspen pole. Ahead of her, it tapered to a point, on the other side the same thing, and between them was an unanchored span of some twenty feet, slung roughly with saplings and rotting rope, badly sagged.

The first rifle shot hit the air. She lurched and fell screaming against one of the hand ropes, slid to her knee. The drop below her was fifty, sixty feet. Mist rose from some unseen source of water, and she hung there suspended over it, gazing into the depthless white. The bridge rocked gently like a hammock. The percussion of the rifle was still in her ears. Her fingers closed round the simple, solid rope. She could hear her heart, hear herself swallow. And him at her heels. Following. No, he was dead and could not follow. He was not there. A strange calm went through her. Up she came in a rush.

"Stop, Mary!" came a voice, almost pleading. The echo of it carried on the hollow air. She did not stop but struggled on, carefully, conscientiously, until she was nearly at the other side. But as she hit the far side and began to run, to scramble up the cliff's crumbling switchbacks, there came a cannonade behind her. Trunks of trees exploded in pale coronas of splinters. Something ripped past her temple and her hair briefly burned. Her pantleg yanked hard where a bullet slapped through. And yet, it would seem, these hunters were as poor marksmen as she herself was, for every one of their shots missed, and she still ran, still alive. And then she was in the trees and invisible to them.

She ran until she could not run any more, nor breathe nor think, and then she ambled along on jouncing, shaking legs, blood clabbering in her veins, willing herself to keep going, until finally her knees gave out, and she knelt with a thump on the ground, empty-headed and desolate. Thirsty, thirsty. A waking dream of bending to a mountain stream, drinking the way a horse does, sucking at the surface, a painful coldness going down.

She didn't know how long she stayed in the clearing, motionless and empty as a nun in patient contemplation. A Cooper's hawk regarded her from its nest. It stood straddle-legged and levered over the edge, a curious onlooker, a low purr in its throat. The widow stared dumbly up at it, seeing the feathered pantaloons and the smooth, ermined chest. Black inquiring eyes. The neck seeming jointless and fluid with each small tilt of the scowling head. She wondered momentarily whether this creature was her watcher, her keeper. But the thought fell in on itself, because the widow knew she had no keeper.

She put her face in her hands and wept dryly while the forest heaved skyward in green and swaying protection.

In profound blackness that night, the widow ventured forth with her arms out before her, proceeding as slow as mist along the ground, her eyes warring with a

371

blindness she could scarcely believe. The world revealing itself in pure sound, the movements of small animals, wind above her in the trees, and something more, some hint in the air that describes topography, a hollowness in the draws and gullies, while up on the ridges sound goes wide. She would stop for minutes at a time and listen. Small chirrups from above. Two cedars creaking together. Here she was again fleeing in the dark, her heart cored out and empty, too tired even to cry. Only now she had nothing. No little grey mare, no coat, no food. No rifle. No William Moreland coming to snatch her away from death. Even the little Bible was gone, lost in the landslide. What could it give her now? Could it light her way? Could it garrotte a rabbit? Alone again, with only the clothes on her body, she stood among the murmurings. In another time she might have wished herself by her father's side, attending to his lectures on science and nature, but that life was also gone. She could no longer recall clearly her father's face.

Close to morning she smelled something rank on the air, an acrid sweetness burned off to its essence and soaking in the dew. She followed it until she reached a scorched line of grass, like a black rivulet along the ground. Just beyond it was another, running along in the same direction, blown by the wind. She followed these till they ran out to nothing, then she turned and followed them back the other way. Small licks of blackness crawled up the trunks of trees, some as high as her knees — scorch marks where fire had been. The

372

smell absurdly strong, peculiar. When she came upon the blackened clearing she suspected where she was. She cast about for some proof and there it was — Giovanni's ruined still. She had stumbled upon the cat skinner's home. No one else had ever seen it.

Nothing moved in the clearing. A raised, V-shaped wooden trough ran downhill and along it gurgled a constant thumb's width of water. She stepped over this and into the clearing. Everything was black or grey. Incinerated grass lay flat along the ground, stiff and colourless. The copper kettle was the size and shape of a fat man's torso. It had been standing within a low stone furnace, enclosed to its widest point and probably boiling mash when the shaking earth caused it to blow off and land twenty feet away with burst welding brads, a bent cap, and its steam pipe pointed skyward. The furnace on which it had stood was made of rock and clay, now scorched and topless, the mortar between the bricks baked to a chalky white. A condenser coil hung from a tree branch, like some enormous Christmas ornament. Here and there a shattered gallon bottle, several metal hoops on the ground among the charred remains of barrels. From the source of the explosion, which was the furnace, fire had spread out downwind in an ellipse. The trees around the still were bare of leaves and their trunks were runnelled with seams of black.

The widow called out, "Giovanni?" then immediately regretted it. Who else might hear her?

Nothing moved. No sound came from the trees.

She spent the morning scrounging among the ruins for useful things. She found very little, for it seemed the cat skinner, despite the chaos of his appearance, was a frugal, tidy man. She discovered a blackened knife with a brass tang where the wood handle had burned away. Several leather gunny sacks cooked hard. Tin cups and plates, a pot, an iron frying pan, neatly stacked and striated with ashes. Here and there he had tacked up small skins to cure on tree trunks. Rabbit, perhaps a marten, all hairless now, and smoked.

She followed the little water trough uphill and after a short climb discovered a small, dry springhouse, a cold box with a metal lid built over a natural spring. It would keep food cool in summer and unfrozen in winter. The widow fished it open and peered inside where it was cool and dank. It was empty but for a can of coffee grounds and a stained bag of flour. Trailing the trough uphill, she paused to palm up a little water to drink. Turning to flick her fingers away she saw something move — a door hung with some kind of blanket that swayed in a breeze. She had found Giovanni's living quarters. She might easily have wandered past it, for it was thickly camouflaged and partially dug into the hill. The fire had not reached here — Giovanni was sensible enough to live at some remove from his still. She approached the strange, half-buried building. It was a towering lean-to with a door made of thick hide and appropriate in size to a giant, and surprisingly spacious inside. The widow ventured in, whispering his name, but the room was empty.

Everything was unearthly silent, and slowly there rose to her nostrils a funk of human odour, profound and intimate and complex. Eventually her eyes adjusted to the dim interior light and she saw the contours of Giovanni's furnishings. Most of the room was bed, a wide, deep platform lavishly strewn with blankets and hides and two strangely homey pillows. All along the wall stood a row of books, every one in Italian, or so she guessed. There was a small fireplace at the back whose chimney must have poked out somewhere uphill, hidden among the trees. Along the mantel he had set out a line of fanged skulls, most of which the widow judged to be cats. A fox and a raccoon among them. A line of waxen grimaces, one of which held a cigarette between its dry jaws. The widow snorted.

She sat on the bed listening intently to the world outside. Not a footstep, not a breath. She remembered a time when she had relied on her little horse to alert her to the presence of other animals. Now she relied on herself. If anyone came, what could she do? She had no defence but to remain still, a rabbit in the underbrush trusting the murmuring instinct of its blood.

She woke with a start. Shot up out of the bed and froze. It was dusk and it was silent. The widow had no recollection of falling asleep, nor of what had woken her. She stood in the strange, capacious hovel, her heart pounding and a familiar nausea rising in her. Hungry. She was hungry. She stepped from the lean-to and made her way slowly to the clearing. The sun had faded to nothing — a pale evening sky in which hung a crescent moon, while here, under the cover of the forest, shadow reigned. It was the time for animals to come out.

In the dusk she made her way back up to the springhouse, where she reached in and collected its contents. The bag of flour smelled vulgar, but it seemed dry, free of bugs. She clumped back down to the empty clearing, went to the furnace, scraped ashes out of its guts, and built a fire in the firebox. It was hard to find wood that hadn't already been burned. Here she sat before the low, glowing firebox, mixing flour and water into a ball of unleavened dough for hardtack bread. With no leavening agent she was obliged to knead relentlessly. On the upper surface of the furnace she had placed the tin cooking pot, now brewing coffee. She sat with the bowl between her enclosing legs and bore down on the dough with both hands, watching the whitish, larval substance roll and squelch under her knuckles.

Abruptly, she leaped up and strode a few paces away before retching dryly over the ferns. Tears in her eyes. She spat, sighed hollowly. A racket of birds came from somewhere far uphill. Then the widow returned to her bowl and blew a few ants away from its rim and went back to work. She was so hungry.

When full night came she was watching the bright, little firebox, lost in meditation, hunched and half-lit, like some infinitely old, primeval creature turning its tired back on the dark.

She remembered a cold hand, once, holding hers — some old church woman taking the miserable child on an outing to give her parents one moment of peace.

376

The woman had led her through the gates of a travelling fair and into an enormous crowd. They had hurried past a cacophony of little booths and tents in the failing light of a fall afternoon, the girl craning to see stuffed animals and wax-faced dollies swimming past. Tripping on her shoes. The cold hand leading her urgently onward, then stopping suddenly to queue outside a large tent. An enormous pot-bellied man with jacket and vest, holding a roll of tickets, looked down at them.

"Little one won't like it," he said. "And she's too young."

"She's twelve."

"She isn't, either. You can leave her here."

"I can't leave her."

He looked down and sniffed, the tickets coming slowly from the roll. "Well, she won't like it."

So in they went, along a dark canvas tunnel hung with posters and placards showing roaring beasts and recoiling women. And then they entered a small room full of benches crammed with people — a scent upon the air, part sawdust and part rot, reminding her of a butcher's shop. There was a barker whose diction was antique, and he strutted the stage, bellowing about the wonders about to be revealed. Finally, out ran a naked man slung with masses of weedy hair, incredible amounts of hair, which obscured even his face and feet, and he roared and shook a bloodied rabbit, trying to terrify the women in the front row, who merely pulled their chins in and fanned themselves. Mary was not afraid at all, for she assumed he was wearing some kind of ridiculous suit and that it was a ruse. So she sat among the crowd and scowled as they did.

Perversions of nature were followed by the wonders of science, the barker holding out his hands, inviting the assembled to imagine a benign future in which every malady has its parallel cure, and even death might be conquered. Her caretaker seized her hand and bent to whisper, "Oh, Mary, wait till you see it!" There came the thin wail of an infant, and the old woman's hand shook hers in pure excitement. Through a door to stage right came a slatternly, middle-aged woman done up like a nurse in aprons and a stiff bonnet, wheeling before her a table, and on the table sat a bizarre glass box festooned with pipes and bellows. Inside lay a squirming baby. The barker hurried behind this woman, helping to lift and drag along an umbilicus of insulated wires. In an instant there was a crush of onlookers around the object. Mary was dragged from her seat to go and see.

A peculiar noise emanated from the box, a mechanical *whup-whup-whup*, and the baby's angry cries were strangely muffled. Mary put her fingers against the glass; it was warm, with a slight accumulation of vapour on the inside. The baby was impossibly small and had a bad colour. The barker's patter diminished, and subsided in theatrical revelation, whispering that this otherworldly glass object, despite its frightful look, was as warm and nurturing as the mother's body, and that the child would die the moment it was taken from its embrace. Quiet fell over the people, and they all gazed down on the infant, and the baby, too, seemed to stop its struggles and open its fists. It appeared to be attending to the movements of crowd, the whispering female voices just beyond the glass. And then, almost abruptly, the moment was over, the barker swooping down on them with gestures to depart, and they were ushered outside, goodbye goodbye, tell your friends, tell your neighbours. The exit door loomed. Then Mary found herself walking alongside the muddy skirts of her keeper. It was already growing dark.

Together, they settled side by side at a little tea tent. The waiter brought them sugary sodas, and the old woman splurged on a cream bun, which they tore into pieces and shared. She dabbed constantly at Mary's face and dress, worrying about bringing her home a mess because someone else would have to deal with it, and what's the point in offering help if you just make more work for people? The gentle hand touching her face, the woman's soft voice, her bare wrists emerging from the frilled black cuffs, so unlike her grandmother's, no jingle of charm bracelets, no scolding. How to prolong this visit? How to stay with this woman? The child looked into her soda, as if she could divine the answer from the drifts of sugar at the bottom of it — the spoon going clockwise or counter-clockwise, the number of stirrings, the left or right hand holding the spoon; everything seemed significant.

A raised voice behind them said, "Well, I think it's a miracle."

379

"Oh, my eye," said another. "They just put a sick baby in a box and call it science. The whole thing was a crock."

Mary had looked up at her babysitter with inquiring eyes and the old woman looked down at her with something of the same curiosity. "I *think* it was real," the old woman said.

"But he was a fake hairy man?"

"That was genuine, I'm afraid. It's a disease of some sort."

But the girl's heart knew otherwise. Deception hung everywhere around them, in the lanterns and painted signs, the music and voices, the antic delight of it all, the dusty, costumed barkers and the wretched touts full of practised charm. Even in this kind old woman. It was all a diversion, an artifice that stood in brief defiance of the real. By the fairground fence, a ring of exhausted Shetlands with dirty manes slept on their feet. Someone had draped their shoulders with bright garlands of paper flowers, and there was a lantern hung from the fence, and a sign she could not read.

This had been her last image of the fair, for soon the old woman took her by the hand and together they hurried along the graded road to home, where a maid met them at the door and Mary was hustled off to bed.

Now, the widow put a weathered hand to her cheek and stared into the fire, seeing again the waiting beasts, and the inscrutable sign, its message forever undeliverable. Try as she might, she could not recall the words. Impossible, too, to lean close to the little girl and whisper warnings or counsel in her ear, to tell her the course of things. But if she could have, what then? What great benefit would come of that magic? Time would pass just as surely, day turn to night. The hand on this cheek might be softer, these trees not here. The Reverend would be unknown to her, and still dead. Her baby boy would not have existed, just as he didn't exist now.

Because the widow was lost in these thoughts, she failed to attend to the sounds coming through the trees. And when she did, it was too late. The darkness was suddenly full of noise and movement, all of it rushing toward her. They had come! They had followed her! She got to her feet, but there was no more running in her, so she simply stood and waited. Not bothering to blink or breathe or get on with her life in any way, bracing herself for the gunshot. It was so black. Where were they? And then one of the twins materialized out of the night and came at her with his rifle raised, moving slowly now, the way a dog stalks a squirrel. Moonlight on his hat, his long upper arms, the long barrel. He was within feet. She could smell him. She could hear his breath coming and going. And then they were together, joined by the rifle's cold muzzle where it touched her above the left eye. Somewhere out in the dark, the other twin was making his slow, stumbling way toward them.

"Go ahead," she said, willing her knees to keep her standing.

But he just looked at her, his eyes shifting leisurely in the firelight.

★　★　★

The Ridgerunner sat primly on a log by the enormous fire holding a fistful of bannock and trying not to make eye contact with the dogs. There were at least eight of them and they circled him the way wolves do, heads low, making small yips to one another. The woman had gone away to gather a few things he might like to trade for, and a moment later these dogs had come out of the dark. The Ridgerunner did not move, but he watched them with his peripheral vision. If worse came to worst he could throw his bread. It wouldn't work on wolves, but maybe it would on dogs.

The woman, Helen, had not been able to give him any information. She'd never heard of Mary Boulton, and she'd not seen another white woman in many months. Maybe years. He had nearly slumped when she'd said it. If not for these dogs, he would have hiked up his packsack, slipped away into the darkness again, and vanished. For what was the point in staying? But now he was pinned down by a pack of stealthy, slat-sided Indian dogs who neither knew him nor trusted him, and they figured he could do without his bannock.

First one dog turned, then they all froze and looked into the dark. The woman was coming back. They darted guiltily around, backing away from her into the long grass, skirmishing with one another as they went.

"There we go," she sighed and placed on the ground a blanket that was wrapped around various objects. She handed him a bowl of stew with a tin spoon in it. Moreland regretted the offer of food, for he had done this with Indians before and he knew it was rude to eat and buy nothing, and he already knew what he would see inside that blanket — mostly ammunition and knives, but possibly needles and gut for repairs, things to eat, things to smoke, hats, shirts. He didn't need or want any of it. He only wanted one thing. And it wasn't here.

"Eat," the woman said kindly, and she watched as he spooned up the stew. It was ridiculously good, fragrant and rich, and after so long in the cold upper world, Moreland was starving. He beamed a grateful smile at Helen, gobbling too fast to thank her. A man came wandering up and sat down close to her. He was tall and kept his hair in two braids, and his face was distinctly unfriendly. After a long interval he said, "What do you want that woman for?"

The Ridgerunner abruptly stopped chewing, for there was something in the way he had said it — he was asking not why Moreland would want a woman, but why anyone would follow *that* woman in particular.

"I already told him we haven't seen her," Helen said gently.

"Why are you looking?" the man said bluntly.

William Moreland swallowed and held the bowl before him. He was pale and reduced, large-eyed in the firelight, and an expression of deep regret passed over his face. Suddenly, he looked as if he were about to weep. Henry glanced at his wife in alarm, and she put a surreptitious hand on his arm.

"Are you her husband?" Helen asked.

"No. I just . . . I need to see her. Because I owe her an apology."

This statement confounded Henry. But Helen gazed at her guest in quiet contemplation for a long moment.

"William is your name?" she asked.

The Ridgerunner nodded.

"Well, William, perhaps you will take a look at these things I have brought out for you. Some of them are quite good. And then, once we're done, I'll tell you where Mary has gone."

CHAPTER
TWENTY-SIX

Dawn found the widow on horseback, reversed in the saddle, her wrists tied together behind her with ropes knotted round the saddle horn. Misery infused every part of her body, and she could not tell any more what was mere injury and what was the anguish of her mind. They did not speak to her, for she was nothing to them but an unfinished task, and they were much like John, they had his aloofness. It was with some incredulity that she realized their horses had been purchased from the Cregans. She herself was mounted backward on Sean Cregan's clever little mare. This fact wounded her more than she could admit, but she told herself she should not be surprised, for the eight boys were thieves and businessmen.

At first, the twins had split up, one leading the way, the other riding behind, guarding her. In this way, she was face to face with one of them. Jude or Julian, she didn't know which — so similar to John it was unnerving to look at him. His face was bloodless, ashen, his massive shoulders hunched over the saddle, and he glowered at her. All she remembered about these two was her husband's directions to her before they had arrived at the cabin for one of their few visits.

"Don't contradict Julian," he said. "He doesn't take it."
A simple statement, but in the shorthand of that family
a potent warning.

They rode down a winding path through the cedars
where there was no underbrush and the ground was
light as cured hide, smooth and carpeted with leaves. As
they went, the widow shifted on her mount as if to
adjust her seat to a more comfortable position, but she
was working at the ropes behind her.

"Cut it out," he said. She heard something in his
voice, some hint of pain or inner gloom. She looked
closely at him, saw the coat flap bow open with each
hooffall, revealing the fine shirt inside, on which had
spread a dark stain. The same shadow crept the edges
of his long coat, where blood had soaked the lining and
now mackled the outer cloth. He saw her looking,
pulled the coat closed. She knew then which one he
was — Jude, the lesser twin, for he bore his injury as
patiently as a dog.

"Does it hurt?"

"You shut your mouth."

A wrathful flush to her cheeks. Not a wink, not a
shift of her gaze, for she was no longer afraid. Instead, a
fury had come over her. She could not take her eyes off
him, and in her mind she was leading him again — the
quarry rushing low and awkward, following the rifle
barrel, running toward that moment. Perhaps he sensed
her thoughts, because he blurted out, "All this, all of
this hell, is because of you. Are you proud of what you
did?" He had spoken only to galvanize himself against
her stare. She realized there was something about her

that he had not expected, or had forgotten, and it was draining the purpose from him.

"No," she said. "I'm not proud of what I did."

"But you're not sorry, are you? Do you feel any regret at all?"

"A little."

"You are an abomination," he said.

"And what are you?" she spat. "*Half* a man!"

His expression froze and, bit by bit, he sank away from her. Half a man, and fading. He simply drew his coat closer, as if she had never said a word. After a few miles he chucked his horse forward and joined his brother at the front, leaving the widow to her thoughts.

She swayed with the converse gait of the horse, watching with dull eyes as her home drifted away. Well, after all, what home did she have now that Bonny was gone? Now the town was gone? There was nothing left. Like the Ridgerunner, she had been hobbled by misfortune and finally caught.

The trees thinned out as the mountains withered and lost character and became merely blue. When she craned around, she could see the beginnings of fields, sloped and undulating areas of cultivation marked out in shades of white or yellow, cut by incursions of leafy trees. Farmland. She spied houses, smoke rising. The air was warm and muggy, and she began to sweat in her hide clothes.

They passed through a grove of massive poplars with wind-bent trunks. She looked up. Every leaf was moving furiously, a sourceless churning, and the sound was like applause. The horses stepped along, Queen Anne's lace reaching to their bellies. Their trail was visible through the long grasses, and it streamed back to where she had been. This is the progress of life, she thought sadly, seeing only what has been and is now gone, dragged away from our beginning, a child riding the resolute shoulder toward bed.

"You're here for three days," the man said. "Just till the judge comes, and then you and them two are off out of here." He stood in the hallway just beyond the door, which was made of metal bars.

"What is this place called?" the widow asked.

"This? Nothing. This is the old bank. We got a new one now, made of brick. Just up the street there."

"No, I mean the town."

"Oh. You're in Willow Cane." He stared at her through the bars a moment while rain steamed on the barred sill behind her. She could smell it, the scent of hot dust and water. A stale but living smell.

"Did you do it?" he asked. His tone was so casual the widow didn't at first know what he meant. And then she did. It hadn't occurred to her that anyone might ask that question, her guilt being so patent it must be part of the air she breathed. And yet here he was, asking, and he seemed truly curious.

"Yes," she said, "I did it."

"I wouldn't have guessed it, you being a girl. What'd you do it with?"

"His rifle."

"Not so? The man's own rifle." He took off his hat and held it before him as if in the presence of someone above him.

"Where'd ya shoot him? In the head?"

Despite herself, the widow winced. "No."

"Where then? Not in the back?"

"Do you really need to know?"

"Not so much. I'm just . . . well, I'm curious."

The widow sat down on her pallet with a sigh. "In the leg." She put a hand across her thigh like a cleaver. The man pondered that for a while, spinning his hat in his hands like a little wheel, churning through the conundrum.

"How long'd that take?" he said. It was like he was asking how long it took to get to the next town. "Must've taken a while, just bleeding like that."

"No," she said. "Not long at all."

"Was he bad to you?"

The man's inquisitive face, bland and waiting beyond the bars, was like a sign held up before her, full of wordless meaning and promising retribution. A feeling like panic rose in her throat and her head began to pound, a painful surfeit of blood pumping there. No more answers for the merely curious. For they would provide her with nothing, and there was no escape. She sat mute upon her bed.

"Well," the man said to himself, pensive, "I never saw a murderess before." A thin rumble of thunder passed somewhere far away. Rain hissed. "You don't look like one," he offered and walked away. Almost immediately

389

he was back, looking through the bars again. When he spoke, his voice was friendly.

"If you know what's good for you," he said, "you won't tell them what you told me. Just keep saying you didn't do it."

The rain continued through the afternoon, hissing through the trees and pooling in the grass. Mary sat on her bunk and ran her hands down her thighs over the soft deerskin, her fretful fingers checking and rechecking the seams unconsciously. Despite the heaviness of the air, she began to smell cooking, a chicken roasting. She had nothing to do. She was not expected to cook or do laundry, she did not have to chop wood or stoke the stove or sweep or hunt or try to stay warm or plan in the least degree for anything. In her head a little chime kept going off — *do something, do something*. But her survival was out of her own hands now. She was expected only to wait. Little surges of dread rose and subsided within her, and she attended to these waves and endured them.

She sighed and stood up. There were shutters on the window that looked like they had never been used. Their hinges had rusted open. If she pressed her face to the bars, she could see a sliver of the street. Once in a while someone would hurry by, a hunched blur, and then they were gone.

Over the next hour the rain stopped. It grew dark and the lights went on in houses nearby so the canopy of the trees lit up. There came the voices of children. Dinner was over. A hammering sound echoed from somewhere across the street, metal on metal. She stood by her window and breathed the wet air in deeply, felt on her face the breeze that came and went as it wished, right through the bars. Little spatters from the trees blew in over her bed and into her face. She pictured the Ridgerunner, decades ago, pacing his cell, maddened by confinement, while the barred door stood open to him. Why had this man, so adept at escape, not fled the courthouse jail? He did not belong to this world, he never would. Why had he tolerated the grinding process of the law? Curiosity was the only answer — William Moreland, a hermit of grand proportion, who could not stand the trappings of civilization, the fences and roads and rules, was curious about people. It was one thing she did not share with him.

She looked about at her own cell. A heavy metal door with bars, a well-framed oak door jamb, and a brass lock. Several pale circumscriptions on the walls suggested long-resident furniture, now departed — so it had perhaps been an office or even a counting room, unwisely equipped with a window. She put a hand round one of the bars and shook it experimentally. A dry grinding issued from the mortar, and dust filtered down along the wall's uneven plaster.

There was a noise behind her and she turned, startled. A young woman stood in the outside hall beyond the barred door, a tray in her hands. The man from earlier was somewhere down the hall, noisily going through drawers. The girl seemed uncomfortable with the waiting. After a long moment, the man

391

appeared at the door and worked the lock open, and the girl took one step inside the cell and halted.

"Go on," he said, "she's not going to eat *you*."

The girl blushed deeply and forced herself forward to the spindly chair by the wall where she set the tray down. The food on the tray smelled familiar, and the widow reasoned that its cook must live nearby. Then the girl hurried from the room, turning the corner so sharply she caught her sleeve on the doorframe.

The man stood with a bemused look on his face and watched the girl as she left the building. Rolling his eyes at the widow, he stepped back and locked the door again. "Just like a squirrel," he said, "scared of everything." He went jingling down the hall.

The widow heard a drawer rasp open somewhere, followed by the hollow sound of keys being dropped and hitting wood. An empty drawer. She listened intently, her eyes going unfocused. A few footsteps. A thump. Then silence for a long time. Had he left and gone home too? Was the building empty, then, utterly functionless except to house her? She called out, but no one called back to her. Some airborne sweetness drifted in through the bars behind her, some late summer tree in bloom, erupting with the recent rain. A sweetness that mixed with the scent of the cooling chicken on her tray and leant the little cell an air of putrefaction.

She went over to the chair and looked down at the food. A glass of milk. She took it up and drank slowly, unable to remember the last time she had tasted milk. Carrots and yam and roast chicken, presented prettily on a bone china plate decorated with a cramped pattern of tiny gold and green roses. Someone had decanted a little gravy into what looked like a tea creamer and set it beside the plate. A bowl with angel food cake stained deeply by ripe blueberries. The widow's expression was that of a woman about to descend into a dank basement — part dread, part determination. She longed to eat but worried the food might not stay down. She bent to see under the cot, where there was a small bedpan. She fetched it out with the toe of her boot, just in case, and then she sat down and placed the tray over her knees, and took up the knife and fork.

The old doctor stopped rooting in the bullet hole, removed the bloodied forceps, and peered closely at the wound. His face was inches from the patient's chest so that his breath blew across the ginger hair. Jude sat up, panting on the table while his brother held his naked shoulders to steady him. His entire chest was black and blue. A dark puncture near the collarbone.

"Huh," the doctor grunted.

"What?" Julian's anxious face appeared over his brother's shoulder. "What's wrong?"

"Don't know." He slid the forceps gently back into the trickling wound and began scrounging again while Jude held his breath. There was a barely audible sound of metal on metal. And then the doctor withdrew a tiny shard of the bullet, no bigger than a lost tooth filling and just as shapeless. Jude put his hand out and the doctor dropped the shard into it. All three men looked at it.

"I was afraid of that," said the doctor. "Lots of little pieces in there. Doubt I can get them all."

Someone came into the outer room and called, "Dad?"

"Here!" he bellowed. Then he rose from his seat and strode to the cabinet to get some sterile pads, holding the probe behind his back while he searched. A young man peered around the door frame — he looked at the brothers and did a doubletake. Quickly he withdrew again.

The metal stool spun slowly from the force of the doctor's departure. The brothers remained where they were, one holding the other up.

Julian's voice came quietly. "How do you feel?"

Jude shook his head. "Only half dead."

CHAPTER
TWENTY-SEVEN

In the dying moments of twilight, when the widow's cell was dark and the outside sky presented itself as pink and misty and cut by bars, there came over the muggy air the sound of bats, their voices dry metallic clicks, like someone trying to wind a rusty clock. The widow lay on her back on the bunk. Her fingers played with the grit that clung to the blanket, rock dust that had sprinkled down from her vain attempts to shake the window bars out. She could not stop considering the objects in her room as some kind of disassembled key to her escape: a chair, a cot, a dinner tray, a bedpan. She went over them all in her mind, unable to stop searching for a solution she knew was not there. A dog barked disinterestedly from inside some echoing place, a barn or shed, answered by other dogs in the dusk.

She sat up, took the tray from the floor, and set it on her lap again, trying to get a little more food in. She had eaten the angel food cake slowly. It was dry and fragrant and weightless. Now she began to work on the white slabs of chicken meat, dipping each slice in gravy. Pausing before putting it in her mouth. It tasted wonderful, and slowly the nausea subsided. Perhaps the sickness had to do with lack of food rather than the food itself.

She began to hear things. A woman's voice. A thump.

Down the hallway came candlelight, trembling, growing in intensity. There were two voices. Then came the sound of a drawer being opened, a few words of argument between a woman and a man. The keys came out, and the light came up the hall toward her cell. The man was at the door again. He unlocked it and went away again, leaving a woman. She was slim and grey-haired and fit, holding a candle. She waited for a moment by the door, seeing the widow still at work on her dinner, and then she went and sat by the wall on the little chair. Prim as a schoolmistress, a woman of long hands and face, wasp-waisted.

"Is the food not good?"

The widow had heard that tone in her own voice, the undercurrent of bafflement that after such efforts in cooking the dinner was not appreciated. She nodded vigorously, still chewing.

"It'd be cold by now," the woman said, dubiously.

"No, it's very good. Did you cook it yourself?"

"Yes."

"Then you live near here?"

The woman was silent for a moment, wondering, her grey eyes twinkling in the poor light. Then she laughed.

"You could smell it cooking! Of course."

The widow picked delicately at the scraps on the plate, caught up the last of the yam with her fork, put the bowl down and the tray to one side and checked her mouth for crumbs, and sighed with contentment, despite her watcher.

The woman leaned out the open cell door and bellowed, "Allan, will you please come and get the tray?" There was a muffled curse, and the man came down the hall. He took up the tray and was about to collect the candle, but the woman said, "No, leave that."

"Does her majesty want anything else?" he said.

She gave him a withering look, and he left again, trudging carefully down the darkened hallway, the tray jingling slightly, like dull bells. When he was gone, the woman leaned forward and whispered, "You know they're out there, don't you? Both of them."

The widow didn't have to ask who she meant. "Where outside?"

"Right on the stoop, sitting on chairs. *With* their guns, if you can believe it. It'd be funny if it weren't so weird. They give me the screaming crawls, those two." The woman looked quickly over her shoulder as if the twins might have impossibly good hearing and could take offence at her words. The widow smiled.

"Are they your brothers?"

"In law."

"Brothers-in-*law*," the woman said as if that made all the difference in the world, as if it explained away some niggling worry that had been afflicting her. She seemed much buoyed by the news, happier to be in her present company.

397

"Are you warm enough, my dear? Would you like another blanket? My husband has a few sweaters that might fit over that . . . outfit of yours."

"I'm fine, thank you."

"Can I bring you a little milk for overnight?"

"Don't bother yourself," the widow said.

The woman sighed and put her hands on her thighs as if to get up, but she was debating something silently. In this posture, hesitant and tense, on the verge of speaking, the widow could see that she was in fact the mother of the girl who had run out earlier. Here were the same long cheeks, the same hooded eyes, only more deeply carved. Eventually, the woman stood up. Whatever thoughts might have been at work in her head, they had been pushed aside. "I'm sorry," she said, taking up the candle. "I can't leave this for you. They say you might burn the place down. I don't think so, but no one listens to me."

She called for the man. After a long interval he arrived, and together they locked the door and he shook it to test the lock, and they went away with the candle so the light faded and then there was only darkness. The sounds of the arguing voices and the drawer and the keys repeated themselves in reverse order. She waited for the thump, and after a moment, there it was. The widow lay curled on her bed, listening to the sounds that came in through the barred window, attending to every animal call, every gust of wind through the branches, every distant voice. She listened for the voices, but knew that she would not hear them.

The widow put her hands over her face and began to laugh, quietly and deeply, a laugh that verged on tears, and when she was done, her hands remained there, keeping the dark out, keeping a small, delicate light in.

The couple came again after dawn, bearing a breakfast tray, heralded by marital peevishness as they rambled down the hall arguing. They found the widow standing by her bed in her outlandish savage costume, the bed made perfectly as if awaiting inspection. It was the only house chore available to her. The couple bustled in like two wrangling dogs, nudging and contentious, worrying the tray and the widow and each other until the wife bluntly told the husband to get out, and he did. He retreated down the hall, grumping under his breath.

"My land," the woman said tartly, sitting herself down with a defiant thump on the little chair. He had lost, she had won, and now she had taken residence. Because of this, the widow intuited that her presence offered something of a spectacle in the town. How could it not? A murderess, dressed to all appearances as an Indian, arriving restrained with ropes and sitting backward on her saddle, the horses strolling through a gauntlet of staring faces, some men following along on the sidewalk under the awnings to get a longer look, children running up through the mud to touch her horse or speak to her until shrilled back by their mothers. And now the two redheads sitting in bizarre vigil at the door of this abandoned bank, their rifles still across their backs. She was a curiosity, certainly, and this woman was likely being pecked to death with

399

questions about her. During the night the widow had heard whispering at the window above her bed, the sound of young men's voices, one saying, "I don't see her," another saying, "Here, get out of the way." She had lain perfectly still, expecting a gunshot, or, if she was lucky, merely something vile dropped through the bars onto her where she lay curled on the bed. But nothing came and after a while she knew they had gone away. Her heart was frozen in her chest. They had called her name: "Mary Boulton."

"Have your breakfast, dear. You must be starved."

The woman's voice was gentle. The widow sat down on the cot and carefully transferred the tray to her knees, contemplating the food on it. Eggs on two thick slices of seared ham, a cool slice of buttered toast, a glass of milk, tea. She took up the knife and fork and delicately sliced a wedge of ham, poked it into the steaming dome of the egg, bursting it, and drew the dripping result to her mouth. Every fibre in her body was grateful.

The woman watched this procedure with uncommon attention. After a moment she realized she was staring rudely, so she extracted a little wad of lace and a crochet hook from her pocket and set upon it with pinched efficiency. She put the unravelling ball of thread in the lap of her dress and held it there expertly as it jerked and hopped. Then, as if in the presence of an intimate, she held forth. "They're out there again, those two, sitting like stone lions at a gate. You couldn't get a smile out of either one of them if you paid him. It's absolutely ridiculous. As if a girl like you could possibly get out of here on your own. You'll be as perplexed as I was when I tell you they were here till ten o'clock before they finally went off to the hotel — ten o'clock! Allan thinks they're the best thing he's ever seen. He can hardly sleep for it. Neither can I, frankly. I've never understood what motivates a man. It's a pure mystery to me. The older I get, the less I know about them. They seem simple enough when they're little boys, don't they? There's no difficulty in seeing what ails them, it's written on their faces. I just don't know what happens to them when they grow up."

The widow had known many women who did this kind of thing, nattering energetically over their work, although the usual subject was the shortcomings of other women. Her grandmother used to call it gassing. Sometimes it was a way to burn off excess energy, to exhaust a lingering anger by talking it out. Sometimes it was a way for an overworked woman to stay awake when her leisure time had finally come. One simply talked, the way those who stand in the cold will step from foot to foot. No response was required. A drowsing husband, a cat or a dog, even a playing baby would do as a confidante. But in this case, the widow could see that something more urgent was at work. This woman was talking her way around some larger worry. The crochet hook stabbed anxiously at the little patch of potato-coloured lace, moving too quickly. The widow noticed that the woman was often obliged to stop and pull out sections and redo them. "What day of the week is it?" she asked.

"Tuesday the eighth. Already Tuesday. You have two days before the train comes."

The woman did not look up when she said this, but her long cheeks were flushed. The ball of cotton skittered about the skirt, caught between the twin abutments of her equine legs.

The widow sat on her cot beside her now empty breakfast tray, waiting to see what was coming, working a finger into the little bullet hole in her pant leg. The edges of the hole were hardened, burnt to a crust by the heat of the bullet. Her finger touched the warm skin of her leg. She remembered the bullet whizzing past her cheek, the smell of her hair burning. John's brothers had come so close to killing her — and she to killing them. Perhaps now they were even, a balance struck between two failures.

No murder but the first one. The bang. A mist on the air. Blood pumping from the meat of his leg, a viscous puddle spreading like honey. The widow yanked her finger out of the hole in her pantleg. She shook herself.

Her companion was watching her thoughtfully, the lacework forgotten, the little blunt hook rolling slowly between her fingers.

"How do you feel?" the woman said. It was not a casual question.

The widow's heart leaped and she wondered if she had spoken out loud.

"Are you feeling very sick?"

"Sick?"

The woman inclined her head toward the bedpan that stood at the far end of the bed, into which the widow had retched that morning. There was nowhere to hide anything in this barren room.

"How far along are you?" the woman said bluntly.

There was silence for a moment. The widow sighed. Some women can tell, almost as if they can smell it on you, see it floating about your body like a cloud of fireflies. "Far enough," she said.

Of course, she had suspected for some time that she was pregnant. Suspected but not been sure. She had recognized the feeling: the sore and laden breasts, the bottomless fatigue, a welcome serenity invading her worried mind. A glimmer forming in her heart; how grateful she would be to know it was true. This woman, with one breath, had brought it out of the dream and into the real.

"Oh, my dear," her companion said, suddenly overcome with emotion, "what are you going to *do?*"

The Judge's dog clambered up the steps of the Willow Cane Hotel and trotted straight through the open doors into the lobby like a paying guest. He did a tour of the armchairs and chesterfields, then made for the manager's office, which was already full of people.

"He's here!" shouted the desk clerk.

The widow was sitting up front, next to the manager's desk, with her wrists tied to the chair's arm and her twin keepers behind her. The dog walked amiably among the crowd, scenting each pantleg, tail wagging in basic goodwill. A hand or two reached out to thump him on the back.

Then the judge arrived. He trudged slowly up the steps, his nose in a handkerchief, leather case under his arm, a short, bespectacled man in rumpled jacket and a homely knitted scarf. He, too, headed for the office, then turned on impulse and made for the front desk.

"Tea, please. Very hot, and nothing in it."

"Yes, sir."

When he entered the small room, many people were already standing. The others, the widow included, took the cue and rose as well. He settled himself gingerly behind the manager's desk, put the case on the floor, and said, "Come." The crowd fluttered a little in response, but it was the dog he was calling, and it came wagging to him, circled a few times, then lay down with a groan. There was silence as the judge sniffled. He regarded them all with a rheumy gaze — and one artificial eye. Its colour was a poor match for the other one, and it seemed to roam of its own accord, to roll and wander.

"All right, sit down," he said. "Court is in session." There was a shuffling and scraping of chairs. He looked at the papers on the desk for a long time, reading a page, then holding it to his chest while he read the next. He hung over one page for a long moment, then he looked up at the widow, and his gaze drifted to the ropes around her wrists, then to the two big men behind her — one of whom was distinctly green in the face. He went back to his papers, read a little more, then laid them in a rough pile and put his elbows on them.

404

"My name is Justice Ulrich. I am what's called a circuit court judge, which means I go from town to town hearing cases. This is not a trial today. We have an arraignment on a charge of murder. What else do we have, Allan?"

Allan had been too busy watching the twins and was caught off guard. He made a floundering motion before bolting out of his seat, while his peeved wife shifted her chair away from him, out of harm's way. "They . . . they're not here yet, Your Honour. We got a man and a woman having a cat-fight over a fence that runs between their houses. Neither of 'em will back down. Woman says she wants to sue him for trespassing, and neglect, and whatever else she can think up. The problem being, they used to be married."

"Dispute over a fence?"

"Yes, sir."

"I see. Let's say we'll deal with the murder today, and I'll come back next week to hear all about the fence. How does that sound?" His eye wandered toward the ceiling, and the audience watched it go.

"Good, good!" Allan said, then sat again, wringing his hands.

The judge's tea arrived on a silver tray, and there followed a long interval during which everybody watched him slurp at his cup and blow his nose. The widow regarded this man with undisguised despair.

"Mrs. Boulton," he said finally, "do you understand that you are being charged with murder?"

She nodded slightly.

"Did you kill your husband?" He waited for a long moment, taking in the closed and hopeless face before him, then went on. "In the absence of an answer, I must enter your plea as not guilty. Just let me write this out . . ." He bent over a page and wrote in a quick, graceful hand. Without looking up, he said, "Everyone will leave the room now, except Mrs. Boulton." There followed a short, confused pause, followed by a creaking of the floorboards as the crowd exited the room. The dog lifted its head only briefly before dropping it again and closing his eyes.

"Everyone, please," said the judge. The twins, who had not moved, rose with reluctance and went to stand in the lobby just outside the door. The widow could hear murmuring behind her and the scratch of the judge's pen on the paper. When he was done, he set the pen down and leaned over the table and addressed the widow in a low voice.

"Someone has been very helpful and written me an anonymous note saying that you are pregnant." He put his index finger on one of many crumpled papers on the desk. "If this is true, it could be in your favour. However, let me be honest with you. A conviction on murder carries an automatic penalty of death by hanging, and from what I can see of your case, those two men will have no trouble getting a conviction. Not least because you confessed to Allan. A jury may look kindly on an expectant mother. Or not. It's impossible to tell." Here he leaned closer to the desktop and lowered his voice even further so that the widow was obliged to lean toward him, and they sat together in the empty room like conspirators.

"There is a possibility," he said, "that they will wait until you have given birth before they execute you."

The widow's head began to swim. "No," she said weakly.

"The child will most likely be taken from you immediately and given to your brothers-in-law, since they are its next of kin. You may never lay eyes on it."

At that, the room began to pulse. She looked into the judge's bizarre face, his eye almost properly focused on her, and let out a short gasp, a single syllable of anguish.

"I'm sorry," he said and sat back, gesturing for the crowd to come back into the room.

That afternoon there drifted through the bars of the widow's cell a faint taste of dust on the air, and she could hear many voices in the street and the sound of wagons. The voices came and went, and there would be long periods of silence before she heard another voice, or the snort of horses and jingle of their traces, or children laughing and being shushed. The widow sat on her bed or paced her cell, her face vacant, her eyes constantly welling. Minutes would go by and she had not a thought in her head, as if all thought had been forced out by the one black, ghastly fact. Only it resided, only it mattered. *You may never lay eyes on it.*

The day was warm and dry and clear, sun falling through the trees overhead and moving on the grass in lavish, bright scraps. When she pressed her face to the bars she could see milling groups of people in the street. Women carried shopping baskets, their shapes passing vaguely in the shimmering day. Some voices seemed to leap out, sharp and urgent, the words clear as if they were spoken to the widow herself: "Never had that happen, did you?" and another voice as if answering, but it could not be answering: "Fourteen dollars!" She listened for anything that made sense, but none of it did. The widow sat back on her cot. After a moment she heard music on the air. There was a band somewhere in town.

Over the next few hours, the voices grew less frequent, and the sense of people on the road faded, and she now heard no horses, no children, and then it was quiet and solitary and there came only wisps of music, as if the town itself was slowly spinning away into space, whatever festivity might be at hand gradually unravelling and floating away on the wind. Mary lay on her bed as if almost asleep, but her heart was pounding and her hands cold and numb with panic. *They are its next of kin.*

She clawed her way out of the bed and went to the heavy, barred inner door, put a hand round one of the bars, and gave it a slight push. Nothing. So she seized it in both hands and gave it a terrific shake. It was so solidly made it did not rattle or grind or make the slightest sound. She could smell new oil in the brass lock. She put her face against the bars and looked down the inner hallway, but it was dark and seemed endless and she could sense nothing beyond it.

408

★ ★ ★

The Ridgerunner came along the uneven crest of the rockfall in the moonlight, thumbs in the shoulder straps of his pack, picking his way carefully over the stones. He stopped to gauge his direction. What he stood on amounted to a natural dam created by the recent landslide. On his right was a new lake, glassy and reflecting the night clouds in flat and eerie greys. To his left was an expanse of ragged boulders and rocks, a packed mass through which ran streams and trickles and even jets of water, forcing their way through the loose rock. Some distance away he could see the original riverbed that stood low and empty now, wide and slick and strewn with debris, and down its middle ran a scrawny stream, lifeless and foul-smelling. William Moreland went on scrambling over the boulders as surefooted as a mountain goat and his shadow went with him, plunging in the crevices.

Soon he gained the far side, where he turned and followed the shoreline until he came upon the railway tipple that jutted into the water like a dock. Somewhere beneath the staring surface of this endless water lay metal tracks, and the Ridgerunner searched for them, even knelt at the edge to peer down into the dark water, but all that shone back at him were the huge silver sky and the clouds in motion. He rocked his head to find his own reflection, but could only discern a dark silhouette of mountain, weird and vacant, and behind that the shimmer of moon and cloud. It was as if this lake held another more sober world within it, and he could not find himself in it. The silence of the place was beyond even his considerable experience. He could almost hear his own heart. It struck him suddenly, ridiculously, that this place would not acknowledge him, even in reflection. The human world erased in one brutal swipe.

A profound sense of unease invaded the Ridgerunner. He turned and gazed up at the collapsed and now unrecognizable mountain face, tracking the devastation of the slide in the moonlight. Finally his excellent eyes picked out a few small lights uphill, each one a tiny glimmer, perhaps nothing more than a lantern. People, alive. And maybe Mary. He hiked his rucksack up and went on uphill, bent and cautious, a shadow among other shadows.

Several revellers sat in chairs on the platform of McEchern's store, the dwarf among them, cups of booze held hovering, staring apprehensively into the dark. They had been carrying on as usual but had fallen silent as something nimble and quiet approached through the mist and broken trees, over the uneven ground, hopping and trotting along. The men leaned out of their chairs, or slipped from the trading post's wooden platform to step a little out into the dark to listen — some almost eager, as if they awaited a friend. Spending time among the recently dead had made them thoughtful about what the dark might hold.

Finally, Moreland walked out of the trees, looking in the moonlight like some terrible, hunchbacked revenant. And indeed he was much like a ghost, carrying the burden of his existence upon his shoulders, drawn by curiosity to the hearths of men.

The dwarf sat back with a thump in his chair. "Shitfire, you scared me," he said, a hand pressed to his chest in relief.

Moreland was grinning now to see the effect he had produced, and he dropped the pack to the ground.

"Gentlemen," he said, "I'm looking for a girl."

CHAPTER
TWENTY-EIGHT

It was Mary's final night, past midnight. The train was due in the early morning. She looked closely at her bleeding hands, held them palm upward to the window, where the blood looked black in the moonlight. On the bunk beside her was a silver dinner knife, filched from her tray and not missed by the woman who had brought her food. The knife, too, was bloodstained from the widow's frantic digging and chipping at the mortar around the window. She held her fists closed and squeezed into the pain. Her breath was frozen in her chest and she fought the urge to sob. Mere hours. That was all she had before they came to get her. The damned woman had come twice that day and stayed longer than she usually did, to keep the doomed girl company, worrying aloud, kindly but powerless, and ultimately impeding the widow's work — the work of getting the bars out of the window.

For two nights she had been shaking and twisting the square of metal in its mortar frame, tidying up the evidence before morning. And now she had the knife. Small chunks of stone came out with dull clicks and fell away outside onto the grass or flew up against her shoulder. She stood on her bunk and pressed the edge of the blade into a crack and bore down on it with her weight. The old knife with its faded family crest on the nub of the handle had snapped twice already, little tongues of silver tumbling to the cot's blanket and the coppery base metal inside showing at the break. She had used the sharp edges then, finding smaller fissures and cracks to wedge the blade into. They came away in anticlimactic clicks and pops. And now it was all gone. *All* the mortar had been chipped away, nothing held the bars in place any more. And yet they would not come loose. Pacing her resilient cage, she gave the bars a hate-filled look and held her injured hands to herself. What to do? What to do?

She had imagined many impossible ways of escape. Over and over, someone came to free her. Strangers. People she knew. In one fantasy, she imagined herself looking out to see William Moreland standing on the grass in the shade of a tall tree, looking right back at her. In this waking dream, he came up to her window, sauntering casually with his head down and his hands in his pockets as a man might who only wished to check the foundation for leaks. Everything was quiet, even his footfalls in the grass came soundlessly. He went past her window, and as he did, he whispered, *We'll pull the bars off with horses. Get ready.* In other imagined escapes, it was the woman who released her. She would arrive at night and carry no candle. A shade among shadows. She would slip the key into the lock and open the door and sweep in on bare feet, pressing her mouth to the widow's ear, the words coming hot and alarmingly loud as whispers do, *I'm letting you go.*

Together they would hurry out into the utterly dark hallway, the woman leading the girl by the wrist, pausing in the gloom and listening before going on, step by step. Then there would come a noise she knew well — the desk drawer being drawn open and the key touching down on the wood bottom. Slow grinding of its closing. Finally, the front door would open and they would go out into the bright moonlight, hunched and close together, guilty as thieves . . .

But these were dreams, childish wishes from what was left of the child's mind. No one was coming to save her. And if the two brothers came in the morning and found her still in her cage, it was the end of everything.

The widow seized the bars with wincing hands and threw herself into her task again. Pushing and pulling, shaking wildly at the thing. Back and forth, the grinding and scraping of some unseen but tenacious bond. Nothing held it there and yet it would not budge! No more mortar, so perhaps metal? She stopped for a moment and bent to peer under the metal frame. All was dark. She considered the problem in silence for a second. Something curious about the sound it was making, the way it was loose and not loose. As if some part of the metal frame extended deep into the wall. Then the widow clambered onto her cot and put both hands on the left side of the bars and pushed with all her weight. Almost without resistance the thing swung out into the night. She nearly fell through.

The widow stood back, stunned. The bars now stood at right angles to the window frame, as if louvered there. And on both sides there was enough space for a small body to squeeze through.

A career drunk sat at the edge of the boardwalk swinging his feet, having been ejected from a sad and miscreant little bar down the street. He was now waiting with a drunk's impatience for the worst of the black whirling in his head to pass so he could totter home. His hat was tilted far back on his sweating head. To his left were the dark and motionless forms of four horses, drowsing alongside their human companion, hitched to an old railing and standing delicately among mounds of their own shit. The drunk sat humming, and he regarded the dark street with some suspicion, for he was a believer in witches and haints. This moonlight in particular seemed to impart to the hooded buildings across the street a sinister air, a sense of waiting intelligence. For who has not wondered whether everything in this world might be alive? Though it be made of stone or wood or metal, there might be life in it, or opinion or, worst of all, resentment. The hewn boards of any boardwalk, did they recall the bite of the saw? Does memory linger in them? Perhaps the forge's fire still dreams in each nail. A building might be made entirely of injured and brooding things. The drunk waved a dismissive hand at the shrouded brow of the old bank across the street.

"Ah, fuck off," he said. And then, in craven reassessment, seeing himself surrounded by unresponding shadow, gave the night a comradely smirk that said,

All's fair between friends. He went back to swinging his feet, squinty-eyed.

It was then that the widow came melting out of the dark, her long hair hung about her shoulders and her eyes hollow in the moonlight. Seeing her, the drunk did a comic doubletake, his head bobbling loosely on his scrawny neck. He watched the spectre come — dressed in no kind of costume he'd ever seen before — but she was clearly a girl, her face streaked with pale mortar dust, and there was dust down the thighs of her deerskin pants. Like an Indian clad for battle, smeared with frightful warpaint. There was determination in her stride, her eyes on the old man where he sat with his head swimming. As she grew nearer, he heard her terrified breathing, deep and regular, like a runner coming to a stop.

"Eah!" croaked the old man.

Mary put her finger to her lips to shush him, and after a moment he nodded in assent, tapped his nose in the shorthand of all old soaks. He kept up this sage nodding and winking while she went quickly among the horses and chose one.

She slipped the stirrups down and unwound the reins from the hitching bar. Then she pushed against the animal's chest and backed it into the street. It was a calm horse, big-headed and powerful; she had chosen a good one. Though if she hadn't done so, the sheer authority of her need to escape would have been forcefully clear to even the most disobedient of animals. The other three horses stamped and blew, swinging their heads around to watch this process. The widow

416

mounted quickly and drew the reins in, her palms stinging from the salt in the leather from someone else's hands. She yearned to gallop, to flee the place without thinking, clattering down the street in panic. Instead, she walked the horse up to the drunk and gazed down upon him with eyes made feral by the terror that was running through her. He mutely returned her gaze. She leaned out of the saddle and deftly plucked the hat from his head and put it on her own. It was malodorous and damp.

Too late the drunk clasped a hand over his pate and then chortled in foolish surprise, swinging his feet again. He watched the widow walk her horse quietly up the street, heading south. "Hey," he called, "give it back!" Even as drunk as he was, she hoped he would remember the direction she had been heading if he was asked later. He might point up the street and say, "She took my hat!"

She went on, agonizingly slowly, the horse shouldering and stepping high with anticipation, and the widow willing herself not to look back, not to crane round and see imagined pursuers, furies, twinned shapes in the dark. Toward the end of the block she edged the horse closer to the buildings. Knifelines of crisp shadow fell over her, the forms of buildings looming huge and malformed on the pockmarked street. The last store on the block was a grocery, with dried beans hung in its windows, dangling like garlands of offal in the lightless interior. Together, horse and rider melted into the long shadows cast by this establishment. They turned the corner and went down another block, past long, windowless brick walls painted with ornate advertisements for tonics and dopes, then turned again and went down a narrow alley, doubling back the way they had come. Heading north now, the opposite direction, toward Frank.

The animal's hooves were shod and might make noise on gravel or rock in the alley, so the widow took it in a serpentine route over grassy areas, avoiding rain barrels and piles of lumber, past unlighted windows and locked back doors, bending deep to avoid the jut of low roofs, clotheslines. She took off the hat and hung it on the saddlehorn. If she dropped it in a rain barrel, as she longed to do, it might be discovered, along with her trick of misdirection. Her heart was beating so fast she was afraid she would become faint and fall from her mount, so she bent at the waist and pressed her cheek to the horse's neck and whispered entreaties to it. Prayers to the real, living ear.

She remembered pressing her lips to William Moreland's throat and whispering. She remembered his hands on her shoulders, warm in the chilly air. For a moment, this seemed to be the only true thing in the world. Everything else was antic and false.

She and the horse emerged from the alleyway onto a long dirt road hemmed by listing fences. It was the road she remembered coming in on; in fact, she had been facing this direction all the way. No sound came from the slumbering town behind her. No cry of alarm. No shouting. Not even a dog barking. Just the soft clop of hooves in the dirt and her own whispers. She looked up at the sky — still mouthing incantations against disaster, a hushed plea to the very air — and the brightness of the moon seemed auspicious. Each step was toward freedom, and with each hooffall she felt her body loosen and relax, felt the air enter her lungs, and the sky over her head seemed to hang a little higher. She was following a vague thread back home, back to McEchern's store and its vital supplies. After that, she knew not what she would do, or where she should go. She felt the rising of exquisite gladness, a pride bursting inside her, for with any luck, her life was now her own, no one else's. The great fortune of it!

All the dead who had been with her . . . inside her. All the ghosts, the portents and omens, the mourning, the roaring darkness. She told herself: *Let it go. All of it*. And she held instead to living, to this small twinkle of hope in her.

At the edge of town a silvery form darted across her path and froze — a little grey fox. They looked at each other amicably for a moment or two. Then the animal turned and went trotting down the road, its little haunches shaking, halting occasionally to look over its shoulder, as if it would show her the way. But the widow knew where she was going.

At dawn there came an annoyance of shoes down the empty hotel corridor, two people clip-clopping in syncopation, and then a hammering on the door. Beyond the thin veneer, a woman's voice hissed, "They can't do anything *now*. Let them sleep a little longer!" But whoever she was speaking to would not, and he thumped on the door again.

One of the brothers raised himself from the bed and threw the covers aside and went across the floor to open the door. The man outside was already speaking to him, as if the door wasn't even there.

". . . ask me how, but she's gone! She's got out somehow."

"What!?"

"She's crawled out the window and lit out of here."

"Jude!"

His wounded brother was struggling to rise from the damp sheets, his wide, strong torso was bound in fresh white bandages, at the edges of which bloomed an enormous bruise.

"How the hell did she —"

"I'm telling you. Right out the goddamned window!"

The woman stood behind her husband, and there was a distinct air of glee radiating from her. The two redheads lunged around the room snatching at clothes and boots, the sail-like flapping of white shirts hurriedly pulled on.

The husband kept up a constant babble. "Dug out all the mortar, pushed the bars open, and out she goes! A little girl like her, didn't look like she could lift a cat."

As a group they stormed from the room, thundered down the stairs to the lobby, and rushed out into the empty street that lay washed in the weak light of dawn. They hurried to the side of the bank where the ruined window stood ajar still, and one twin peered through into the empty cell, then seized the window bars and slammed them shut with a terrific whang. They went back out into the street, where they halted like

420

bookends, one looking down the street, the other looking up it, as if they might catch the widow yet, see her still fleeing. They were in shirt sleeves and rumpled pants, blinking, their identical faces bereft. And one of them was bent in pain.

"Well? What'll you do now?" asked the woman from the hotel's porch. Her face triumphant, and her hand at her husband's shoulder to hold him back, keep him from them. There was a smell of cooking in the air, bacon and eggs, coffee, wafting out from the hotel's kitchen. Life going on regardless. Man and woman looked down on the two brothers, who stepped and swayed in the street below. They were addled and alarmed, exhausted. Their shirts were frayed, boots worn and nicked and faded, their very hands and faces wrinkled. And in their eyes something awful, some cognisance of a force more relentless than themselves. Weather. Rain. Nights spent freezing. The trackless eternity of trees . . . Her.

"We'll get her," said Julian. And his voice sounded almost convinced. But still, they remained where they were, in the empty street.

"Why should we?" said Jude finally.

His brother turned and looked at him in disbelief. "Have you forgotten? We have to."

"Look at me. Look at us," he said, sadly. "We've done enough, Julian." And with that came a rift between them, alarming and new. The follower had ceased to follow.

"He won't understand."

"I don't care what he wants. Not any more."

They simply looked at each other, a ferocious communication running between them, wordless and elemental, rushing onward. Which would it be: union or dissolution? The watching couple held their breath, as people do at a play, each wondering what the players will do next, and each with a different hope for the outcome.

"Well?" said the man from his spot on the porch. "What's happening?"

And it was a good question. But neither brother knew what was happening. Not remotely. They turned on him two identical gazes of such grief and humiliation that his eyes fell to the floor and he shuffled in shame.

CHAPTER
TWENTY-NINE

Among the windblown bushes the widow knelt, unmoving, waiting as an animal waits and watches. She was up on a slight ridge behind McEchern's trading post. She could hear the dwarf's voice, an incessant soprano cut by gusts of laughter. Overhead lay a sunset of intemperate beauty, a pink and orange flush that refused to subside, its warmth caught among the shivering bushes that ringed the widow like a living halo. She waited silently, crouched there. Never again would she simply walk into a place without knowing what awaited her. The sick take to their beds, prisoners wait, and the hunted must hide.

All that day she had ridden the horse with this one moment in mind. And so, after galloping for a few miles, she had walked the horse, willing herself not to look over her shoulder more than once every ten minutes, thinking, "This time, when I look, they will be there, a dark spot in the distance." But it had never happened. The wind had risen and the air was bright. She went past that same racketing palisade of aspens, the identical journey ravelling back onto the spool, the widow in some ineffable way undoing the day. Her horse was blandly contented with her, or perhaps with any rider, the picture of animal equanimity, like a friendly dog, faithless to its previous owner.

They had ascended into the hills that mid-morning and by noon were among the pines, where the air was crisp and damp. Water pooled in the hollows, and the horse bent and sucked noisily while she leant back in the saddle and held the reins loose so it could reach. Then they had gone on, among crags and fissures, following the worn path uphill. The widow running her fingers through the stiff mane before her, drowsy and weary, for this was the time of day when the pregnancy weighed heavy and dazzling, running like dope through her veins.

Gradually, a plan formed in her head. Or the beginnings of one. First was a tent. Wire for snares. Furs to make a decent coat. Pans, a knife, a hatchet, flour, lard, yeast cakes, matches . . . What else? She leaned and patted the animal's muscular neck and spoke gently to it. For a while, she considered naming the horse but could come up with nothing. It was as nameless to her as she was to it.

They went on across the alpine meadow on which the Cregans had camped, for there were the fallen stays of their little corral, looking like artifacts from a past millennium, a lost people. The end of the world, come and gone. She drifted past their old fire, windblown leaves caught and eddying within the ring of cold stones. From there, the path faded and broke apart, some tributaries going uphill, some downhill, and from this she knew she was nearing the town of Frank. And so the widow steered them off the meadow and into the

424

trees, cutting downhill and away from the open ranges of the landslide. Finally, she had dismounted, tethered the horse to a tree, and gone ahead on foot, making for the trading post.

Now, as she waited, crouched downwind among the bright bushes, she became aware that she could no longer hear McEchern's voice. The tent wowed and ruffled in the breeze, but there was no more talking. She needed food. She could not wait much longer, and might have to simply walk in there and face it. But just then the dwarf emerged onto the platform, a small dark form that hopped down nimbly and went among the blowing bushes and stood there for a moment having a piss, his hat tilted back. He whistled. When he turned and began to make his way inside, the widow leaped up and skied in her boots down the embankment in a slide of pine needles. She trotted to a stop before him.

He was speechless for a moment, his white face crumbling into annoyed relief.

"Jesus Christ!"

"Shh!" she said, stifling a laugh.

"I thought you were a cougar!"

"Oh, Mac, I'm sorry."

"First him and now you. People jumping out at me from all sides!"

He released a long sigh, coming back to himself after the fright. Then a joyful smile spread over his face — suddenly he realized how extraordinary it was that she stood before him. The widow went down on one knee and he walked into her arms, and she held him as one holds a child, as one presses one's face against the solid, warm head and feels the small returning embrace.

"I thought you were dead," he said to her shoulder.

"So did I."

Then he stood back from her. She saw the fine white hairs in his moustache, and saw her own dim shape reflected in the clear pools of his eyes, one in each, twin spectres floating there in another world.

"Come on," he said, "there's someone inside you'll want to see."

The widow woke at dawn to the sound of some low, deep exhalation, a sigh that she assumed had come from the Ridgerunner, who lay beside her. But after a moment she realized it could not have come from him. It must have come from her dreams. She sat up and gazed at his face. It amazed her how much more beautiful he was than in her imagination. The closed, serene eyes, the lips parted slightly, not a trace of tension in his brow, his unguarded face dazzling to her. She resisted the temptation to kiss him. As she had the night before. Straddling him, allowing him to enter her. Now there was no point in being careful, so they had dashed themselves with joy against each other, and then collapsed. She had told him her condition. At first, he had only been interested in how his prophylactic method had failed. Otherwise, and because it meant they could have sex as they wished, he had accepted it lightly, as one does who does not fully apprehend the future. No matter, she thought. That was one thing they shared: not knowing.

Don't kiss him, she told herself. She backed silently out of the tent they shared, naked, clutching her parcel of clothes, and looked up at the listing peak of McEchern's tent. No smoke yet. So the dwarf was also asleep.

An hour later, Charlie McEchern was stoking his stove, a pot of coffee beginning to warm on its top, when he looked up to see the widow standing at the back doorflap of his tent. A queer look on her face. She giggled and skipped about the store, girlish and giddy, then hurried to the front doorflap to check that Moreland had not yet risen from his tent.

"What's with you?" he said.

"Nothing."

She was peeking out the door, smiling. McEchern came and stood by her, looking up at her earnestly.

"You're leaving, aren't you?"

Of course, he must have seen her tending to the horse out back, which was now saddled and heavily packed, almost expertly, with all the provisions he had given her, or loaned to her on the promise of payment that both of them knew could never be made. The widow nodded. She was indeed leaving.

The dwarf didn't know what to make of the sly smile on her face. He scowled and put his hands on his hips. "Well, I'm leaving too, you know?"

She let the canvas flap drop. "What! Why?"

"What'd'ya mean why? I can't sell whisky to the goddamn trees, Mary. There's nothing left for me here. Soon as those Cregans take off, the place'll be as

427

deserted as a church. Frankly, it gives me the creeps, already. I figure it's time to go."

"But where?" She sounded bereft, which seemed to please him.

"Yukon," he said. "Lots of people there, mining, drinking, all that. I hear they even have a library. I was going to ask you to come with me . . ." He reddened. "But I suppose you have whats-his-name there to look after you."

"I don't need looking after, Mac."

The dwarf looked dubious but didn't argue. There was a brief silence, a little seam of cool through the warm.

"Where is Yukon?" Mary said finally.

"North of here. A long way north. And west."

"Isn't it cold?"

"About the same as winter here," he said, "but year-round." They both laughed.

"Have I ever thanked you?" the widow said.

The dwarf made as if pondering for a moment, stroking his moustache. "Nope," he said.

She nodded. "Interesting," she said.

He snorted. "Think you're cute, don't ya?"

The Ridgerunner half-woke to see that the light in the tent was high and cool, a squirrel chittering to his left, and the hiss of wind through trees — all of it bespoke a late rising, midday . . . He had slept in! He sat bolt upright in a tumble of blankets and, like a blind man, groped about the empty tent for her, his hands patting the blankets as if the widow might have shrunk in her

428

sleep and was lying unseen and nut-sized among them. Then he scratched his back and waited for his head to clear. In his mind they were still in the mountains and alone, and she was surely just outside smoking her pipe, awaiting him. He was still half asleep, dream-addled. He sighed and ran a hand over his face. Alone again and just imagining her? Still, the body radiates contentment, release. His unhurried mind ran back to the night, the tent, the blankets, and her — suddenly there was a cavalcade of salacious scenes, ruinously beautiful, and . . . He rubbed his eyes . . . True! He'd found her! Or she'd found him. He wasn't sure which.

Suddenly, he remembered everything.

McEchern telling him, "Drop it. She's done. Who knows who they were. Who knows where they took her. And even if you knew" — he spread his small hands out — "what could you do? Are you Sam Steele?" The two of them drunk for two days, until the Ridgerunner could drink no more, and merely sat holding his head. Then a long, sorry, sober night during which the dwarf had chattered to stave off his companion's unnerving silence, telling story after story, every one about her. Wondering at the particulars of her past, the whiff of crime, her dreadful pursuers, recounting the incredible fact of her firing upon them. Questions that were unanswered and unanswerable. It had been a wake. They the mourners, and Mary Boulton the corpse.

And then she had walked in. Dressed like an Indian. She had walked right in and stood smiling at William Moreland.

He had scrounged excitedly round the tent and struggled with the opening. She had looked different, somehow. Was it in her gait or her voice . . . her eyes? He wasn't sure. But it was familiar, a thing he'd only seen in certain men.

"Mary!" he called out. He heard only the wind in the trees. At that moment his hand strayed across something that crinkled and folded against his fingers. A piece of paper. The Ridgerunner held it to his sleepy eyes and read it, and there he saw what he could not have known were the first two words the widow had ever written.

Find me.

Also available in ISIS Large Print:

Restitution

Eliza Graham

February 1945. Europe is in ruins and the Red Army is searing its way across Germany, revenging itself upon a petrified population. The War is over, but for some the fight for survival is only just beginning.

Alix, the aristocratic daughter of a German resistance fighter, is alone and desperate to flee. But when a ferocious snowstorm descends she must return to the shelter of her abandoned ancestral home. There she is shocked to find her childhood sweetheart, Gregor. As old passions are rekindled, a couple break in to hide — the man, in Gestapo uniform, is a stranger, but his companion is more familiar.

By morning the woman and her Nazi escort are dead, and Gregor has vanished. Terrified, Alix runs for her life. It will take six years and the fall of Communism before the riddles of that fateful night can be deciphered.

ISBN 978-0-7531-8370-0 (hb)
ISBN 978-0-7531-8371-7 (pb)

The Other

David Guterson

It is 1972. Neil Countryman is from the high school in north Seattle. He slumps at his desk all day and gets high in the park at lunchtime. John William Barry is from Lakeside, a private academy for the more privileged of Seattle's youth. He is an earnest, fiery young man, and his family background is one of material wealth and emotional deprivation.

When their lives collide for the first time, it is the beginning of a friendship that is both fraught and intimate. Both boys have a taste for the wilderness, and together they explore the most remote areas of the mountains. But as they grow older, John William's intense intelligence and craving for isolation mark him out as an eccentric. As Neil begins to accumulate the more conventional comforts — a wife, a steady job — their lives begin to take radically different paths . . .

ISBN 978-0-7531-8204-8 (hb)
ISBN 978-0-7531-8205-5 (pb)

The Witch's Trinity

Erika Mailman

Germany, 1507. In a time when famine is rife and panic spreading, people resort to desperate measures in order to survive. When a Dominican friar arrives in the small town of Tierkinddorf, convinced that witchcraft is to blame for the people's plight, no woman is safe from the pointing finger. Having witnessed her best friend being burnt at the stake, Güde knows she could be next. But when the accusation of witchcraft comes from her own daughter-in-law, who relishes the prospect of having one less mouth to feed, Güde's strength and faith are tested to their limits.

The Witch's Trinity is a powerful story of injustice and betrayal; of women becoming the victims of desperate circumstance.

ISBN 978-0-7531-8142-3 (hb)
ISBN 978-0-7531-8143-0 (pb)

Fire in the Blood

Irène Némirovsky

A morality tale with doubtful morals, a story of murder, love and betrayal in rural France

An old man looks back on a chequered life with secret regrets, concealing a truth he will not reveal until the end. Fire in the Blood is a small and beautiful chamber piece which starts quietly, lyrically, but then races away with revelations and narrative twists in a story about young women forced into marriages with old men, about mothers and daughters, stepmothers and stepdaughters, youthful passions and the regrets of old age, about peasant communities and the way they hide their secrets.

ISBN 978-0-7531-8154-6 (hb)
ISBN 978-0-7531-8155-3 (pb)

Where Three Roads Meet

Salley Vickers

At the end of his life, an old man waits in his office for a stranger to arrive. Over the next few weeks, Teiresias will visit again, making his way across the heath to relate the story of his life. As these two men sit together, a remarkable tale unfolds.

The compelling story of Oedipus, who, unknowingly, kills his father and marries his mother, is probably the most influential of all the Greek myths, having furnished Freud's theory of psychoanalysis. Bestselling novelist Salley Vickers, herself a former psychoanalyst, takes the ancient story of patricide and incest and explores it through the vision of Teiresias, the blind seer, who alone"sees" the truth about the protagonists' terrible past and their place in the cosmic order.

ISBN 978-0-7531-8064-8 (hb)
ISBN 978-0-7531-8065-5 (pb)

Jo

ISIS publish a wide range of books in large print, from fiction to biography. Any suggestions for books you would like to see in large print or audio are always welcome. Please send to the Editorial Department at:

ISIS Publishing Limited
7 Centremead
Osney Mead
Oxford OX2 0ES

A full list of titles is available free of charge from:

Ulverscroft Large Print Books Limited

(UK)
The Green
Bradgate Road, Anstey
Leicester LE7 7FU
Tel: (0116) 236 4325

(Australia)
P.O. Box 314
St Leonards
NSW 1590
Tel: (02) 9436 2622

(USA)
P.O. Box 1230
West Seneca
N.Y. 14224-1230
Tel: (716) 674 4270

(Canada)
P.O. Box 80038
Burlington
Ontario L7L 6B1
Tel: (905) 637 8734

(New Zealand)
P.O. Box 456
Feilding
Tel: (06) 323 6828

Details of **ISIS** complete and unabridged audio books are also available from these offices. Alternatively, contact your local library for details of their collection of **ISIS** large print and unabridged audio books.